Promise Me Forever

PAIGE WEAVER

Promise Me Forever

Published by Paige Weaver LLC
P.O. Box 80016
Keller, Texas 76244

ISBN 978-1-5232424-5-0

Cover design © Sarah Hansen
okaycreations.com

Promise Me Forever

A Novel

Extraordinary people survive under the most terrible circumstances and they become more extraordinary because of it.

~ writer Robertson Davies

Prologue

-Cat-

Dying never scared me. It was living that I was frightened of.

Alive, you feel every heartache, every loss. You cry. You hurt. You suffer and grieve. I didn't want to feel those things. So many times I wanted to give up and close my eyes. I wanted to disappear into the darkness and never return. But as I fell to the ground, pain exploding in my side, it was living that I suddenly wanted to do.

"Cat!"

I heard him roar as the back of my head hit the concrete. The shouts of the men faded. Wet warmth spread across my side.

"Don't you do it, Cat! Don't you fuckin' die on me!"

Cash's face appeared above me. He was mad, his eyes full of rage and panic. He was pressing on the open wound below my ribs, hurting me and screaming at someone. I couldn't understand him – I hurt too much – but I could feel his desperation.

When he looked down at me, his mouth moved. He was telling me something but what was it? *Focus, Cat, focus.*

"I'm not going to let you die. You understand me? I'm not going to let you die!"

But it was too late.

My eyes drifted closed. Blood ran from my chest. As I started to lose consciousness, a loud boom detonated above me.

I opened my eyes.

There was chaos, smoke, and pain. So much pain. Agony cut through me. I cried out and bowed my body.

Cash gathered me in his arms as gunfire erupted around us. I wanted to tell him to save my brother instead but I couldn't. My eyes refused to stay open. My mouth refused to work.

"Stay with me, Cat. Please, stay with me," Cash whispered, cradling me against his chest.

But I couldn't fight any longer.

My head lolled back against his arm. The darkness descended. I heard Cash plead but then I didn't hear anything anymore.

This was it. The end.

But I wasn't ready to go yet.

Chapter One

-Cash-

Minutes Before

I'm not scared, cowboy."

"Then say it," I whispered in her ear. "Just once let me hear it."

Cat shivered and stared up at me with crystal green eyes. "I love you, Cash."

"I love you too, Beauty Queen."

I took her lips fiercely, wanting to stretch her out on the bed behind us and take what she was offering.

She leaned into me, pushing her breasts into my chest. I wanted to reach up and cup them, feel them react to my touch. She was amazing. Her body was perfect. She was mine.

And she loved me.

I ran my hand around her waist and tugged her closer. My hardness strained against my zipper, nudging her stomach. Showing her just how much I wanted her. She moaned and pressed against me, urging me to do more. I resisted, but shit, it was hard. My brain finally won out over my body. I needed to get her and my sister, Keely, out of town. My dick could just settle down. Fuck, who was I kidding? That was impossible around Cat.

I lowered my hand, letting my fingers trail down over her ass. Cupping it, I kissed her deeper, pressing her into the rigid length under my jeans. She whimpered against my mouth. God, I loved that sound.

Reluctantly, I broke the kiss off, letting my lips slide from hers. Getting her naked and making her come would have to wait. We needed to leave.

"Let's go home, Cat," I said in a gravelly voice I didn't recognize as my own. Is that what love did to a man? Turn him inside out and make everything sound different? Feel different? Look different?

Cat pulled her lower lip through her teeth, tasting me on her lips. Nodding, she looked up at me through her long, dark lashes. "Okay, cowboy."

I took another second to stare at her. The night we met, I found myself mesmerized by a girl that wasn't my type. She was spoiled and rich and too high maintenance for a cowboy like me. I was a salt-of-the-earth kind of guy. She was a daddy's princess, used to getting her way. One night together was all we planned but we found that once would never be enough.

I reached up and ran my thumb over her bottom lip. God, I loved her. I loved the way she looked. The way she tasted. The way her body clenched around me when I thrust into her. I loved the way her eyes snapped with fire when I made her mad. I loved everything about her.

And that's why I had lied to her.

I wasn't going to leave town without killing the men that had hurt her and Keely. I wanted them to suffer. I wanted my hands red from their blood. The last few years trying to survive in this wasteland of a country had turned me into a dangerous man. One that would lie to get revenge. As soon as Cat and Keely were safe outside the town's walls, I would double back. The two men who had touched them would find out how deadly I could be.

The bastards were right outside, celebrating their return to the fucked up town of Hilltop, Texas. It had been my idea to check out the community. Terrorists had ransacked the country and an electromagnetic pulse had taken out every conceivable piece of electronics in the U.S. Half the population was dead thanks to disease, hunger, and war. The other half wished to God they were sometimes. Supplies were scarce. People were starving. I had heard that Hilltop had running water, ample supplies, and electricity. In a world gone dark, a town like that was an anomaly. I had to check it out.

We had arrived two days ago and were greeted by a tall metal wall made out of shipping containers. Walking in hadn't been a problem. We were greeted by a preacher and two mean-looking men. They took our horses and led us to a hotel – the same one Cat and I stood in now. A woman named Mary fed us and welcomed us with open arms. But I didn't trust her or anyone else in Hilltop.

Something nagged at me to get the hell out of town. I ignored it and had gone to gather supplies. My friend Gavin and I were trading bullets for medical supplies when Cat's younger brother, Tate, ran up to us. He was out of breath and unable to speak. I almost wrung his neck, waiting for him to spit the words out. I knew Cat was in trouble. I could feel it in my bones.

When he finally caught his breath and said the leader of Hilltop was back with an army of men and two of them were the ones that had hurt Cat and Keely, I didn't wait for him to finish. I took off running. I had to get to Cat.

I took to the streets at a dead run. My heart was in my throat, fear eating me alive. I was so relieved to find Cat standing in our room, I told her the truth.

I loved her.

But now it was time to go.

Juggling my shotgun in one hand and holding Cat's hand in the other, I led her into the hallway. My backpack was slung over my shoulder. Hers was on her back and she carried our other gun. All of our belongings were in two bags. All that we owned.

"The men were heading toward the town's square," she said behind me as I listened for any commotion downstairs.

"I saw 'em," I muttered, keeping a tight grip on her hand. No way in hell would I let her go. "Gavin went to get the horses. We're going to ride like hell out of here."

It was a lie. There was no *we*. She was going to ride. I would stay and send those men straight to hell.

Our strides were quick as we rushed down the hallway. I felt something pushing me, urging me to hurry. I could almost hear the seconds ticking down until I exploded and went on a rampage. No one touched Cat. No one but me. I just hoped to God that Gavin was able to get the horses and Tate was doing what I had told him to do, which was gather our supplies and grab my sister, Keely. I needed them to do their job so I could do mine – feed my vengefulness and protect Cat.

"Where the fuck is he?" I muttered, glancing in Tate's empty room when we walked past it. Teenagers could be irrational, especially him.

On the way back to the hotel, I almost had to tackle him to the ground. He had seen what those men had done to Keely and Cat. He had been there and wanted revenge in the worst kind of way. I couldn't blame him but I didn't want to have to tell Cat that the only family member she had left was dead. If he had done something foolish, like go after them himself, I would kill him myself.

I was beginning to worry it might come to that, when the door on my left swung open.

"Cat!"

Tate stepped out of the room, followed by Keely. He dropped the backpack he was carrying and rushed past me to wrap his long arms around his sister. I refused to let go of her. There was just something in me that needed to touch her as long as possible.

"I'm okay," Cat said, wiggling out of his arms. "You ready?"

Tate backed away and nodded, his long brown hair falling into his eyes. "Always." He lifted the edge of his shirt, showing the pistol stuck in his waistband.

For a teenager, he was cold. Accurate with a gun. He was also a smartass with a chip on his shoulder. That made him very dangerous.

I glanced at my sister standing next to him. For years, I had searched for her. She was the only family I had left after the EMP struck and terrorists invaded the country. When I finally found her, I had found Cat too.

"You got everything?" I asked Keely.

She nodded, not saying a word. She hadn't since Hightower touched her. Just another reason to end his life soon.

I glanced back at Tate. "Keep the girls between us at all times and shoot to kill. Understand?"

He picked up the backpack from the floor and slung it on his shoulder as he nodded. "I won't hesitate. Not this time."

He was still beating himself up for not pulling the trigger on the man that had killed his older brother and hurt Cat. But he just might get his chance. So would I.

We made our way downstairs, carrying our meager belongings and not making a sound. We were experts at sneaking in and out of places. We had to be in order to survive.

The night the EMP hit the world changed. Life became harsher. Deadlier. It was either fight or be killed. Steal or starve. Adapt or give up. The choice was always obvious to me. I chose to survive. Millions of weak souls hadn't been so lucky.

The stairs opened up to the hotel's dining room. It held six or seven good-sized tables covered with yellowed tablecloths. I led the way across the room and to the swinging doors of the kitchen. The front door wasn't an option – where the townspeople were gathered. I could hear them, laughing and talking. Welcoming home the men that stole and pillaged for their precious supplies.

A cold bead of sweat rolled down my back. If something happened to Gavin or me, Cat and Keely wouldn't stand a chance of getting out. Not against a town full of dangerous men. The town citizens wouldn't help, even if they were two unarmed girls – they were under the leader's thumb. No, the front door was out of the question. That left the back door as our only option.

We headed into the kitchen, moving fast. It was large and industrial-sized, meant to feed a hotel full of guests. Stainless steel appliances and a large butcher-block island took up most of the space. Near the back there was a large service door.

Perfect.

Bright sunlight blinded me as I swung it open. An alleyway greeted me. Down one side were turn-of-the-century buildings, including the hotel. On the other was the metal wall of the town. I looked up at it. Shit. It had to be at least nine feet tall.

Gravel crunched under my boots as I stepped outside. It was quiet and empty as far as I could see.

Cat followed, shielding her eyes against the sun and holding onto her backpack strap and the gun. Keely and Tate stepped out of the hotel behind her and glanced around, a survival instinct born out of years of living in a war torn country.

We kept our backs to the buildings and our ears open for trouble as we rushed down the alleyway. I could hear commotion in the town square. Loud. Joyful. Fucked up crazy.

We were a few buildings away from the hotel when I saw Gavin. He was up ahead, holding the reins of two horses as they danced around. I was so busy concentrating on him that I didn't see the man.

He appeared out of nowhere, walking between two buildings. His head was down but when he heard us, he jerked his gaze up.

"Oh, shit!" Tate exclaimed.

I yanked up my gun and stepped in front of Cat. "Go!" I yelled at her, taking careful aim at the man.

"No!" she screamed, scrambling to grab hold of my jacket.

The man's expression went from alarm to terror. He spun around to run and alert the others.

"Shit!" Lowering my gun, I took off after him. A gunshot would have the whole town on us in seconds. I had to catch him instead.

I sped up until I was right on him. Reaching out, I grabbed the collar of his jacket and slammed him back against the brick wall of a building.

"THEY'RE HER—" he started to shout.

I raised my gun and smacked the butt against the side of his head, shutting him up. He folded like a lawn chair, dropping to the ground.

Standing over him, I breathed hard, gripping my shotgun firmly. Tate walked up and kicked the man's boot, making sure he was out.

"You're a fuckin' badass," he said, squinting at me.

Whatever. I did what I had to do.

Sweating despite the cool weather, I wiped a hand across my chin and headed back to Cat.

"Let's go," I muttered, taking her hand and dragging her along.

I had seen the look she gave me. Like I was a freak of nature. Maybe I was. I had killed for her. Injured for her. And I would do it again.

We were halfway down the alleyway, moving at a quick pace, when I saw them. Five men. They appeared between two buildings. Puffs of white smoke rose above their heads. Weed. I could smell it when the wind changed directions.

They were looking down and talking. Not paying attention to shit. At the edge of the building they stopped, their backs to us, their heads bent.

I slid to a stop and held out a hand, stopping Keely and Tate. Cat bumped into me, her soft body hitting my back.

My damn cock always responded to any touch from her but I had bigger problems. There were too many men and they held AK-47s. Too much firepower against our old shotguns and pistols.

Turning, I grabbed Cat's forearm – probably too hard – and rushed over between two buildings, pulling her with me. Keely and Tate followed at a quick run, trying to make as little noise as possible.

I pushed Cat against the brick wall of the building and stood over her, one leg on either side. My priority was protecting her at all costs. Even if it meant a bullet to the back.

Keely pressed herself next to Cat and Tate stood guard on the other side of her. Tightening my grip on my gun, I peeked around the edge of the brick wall.

Crap, we were stuck. We had men in front of us and the street behind us. Screwed was putting it mildly.

I eased back and looked down at Cat. Her nose was red from the cold and her eyes were wide. "What now?" she whispered.

I nodded toward the front of the buildings. "We take the street and circle around. Act like we belong here and we're just going about our day."

Keely started shaking her head and pressing back against the wall, little whimper sounds leaving her. The monster who had raped her was out there. Who had taken her voice and gave her nightmares.

I grabbed the strap of her backpack and pulled her away from the building. "I'm getting you out, Keely. I promise."

She shook her head again but there was no time to argue. With a clenched jaw, I let her go and led the way down between the two buildings. All I wanted to do was find the two men who had touched her and Cat and send them to an early grave. Put the motherfuckers six feet under with holes in their heads.

But I reigned in my temper and walked at a leisure pace, leading Cat, Keely, and Tate.

We emerged on the sidewalk. Across the street, people were gathered. They wore faded clothes and homespun knit hats. Children ran through the maze of excited adults, squealing and laughing. I hadn't seen the men's leader but Tate said he was older. That's okay. My gun wasn't picky and neither was I.

I kept my head tilted just right to hide my face under my cowboy hat, but I kept a sharp eye out for trouble. I made sure Cat and Keely stayed behind me and Tate remained calm. My body was wound tight. My senses were heightened. I was ready for anything.

But hell was about to find me first.

We passed what looked like had been a diner before the EMP strike. The words 'Burger and Shakes' were painted on the big picture window in front. They were faded now, some of the letters almost gone. Through the filth-coated glass, I could see chairs stacked on tables and movement in the room. I stared straight ahead and kept walking. Casual. Relaxed. Making sure Cat and Keely were well protected behind me.

Gavin appeared up ahead. He was at the corner of the last building, near the entrance cut into Hilltop's wall. Walking over, he slid the gate open, ready for us to make a quick getaway. I figured we could reach him in ten minutes flat.

But that was not going to happen.

An itch started between my shoulder blades. The kind that had kept me alive since the world ended and World War III started. The hair on the back of my neck rose. I heard a door open and a little bell ding. The sound of boots shuffling on the sidewalk came from behind me.

"I heard we had visitors," a deep voice boomed. "Welcome to Hilltop."

Shit. We were in trouble.

Chapter Two

-Cash-

My hand clenched around the shotgun. I recognized the voice. I had heard it another time. Another place.

Slowly, I turned.

Five men stood under a tattered, storefront awning. They had malice in their eyes and guns in their hands.

Cat stood in front of me with Keely beside her and Tate not far away. I grabbed hold of Cat's backpack then Keely's arm and pulled them behind me. Tate stood still, his gaze glued to the men.

I spotted the leader right away. He was older than the others. More distinguished looking. His dark hair was peppered with gray and his cheeks were covered with a thick, wiry beard. From the way he stood, to the look in his eyes, he exuded power and control.

He hadn't changed much from the last time I saw him. He was the same man who had raided Ryder's ranch. Leader of a militia. Cocky sonofabitch nut. He had threatened my friend, Maddie, and ordered his men to take all of our supplies and food. We were left hungry for weeks. Now I knew where it had all gone – to feed the town of Hilltop.

"Welcome," he said again. "I'm Frankie. And you are?"

"We're leaving," I said in a deadly voice.

The old man didn't look happy with my attitude but played nice and smiled. "I hate to see you leave. We're always happy to get visitors here. Especially young Americans like yourselves."

Tate snorted, widening his stance. "That why you've got a wall around your town? Because you're happy to get visitors?"

Frankie frowned and turned his gaze on the kid. "Watch yourself, boy."

Cat stepped out from behind me before I could stop her. "Why don't *you* watch yourself, you sonofabitch. No one threatens my brother."

Frankie chuckled and ran a hand over his bearded chin, glancing up and down her. "Hello there. You look mighty familiar. What's your name, darling?"

I pulled Cat behind me again, rage pulsating through me. "Her name is none of your damn business."

Frankie smiled wider and started strolling toward us. "Don't get your panties in a wad, young man. I'm just asking. Women are worshipped around here. They will bring forth a new generation of Americans. We hold them in the utmost regard."

I eased my finger over the trigger of my gun. "I don't care who the fuck you worship. It won't be her."

The smile died on his lips. Anger flared in his eyes. He stared at me hard, his hand hovering over his own gun. "I don't like the tone of your voice, young man. Sounded like a threat to me."

Fuck. This is not what I wanted. Not with Tate, Keely, and Cat here. But I wasn't going to back down and show weakness.

I tilted my head, staring at him under my hat. "Yeah, guess it was. You better throw us out of town for threatening you and all."

Frankie snorted. "You think I'm a fool, boy?"

I shrugged. "Well, maybe."

His face grew red and his hands clenched. I was wondering what were our chances of making a run for it when two men strolled out of the building beside him. One was thin, average height. The other was huge, his head shaved.

The thin one was walking toward Frankie. "Hey, boss, we got…" His voice trailed off when he looked up and saw us. "What the fuck?"

Malice ripped through me when his eyes slid over Cat.

"Well, well. Hello little bird. Hellooo."

Cat grabbed the back of my jacket. "No. No," she whispered in a terrified voice. She was shaking, her hands gripping at me in fear.

Keely let out a soft cry and started backing away slowly, whimpering and hunching her shoulders as if invisible hands were hurting her.

That's when I knew. These were the fuckers. The two men that hurt Cat and Keely.

Time seemed to stop. My heart rate slowed down. I could hear each breath I took. Each time I drew air into my lungs. A roaring started in my ears, blocking out other noises. My vision zeroed in on the thin man.

Him first.

I dropped my backpack and reached back, shoving Cat to the ground. She hit the concrete hard, dropping the shotgun. The bag on her back took the blunt of the fall. I couldn't worry if she was hurt. I needed her safe.

Tate grabbed Keely and pushed her down. With them out of the line of fire, I swung my gun up. At the same time, Tate pulled the pistol from his waistband and another one from the back of his jeans.

"Shit!" the thin man roared, reaching for his gun.

But I was faster.

I pulled the trigger. The gun exploded and kicked back against my shoulder. The blast was loud as the shot left the chamber.

"OWWW!" the thin man screamed as the pellets found their home in his shoulder with a sickening thud. He fell back a step and clasped the wounds. Blood ran down his arm.

He lifted his hand and saw the blood. "You fucker!" He lifted his gun and fired.

"NOOOOO!"

The scream came from behind me. Cat.

Shrugging out of her pack, she scrambled to her feet and dived in front of me. I reached out to wrap my arm around her waist and yank her back but it was too late.

The bullet found her instead of me.

Chapter Three

-Cash-

Cat jerked as the lead buried in her body. Her legs folded. The back of her head hit the concrete as she fell.

Keely screamed and crawled to her on all fours. I saw the blood on Cat's jacket and lost it.

Roaring, I opened fire on the men. Fury made me pull the trigger again and again, spraying lead through the air.

Blasts came from beside me. Tate. He released a volley of bullets from the two pistols he held, looking like Billy the Kid in an old timey flick.

The men returned fire, some dropping to the ground for cover. The air filled with the sulphur smell of gunpowder. It filled my nostrils and tasted like metal. Smoke rose from the barrels. I squinted against it and pumped my shotgun then fired.

Two men went down. Another ran for cover behind a building. The kid and I were holding our own but more men were racing toward us. We needed help.

And it came in the form of Gavin.

He appeared out of nowhere, riding up on the horse like the hero in a Spaghetti Western. His dark hair was tossed wildly in the wind and his eyes blazed down on the men. Raising his bow, he let an arrow fly.

I fired off another shot then dropped down beside Cat, letting Tate and Gavin take over. But before I could take care of her, a bullet whizzed by Keely's head.

"Gavin, get my sister out of here!" I shouted, ducking over Cat's body when a shot hit the ground close to her.

Gavin slung the bow to his back and turned his horse. With a firm kick to the ribs, he spurred it straight for Keely. Hooves thundered as he rushed toward her. When he was close enough, he leaned down and swooped her up. She kicked and screamed, terrified, but he held onto her and plunked her down in front of him in the saddle.

"What about y'all?" he shouted, holding onto her with an arm around her waist and protecting her with his body.

"Just get Keely as far away from here as possible!" I yelled, picking up Cat's gun and tossing it to him. "Go!"

He caught the gun with one hand and gave a firm nod. Digging his heels into the horse's sides, he swung around. The gelding shot off, its eyes rolling back in its head with fear. They headed toward the opened gate, traveling at a full gallop. Gavin kept an arm around my sister, holding her in front of him. When a man appeared, racing toward the entrance to close the gate, Gavin raised the gun and fired a shot. The man dived, narrowly missing getting hit. With the gate cleared, Gavin spurred the horse to go faster. They flew past the gate and under the constructed wall. Within seconds, they disappeared among the abandoned cars and overgrown trees outside Hilltop.

I could trust Gavin to get Keely somewhere safe and not turn around for me. He and I made a pact once. If we were ever in a sticky situation, we would do whatever we needed to do to protect our family, even if it meant one of us might be killed.

With them gone, I picked Cat up in my arms and started running. We needed cover. Some kind of shelter. Jesus, she was so limp. And something warm soaked into my jacket. *Fuck, this is not good.* I tried not to freak, my mind going a million miles a minute. Bullets were ricocheting all around us. There. A little bistro table set in front of an abandoned building. It would have to do.

"Tate, get your ass over here!" I yelled, turning the table onto its side and laying Cat behind it.

Tate ran for us, firing at the men. They answered with bullets. The rat-a-tat-tat rang in my ear.

When he slid to a stop beside us, he looked down at Cat and whispered, "No. No. Save her."

"I will," I answered, leaning over her. But shit, she looked bad. Blood was pooling under her and made her jacket a sticky, red mess. I wanted to scream and cry and shake her until she woke up, but first things first. We needed to get out of here.

I leaned over and tried the door of the abandoned building beside us. Locked. Damn. We couldn't make a run for the town wall without being a moving target.

I was looking for another option when bullets blasted the table. Ducking, I emptied my chamber over the edge, taking out a few more men.

Tate was still frozen, staring down at Cat. His long, shaggy hair covered his eyes but I could still see his fear. His sister had been shot. She might be dying.

"Tate!" I roared as bullets pinged around us. "Tate, get your shit together and shoot them!"

He tightened his jaw and raised his guns. Bullets flew by him like he was invisible, but he didn't even blink as the whizzing metal zipped by him. He just fired shot after shot.

I fired my last bullet and tossed the gun aside. Looking down at Cat, I tried to keep the panic at bay but shit, it was hard.

She had been hit somewhere in her midsection. Her skin was pale, her lips bloodless.

"Fuck. Fuck. Fuck."

I ripped open her jacket, looking for the wound. It wasn't hard to find. A hole was in her left side, below her ribcage and above her hipbone.

I put both of my hands over it and pressed down. Blood oozed between my fingers, coating my hand. When I saw that bullet hit her, I saw my life flash before my eyes. Now, I saw my life slipping away from me.

I pressed harder on the wound and looked up at her face.

"Don't you do it, Cat. Don't you fuckin' die on me!" I yelled.

I yanked my jacket off and bundled it into a ball. Ignoring the sticky blood on my hands, I pressed the jacket against the wound.

Her eyes fluttered open. There was peace in them and acceptance. She was dying.

"No." I shook my head, tears filling my vision. "You can't."

But her eyes started to close anyway.

Anger filled me as I pressed on her wound. It was *their* fault. *They* had put a bullet in her. *They* had done this to the woman I loved.

I looked up over the edge of the table. The thin one who had called Cat 'little bird' was crouched low, running for cover. He was the one who had shot her. The one who had tried to touch her and take what was mine. A low, predatory sound erupted from my chest.

His arm dangled uselessly at his side. Blood dripped from his fingers. He was shooting with his other hand but his shots were going all over the place near Tate's feet.

I reached for my shotgun. My hands were shaking and slippery with Cat's blood but they gripped the metal easily.

With trembling fingers, I reached into my jeans pocket and pulled out the only shell I had left. I loaded it into the chamber and pumped the gun. Coldness turned my blood to ice. I became distant, unemotional. Deadly.

Lifting the gun to my shoulder, I aimed over the table. The man was running toward the building where Frankie disappeared. I had seconds. I squinted down the barrel, taking perfect aim. But Tate beat me to it.

He pulled the trigger. The bullet hit the doorframe above the skinny man's head. Wood splintered. He yelped and dove inside.

The shot must have jolted Cat awake. She cried out and opened her eyes.

I set the shotgun down and leaned over her. "Cat? Babe? Talk to me."

But she didn't. Her eyes started to close.

I cupped her face and turned her head my direction. "Look at me, Cat. Stay awake," I shouted over the gunfire.

When she didn't, I pressed down on her wound again, using my jacket as a compression.

"Tate! We need to get out of here!"

I grabbed my shotgun and tossed it to him. He caught it mid-air as I gathered Cat in my arms.

Her head lolled back against my arm, her dark hair falling over it. She was in bad shape but we needed to find better cover. I just didn't know where that would be.

But my luck was about to change.

The sound of an engine came from outside the town walls. It was loud and clunky, shaking the earth and filling my ears with a sound that was foreign. A running vehicle was a phenomenon when the EMP had fried most of them.

A second later, a large truck burst through the open gate. Roaring into town, it flew up on a curb and bounced over a neatly trimmed shrub. A mailbox was next. Nothing was safe from the truck obliterating everything in its path as it sped toward us.

It was in full throttle, heading straight our way. At the last second, the driver jerked the wheel to the right. Tires shrieked. Rubber burned. The truck skidded sideways then slammed to a stop in front of us. The passenger door flew open.

"Get in!"

Hilltop's preacher, David, was leaning across the seat, motioning us in the truck. I didn't hesitate. I gathered Cat in my arms and ran.

As soon as I reached the pickup, I climbed in with Cat in my arms. She moaned when I settled in the middle of the seat with her in my lap.

David didn't ask what happened to her. He yelled at Tate. "Get in, son!"

Tate dived for the truck, dodging a hail of bullets.

"Where's the rest of your group?" David shouted.

"They got out!" Tate exclaimed, slamming the door closed. "Go!"

David hit the gas, spinning the truck into a fishtail. Shrapnel sprayed the side of the pickup. Tate grabbed the leather handle dangling from the roof and held on.

"Hold on, kids!" David bellowed. The pickup shot forward.

We bounced over curbs and took out a parking sign. I held onto Cat tightly. Her blood soaked into my jacket more.

"How is she?" David yelled over the roar of the engine, flooring the gas and heading straight for the torn off gate.

I looked down at Cat. She was pale, her skin almost translucent, her lips white.

"Not good," I rasped, swallowing. "There's blood everywhere."

"Where's she shot?" David asked, keeping his eyes on the road.

I didn't answer. I couldn't.

"Cash! Where's she shot?" Tate yelled over the sound of the wind whipping in through the windows. "We gotta know."

"Side," I croaked out. "She was shot in the side."

The girl I swore wasn't my type was in my arms dying.

Chapter Four

-Cat-

"Hold her down."

"Fuck. I can't do this."

"Yeah, you can. Hold her down, boy."

The voices washed over me, increasing the pain in my head. I tried opening my eyes but the agony was too much. I just wanted to return to the darkness where there was no pain, no hurt.

I started to drift away but long fingers wrapped around my biceps and pressed down. Someone else grabbed my ankles and held them firmly against the mattress under me.

"You got her really good? She's gonna fight if she wakes up."

"Just do it," someone growled.

Pain exploded in my side and spread, moving like wildfire through my body. Burning me. Slicing me. Poisoning me.

My eyes flew open. I arched off the bed and let out a bloodcurdling scream.

"Hold her, dammit!"

Hands tightened on me. A sharp object slid into my side. I felt it probing, searching, tearing my insides. I screamed and wailed, fighting the hands that held me down.

"Hurry up," someone snapped. The voice was familiar. A man that swore never to hurt me.

"I can't find it," a man responded. "It's in too deep."

"Listen to me, old man," the voice above me snarled as he held me down. "Get that bullet out of her or I'll put one in you."

There was silence then the older man's gruff order. "Hold her."

Fingers tightened on me. The knife went deeper into my chest. I screamed louder. My body bucked. I kicked out despite the hands holding me down. I had to get away. They were killing me!

"Fuck, Tate! Hold her down!" someone shouted with anger, his fingers clamped on me.

"She's bleeding too damn much, Cash. I...I can't watch her die like this!"

"She's not going to die, Tate. I won't let her," the man above me ground out.

The knife went deeper, cutting through layers of my muscle. I could almost feel it near my bone, scraping along its hard surface. I screamed and arched my body, my vocal cords almost bursting.

"Why isn't she passing out? Goddammit! Do something, Cash!" the person holding my feet shouted.

There was silence except for my cries then a voice. Calm. Unemotional.

"Reverend?"

The man above me went from sounding angry to being frigid. I wanted to scream at him. Bare my teeth at him. Tell him to fuck off for being so goddamn cold when someone was carving my body to pieces.

A gravelly voice answered, one of his hands on my stomach and the other wielding the knife in my body. "If she were unconscious, son, it would be better. I can't get that bullet out with her jerking around. I might puncture something vital since I'm going in blind."

The man above me stiffened. I could almost feel him waiting, holding his breath.

The gravelly voice spoke again. "Do it."

"Shit. Shit," the younger man swore, standing at the foot of the bed.

I didn't care anymore what they did to me. Nothing could save me from the pain. It consumed me. It tore away at my insides. I wailed as the knife dug deeper into my chest.

"Please!" The sound ripped from my chest.

The voice above me was taut. So cold. "I'm sorry, sweetheart."

A hard fist punched me in the jaw. It was the last thing I remembered.

~~~~

I floated in a sea of hot and cold. Darkness pulled me under churning waters. Tidal waves of pain crashed against me. I'm not sure if hours, days, or weeks passed. All I knew was I was dying.

My teeth chattered. My body was on fire. Every cell I possessed seemed to be consumed in flames.

"Come back to me, Catarina," someone whispered in my ear. "Please come back to me."

My body reacted and my heart sped up. I knew him. His voice was like medicine to my soul. His presence was like a drug soaking into my bloodstream. I tried to open my eyes and look at him but I couldn't. It took too much effort.

He touched my jaw, his fingers rough against my skin right where he hit me. "I'm sorry about that, sweetheart."

Something cool brushed across my forehead. It felt good against my hot skin.
~~~~

"God, you're burning up," the voice above me whispered.

"Is she any better?" someone asked, entering the room. He sounded younger and worried. I knew him too. My head just hurt too much to figure out how.

The man above me took the wet cloth away from my head and answered. "No. She's still bleeding and her fever's high."

The words were clipped. Angry. I wanted to open my eyes and see who it was because it couldn't be Cash. I was wrong. Cash was calm and polite at all times. The man above me was cold and forbidding. Pissed and bad-tempered. But if it wasn't Cash, who was it?

The cloth reappeared and ran over my dry, chapped lips. I wanted to turn my head, lick the drop of water that landed near the corner of my mouth, but I couldn't move. The heat and pain controlled me.

"You want me to sit with her a while? You can go eat or something," someone else said, the sound of his heavy boots stopping near the side of my bed. He sounded older, wiser. His voice held all the experience of someone who had seen and done many things, not all of them good. "You need to take a break, son. Get some rest."

The person beside me tensed. I didn't need to be conscious to know it. The air changed, vibrating with warning. Like the air right before an electrical storm.

The wet cloth was taken from my face and flung down.

"I don't need a damn break! I need her awake! I need her to open her eyes and look at me!"

There was silence then the older man's voice.

"Son, it's in God's hands now. All we can do is wait."

A chair was flung back. It hit the wall with a crash. The person beside me jumped to his feet.

"God? Where was He when she was shot? Where was He when that monster tried to hurt her? No, I'll be *damned* if I'm going to wait around for Him to take her from me!" He was angry but underneath it was something else. Fear. "He did this! He let this happen!"

The old man's voice was gruff. "Son, God didn't do this. Men did."

The man above me went still. "You're right, old man. God didn't do this. I did."

~~~~

Fever threatened to burn me from the inside out. I thrashed. Sweat soaked my body. Chills shook me.

I drifted in and out of consciousness, my mind fuzzy. What was real, unclear.

"Cat? Babe, wake up."

I opened my eyes. Every inch of me hurt. Getting run over by a truck wouldn't have hurt as bad.

"Look at me, Cat."

I didn't want to. My head was pressed against something cool. Something that felt good against my feverish skin. Wind whipped my hair around. Strings of it clung to my mouth.

"Cat. Look at me."

There it was again. That voice. I knew it. I had cried over it. Many nights I craved to hear it again. I had to look at him.

I didn't bother pushing my hair out of my face. I lifted my head. My neck protested. My arms were too heavy to move and my hands were useless, lying in my lap.

The first thing I saw was inky blackness. It was dark but the lights of a car's dashboard lit up the night. My eyes adjusted. *Wait. A car?*
~~~~

I could hear the roar of the engine and feel the road under the tires. Yes, I was in a car but how? Barbed wire fences and large oak trees flew by outside the window. I tried to remember how I got there but everything was blank.

"Babe."

There it was again. That voice. I turned my head.

"Luke?" I asked in a croaky voice, my throat raw from screaming and my mouth dry from the fever that ate at me.

He glanced over at me and smiled. "Hey, babe."

I drew a sharp breath. *Luke's beside me. How's that possible?*

He grinned and looked back at the road. I let my eyes roam over him, at a loss for words.

He had one wrist dangling over the steering wheel and one hand on the gearshift between us. His hair was cut short and his body was muscular. My mouth went dry and my heart jumped into my throat. He looked just the same as the night he died.

What was going on?

I glanced into the backseat, expecting to see Jenna, but she wasn't there.

"It's just you and me, Cat," Luke said, his gaze flicking over to me.

I glanced down. I was wearing dark jeans and a jacket. Dusty, scuffed boots were laced up my calves. It was what I had been wearing on the sidewalk in Hilltop. When Frankie stopped us from leaving. When Paul and Hightower appeared.

Dried blood encrusted one side of the jacket. I touched it then lifted my hand. Blood was caked under my nails and stained my hands. It was my blood, I realized, and I remembered suddenly how I lost it.

A bullet to my side.

"This isn't real," I whispered, dropping my hands back to my lap and staring straight ahead.

Luke downshifted and looked over at me, taking a curve in the road too fast. "Real is relevant, Cat. It's not always what you can see or believe."

"So I'm dreaming," I mumbled, trying to comprehend. "Or dead."

"You're hallucinating. Your fever is dangerously high."

I turned my head to look at him. "Then you're not real."

He grinned. "I never said that, babe."

I scrunched my brows together, confused. He didn't explain. Instead, he looked back at the road and shifted into another gear, his fingers tight around the gearshift.

The fever that was making me see Luke so clearly made everything else fuzzy. I licked my dry lips, so thirsty it hurt. Weakness made me rest my head on the back of the seat. The wound in my side grew.

Burning up with fever, I rolled my head to the side and looked at Luke. "Where are you taking me?"

He glanced over at me. "Home."

I shook my head. Beads of sweat popped out on my forehead. My body started shaking violently from the infection trying to kill me.

"I don't want to go home, Luke. I want to stay with you."

Luke's gaze was somber. "You can't, babe. You're not ready. You need to go home."

"I have no home," I whispered, my eyes slowly closing. "Not anymore."

There was silence then Luke's deep voice.

"Yes, you do, Cat. Your home is with him."

My eyes slowly opened. A different kind of warmth filled me. Not the kind from infections or fevers. The kind that Cash caused in me.

"I don't want to leave," I murmured. "I love him but I miss you."

Luke gave me a sad smile. "I know but I'll always be with you, babe, I promise."

I smiled weakly and closed my eyes. The fever took control. My teeth started chattering. My shoulders slumped and my body grew weaker and weaker. The shaking in my limbs turned into strong tremors.

Luke's voice came from far away. "I need you to fight, Cat. Fight and go back to him. He's angry and pissed but he needs you and you need him. Go back."

I wanted to open my eyes and tell him that Cash didn't need someone like me but I couldn't. I was losing consciousness fast.

Luke's voice came back one last time, swirling in my mind. Whispering. Persistent.

"Listen, Cat. Do you hear it? Home is calling you."

I furrowed my brows, listening. *There. A voice.* Luke was right. I didn't hear it before but now I did. It was faint but grew stronger and stronger. Angry. Desperate. It grabbed my attention and wouldn't let go.

The sound of the wind rushing into the car disappeared. The roar of the engine grew silent. I heard the voice in my ear as clear as day.

"Don't leave me, Cat. Please don't leave me."

My eyes fluttered open. Luke was gone. I was no longer in his car. I was in a bed.

The voice belonged to the man sitting in a chair beside me. His face was in his hands. His hair was disheveled. His chin was covered with a thick growth of beard and his clothes were wrinkled as if he had slept for days in them.

He looked tired, weary. His shoulders were slumped with despair. He was a man suffering, worn out with worry.

It was Cash.

And he was my home.

Chapter Five

-Cash-

I rubbed my hands over my eyes. Exhausted. At my wits end. My world had fallen apart. The last week had been hell.

I didn't know where Gavin and Keely were. There had been no sign of them. When we left Hilltop, we kept an eye out but hadn't spotted them. Part of me screamed to go find my sister – I had finally found her after all these years and didn't want to lose her again – but Cat was bad off. I was afraid if I left her, she would slip away from me. I just had to trust Gavin to take care of Keely.

Sending my sister with Gavin was tough but watching David dig the bullet out of Cat's side was the hardest thing I've ever had to do. I stood there and held her down. Subjected her to pain and watched her bleed as he took a knife and tried to locate the bullet buried in her. She screamed and thrashed around until I thought I would go berserk. I wanted to knock the old man's teeth out for hurting her but he was the only one who knew what he was doing.

When he slammed his truck to a stop in front of us in Hilltop, I wasn't sure if I could trust him but I had no choice. Cat had been in my arms, wounded and bleeding. Maybe even dying. I was frantic. I needed help. The decision was simple. I had to trust him. Now here we were, in a small cabin he had taken us to miles and miles from town.

It wasn't much to look at. It had two bedrooms and a kitchen with a large porch out front. It was set back against a hill, a barn off to one side and an outhouse on the other. The preacher had been stocking the place for years, stealing from Frankie what he had stole from others. When we got to the cabin, I didn't give a damn why he had it. My concern was Cat.

"Take her to the bedroom," David – the preacher – instructed, nodding to a sheet-covered doorway as I carried her into the ice-cold cabin.

With Tate behind me, I headed toward the room as David lit a kerosene heater and went to a cabinet in the kitchen. I heard him rambling around in it as I pushed past the sheet. The bedroom was small, just big enough for a bed, a nightstand, and a dresser.

I laid Cat down on the faded quilt, careful not to jar her too much. Blood soaked my jacket and drenched her side. A smear of it was across her cheek.

I was on the verge of freaking out. I wanted to scream and throw something. Shake her and tell her to wake the fuck up. *This couldn't be happening.* I was in hell and watching her bleed was my punishment for all the bad things I had done.

David walked in with a bowl of supplies in one hand and carrying the heater in the other. He rounded the bed and set the heater on the floor and the supplies on the nightstand. When he turned to Cat and started to reach for the top button of her jacket, I grabbed his wrist in a bone-crushing grasp.

"Don't touch her," I growled through clenched teeth. My hand was bloody and my mood was dark. No one touched Cat but me.

David looked up. "I'm a doctor, son," he said in a calm voice. "It'll be okay. I'm not going to hurt her."

Doubt played with me. I glanced down at Cat and saw the blood soaking the bed under her. I fought the possessiveness in me that wanted no one to touch her and hurt her more.

Relaxing, I let the preacher go. "One wrong move and my knife will find your jugular. It's as simple as that."

His wrinkled, square face went white. "I took an oath, son. I'm a doctor, not a monster."

"I thought you were a preacher," Tate piped up from the end of the bed, staring down at his sister with a pale face.

David stood up straighter, almost giant-like in the small room. "I am a preacher but I'm also a doctor," he explained, unrolling the towel that held his supplies. "Well, I was an obstetrician to be exact."

Tate shifted to his other leg with uneasiness. "She ain't pregnant, Doc." He paused and looked at me, his face going slack. "Or is she?"

I avoided his eyes. "No, she's not."

I started unbuttoning her blood-soaked jacket, anything to keep my fists from finding a wall. The truth was I wasn't sure if Cat was pregnant. We hadn't used any protection. Condoms were impossible to find, thanks to the lack of supplies. Nothing was being manufactured and nothing was being shipped into the U.S. Birth control was nonexistent except for abstinence and pulling out. One was damn hard to do and the other was not fool proof.

Shit, I didn't want to think about her lying there bleeding, maybe even dying, and possibly carrying my child. My hands started shaking. I got weak in the knees. But one thing at a time. We had to get that bullet out of her.

I unbuttoned the last button on her jacket and pushed the edges back. Bile rose in my throat when I saw the blood soaking her side. It turned her shirt a dark red and made the material stick to her. Her chest rose and fell slowly. Too slowly. I counted each breath she took then I prayed for her to take more.

Swallowing hard, I let my gaze travel to her face. God, it was pale. Her dark lashes lay against her colorless cheeks. Her dark hair spilled behind her on the bed. She was beautiful and she was dying.

All because of me.

I felt my stomach roll and the room spin. Not from nausea. From the fear and disgust knowing she was lying there, bleeding and unconscious, because of me.

I reached for the buttons on her shirt with shaky hands. *I did this. I caused her to get shot and bleed.*

I peeled back the edges of her shirt, exposing the hole in her side. Blood ran from it, soaking the quilt under her. David handed me a rag and I started wiping it away but it kept coming. Pouring.

I did this.

Fury had me clamping my jaw shut. My fingers gripped the cloth, my knuckles turning white.

Me.

The clink of metal interrupted my thoughts. I looked up, anger rippling through me and looking for an outlet. David was arranging his equipment on the bed beside Cat. There was a half-empty bottle of alcohol, a paring knife, tweezers, a tube of antibiotic cream, and a needle wrapped with thick black thread. A sorry excuse for a doctor's stash of supplies.

I felt sick, seeing that needle. The thought of someone stitching Cat up made me want to puke. I didn't want to watch David stick a needle in her skin but I damn sure wasn't going to leave her side.

He picked up the paring knife and poured some alcohol on it. That's about as sterile as it was going to get, being out in the middle of nowhere without a working hospital.

His hand shook as he set the bottle aside. I watched as he ran his hand over his whiskered chin, holding that damn knife in his trembling hand and looking unsure.

What the hell? He's nervous?

He must have seen the look in my eyes – the one that said you better get your shit together – because he cleared his throat and looked at Tate.

"Kid, under the sink there's a bottle of Jim Beam. Get it for me."

Tate spun on his heel and left. I took a step closer to the bed, ready to tackle David if he put that trembling knife anywhere near Cat's body.

"What's going on, old man?" I asked, my voice like death warmed over.

He glanced up, sweat coating his upper lip. "Just give me a second. It's been awhile."

I tilted my head, staring at him under the brim of my hat. "Not sure we've got a second but do what you've gotta do. You got a minute then I'm putting a gun to your head and making you."

He nodded nervously and fiddled with the medical supplies. Tate reappeared with the alcohol, almost tripping over his own feet. The bottle of booze was dusty and looked older than me. David grabbed it and unscrewed the top. Tossing the lid on the bed, he lifted the bottle and took a long drink. After half of it was gone, he offered it to me.

"You'll need it," he said.

I was tempted but I shook my head. "I need her more."

David eyed me then recapped the bottle. "Your call. But if you're not gonna drink, I suggest you pray. It might be the only thing that gets you through this."

He put the whiskey bottle beside the bed and grabbed the rubbing alcohol. After dousing both of his hands with it, he set it aside and looked down at Cat.

"Okay. Hold her, boys."

I tossed my hat to the corner of the room and grabbed her arms. Tate grabbed her ankles. She was unconscious but that changed when David started poking and prodding her with the paring knife. Blood poured from the half-inch hole in her side. She started screaming and fighting. It almost killed me, seeing her like that.

She bowed off the bed, a loud wail escaping her, as David dug deeper into her side. He was sweating. Blood coated his thick fingers.

Tate and I held her down, pushing her into the lumpy mattress. She thrashed about until I was afraid David would nick something vital. Tate was having a fit and I was about to lose it.

"Do it," David told me when she continued to fight.

I didn't want to but hell, I couldn't take seeing her in agony any longer. When she screamed 'please,' it gutted me, leaving me raw. Saying a silent prayer for her to forgive me because I damn sure would never forgive myself, I whispered, 'I'm sorry, sweetheart,' and cuffed her on the chin. It was just enough to knock her out but it still left a nasty bruise on her jaw. I had stared at it for days, sick with what I had done. Furious that I had caused all of it to happen to her in the first place. As I sat there beside her bed, day in and day out, I hated myself more and more.

That's where I was now. Sitting beside her bed with my head in my hands. I hadn't slept in forty-eight hours. I hadn't eaten in twenty-four. Cat had been out for a week. I had lost count of the days after three. David had gone looking for Gavin and Keely a few times. Each time he came back with no news. I left Cat only long enough to take care of personal business then I was back in the chair, silently begging her to wake up and return to me.

"Anything?"

I dropped my hands from my face and looked up at Tate as he walked in. He appeared scruffier than usual and dirtier than normal. There was dirt on his jacket and mud on his boots. I didn't bother asking what the hell he had been doing. I didn't have it in me to care.

"She's still burning up," I said, leaning back in the chair. "Nothing's changed."

Exhausted, I rubbed a hand down my face. I was worried about Gavin and Keely. Worried that the militia would find us. Worried about losing Cat.

I had cleaned her up, wiping away the blood. The water in the bowl had been red. My hands were still stained with it. She was clean but I was far from it. My clothes were the same ones I had been wearing for days, stiff with dried blood.

I felt Tate staring at me warily. I knew what he was thinking. He thought I had lost my fuckin' mind. After David got the bullet out of Cat's chest and dropped it on the quilt, I had stormed from the room and raised bloody hell. I had cussed and thrown things. Had a real tantrum that my mom and dad would have been ashamed of. Cat had been shot. She had jumped in front of a bullet for me. *Goddamn it. For me.* I had led her to that town. I had made love to her in that hellhole. I had lost my head and pulled a gun on that asshole, ready to deal out some retribution for Cat and Keely. Instead, I gave her a bullet and a fight for her life.

I started taking out my frustration and fear on Tate and David. Day in and day out for the past week, I snapped at them whenever they tried talking to me. I roared at them when they tried to get me to leave Cat's side. I wasn't that calm, gentle cowboy that she had met years ago. I was mean and angry. So when Tate started talking, I tuned him out until his words got through to me.

"So I got as close as I could to the town. There's no way I can get in and get our supplies and I didn't see any sign of Gavin or Keely," he said, sounding older than his fifteen years. "I'll try again soon."

I snapped my head up, glaring at him. "Who the hell said you could go near town?"

He ground his teeth, always ready with an attitude. "No one, but I ain't looking for permission. I'll do what I want and what I want to do is find Keely."

I shot to my feet. I wasn't one to lose a handle on my temper, but something happened to me as I watched Cat get shot. Something inside me just…

Tore apart.

I got in Tate's face. He was tall but I was taller. I had seen more and done more. He might be a badass kid but I was a deadly man.

"You don't think I'm worried about my sister too? You don't think I want to climb in that truck and haul ass out of here to find her? Fuck kid, I do, but I'm not moving until Cat wakes up and I sure as hell don't need you with a bullet in your side too. So don't walk out that damn door without asking me," I said in a controlled voice that was laced with fury. "In fact, don't even take a leak without checking with me first. Got it?"

Tate thrust his chin up. So much like his sister that I felt a punch to my gut.

"Who died and made you boss?" he snapped, defiant little shit.

As soon as the words left his mouth, he realized what he had said. His tanned face went white. His gaze swung to Cat. "Shit," he croaked.

I suddenly felt guilty as hell. The kid had lost his older brother, Nathan, and he had never had much of a father or mother to speak of, according to Cat. That left only one person to boss him around and God only knew if she would survive or not.

I let out a breath and ran my fingers through my hair. "Sorry, kid. Just…just don't wander off, okay?"

Tate gave me a guilty look from behind his long brown hair. "Yeah, okay."

We stood there a minute, not talking. Worried. Exhausted. I rubbed a hand over my eyes, trying to keep myself alert.

"You look like shit. Go to sleep. I'm gonna go talk to the preacher," Tate said, pushing his hair out of his eyes.

I nodded and went back to my chair as he left. Resting my elbows on the arms, I slouched down and ran my fingers over my brow, barely holding onto my sanity. I wanted to throw the chair across the room and ram my fist through the window. I wanted to get in the truck and race back to Hilltop, destroy the men who had done this to Cat. Instead, I stayed in the chair and stared at her.

Minutes past. Dark thoughts swirled in my mind the longer I sat there. I was sorry for not protecting her. Sorry for taking her to Hilltop. Sorry for loving her and getting her in this mess. She deserved better than a bullet wound and a lumpy bed in a two-room cabin. She deserved better than me.

My helplessness turned to fury. It grew and churned in me. It ate away at that place where I had once been easygoing and calm. Cat was unconscious because of me. She was hurt because of me. The thought made me angrier than ever before.

That's when I lost it.

I shot to my feet and started pacing beside the bed. My strides were furious. My fists clenched and unclenched.

"Damn you, Cat," I muttered between tightly gritted teeth. "Wake up. Wake up now and tell me that you hate me. That's an order."

She didn't move and I grew more furious. At her. At me. At this goddamn world.

"You're a spoiled, little brat that always gets her way. Well, princess, you got your way. You saved me. You jumped in front of that fuckin' bullet and saved my life. You got what you wanted. Now wake the hell up so I can get what I want!" I shouted at her. "Now, damn you! Wake up!"

Still nothing. She lay still and quiet. Her eyes didn't open and glare at me. Her eyebrows didn't arch haughtily.

I stood over her and clenched my fists, my chest rising and falling with rage. "Fight, Cat," I ground out between a tightly clenched jaw. "Fight now."

When she stayed still, all the anger left me in a whoosh. My exhaustion caught up to me. I fell into the chair and put my face in my hands.

"Don't leave me, Cat," I whispered in a broken voice. "Please don't leave me."

Anger and grief suffocated me.

"Fuck," I said hoarsely as my hands started shaking.

At that moment, I started making deals with God. I would die in her place. I would walk into Hilltop and surrender myself to Frankie and his men. I would let them tear me apart limb by limb and not lift a hand.

I would stop loving her if He only returned her to me.

As soon as I swore the last one, I heard movement from the bed.

"Cash?"

My heart stopped. I lifted my head.

Cat was staring back at me.

Chapter Six

-Cat-

He was sitting beside my bed, looking larger than life. His elbows were on his knees and his legs were spread wide. Carefully controlled power radiated from him, leashed and barely contained.

He was holding his head in his hands. As I watched, his fingers plunged violently into his hair. I wanted to touch his strong jaw and firm lips. Run my fingers over the whiskers that grew near them. I wanted to prove that he was real and I hadn't died and gone to heaven.

The idea of pearly white gates almost made me scoff. I would go to hell when I died, I was sure of it. The devil would be waiting for me at the fiery entrance and welcome me with open arms. I had done some terrible things in my life and never cared if they were right or wrong. Lying. Drinking. Fucking. Swearing. Men swore I had no soul. My grandmother deemed that hell was the only place I would go. I knew what eternity had in store for me and it wasn't halos and golden wings. It was fire and brimstone.

So if I were dead, I wouldn't see Cash. He was the white knight to my black soul. He would go to heaven while I was on a one-way path to hell. It must mean I was very much alive.

I laid still a moment, assessing my surroundings. The hum of a heater came from somewhere on the floor, making the room toasty warm. The bed I was on was soft and covered with a faded blanket, the edge pulled up around my chin.

I moved then grimaced. My side felt like a white-hot poker had been stabbed in me repeatedly. I felt the pain down to my marrow and in every muscle and fiber of my body. It was agonizing. The kind of hurt that made you sick to your stomach.

I bit my lips to keep from crying out and curled my fingers into the sheet. Gripping the threadbare material hard, I whispered the first word that came to me.

"Cash."

He jerked his head up, his gray eyes going wide.

"Cat?"

He dropped his hands between his knees. His hair was spiked and standing up in all different directions. There were dark circles under his eyes and worry in his storm-colored gaze. Despite it all, he had never looked so good.

I smiled weakly and said the second thing that came to me.

"Cowboy."

It wasn't much, but it was all I could gather enough energy to say.

He didn't smile. I didn't even get one little quirk of his mouth. His eyes went from light to dark in seconds.

"God, Cat."

Hearing him say my name never sounded so sweet. His voice could soothe me. Make me come one second and center me in reality the next. I needed to hear it like I needed air to breathe.

"Say my name again," I whispered. "Please."

He stood up slowly, rising over my bed. He was large and lean, towering over me like some kind of powerful warrior out of a video game that Keely had probably played. He put a hand on either side of me and leaned down.

"I'll say it a hundred times if you want me to," he rasped, so close to me I could see the gray specks in his irises. "Cat."

"Again," I demanded, my voice hoarse and scratchy from misuse.

His gaze dropped down to my lips. "Cat."

I reached up and wrapped my arms around his neck, pulling him down to me.

"You're real. You're real," I repeated against the warm skin of his throat.

He ran his hands up my arms and to my back, careful of the bandage on my side.

"I'm real," he muttered, his lips against my hair. "And I'm holding you."

His fingers burned my skin and slid over me with possession. One of them moved to grasp the back of my neck and the other traveled across my back. They were gentle. Strong. Burying under my matted hair. Touching on the edge of my jaw. Tracing the top of my spine. Proving I was alive.

I tried to look around as he held me, afraid we were still in Hilltop.

"Did we get out? Where are we?" I whispered with panic, afraid Frankie or Paul would appear.

Cash's voice was deep. Calming. "We're in a cabin, safe for now."

I grasped at his jacket frantically. "Where's Tate and Keely? Did they make it out too?"

Cash held me tighter. "Tate's here. Keely's with Gavin. He got her out but we haven't seen them since."

Tears fell down my cheeks as I buried my face in his neck. The slight movement sent pain shooting through me.

I grasped him tighter as waves of agony hit me. My abdomen felt like spikes were being driven into it. My breath caught when it grew worse and worse. Feeling something warm on my stomach, I pulled away and looked down.

I was wearing a shirt but it had ridden up underneath my breasts, leaving the white bandage wrapped around my middle exposed. Blood was spreading on it, turning the bleached white a bright red.

The pain became excruciating. Weakness made me go limp. The little bit of energy I had disappeared. I couldn't fight it any longer. My arms dropped away from Cash and my eyes drifted closed. I started to lose consciousness when a harsh voice brought me back.

"No!" Cash swore with panic.

He lowered me back to the bed quickly and reached for the bandage on my side. When he peeled back the edge, blood started running down my body.

"David! Get in here!" he shouted. "Hurry!"

I flinched when he pressed something to the wound. It sent a stream of fire through me. I was losing consciousness fast but I fought it. Just like Luke told me to do.

I heard the thump of heavy boots then the sound of voices in the room. One was angry, the other calm. Hands touched me, poking at the wound and wiping blood away.

"I did this," Cash spit angrily. "She was okay until I touched her and held her. Shit, what have I done?"

"It's okay, son," a calm, gravelly voice responded. "She's lost a lot of blood and she's burning up with fever. Give her time. She's getting better. She's just weak."

"No!" The word was slashed out like a weapon, cutting through the air. "It's my fault! I never should have touched her!"

There was a shift in the air. I felt something fly by. It hit the wall with a bang and shattered. Someone roared. Another person yelled.

I forced my eyes open. Cash was standing over me, breathing hard. His chest rose and fell, drawing in quick bursts of air. His fists were clenched. The look in his eyes was fierce and wild, the bunching of his biceps violent.

He had been the one to throw something. It was in the way he held himself. In the way he stared across the room. Fury rolled off him in waves.

"Fuck, this is my fault," he said, his voice broken. "I never should have loved her."

There was so much anguish and self-hate in his voice that my heart cracked. My eyes closed. A single tear escaped from one of them.

Then the darkness claimed me again.

Chapter Seven

-Cash-

I stared down at Cat. My blood ran cold. Seconds ago, I had held her and whispered her name. Now I was watching her bleed and lose consciousness.

My throat closed up. My body went stiff. I went cold and hot at the same time. It was my fault she was in pain. My fault that she was suffering. I wanted to punch something or someone. I was so fucked up on the inside that I didn't know which way was up or down. I wanted to drop to my knees and touch her again. Whisper her name and feel her breath against my cheek. But something inside me shut down.

"She's okay, son. Just let her rest," David said quietly, putting a hand on my arm.

I fought the urge to twist it off. Instead, I lifted my gaze to his.

"I'm not your son," I spit.

Grabbing my cowboy hat from the corner of the room, I glared at him as I stalked past. Reverend or not, the man could go to hell.

Tate was rushing into the room as I was leaving.

"What's wrong?" he asked, his eyes wide with fear as they went from me to David.

"Watch your sister," I snapped. "Don't leave her side."

"Where are you going?"

I cut my eyes over at him. "To track my sister and Gavin."

He took a step closer. "I'm coming with you."

"Over my dead body." I pointed at the bed. "Get your ass over there and don't leave Cat's side."

He narrowed his eyes at me. "I said you ain't the boss."

I took a step closer to him and lowered my voice. "You leave her side or follow me, I'll rip you a new one, Tate. Watch her!" I barked, thrusting my finger at the bed.

He fell back a step, looking at me like I was demented. Maybe I was. I hadn't left Cat's side for a week. Suddenly, I needed to get away. But I had to know that she would be safe and the kid would stay out of trouble.

When he backed down, I shot out of the bedroom and across the cabin. The living room was the size of a postage stamp. Tate had been camping out on the couch. David had taken the tiny second bedroom. I had spent my nights in the chair next to Cat's bed. But Tate could take over. I needed to put space between her and me. It was for the best. I had gotten her shot and put her in danger. Me.

I hit the heavy wooden door with the palm of my hand, slamming it open. Sunlight and a gust of cold wind greeted me as I stalked outside. Jumping off the porch, I started across the clearing, my strides angry. Pissed.

I clenched my fists. My muscles grew taut. I couldn't handle seeing Cat lying there bleeding anymore. I had lost my parents because I couldn't save them. I had lost my home and my land. I had seen things that would make a grown man cry and done things that would make one shudder. But I couldn't take seeing the woman I loved hurt because of me.

Looking down, I flexed my hand, knowing what I had to do. I had to stay away from Cat and stop loving her. For her safety and my sanity. It's what I deserved for getting her hurt. It's the deal I made with God if He returned her to me.

I just had to figure out how to survive it and get her to stop loving me.

Chapter Eight

-Cat-

Cold air forced me awake. Strong gusts of wind rattled the window. I opened my eyes with a white ceiling meeting my gaze, a wide crack running down the middle.

It all started to come back to me in a flood of images. Paul. Frankie. Hilltop and the hotel. Cash. The bullet. Keely and Gavin. My pain. His anger.

I drew in a great gulp of air. My side hurt, a sharp pain extending to every limb of my body.

I winced and realized with a start that I was only wearing a man's flannel shirt. It hit me mid-thigh. A bandage of some kind was wrapped around my middle. I reached down and felt it. When my fingers grazed over the left side, a hiss left me.

That's where the bullet struck. I felt queasy, remembering the thud it had made when it hit me and the excruciating agony afterward.

I started to push the blanket off me to look at the wide bandage but a soft snore startled me.

Tate was asleep in the chair beside the bed. His hand supported his head on the arm of the chair and his mouth was hanging open.

I remembered what Cash had said – Gavin got Keely out but he hadn't seen them since. I was worried but at least Tate was here. I didn't know what I would do if something happened to him.

Another snore escaped him. His chin dropped off his hand and his eyes opened. When he saw me, he blinked then blinked again.

"Cat?"

"In the flesh," I whispered weakly. "Can I have some water?"

Tate jumped to his feet, almost toppling over the chair. He rushed out of the room in a tangle of feet and gangly legs.

I heard him talking to someone outside the bedroom. A minute later, he reappeared carrying a crumbled plastic water bottle.

"I'm so glad you're awake!" he said in an excited voice, handing the water to me. "I thought for sure you'd go into a coma or die. We were all so worried that you wouldn't make it. You scared the shit out of me, sis, I swear."

"I'm okay," I lied, taking the bottle with a shaky hand. "Just thirsty." And in pain.

Raising the container, I took a long drink. Metallic-tasting water slid past my cracked lips and down my parched throat. I gulped and gulped, unable to get enough. Dying of thirst.

"Not too much. You'll get sick," a deep voice boomed from the doorway.

I lowered the bottle, my blood going cold at the sound of the man. The preacher from Hilltop stood near the foot of my bed. David.

He had a smile on his face but worry in his eyes. I remembered him as the man who had welcomed us with a grin. Tricked us into believing Hilltop was a friendly place. As far a I knew, he worked for Frankie. He was guilty by association if nothing else.

When he took a step closer to the bed, my fear of him turned into rage. Rage for what they did to me. Rage at feeling helpless when I saw Paul and Hightower.

I sat up and reached for the pistol sticking out of Tate's waistband. The world tilted and my vision blurred but I grabbed the gun and pointed it at David.

"Don't move, mister."

Tate looked at me wide-eyed through strands of his long hair. "Cat, he's cool. Put the gun down."

"Shut up, Tate. He's one of *them*," I spit, keeping my gaze on the old man.

The preacher's smile wavered. He raised his hands, showing he was no threat.

"I see you're feeling better," he said. "But you're looking a little pale. You must be in a whole lot of pain. I got something—"

He started to reach into the front pocket of his jacket but I pulled the hammer back on the pistol.

"I said not to move."

He paused and raised one bushy eyebrow. I licked my dry lips and tried to concentrate on holding the gun steady. The pain was getting worse. A dull thumping agony beat through me.

The man must have known it because he reached toward his pocket again. "Don't shoot me, honey." A second later he tossed something on the bed beside me.

"From your boyfriend," he said in way of explanation, nodding down at the bottle.

I looked down. It was a prescription bottle. A couple of white pills sat inside. If they were painkillers, I needed them. But I wasn't ready to trust the preacher just yet.

"Where is he?" I whispered, leaving the bottle untouched.

David shrugged. "Your man? He's gone."

The gun faltered in my hand. Panic bubbled up inside me. I glanced at Tate.

"Where's Cash?"

Tate avoided my eyes, hiding behind his long bangs. "You gotta understand, sis…"

I interrupted him, growing desperate and angry. "Where is he, Tate? Tell me!"

He pushed his hair out of his face and ducked his head. "It's just…well…he's just not the same since you got shot. It's like…seeing you bleed all over the place, it…well, it changed him. Made him mad."

Hurt twisted inside me.

"So he left?" I asked, forcing the words out. "He just packed up and rode off?"

Tate frowned. "Nah. He keeps his distance. That's all. Says it's for the best. He's around. He just stays clear of you most of the time and it keeps going out, looking for Gavin and Keely."

"He hasn't found them?" I asked with a whisper.

Tate shook his head, looking upset.

Anguish squeezed my heart and made my eyes water. The preacher started to move toward me again but I raised the gun higher.

"Don't come any closer," I said, staring at him through the tears clouding my eyes. "I'm not warning you again."

The threat was weak and he knew it.

Moving closer, he kept his hands up. "I'm a doctor. If I wanted to hurt you, I wouldn't have dug that slug out of your side. I would've let you bleed out instead." He nodded at the gun in my hand. "Now, put it away before you shoot me on accident and someone's got to dig a bullet out of my ribs."

I glanced at Tate, unsure. The preacher couldn't be trusted. I was almost certain of it. But Tate nodded.

"You can trust him, sis. He ain't gonna hurt you."

And just like that, my energy disappeared. I let out a breath and dropped my hand. The gun was suddenly too heavy. I was too weak. The pistol fell into my lap, my fingers going limp around it.

I started to collapse back to the bed but the preacher raced to my side. Putting an arm around my shoulders, he eased me down.

"She's freezing, kid. Get another blanket and heat up some of that soup," he instructed, glancing over his shoulder at Tate.

"Yes, sir." Tate jumped to attention.

"And go get Cash. He may not want to be here but he'll want to know she's awake and lucid," David added.

Tate nodded and disappeared behind the blanket that hung between the bedroom and the rest of the cabin.

As he did, David grabbed the bottle of pills from beside me and shook one out in the palm of his hand. "I didn't ask where Cash got these from but praise God he did. Painkillers, darling. Take one," he said, offering it to me in the palm of his hand.

I took it and the water he handed me, my fingers numb with cold. The pill felt like a stone going down my throat but the water felt amazing.

I took small sips, hoping the painkiller did its job quickly. The wound was throbbing, sending agony through me. Beads of sweat popped out on my upper lip and hairline. I felt like I had been run over by a freight train and speared by a harpoon.

When a violent shiver ran through me, the preacher reached for the blanket that had fallen down around my waist.

"May I?" he asked pausing, his fingers inches from the faded quilt.

I studied him through the dark strands of my hair. Everything in me screamed not to trust him. But if Cash and Tate did then I would too.

"Okay," I whispered, giving in.

He started tucking the blanket around me. "Gotta say that you're one mighty strong woman. Stubborn, I might add, but strong. You fought us tooth and nail when I tried to get that bullet out of you. That man of yours had to knock you out. About tore him up. I ain't never seen a man so broken before."

I reached out from under the blanket and touched my jaw. A vague memory of Cash doing the same came to me. He had run his fingers over my chin and whispered he was sorry.

"Tell me the truth. How bad was I?" I asked, dropping my hand away.

David tucked my hand under the covers, frowning when he felt my cold fingers. "Bad enough that Cash didn't sleep a wink or leave your side for a week."

My heart thumped harder. Cash had sat beside me the whole time? A week? I blushed, thinking of him taking care of me. Wiping my brow. Watching me sleep. So why was he staying away from me now?

David patted my shoulder and turned to leave. "Get some rest. I'll check on you later." He was almost to the door when I spoke up.

"Wait. Can I ask you something?"

He turned and looked down at me, a gentle smile on his face. "I'm a man of God and a doctor. Questions and confessions are my specialty."

I didn't return his smile. I had only one thing on my mind.

Cash.

"Does he really want to stay away from me?" I asked, almost afraid to hear the answer.

David opened his mouth then clamped it shut. Walking to the end of the bed, he rubbed his chin and looked down at me.

"He's fighting his own demons. He'll come around," he said, sounding sure and confident.

"And if he doesn't?" I asked.

David shrugged. "Then you fight the demons for him."

Chapter Nine

-Cat-

I woke up sometime later. The bedroom was dim. The sun was setting. The chair beside me was empty. There were no sounds coming from the other room. I stayed still, listening. There was nothing. Just silence.

I shifted and my bladder protested. I needed to find a restroom quick.

I pushed to a sitting position, careful not to move too fast. The room spun then righted itself. I moved a lock of my hair back. It felt matted and dirty but it was the least of my problems. I had to get out of bed.

Taking a deep breath, I shoved the covers off my legs with my feet. Cold air hit me. I eased my feet over the side of the bed. By the time they dangled to the floor, I was breathing hard and sweating. Weak.

I sat at the edge of the mattress for a moment. When my breathing returned to normal, I pushed to my feet. As soon as I was upright, my knees started to buckle. I cried out and grabbed the bed, catching myself before I fell.

When the room stopped spinning, I let go of the bed and straightened. This time my legs supported me.

The shirt I wore hit me at my knees. My feet were bare, the scuffed, wooden floor cold beneath my toes. I glanced around. I didn't want to walk around without pants or underwear, but I didn't see any other clothing. The shirt would have to do.

I took a faltering step then another. It felt weird to stand after being in a bed for so long. My legs felt like Jell-O and being upright felt odd.

I took careful, slow steps toward the door. When I got to the faded sheet that hung from it, I pushed it aside and stepped out of the bedroom.

A small living room greeted me. The walls were rough planked board. The windows were covered with faded curtains in green. The room had a rundown couch shoved against a wall and a faded recliner in the corner. On my right was the kitchen. Four mismatched chairs sat around a scarred table. A small hot plate rested on the cracked butcher block countertop and a stack of dirty dishes were stacked near it.

I averted my gaze, my stomach rolling at the thought of food. Tate had brought me soup earlier but I hadn't managed to keep it down.

Fighting the ill feeling again, I held onto the wall and made my way across the room. My legs were unsteady but I was determined to find the bathroom or what counted for a bathroom when modern plumbing didn't work anymore. The cabin was rustic, more for camping than for living. I realized quickly that there had never been a toilet or even a shower. I would have to go outside, barefoot and half dressed. But I *had* to go.

The thought of using a tree or a dark, dank outhouse would have made the old me stomp my Louis Vuitton heels in frustration and whine like a spoiled princess. I once lived in the biggest home in the county. I could snap my fingers and get what I wanted. My father was a bigwig in the oil business. His daughter wouldn't be caught dead using an outhouse or wearing a man's flannel shirt that hung on her like a sack.

But times had changed. I hadn't seen my dad in three years. I gave up heels for boots. I ate whatever I could find and lived wherever it was safe. Running water was a luxury very few had. Using an outhouse was now normal.

I made my way to the front door, listening for any sounds of activity. There was none, not even the sound of someone breathing. Where was everyone?

I felt alone and that's a feeling I didn't like. It could get you killed in this world, not having someone to watch your back. The war and the EMP had brought out the worst in people. The inability to produce and distribute antipsychotic drugs made it impossible to keep the crazies sane. The absence of law enforcement enabled rapists and killers to roam free. People shot you in the back for something as simple as a bar of soap. Yes, we had no electricity but it went beyond that. The ripple effect of the EMP was massive. Rumor was, the U.S. would never recover from it.

I didn't know if that was true or not, but I didn't like being alone. Bad things happened when you were by yourself. People like Paul and Hightower found you.

Forcing them out of my mind, I pushed open the front door and stepped outside. A gust of wind wrapped around my legs. My hair whipped across my face. Thick woods surrounded the cabin. Leaves blew across the clearing in front.

I held onto the rough-cut timbered structure and made my way across the porch. I could see the outhouse. It was set back a few yards from the cabin, surrounded by tall pine trees.

I tried not to think about how far away it was as I stepped off the porch and into the tall weeds. Despite the cold, a thin sheen of sweat dotted my forehead and upper lip. My knees almost gave out. Blades of dead grass pushed between my bare toes and my feet sank into soft earth.

I took a few hesitant steps. Somehow, I made it to the outhouse without falling. I did my business and headed back, feeling weaker and weaker. Holding onto the rough bark of trees as I went for support.

I was almost to the cabin when I heard a twig snap behind me. My body went cold. The little hairs on my arms stood up.

"What the hell are you doing?" a deep voice exploded.

Relief almost made me collapse. My heart beat a rapid, crazy tempo as I turned.

It was Cash.

And god, did he look pissed.

His head was tilted, the brim of his hat shielding his eyes from the sun and me. His body was strung tight. His gray, cold gaze was staring at me.

A few yards behind him was David. He was walking toward us, watching us with interest. His tall, giant-like body moved slowly. In one of his hands a skinned chicken dangled. In his other was a bloody knife.

I looked away from the dead bird and at Cash.

"Ummm." My mind went blank when I saw the anger in his gaze. I knew he wouldn't hurt a hair on my head but he was staring at me with such animosity.

Cash raised one eyebrow, waiting for me to explain. I saw his eyes. They were cold. Hard. Staring back at me with rage. I had never seen him look so furious. I felt a pang when I remembered what David had said. Cash was fighting his own demons.

And apparently I was one of them.

He took a step closer, the toes of his boots inches from my bare toes.

"I asked you a question, Beauty Queen. What are you doing out here?"

My chin quivered, but I jutted it up anyway. I was cold and godawful weak. My teeth were on the verge of chattering and I was fighting the urge to collapse. Pain throbbed in my side and a damn rock had poked me in the arch of my foot.

I wasn't in the mood.

"I'm happy to see you too, cowboy," I said as sweetly as I could, considering I was about to pass out.

David chuckled and walked past us on the way to the cabin. A tic appeared in Cash's whiskered jaw as he ignored the preacher and stared at me. His eyes turned a darker shade of gray. They made a quick pass over me, taking in my bare legs with no hint of concern.

"I didn't ask if you're happy to see me," he said in a clipped voice, sounding impatient and pissed. "I asked what you're doing out here by yourself. It's cold. Where's Tate?" He glanced past me to the house.

"I don't know," I answered, wondering that myself.

"Shit. I'm going to kill that kid," Cash snarled between clenched teeth, rushing past me.

I opened my mouth to tell him not to but a strong gust of wind hit me. The end of my shirt flew up. I slapped a hand on it to keep it down. When I did, pain exploded in my side, right above the bullet wound. I wrapped a hand around my middle and cried out, doubling over and seeing stars.

Cash spun around. "Damn it to hell," he scowled, taking one look at me.

He marched back and swung me up into his arms.

"What are you doing?" I cried out in a weak voice as he started for the house with me cradled against his chest.

"What do you think I'm doing?" he growled, his mouth set in what might be a permanent scowl. "I'm taking you back inside where you should be."

The muscles in his arm were tense under my thighs as he held me. His jaw was clamped so hard I was surprised I didn't hear his teeth grind together and crack. He was furious but he carried me carefully, making sure not to hurt me.

I stuck my jaw up, fighting weakness. "Cash, you don't have to—"

He cut me off. "Shut it, Cat. You're white as a sheet and your damn wound is probably bleeding again. You feel like you're burning up with fever and it's fuckin' cold out here. If I ever catch you alone outside again, I'm going to hogtie you to the bed. Understand?"

I stared up at him, wide-eyed. He had never said anything like that to me before. He really was pissed.

His strides were long and angry as he carried me to the cabin. The wind picked up and tossed my hair into my face. We didn't talk. He fumed. I stared, my body weak but my mind racing. What was wrong with him?

The pain in my side became worse but it didn't hurt as much as Cash's coldness toward me. When we reached the porch, I couldn't take it anymore.

"Put me down," I insisted in a faint voice, the last of my strength disappearing.

"I don't think so, sweetheart. Stay still," Cash muttered, tightening his arms around me. "You're going to hurt yourself."

"I'm already hurt. Put me down," I said through clenched teeth.

Cash didn't bother stopping or looking down at me. "No!" he snapped.

The word slashed through the air like a whip. His tone left no room for argument. His arms tightened around me as he took the porch steps two at a time. When he got to the top, his boots made heavy, angry thuds as he crossed to the front door.

Before we got there, Tate bounded around the corner of the cabin.

"What's up?" he asked, his gaze darting from me to Cash.

I opened my mouth to respond but Cash beat me to it.

"Get in the house now, Tate!" he ordered, the look on his face so dark that I shrink back in his arms.

"Yes, sir!" Tate jumped to attention and saluted Cash. Always the smartass, he snapped his heels together and reached out, yanking open the door for us.

Cash paused in the threshold, inches from my brother.

"Kid, I'm warning you," he hissed. "I'm not in a mood for your horse shit right now."

Tate's eyes flicked to me, ignoring Cash's threat. "She break her leg or something? Why are you carrying her? Why's he carrying you, Cat?"

I couldn't help but grin. Leave it to my brother to never know when to stop.

Cash grumbled and carried me into the cabin.

"No, she didn't break her leg," he muttered as Tate followed close behind us. "Stop with the questions."

"So what happened?" Tate asked. "She hurt or is this some kind of romantic shit? Do I need to give you two some privacy? You not afraid to be around her anymore, Cash?"

Cash's jaw clenched. The tic reappeared. He stopped. Facing Tate with me in his arms, his cold eyes centered on my brother.

"Where the fuck were you? I told you not to leave her side. She's not fully recovered yet."

Tate flipped his bangs out of his face, unfazed by Cash's fury. "I went out for just a second. Thought I heard a noise."

Cash bristled. I swear fire shot from his eyes.

"What part of 'don't leave her' do you not understand?" he snarled. "That was the only job I gave you."

Tate shrugged. "Well, guess you should have watched her yourself then, huh?"

Cash let out a low growl at Tate's veiled meaning. With a dark look, he started for the bedroom again, his arms tight around me. His stride was quick and purposeful. Livid.

"What's the big deal?" Tate argued, catching up to us. "It was just a split second. She looks fine to me."

Cash stopped. Cradling me against his chest like I weighed nothing, he turned and glared down at Tate.

"It took one second for the bullet to find her," he said in a voice so low it sent shivers down my spine. "One split second for it to bury in her side. You want something like that on your conscience? Keeping you up at night? Eating away at your soul? Believe me, it isn't fuckin' fun."

Tate went white. His Adam's apple bobbed up and down in his throat. For once, he didn't know what to say.

But I did.

"Cash, I'm okay," I said weakly. "You shouldn't—"

He cut me off. "Shut up, Cat. Just shut the hell up."

He started for the bedroom again. Tate didn't move, still rattled. I looked up at Cash as he carried me, wondering what had happened to him. To us. The pain in my side was severe but his anger toward me was agonizing.

"Put me down," I insisted as soon as he pushed past the sheet hanging in the doorway. "I don't want you touching me if you're going to be like this."

He slammed to a stop at the foot of the bed and glared down at me.

"You want down?" he quipped.

"Yeah." I nodded.

"What the Beauty Queen wants, she gets."

He set me down, his hands warm as they slid over my legs. His arms, so strong around me seconds ago, let me go. When they did, all the blood rushed from my head. The room tilted.

"Damn," I whispered, swaying.

A soft curse left Cash. He scooped me up again.

"You stubborn, little spoiled brat," he hissed in a rugged, raspy voice. "Maybe one day you'll listen to me."

I mumbled weakly as he laid me on the bed, "What would be the fun in that?"

He let out a soft grunt of irritation and planted both of his hands on either side of me.

"I'll warn you one more time. Don't mess with me, Cat."

I didn't move. Didn't breathe. Didn't think of anything but him looming over me.

"What happens if I do?" I asked, just a whisper on a rush of air. "What will you do?"

Cash's jaw tightened. "I won't be responsible for my actions. That's what I'll do."

He looked so angry. So annoyed. But I had never been afraid of him.

I reached up and grabbed the front of his shirt. With one pull, I tugged him closer to me.

"What happened to you, Cash? Where's my cowboy?" I whispered, struggling against the exhaustion and pain that was quickly winning.

Cash's gaze traveled over my face, touching on each of my features. My lips. My jawline. The way my hair fell across the pillow. When he looked back into my eyes, his were piercing. Full of fire and ice.

"He disappeared the moment that bullet hit you, Cat," he rasped. "He's gone."

He reached between us and unhooked my fist from his shirt, prying my fingers free. My heart beat against my ribs. My throat closed up. As he pulled away, I struggled to push myself upright, wincing when throbs shot through my left side.

"You're being a stubborn jerk," I whispered in a shaky, weak voice. My energy was completely gone. Lightheadedness was making the room spin. The pain was back in full force and so was my fever.

But I was going to fight him.

"No, a jackass," I corrected myself. "I like that better. You're being a jackass, Cash, and I don't like you very much right now."

He looked down at me, the side of his mouth quirking up in a cold smile.

"Like me?" he whispered. "Hell, sweetheart, you should hate me."

Before I could say anything, he turned around and strolled from the room like he didn't give a damn.

And I was afraid he suddenly didn't.

Chapter Ten

-Cat-

"Son of a bitch," I whispered, breathing hard. It had been days since Cash had caught me outside. Now, I was sick to death of being inside.

My fever was gone. I was getting my strength back. I had managed to give myself a sponge bath using water Tate had dragged in from a nearby creek. My clothes were back on but my boots were giving me hell. I had managed to step into one but because of the wound in my side, I couldn't bend down and tie the laces.

I blew out a frustrated breath. David had wrapped my middle in a tight bandage. I wasn't happy about it. I argued with him viciously. I tried to make him see reason. I just needed a little covering over the wound and I would be fine.

But he refused to listen. Just sat there with a calm expression on his craggy face and wrapped a strip of an old sheet around my middle. He said if I was going to move around, my side needed to be wrapped good and tight so I wouldn't reopen the wound.

It didn't matter what his reason was. I had thrown a huge tantrum. I was tired of being locked up in a room, hovered over by David and Tate like I was a piece of china that might break. I was tired of being avoided by Cash and I was worried about Keely. I wanted out of the cabin and I didn't want to be wrapped up like a mummy in bandages. But my fit ended when Tate poked his head into the room and said Cash was pacing the floor and looked like he wanted to kill someone. That made me shut up real quick.

I took a deep breath, bit down hard on my bottom lip, and leaned down, bending my body in half to reach the laces. I was determined to leave the room and pull my weight around the cabin. Do my part and show them I was well.

But pain shot from the wound in my side. I hissed, squeezing my eyes closed. I was better but it still hurt, more of a dull ache than sharp pain like before. I had refused to take any more painkillers. David wasn't happy about it but something was telling me the clock was ticking down until Paul and Hightower showed up. I had laid in bed for days, antsy and thinking about it. They wouldn't give up easily if they knew we were close. It was only a matter of time before they found us again and I didn't want pills clouding my mind.

"Shit!" I shouted with irritation, glaring at the laces. I needed to get dressed!

The sheet that hung in the doorway flew back. I looked up. Cash was standing there, looking large and forbidding.

Sulking, I plopped down on the edge of the bed. "Leave me alone."

I was pissed that I couldn't take care of myself and angry with him for being so damn cold.

Cash took one look at my unlaced boot and headed straight toward me.

Oh god.

His hair was sticking up. The stubble on his jaw was dark. Not knowing where Keely was had to be killing him.

I forgot that I was only wearing one boot and it was unlaced, that I was recovering from a bullet wound and was still woozy sometimes. I hopped off the bed and faced Cash as he closed the distance between us.

His eyes blazed. His body was taut, ready to attack. He stopped a foot from me. His gaze drifted down my figure slowly. I burned. I ached. I felt drawn to him like never before.

The need was overpowering. The desire was almost too much. I stood still, wondering what he was going to do. He had been so distant. So unfeeling. I didn't know this man in front of me but I was intrigued by him. Maybe even more than before.

"Cash—" I whispered, needing him to say something. Anything.

But he didn't. He clenched his jaw and went down to one knee at my feet. I drew in a sharp breath when he grabbed the laces of my boot and started to tie them.

"Just be quiet, Cat," he said when I opened my mouth to protest.

I clamped my mouth shut and pulled my bottom lip between my teeth. When my boot was laced, he reached for the other one lying nearby. His eyes flicked up to me once but he didn't say anything. He just took my ankle in his hand and lifted my foot to slide in the boot.

I grabbed his shoulders when I started to lose my balance. He tensed, his muscles growing taut under my hands.

A second passed then another. Tension filled the room. I wanted to say something but I couldn't. His hand was grasping my ankle. So intimate. So possessive. I wanted him to move it higher. Keep going. To the zipper and button on my jeans. I wanted him to yank my pants down. Pull me beneath him on the floor. But he did none of it. Instead, he slid his hand up to my calf and pushed my foot the rest of the way in the boot.

Depressing.

Letting go of my calf like it burned him, he laced the boot up with hurried, angry jerks.

"No sign of Keely and Gavin yet?" I asked, filling the silence.

"No," he clipped out, yanking one lace too hard.

I worried my bottom lip. "You think they're okay?"

A muscle ticked in Cash's jaw. "Gavin will guard her with his life."

"But you're still worried?"

He let out a humph – his new form of answering.

"Where is everyone else?" I asked, wanting him to just talk to me.

He glanced up, the coldness in his eyes mixing with the heat that burned in them. "Hunting."

"So how'd you get stuck babysitting me?"

"Luck," he deadpanned.

"Hmm. Don't sound so excited."

He grunted and finished tying my boot. Great, now we were reduced to grunts and one word answers.

"Well, thank you for this," I whispered, pointing to my boots. "I couldn't do it with the wound. Makes me feel like a complete invalid."

He grimaced, as if my words hurt him. But a second later, if he felt any guilt it was gone. Glaring up at me, he took my hands off his shoulders and let them drop to my sides as if he couldn't stand for me to touch him. I had to admit. That hurt. The heart he had mended was now torn apart.

Taking his time, he rose to his feet. His warmth invaded me. His body called to mine. He made no effort to move away. No effort to touch me.

Looking down, his gaze moved to the place where my bandage was hidden under my shirt. A frown marred his face. When he glanced back into my eyes, it was with aloofness.

"Keep your thanks, Cat. I don't want it."

Hurt ripped through me as he turned and walked away.

My heart hammered against my chest. My hands shook. A lump formed in my throat.

And I was left standing alone.

Waiting. Just waiting for the cowboy I fell in love with to show back up again.

~~~~

The longer I stood there, the angrier I got. I let myself fall in love with Cash. I let myself feel something for him. I was supposed to be the mean one. The bad seed, as my grandmother liked to call me. Cash wasn't supposed to turn his back on me.

And, dammit, I wouldn't let him.

Stiffening my spine, I shoved the sheet hanging in the doorway out of the way. I had no idea what I had done but it was time we settled this.

Cash was standing by the kitchen table, loading his shotgun. His hip was cocked and his arm flexed as he shoved shell after shell into the chamber. He looked so damn good but he was still pissed. It showed in the rigid lines of his body. In the set of his mouth.

Well, I could be pissed too.

I shot across the room. Cash set the shotgun on the table carefully and looked up, not surprised to see me.

I flew to a stop in front of him and pulled back my hand. Without thinking of the consequences, I slapped him as hard as I could. My palm connected with his cheek with a resounding smack, echoing across the room.
~~~~

Cash's head snapped to one side and a hand print appeared on his face. When he looked back at me, fury glowed in his eyes.

"What the hell was that for?" he snapped.

I wanted to recoil from the hate I heard in his voice but I stood my ground. "That's for being an asshole and this one is for being a coldhearted sonofabitch."

I raised my hand and swung again but he caught my wrist. His fingers dug into the bone without mercy. I refused to flinch and he refused to care. The anger that had been in his eyes was now blistering rage.

"I'll show you a sonofabitch," he ground out between clenched teeth. "Then maybe you'll regret stepping in front of that bullet for me."

He jerked me to him with his hand around my wrist. I fell against him and yelped but he silenced it quick with his mouth against mine. It was a harsh, ruthless kiss. Demanding and brutal. My teeth cut into my lips. My lungs forgot how to work.

I fought him but he refused to let me go. He was punishing me. Showing me not to mess with him. But I was not easily scared off.

I bit his lip, drawing blood. He growled, a rumble deep from his chest. Letting go of my wrist, he grasped the back of my head, yanking me closer.

I tried jerking away but his fingers fisted in my hair. His mouth ravaged mine. I felt owned, broken, and devoured all at once.

He pushed me back against the table, ramming my hip into the edge. I forgot about the pain radiating from my wound. His tongue licked at the corner of my mouth before plunging back inside, making me forget everything but him.

I hated him for making me feel something. I hated him for being so mean when I needed him most. I tried to push him off me, but he held me immobile. His teeth clashed against mine. His hand fisted in my hair tighter. He reached down and grasped the curve of my hip.

"You're going to regret ever loving me, sweetheart. I'll make sure of it," he rasped roughly against my mouth.

Tearing his lips from mine, he spun me around. I didn't have time to react before he wrapped his hand tightly around the back of my neck and forced me down on the table.

Oh god. He was going to take me like this. Over the table and from behind. His crotch nudged my ass. I could feel his hardness under his jeans. It was just as powerful and demanding as he was.

"Cash, please," I pleaded, my voice shaky but my body growing wet for him. I needed this. I needed him in me.

"Shut up, Cat," he growled, reaching around me for the button of my jeans. "This asshole is going to show you why you should never have fallen in love with me."

He unbuttoned my jeans and shoved them down my legs. I didn't fight him because…shit, I wanted him. I wanted to feel him stretch me and sink deep inside. I wanted him to use my body and fuck me like a man possessed.

I wiggled my hips against him. He let out a soft hiss and tightened his hand on my neck, keeping me pressed to the table.

"Stay still."

As soon as I did, his fingers turned gentle, almost a caress along my neck. His other hand slid along the cheek of my ass. My mouth went dry. My body trembled. I was so close to begging for him to touch me that a whimper escaped past my lips.

"Are you in pain?" he asked in a harsh voice, cutting and cold.

"No." I shook my head.

"Would you tell me if you were?"

I bit my lip and nodded.

"Good girl."

He dipped one hand between my legs. I let out a soft mewl.

"Impatient?" he taunted, moving his hand lower.

"No," I answered hoarsely. Impatient wasn't a strong enough word. Crazed seemed too mild. Desperate seemed too lame.

Cash stilled, his hand so close to my core. "No?"

I licked my dry lips. "I'm dying for you."

He let out a throaty groan and slid his finger over my clit. Jolts raced through me, electrifying my body.

"Oh god. Oh god," I breathed, my body pushing against his hand.

He did it again and again, making slow circles with his finger until he was holding me down as I wiggled against the table.

"Don't stop," I whispered. "Please."

"Wouldn't dream of it."

He slid his fingers past my slick folds then smeared the wetness over my clit. I gasped and shuddered. He held me down and made another pass over me with his thumb, going a little deeper. Pushing a little harder.

I clamped down on my bottom lip, trying not to cry out. It was too much but he wasn't done. He added two fingers. They slid into me effortlessly, stretching me. Preparing me for what was to come.

"Do you still love me?" he asked, his fingers working in and out of me, his other hand still holding me down.

"More than anything," I groaned, trying to form a coherent thought. Lost in the feelings his fingers were causing.

A deep sound of disapproval came from his chest. "Wrong answer," he murmured.

His fingers plunged into me hard. I cried out and tried to bolt upright, but his hand on my neck forced me back down.

"This is about punishment and nothing else, Cat. Feel it," he whispered, scissoring his fingers in me. "Take it."

I came hard. The orgasm shook my body in little quakes and made me stand up on my toes.

"Fuck, I *feel* you coming," Cash moaned, thrusting his fingers deep.

As I continued to orgasm, he quickly withdrew. I heard his zipper lower then felt him position himself at my opening. With one push, he slid inside. A hoarse cry escaped me as he went in as deep as he could go, filling me completely. Stretching my quivering walls. Adding to my ecstasy.

"Shit, shit," he muttered as the ripples of my orgasm squeezed and clutched him, stroking his manhood in waves.

"Please," I whimpered, bucking against his hold. Oh god. I had never felt anything so wonderful. I was dying. Desperate. I needed him to move. I was crazy with need.

He let go of my neck and grasped my hip, keeping his cock deeply imbedded in me.

"What do you want?" he rumbled deep in his chest.

Jesus, he was splitting me. Killing me.

I took a shaky breath. "For you to love me."

A low, dangerous sound came from Cash's throat. "Loving you almost got you killed. You get this instead."

He held my hips gently, making sure I didn't get hurt, but withdrew and plunged back into me hard. Balls deep. Rough.

I cried out, my body going stiff. My slick walls were sensitive, having just had an orgasm, and my clit was swollen from his thumb and fingers. It made my body grasp him tighter and my nerve endings scream. I could feel every inch of his hardness. He was so big and thick that every time we made love, he left me sore and tender. This time would be no different. I would ache tomorrow, not letting me forget where he had been.

He plunged into me harder. He didn't give any leeway and I took it greedily, biting down on my lip to keep from shouting.

"You feel that?" he rasped, slamming in and out of me with punishing thrusts, his hips pounding my ass. "I'm fucking you, Cat. I'm using you. I'm not loving you. Isn't that what you wanted when we first met? Just a quick fuck with no emotion?"

"No," I breathed, shaking my head and fighting the orgasm I could feel building again. "I've always been in love with you. Always."

Cash swore softly as if my words hurt him. But a second later his voice was harsh. "Then I'll make you wish you never were."

He drove into me deep. So deep that pain and pleasure rippled over me. It sent me over the edge. I burst into a million, colorful pieces. Spots appeared behind my eyelids. I threw my head back and let out a cry.

He didn't stop, driving into me faster and harder as my body jerked in climax. I managed to turn my head and look at him over my shoulder, small cries escaping me, my body moving against the table.

He had never looked so sexy before. The muscles in his throat were tense, the veins sticking out. His eyes were shut and his lips were parted. Quick, shallow breaths escaped past them. His hair was a mess and his whiskered chin was dark.

He was holding back. I could see it in the firm set of his mouth. But I wanted him to lose it. I wanted to see him break apart and shatter. For me. In me. So I whispered the first words that came to me.

"I love you, Cash."

His eyes flew open. His gaze found mine. The icy gray staring back at me was full of possession. Full of savage need. A primitive grunt left him and his jaw clenched hard.

"Fuck," he whispered, squeezing his eyes closed. "Fuck, Cat."

He let out a bestial growl and thrust into me, forcing himself as deep as he could go. Warmth spurted against my core. A thick stream of cum hit me once, twice, emptying hotly into me. My body spasmed around his, squeezing every single drop out of him. He moaned and plunged deeper, pulsating and forcing his semen to stay in me.

We stayed that way for minutes. I could feel my heartbeat in my fingers and under my skin. My cheekbone felt battered against the table. My hips felt bruised from his fingers. The wound in my side ached.

I throbbed around him, soaked from his release. His hands stayed clasped on my hips, keeping me immobile. Eventually, my body turned limp and my fingers uncurled. I became suddenly aware of a cold draft coming in from under the door and the sound of the wind rattling the windows. Too soon, Cash withdrew from me and tucked himself back into his jeans. He didn't touch me.

Didn't look at me. Didn't help me up when I struggled to push myself to my feet.

My body shook. My muscles felt sore. The area between my legs was bruised and tender, slick with his essence. I tried to bend over and grab my jeans from down around my ankles but the world spun crazily.

Cash reached out and grabbed me before I could topple over. He frowned and pulled my jeans up far enough for me to reach them.

"Get dressed," he muttered, letting them go.

I stood there dumbfounded, still exposed. He leaned past me and picked his gun up from the table. Without a single glance at me, he turned and headed toward the front door.

So that was that, I guessed.

Tears burned the back of my eyes.

"Shit," I whispered, wiping the moisture from my eyelashes and focusing on getting my jeans pulled up over my hips. "Shit. Shit. Shit."

I wasn't crying over the coldness that Cash had fucked me with. I was crying over my own stupidity.

I loved him. I had allowed myself to feel something for him. Hadn't I learned my lesson? Love only leads to heartache and no one wanted to love a girl like me.

I swore under my breath again as I struggled to get my jeans buttoned. *Why won't the buttons cooperate?*

My throat clogged up with unshed tears. The sound of heavy, booted footsteps treading back to me didn't register. I didn't hear the angry stride or pay attention to the way my body grew warmer. I was too lost in my own little pity party.

Suddenly, Cash was back in front of me. Without a word, he set the gun on the table and brushed my hands out of the way. His face was set in firm concentration as he started buttoning my jeans.

I could see every detail of his face. The individual hairs on his jaw. The way his brows drew together when he was frustrated. The little lines jutting out from the corners of his eyes from the long hours spent under the Texas sun. I drank in each feature, unable to get enough and hating myself for caring so much. He was the man who could heal me with just one touch or hurt me with one softly spoken word.

"Did I hurt you?" he asked in a voice as warm as a summer day, slipping the button through the hole on my jeans. As he did, his knuckles grazed my bandage-wrapped abdomen. His nostrils flared at the contact.

It was such an intimate touch – so possessive and careful – that I forgot to answer until he glanced up at me with a cold stare.

"Did I hurt you, Cat? Answer the question."

With a flushed face, I shook my head. "No."

His gaze darted down my body. "Then why are you crying?"

I chewed on my bottom lip, afraid to answer him. I had always bottled up my feelings. It was one of my defense mechanisms along with alcohol and men. But Cash had his way of getting me to talk.

He slid his hand from the front of my jeans to the curve of my hip, pressing the bone lightly with his fingers.

"Why are you crying?" he asked again.

With my heart tearing apart, I stuck my chin up with defiance. "Because I allowed myself to love you."

Cash let go of me and took a step back. Coldness was in his eyes.

"We all make mistakes, Cat. I'm yours and you're mine."

"You sonofabitch," I whispered, my heart squeezing painfully.

A dangerous glint appeared in his eyes. He grabbed the back of my neck and dragged me toward him, careful not to hurt me. Leaning over, he put his mouth near my ear.

"Yeah, I am a sonofabitch. I made you come on my fingers and then on my cock. I held you down and fucked you how I wanted, at the pace I wanted, then I emptied myself deep inside you like I wanted. It was all about me, sweetheart. Your needs had nothing to do with it. So yeah, I'm a sonofabitch. This goddamn war turned me into one. And you know what? I don't give a shit. So hate me because I deserve it."

His words slammed into me. If he had hit me, it would have hurt less. But I jerked away from him and showed my teeth.

"You fucking liar. You care."

He smirked. "Do I?"

I saw red. Not an oh-he-hurt-my-feelings kind of red. A red-hot, fiery depths of hell kind of red. I slapped my palm on his chest, pushing him back a step.

"Fuck you."

He smiled. The corner of his mouth curved up in what could only be described as sexual temptation on overdrive.

"You just did, sweetheart," he said in a smooth, let-me-lick-you voice. "Well, I fucked *you* to be precise."

My pulse skipped a beat. The part of me he had just left, clenched. I was ultra aware of the wetness between my legs and had a sudden vision of him between my legs, his cum making it easy for him to slide back into me again.

He must have read my mind because his gaze burned. The air shifted. He glanced down at me then turned and walked away.

Rage burst in me. I flew toward him. When I got close enough, I hit him on the back with my fist. He turned, glaring down at me.

"Ugh!" I hit him again, this time on his chest, knocking him back a step. Tired of his coldness and distant attitude.

"Screw you, Cash Marshall! You sat beside me day in and day out when I was unconscious and burning up with fever. You hovered over me like a freaking bodyguard so stop acting like an ass and telling me you don't care!"

He stood his ground, taking my abuse as I hit his hard abdomen. His body was like a piece of granite under my hand. I let out a frustrated sound, wanting him to show some emotion.

He leaned forward, his nose going close to mine. "But I don't," he said in a dangerous-as-hell, I-dare-you-to-do-that-again whisper. "And if I did at one time, maybe I shouldn't have. Maybe you wouldn't have jumped in front of that bullet and gotten a hole in your side."

I felt my stomach bottom out. My hands started shaking. I stuck up my chin, not caring if he could see that my eyes were teary.

I became aware of how close we were. How the hardness under his jeans strained against the zipper. How strands of my hair caught on his whiskers when he leaned closer like little strands of rope tying us together.

He must have felt it too. He took a safe step back but I wasn't going to let him go that easily.

"You can deny it all you want, cowboy. You care," I said, crossing my arms over my chest, everything suddenly crystal clear. "That's why you're acting like such a jerk. You're scared that if you love me, I'll get shot or hurt again, maybe even killed. That freaks you out. So you're going to push me away and make me hate you. Right?"

His eyes went dark and pain flashed across his face but a second later it was gone. His lips curved up in a deadly grin that made my knees weak and wobbly.

"That's right, sweetheart," he said, taking a slow step toward me. Invading what little personal space I had left. "I want you to hate me. Despise me. Loathe the ground I walk on. I sat beside that bed and watched you struggle to live. I watched you bleed and scream with pain."

I moved back, desperate to get away from the predatory look in his eyes. But he tracked me like a panther, moving with careful, precise steps. When my back hit the wall beside the bedroom, I was trapped. Cornered. His for the taking.

He stopped right in front of me. I didn't fight when he planted a foot on either side of me, capturing me against the rough-hewn wall. I didn't flinch when he put his hands behind me. But I did jump when he leaned over and put his mouth near my ear.

"It tore me up, Cat, seeing you lying there bleeding. It *destroyed* me. I have no love left. Only a need to fuck you into next week."

Oh, god.

My lips parted. My knees trembled. I was acutely aware of the nearness of his mouth. The position of his hands, flat against the wall behind me.

I reached out, needing to touch him. Needing him to know that I was okay. That I wasn't going to die.

His eyes burned and the muscles tensed in his arms when I put my fingertips against his abdomen, right above his low-slung jeans.

"It wasn't your fault, Cash."

"Yes it was, sweetheart," he rasped, his gaze dropping to my lips. He ran his hand under my shirt, grazing the bandage over my left side. "This is because of me. Don't try to deny it."

I shook my head, tears in my eyes.

Emotions play out on his face. Frustration. Need. Desperation. Anger. But then coldness took over again. A mask of indifference came down over his face.

He pushed away from the wall and backed away, putting a safe distance between us.

"It's over, Cat," he said with cool detachment. "We're done. Stop loving me and start hating me."

With a quick glance down at my lips, he turned and walked away. I watched as he grabbed the shotgun from the table and headed for the door.

I wanted to follow but I stayed against the wall, hurt coursing through me. I never wanted to love him. I was too afraid. So I tried running from him and making out with someone else. I tried to drink his memory away. I tried it all but none of it worked. He was in my blood and a bullet wasn't going to end that.

Sticking my chin up, I took a quick step forward.

"If you want to push me away because you think you're saving me or you've got some kind of guilt, then fine," I blurted out as he paused to grab his cowboy hat from the sofa. "But just know that I can't stop loving you and I'm not going to try."

Cash froze, his hat in his hand. Slowly, he set it on his head and pulled the brim down low. I held my breath as he glanced back at me from under the shadows of the hat, his eyes pinpoints of cold steel.

"Then I'll make you," he said with quiet certainty. "And I'll try my damnedest to resist you every time I turn around."

Without another word, he turned and walked out the door.

Chapter Eleven

-Cat-

For days, I cried when no one was looking and stomped around the cabin with anger when they were. One minute, I was furious and the next, tears were in my eyes. But one thing was for certain. My heart was breaking, one second at a time.

I eased down to the edge of the bed, holding my side. The wound was healing but it was ugly and red. Streaks ran from the edges and the stitches David had carefully pulled through my skin itched. It still throbbed with pain, sometimes bad enough it made me catch my breath. When that happened, Cash would grind his teeth and storm from the cabin. I think that hurt more than the wound.

Sighing, I stared across the empty bedroom. He stayed away most of the time, always telling Tate or David to keep an eye on me and make me stay inside.

I was going stir-crazy, I was sure. I was sick of half-ass bathing, using only a threadbare washcloth and a chunk of weird smelling soap. I wanted a real bath, not something from a bucket of freezing cold creek water that Tate hauled up to the cabin for me.

I was tired of questionable-looking soup and the occasional rabbit someone shot. I wanted a steak from the best restaurant in town, a glass of my dad's best liquor, and the chocolate from Paris he sent me when he traveled there on business. I wanted my clothes, my room, my life back. The one where I didn't scrounge for every little bit of food or supplies. The one where I didn't have to worry about surviving in a world gone mad.

Or loving a man who was trying to push me away.

I stood up and left the bedroom, tired of feeling sorry for myself and tired of hurting from Cash.

David looked up from the kitchen table. He was sipping on something from a metal cup. Even from my distance, it smelled suspiciously like vodka. He had been drinking since yesterday, not enough to get drunk. Just enough that I noticed. Maybe he was feeling the walls closing in on him like they were doing to me.

I ignored his assessing, quick perusal of me and went over to a window. "Are they back yet?" I asked, peering out.

"No. I don't expect them back until dark, knowing Cash. The guy can't seem to stay still for long, I noticed. Reminds me of myself back in my younger days."

No, he's just antsy to get away from me, I thought with a pang of hurt. Every morning he grabbed his gun and left, not saying a word. At night he ate his meals alone and slept in the living room. But today was different. He had left before I woke and took Tate with him. They had been gone too long and I was starting to worry.

I started pacing around the tiny cabin, fidgeting with my jacket. Picking at a broken nail. David watched me through narrowed eyes, drinking from his cup.

"You gonna rub a hole in my rug, girl?" he drawled, pointing to my boots with the drink.

I stopped my pacing and looked down. The rug had so many holes and thin spots in it that I didn't think my pacing would make much difference. So I started doing it again.

Window. Middle of room. Window. Middle of room. I was wound too tight to argue about the quickly fading quality of the man's furnishings.

Each time Cash left, I worried. He may want us to be over but I couldn't stop caring. What if he was heading back to Hilltop? What if he was going after Paul or Frankie? If he went back, he would be killed. I knew it in my gut.

I felt ill at the thought. The room started to spin and I swayed. I heard the screech of a chair's legs as it was pushed back across the floor.

"You okay, kiddo?" David asked, rising to his feet.

I squeezed my eyes shut until the dizziness went away. When I reopened my eyes, I found David studying me. Concern made his face even more wrinkled and drew his gray brows together in one bushy line.

"You're not going to pass out on me, are you?" he asked, wariness in his voice.

"No," I said in a hushed tone, rubbing a hand over my brow. "I'm okay."

A lie. I hadn't been okay since I woke up in bed with a bullet hole in my side. I was barely holding it together. Cash wouldn't look at me when he was around. He avoided getting too close to me. God forbid we accidently touched. It hurt. A lot. But not as much as knowing he didn't love me anymore.

David eased back into the chair, wincing when he had to bend his knees. I started pacing again. I was worried about Cash and Tate. Worried about us. When I saw Paul in Hilltop, the memories came back. I could still feel every revolting touch of his hand. Every disgusting word he said to me and the promise to finish what he started.

"Little bird, I ain't done with you yet."

I shivered with fear. Cash shot Paul but I just knew he was still alive. I could almost feel him coming, searching for me. Leering at me and smiling with anticipation.

I wrapped my arms around my middle and hoped to God he didn't find me. Terror clawed at me, refusing to let go. I was drowning in it when the front door flew open.

Cash.

He was standing in the doorway, his expression hidden under the dark shadows of his cowboy hat. His gaze found me right away.

I was suddenly aware of the roughness of my shirt against my bare breasts. The clenching between my legs. I forgot to be cold. To be ill. To be mad that he said it was over.

I forgot to be anything but his.

"Cash," I whispered, his name just a hushed sound from my lips. It was a name I wanted to say in the middle of the night when he shoved my legs apart. A name I wanted to cry when he shoved his cock deep into me.

I took an instinctive step forward. I wanted to go to him. Feed my addiction and drown in my craving. It was a natural reaction. A pull that I couldn't resist. But I was brought up short when I saw his eyes.

They were cold, gray, and intense. Icy reserve stared back at me. The warning on his face screamed only one thing – stay away.

I stepped back and lowered my eyes, bowing to him in my own fucking way. I wasn't giving up. I was giving in. If he didn't want me near him, he would get his wish.

Cash stalked into the house with purpose. He moved with grace and control, always in power, always with command.

I took an instinctive step back. Not out of fear. Out of self-preservation. Something flared in his eyes. An animalistic warning to stay still. I had seen it before. I knew what it meant. I froze and he kept on walking, brushing past me.

"Catarina," he said in acknowledgement.

The deep timbre of his voice sent shockwaves through me. I grew hungry, not for food but for the one thing he could fill me with.

Him.

I hated him for that. When he said my full name, it always sent me to a different place. One with obsession and craving and carnal desire. I wanted him to fuck me hard, fuck me fast, fuck me however he wanted, just fuck me. Love could wait. It would never leave me. But right now, I needed him to touch me and take away the ache.

Jesus, was my grandmother right? Was I that screwed up? The world was a hellhole and we were barely surviving yet all I could think about was Cash holding me down and sliding into me.

All because he called me Catarina.

He didn't pause but moved past me to the middle of the room. Tate was hot on his heels, a look of excited concentration on his face. *Thank God they are both okay.*

I turned, wondering what the hell was going on. I recognized the look on my brother's face. Something had happened.

Cash stopped at the edge of the rug and squatted down. He laid his shotgun on the floor beside him and flipped the corner of the rug back. I was surprised to see a trapdoor, flush with the hardwood floor.

Cash grasped the metal handle inlaid on the top and gave it a twist. The lock disengaged and he pulled it open.

"What's going on? Did you see anything?" David asked, rising from the kitchen chair and wandering over to where Cash kneeled.

"I didn't see anyone. It's what I felt," Cash answered, reaching down into the hidden hole, searching for something.

A chill went through me. Cash was an expert at hunting and tracking. If he thought someone was out there, then there was.

I wrapped my arms around my waist and took a step toward him. "Do you think it was one of them?"

He ignored me and glanced at David and Tate instead.

"We need to keep a lookout. We'll take two hour shifts tonight. If there's trouble, fire three shots in the air. Tate, you stay in here with Cat. David, you and I will take turns on watch."

I took a step closer and peeked over his shoulder, looking down into the compartment under the floor. Cans of food, boxes of ammunition, and a large canvas bag sat in the hole. Cash reached down and unzipped the bulky bag. At least twenty guns were in there. David had an arsenal. A powerful, deadly looking one.

Cash grabbed a gun and pulled it out. It was long with a wooden body and black scope mounted on the top. He offered it across the hole to David. "You ready for this?"

David looked down at the gun. He was a doctor and a preacher. He saved people in more ways than one. Killing went against everything he stood for.

But times were different.

He grabbed the gun and magazine of bullets Cash handed him. "*Blessed be the Lord, my rock, who trains my hands for war, and my fingers for battle,*" he said, sliding the mag into place.

Cash reached into the bag again and grabbed a pistol. "Just your style, Tate."

Tate took the gun and weighed it in his hand. "I ain't got a Psalm to quote, Preacher," he said, peering up at the older man from beneath a ball cap he had found.

David grinned. "Well, son, you don't need one. You just need a prayer."

Tate gave a short snort and turned his attention to the pistol, checking to make sure it was loaded.

I watched it all with a mixture of panic and horror. It looked like they were preparing to go to war.

"Why don't we just leave?" I asked, looking from Cash to David and Tate. "Wouldn't that be better than staying here, sitting ducks for whoever is out there?"

Cash rested his elbow on his bent knee and pushed his hat back with his finger. His gaze traveled up my body, from my black army boots to the dark curls around my shoulders.

He pushed to his feet and took a step toward me. His eyes drifted down to my side where the bandage still covered me under my shirt and jacket.

"How is the wound?" he asked in a deep voice meant more for the bedroom than for a room bursting with guns and ammunition.

I stuck my chin up and shrugged. "Good enough to run."

His gaze dropped down to the V in my collar then flicked back up to my eyes. "Good enough won't do. I need you better."

I opened my mouth to argue but he pushed past me, careful not to touch any part of me.

I turned, watching him walk away. Tate and David were minding their own business, messing with the guns, but I knew they were watching us. Let them. I didn't care. I was angry.

"I thought you didn't need me at all," I said, staring at Cash's sinew muscular back. "Which is it, cowboy?"

He stopped. His fingers clenched around the shotgun he carried. His shoulders went taut.

Tate and David grew quiet, both of them watching us. I stood in place, staring at the back of Cash's head and waiting for him to explode.

He turned his head, enough that I could only see his stone-cut jaw and whiskered right cheek.

"I don't need you, sweetheart," he drawled, the words rolling off his tongue and wrapping around me. "But I sure as hell could do without wanting you."

Chapter Twelve

-Cash-

Cat's cheeks turned a fierce red. Fury erupted in her eyes. I'm surprised I didn't burst into a ball of fire, as much as she was glaring at me.

That was the girl I had met in a dusty, backwoods bar. The one who riled me up in a swanky Dallas restaurant. She was strong and sassy and took shit from no one, including me. I was afraid I would always love her come hell or high water. And that was the problem. Why we had to be over.

I had come to the decision that she was safer if she didn't love me. If I was nothing to her anymore. But when she stood in the kitchen a few days ago, her eyes spitting fire and her sweet mouth calling me a sonofabitch, I couldn't resist. Kissing her, having her, being with her, were the only things I wanted.

Now here I was – days later, trying to stay away from Cat.

I refused to eat with her. I avoided her as much as I could. When Tate and David showed back up after I bent her over the table, I hauled my ass out of there, refusing to talk to either one of them. I needed to get as far away from Cat as possible. There were things to do. Supplies to gather. We were low on food and kerosene. Plus, our pile of wood to burn at night was growing smaller. I hunted and worked from sunup to sundown and searched for any sign of Keely and Gavin as much as I could. I burned more energy than I consumed but I did it all for Cat.

To keep her safe.

To keep her warm and fed.

To make up for that bullet wound in her side.

I wanted to prove to her that day in the kitchen how much she shouldn't love me. Show her how loving me was wrong. Instead, I proved how much she was still in my blood.

I pulled my hat brim low and headed for the door. What I wanted to do was take off running. Put some distance between the little Beauty Queen and me. But I set my mouth in a firm line and continued on, reminding myself that there was a difference between love and lust. I needed to destroy one and ignore the other before I lost control again and Cat paid the price.

The smell of winter was in the air as I stepped out onto the porch. It was late in the day. The sun was low in the sky, disappearing behind the treetops. I drew in a lungful of chilled air, needing to clear my mind. I had other things to worry about than a hotheaded girl with a body meant for loving. There was someone out in the woods, biding his time. Watching us. I could feel it. Trouble was coming. I welcomed it with open arms. Let the fuckers show their faces.

I would be ready.

Fury burned in me when I remembered that skinny man's gaze on Cat. He looked at her with hunger. Like a hyena with its sharp teeth showing and a deadly grin on his face. It was the undeniable possession in his eyes when he looked at Cat and the knowledge that he had hurt her that made me fire that first shot.

I glanced around, my hand tense on my shotgun. What I wouldn't give to have that bastard appear in front of me right now. But nothing seemed different. Dead leaves littered the ground, looking undisturbed. The small barn that was set back in the woods a few yards away still had branches and leaves on the roof, camouflaging the rusted metal. Things seemed fine but something was telling me to stay alert.

We weren't alone.

I wasn't alone.

I glanced over my shoulder when the door of the cabin opened, the old hinges squeaking in protest. It was Cat and she looked hesitant, her teeth worrying her bottom lip. I fought the urge to grab her, force her up against the outside of the cabin, and suck on that lip. Instead, I faced forward again and started down the porch steps.

She followed. Those heavy boots of hers made enough noise on the porch to announce her presence for miles around. I sighed but didn't stop, striding toward the woods.

"Cash Marshall!" she shouted as I hit the grass and started toward the line of trees, her shorter legs unable to keep up with mine.

I didn't bother turning around. "Go back inside, Cat," I said in a bored tone, keeping my gaze straight ahead.

I heard her blow out a breath in frustration and continue following me. Tall weeds swished against her jeans as she hurried to catch up. For every step I took, she took three. For every foot she got closer, the more I became aware just how thin a hold I had on my resistance to her.

"I don't take orders from you!" she said in a loud voice, stomping through the high grass. "How many times do I have to remind you of that?"

I shook my head, stepping over a rabbit hole at the same time. "Sweetheart, you can remind me all you want. I'm still going to tell you what to do. Go inside before you freeze your ass off. I'm not asking. I'm telling."

By now she was walking beside me, huffing and puffing to match my speed. I kept my eyes locked straight ahead but I could feel Cat peering at me. Pestering me in her own, stubborn way. She should be upset, maybe even sad for breaking it off with her. Instead, she was furious.

I held my calm in check and gritted my teeth. I wasn't going to fight her. Not today. If I put my hands on her, pushing her down on the kitchen table and burying myself to the hilt in her from behind would look like child's play. Neither one of us needed that. Not now. Hell, maybe not ever.

"Why do you feel the need to tell me what to do?" she asked, skirting around a large, prickly weed. "I'm a big girl. I survived three long years after the EMP without you by my side. I ate. I found shelter and water. I didn't lose my ability to think or make rational decisions when you showed up again."

I sighed but didn't answer. My dad once said that sometimes it was best to keep quiet and not argue with a woman. I thought this was one of those times.

I tried to ignore her as best as I could and keep my mind on my surroundings, but the longer I didn't speak, the madder she seemed to get. The girl had always been a spitfire. Might have been why she got under my skin from the first moment I met her. But now I needed her quiet and back in the cabin. That feeling between my shoulder blades was not going away. Someone was watching. Waiting. Wondering if this was the time to strike.

I squinted against the sunlight filtering in through the trees and slowed down. Switching the safety off my gun with one finger, I tried to make as little noise as possible. My muscles were taut, ready for action. My ears were alert for any sound of a gun being cocked or a bullet being chambered. I needed every ounce of awareness I had. I didn't need it centered on the little princess beside me.

She stepped over a large rotten log at the same time I did. Our arms touched. She leaned into me. I almost jumped out of my skin. Damn. I had it bad.

I quickened my pace, skirting around a large oak tree. We were deeper in the woods, the cabin almost out of sight. I could hear her breathing quicker, trying to keep up with me. I should've slowed down. She was still weak and I was still worried about her. But there was this thing called temptation and it wouldn't leave me alone. It chased me and teased me whenever Cat was around and I didn't like it. That's why I had to stay cold.

I had just made up my mind that as long as I didn't have to touch her, I could handle her tagging along, when suddenly she tripped over a rock. I reached out and seized her upper arm, keeping her from landing face first in the mildewed leaves and reopening her wound. My temper flared. My fingers looped around her arm tightened.

"That's it, Beauty Queen, I'm taking you back."

I swung around, pulling her with me.

She jerked out of my grasp. "I'm not leaving. You might as well deal with it, *asshole*."

There was that word again. Asshole. Maybe I was. Maybe I had to be to get her to hate me.

"Fine," I snapped, staring her down and keeping my voice low in case someone was out there.

She muttered something under her breath and started walking again, this time picking her way carefully over stones and twigs. I caught up to her in two strides. Here the trees were denser. The woods were thick, perfect for a man to hide in. I wasn't letting her out of my sight.

People had become desperate since the EMP and terrorist invasion. Food was worth killing over, water was worth dying for, and a woman that looked like Cat was worth stalking and taking by any means necessary.

But they had to get through me first.

I eyed Cat out of the corner of my eye. The tip of her nose was pink but her face was pale. Her teeth chattered and her body shivered. She was cold and, shit, I couldn't help but care.

I drew to a stop and turned to face her. She did the same, glaring up at me from only a foot away.

"What?"

"You're freezing." I unzipped my jacket and pulled it off. "If you insist on staying with me, you stay warm."

She rolled her eyes but didn't resist as I wrapped my jacket around her.

"It's warm," she whispered, giving me a sheepish look. "Thank you, I guess."

I grunted and started walking again. That's about as much reaction as she was going to get out of me on the subject of my body warming her up.

We went a few more yards. This far from the cabin, it was quiet. Almost eerie. A small bird fluttered from tree to tree, hopping along twigs and branches. The limbs above us swayed in the wind, creating a whooshing noise with their leaves. It was my element. The place I felt most at peace. I grew up in the woods and hell, the way things were going, I might die in them too.

Cat was quiet as we walked. I could almost hear her mind churning, thinking of a new way to torment me.

I was waiting for that moment, ready to shut down all emotion and be a coldhearted S.O.B., when a squirrel shot out of a tree a few yards away. Cat jumped a mile high and grabbed my arm.

"Eeek!" Her soft body hit mine. Her breasts pressed into me. It was heaven. It was hell. It was everything in between and I was a bastard for enjoying it.

"Sorry," she said with a frown, letting go of me and springing back when she realized she was grasping me. "Woods aren't my thing."

"Humph. I couldn't tell," I mumbled, shutting down. She *was* the most spoiled rich girl I had ever met.

She didn't bother commenting or coming back with some snide remark. That's when I knew something was wrong.

"You really think someone's out here?" she asked in a whisper, moving closer to me and looking around. "If Paul found me again…" Her voice trailed off. Fuck, she was scared.

I stopped and turned to face her. Anger ripped through me at the thought of that man touching who used to be mine. Scratch that. Who was still mine.

"How did he do it?" I asked with bluntness, harsher than I would have liked.

Cat blinked up at me, confused. "Do what?"

I propped my shotgun against a fallen log then turned back to Cat.

"How was he able to get the jump on you?" I asked, keeping my gaze on her as I straightened to my full height and started toward her.

She glanced everywhere but at me as I advanced. "He…um…he…" She backed up, nervous as hell and as jumpy as a frog.

I grabbed her wrist, stopping her. Wanting her to know she was safe with me. The fright in her eyes almost destroyed me. The feel of her racing pulse under my fingers unnerved me.

I gave her a little tug, needing her closer for what I planned to do. Hoping she realized that I would rather die than hurt a hair on her head.

She came to me easily. I let go of her wrist when we were toe to toe and slowly started walking around her. Taking my time. Showing her I was no threat.

"Did he come up from behind you or from the front?" I asked, stopping behind her, glancing down at the gentle curve of her hips.

She was motionless, her back to me. Her breathing increased. I saw her tremble.

"From the side," she whispered. "He appeared out of nowhere and held a gun to my head."

Rage erupted in me. I wanted to rip the fucker's head off and burn what was left of him. But I used the fury. Welcomed it even. It kept my feelings cold and gave me a purpose. A reason for touching Cat.

To keep her safe and teach her a little self-defense.

I stepped to her side, kicking dead leaves out of the way. She was so small that I could break her with one hand. The thought only made me harden my heart more. I had to be tough on her so she could be tougher.

"Then what did he do?" I asked.

She turned her head and looked directly at me, terror flicking in her eyes.

"He grabbed my wrist and forced my arm up my back, restraining me."

Hell. I wanted to kill the man. I wanted to be his judge, jury, and executioner. Until then, I would make sure Cat was safe and could protect herself.

I reached out and slid my fingers around her wrist. There it was again. Her pulse. Fast and strong.

I held her wrist gently and slowly walked behind her. My breath ruffled the hair on top of her head. I felt her shudder as I stopped so close behind her.

But it was only the beginning.

I tightened my fingers on her wrist, putting pressure on the delicate bones. Very carefully, I started pushing her arm up the middle of her back.

"Like this?"

"Yes," she said. "But he kept pushing it higher."

I forced her arm up more, just an inch. Careful not to hurt her but making her feel it. She hissed and arched her back.

"Did you fight him?" I asked near her ear.

"Yes," she said so quiet I almost didn't hear.

"Show me," I demanded. "Fight me like you fought him. Get me off."

From over her shoulder I saw her tongue dart out, licking her lips nervously. "Okay."

She twisted around quickly and brought her knee up, right in line with my crotch. My arm went around her as I held her wrist, trapping her against me. At the last second, she stopped, her knee nestled right between my legs. Against my boys. Shit. I got the idea loud and clear.

"So you kneed him. Then what?" I asked, trying to focus on what we were doing and not how close she was or how nicely she fit against me.

She lowered her knee.

"He knocked me to the ground," she said, her voice growing stronger, fire lighting in her eyes as she remembered. "With his fist."

I glanced down at her jaw, remembering the bruise I had left there. I still felt sick, knowing I had hurt her, but I hardened my heart. She had to learn better self-defense moves than just a knee to the gonads. These men were not your run of the mill assholes.

I dropped her wrist and took a step back, putting some distance between us.

"A knee to the balls will hurt a man and buy you some time but you need to know how do more. Let me see your hand."

I grabbed her right hand before she offered it and held it out between us.

"This right here," I ran my thumb over the delicate skin on the back edge of her hand, "can injure a man."

I brought her hand to my throat, putting the side against my windpipe in a chopping motion.

"Hit a man like this."

Holding her wrist, I pushed her hand hard against my Adam's Apple, feeling the pressure deep in my throat.

"If you put enough power behind it, you could really hurt someone."

I pushed her hand harder against my windpipe, letting her feel the tendons in my neck and the right place to strike.

She pulled her hand away, resisting, but I grabbed it again and put it against my throat.

"I want you to hurt me. Prove you can do it."

"No." She tried to pull her hand away again but I held on and took a step closer, using my bigger size to intimidate her.

"I'm him. I'm attacking you. I'm going to throw you down on the ground and rip your clothes off. What are you going to do about it? It's either you or him, Cat. Choose."

"Him."

She hit me hard in the throat, unexpected and hard. Stars burst in my eyes and my throat felt like it had collapsed. I fell back a step and drew in a wheezing breath.

"Oh shit! I'm sorry!" She flew to me, her eyes wide and her hand covering her mouth.

"It's okay," I said with a raspy voice, rubbing my throat.

"No, it's not okay!"

Her fingers reached out for my neck. I grasped her wrist, stopping her.

"Don't worry about me. Worry about yourself," I snapped, suddenly angry. Her concern for me was the last thing I wanted. It had almost gotten her killed before and I didn't want to take that chance again. She needed to hate me instead.

She stuck her chin up. Fuck, I wanted to kiss it.

"And who will worry about you?" she asked. "Someone has to."

I scoffed. "No one does and I definitely don't want you to."

Hurt crossed her face. I regretted the sharp words but I had to have a heart like steel.

"Do I need to remind you that we're over, Cat? That means you shouldn't worry about me or care anymore," I said, letting go of her wrist like it stung.

She stuck her chin up and looked me in the eye. "Then you shouldn't worry about me either, cowboy."

I huffed. "Wrong. I'm not going to let anything happen to you, *princess*. I can promise you that."

"Why do you even care? It isn't like you love me anyway."

Low blow. Yeah, I wanted her to think that I didn't love her but hearing her say it out loud sent me to a dark place.

"You're my responsibility," I said, low and dangerous, peering at her from under my hat. "Leave it at that."

One of her eyebrows shot up. "I'm your *responsibility*? Really? You've got some nerve. Just because you got in my pants, cowboy, doesn't mean—"

I swore softly and grabbed the front of her jacket in one fist. With one tug, I yanked her to me, almost lifting her off her feet.

"Enough!" I growled in a low voice.

She fell against my chest. Her hands went flat on my chest. A sharp breath was inhaled between her lips.

I got a big whiff of her. Something clean and sweet. I knew Tate had been hauling buckets of creek water to the cabin for her to bathe with. I had sat on the porch, imagining drops of water rolling down her breasts and over her stomach. I had wanted to jump up and storm through the cabin. Shove my way past that limp sheet hanging in the doorway. Fall to my knees in front of her and lick the drops of water off of her skin.

But I didn't do any of it.

I ran my hand up to the back of her head. Leaning over, I put my mouth right over her ear, planning on telling her what I had the nerve to do to her.

That's when I heard it.

The sound of a twig breaking.

I froze, my body going stiff. My hand stayed on the back of Cat's head. My mouth stayed near her ear. A bird shot out of the trees overhead, startled from its nest. I could almost feel the alarm pounding through Cat.

We weren't alone anymore.

I could feel him behind me. A shifting in the air. It wasn't Tate or David; they would have announced themselves and not been so quiet. No, it was someone else.

"Listen to me," I whispered in Cat's ear, making my voice as low as I could. "I need you to do exactly what I say. We've got company and something's telling me they're not friendly."

She tried to pull away in order to see for herself, but I grasped her tighter, my hand on the back of her head keeping her close.

She nodded, understanding, but I could almost feel her fear. It was a tangible thing, one that left her shaking and the air tense. But I wasn't going to let anything happen to her. No way in hell.

I flicked my eyes down, barely moving my head. My shotgun was just a foot away. I could grab it but the person might have a gun pointed at me. He could pull the trigger before I had mine up and cocked. I wanted him to get closer. Think he had the jump on us. In the meantime, I wanted Cat to do something for me.

"Put your hand on my zipper," I instructed. "Like you're going to unzip me."

Her gaze flicked up to mine. "What?" she whispered with shock.

I reached between us, the back of my hand brushing against her stomach. "Do it."

She hesitated only a second but then laid her fingers near the zipper of my jeans. My body stiffened. My cock reared to life.

Moving gradually and using the closeness of our bodies to hide what I was doing, I slid the six-inch hunting knife off my belt.

"Take this," I whispered, pressing the handle into Cat's hand next to my zipper. "When I say run, do it and don't look back."

She looked terrified but took the knife, holding it in her fist. I relaxed my hold on the back of her head and took a step to the right, shielding her with my body from whoever was behind us but still keeping my mouth near her ear. We looked like two lovers embraced, so caught up with each other we weren't paying attention. But I was aware of everything. Every breath Cat took. Every leaf that fell around us.

When another twig snapped.

With my mouth near Cat's ear, I took a deep breath.

"Run."

Chapter Thirteen

-Cat-

Cash had his hands on me. His mouth near my ear. His body so close to mine. One minute I thought he was going to kiss me. The next, I'm scared and turning to run.

As soon as he let me go, Cash lunged and grabbed his shotgun. He had it up and cocked before I got two feet away. I didn't look back. I didn't pause. I knew what would happen if it was Paul and he caught me.

So I ran.

My feet flew, breaking the leaves under me. My hair flapped against my back and air rushed in and out of my lungs. I jumped over logs and avoided ditches. I ran as fast as I could and I didn't stop. I needed to get back to the cabin and get help.

My heart pumped harder. When I heard a shout, I didn't turn around. It wasn't Cash. I would know his voice anywhere. It was someone else and he sounded angry.

Clouds of chilly air escaped past my lips as I darted around a tree and almost slipped in a pile of wet leaves. Beams of sunlight broke through the branches above me. I held onto the knife, my only weapon. All I could hear was my heart beating in my ears and the blood rushing in my veins.

I picked up speed, jumping over a falling log and ducking under a low hanging branch. The sounds of struggle came from behind me. I heard another yell, this time from Cash. I whipped my head around, looking behind me. I couldn't see anyone but I could hear them. Fighting. Fists colliding with flesh.

With my heart racing out of control, I ran faster. *I need to get help! I need to get help!*

I never saw the barbed wire, hidden under dead leaves. My feet became tangled in it. Sharp wire snagged the bottom of my jeans. I cried out, falling. My body smacked onto the ground. The knife in my hand went flying. My temple hit a rock, sending pain ricocheting through my skull.

I cried out as my bandaged side hit the ground. Agony fired through me. I rolled onto my back and grabbed my side, squeezing my eyes shut.

A small trickle of blood ran from my hairline. The bullet wound throbbed.

Get up! the voice in my head screamed.

I tried not to cry out as I pushed to a sitting position. Every inch of me ached and the world spun but I had to keep going.

I untangled my feet from the barbed wire and kicked it away. Almost face-planting, I climbed to my feet. Dead leaves fell from my jacket. A few fluttered down from my hair. I was a bit unsteady but I was standing upright. *I can do this.*

Bending over, I grabbed the knife then stood up and looked around. I was still alone. The woods around me were thick, the trees bare of leaves for the winter. It looked haunted and eerie. Like something out of a horror film.

"Don't go there, Cat," I whispered.

The wind picked up. I could hear the fighting again. I wasn't sure who was out there or how many there were but Cash needed help.

Forgetting about my injuries, I broke into a run. A stitch started in my side. The bullet wound throbbed each time my feet hit the earth. Another drop of blood fell from the cut on my head.

I ran until I came to the edge of a clearing. It didn't look familiar. Tall, brown grass swayed in the wind. There was a fence, twisted and hanging loose. It looked like an abandoned crop field hidden in the woods, overgrown and forgotten. Someplace I had never seen and had never been.

Breathing hard, I spun around in a full circle, looking for something familiar. I was lost. Oh god, I was lost.

Panic bubbled up inside me. Fear made it almost impossible to think. I whirled around to face the way I just came from. *All I have to do is backtrack. You've got this, Cat.*

I clasped the knife tighter. Bad things happened in woods. People went missing. Bodies were found. Women were hurt.

But I was not going to be one of them.

I started back into the thick woods. I was yards from the clearing when three gunshots ricocheted through the air. Birds burst from the tree in front of me. I jerked to a stop. *Cash!*

I took off running toward where the shots came from. Forget about getting to safety. Cash could be lying somewhere bleeding. Dying.

My lungs hurt, my wound ached, and my head throbbed as I leaped through the woods. Thorn bushes grabbed my clothes and snagged my hair but I didn't stop. I could hear fighting.

A grunt.

A punch.

I flew past a large tree and that's when I saw them. Cash and another man on the ground. Cash was on top. His hat was gone, one of his hands wrapped around the man's throat. The man beneath him was fighting, landing punch after punch in Cash's ribs, trying to knock him off. Cash wasn't budging. He gave no signs of feeling pain as the man's knuckles buried in his side again and again.

I slid to a stop, stepping on a small branch. It snapped. The man cut his eyes over at me, still struggling under Cash.

The earth tilted. My eyes grew round.

I *knew* him.

His hair was longer than it had been years ago. The lower portion of his face was covered with a scruffy beard. Blood trickled from a cut on his eyebrow. A bruise was forming around his right eye.

His clothes were dirty but that wasn't surprising. Mine weren't clean either. He wasn't as muscular as I remembered. The shortage of food had made him lean along with everyone else.

It was his eyes I recognized. They were a brilliant blue. The same ones that looked down at me with drunken lust long ago and stared at me with surprise days later.

It was the soldier. The one I had almost had sex with in a bathroom at a drunken party. The one who had told me to get out of Austin after the EMP struck.

He was here. Now. In these woods.

And Cash was going to kill him.

"Get out of here, Cat!" Cash roared without looking up at me as he tightened his fingers around the man's neck and held him down.

"No!" I cried out, staggering forward. The soldier's face was turning red. I wasn't sure what I was going to do, but I couldn't let Cash kill him.

Cash's gaze snapped up to me as I rushed toward them. It was just the distraction the soldier needed.

He swung fast and hard, two quick jabs to Cash's ribs then temple. It sent Cash toppling sideways, throwing him off the man.

As soon as he was free, the soldier scrambled to get Cash's gun that lay a few feet away. But Cash was unstoppable. He reached back and slid a long knife out of his boot. Just as the man's fingers closed around the shotgun, Cash grabbed him in a chokehold from behind and jerked him upright.

"Don't move," he growled, putting the tip of the knife under the soldier's ribcage and his arm around the man's windpipe.

The soldier looked at me and raised his hands, his face bloody and bruised.

I shifted my gaze away from him and glanced at Cash. There was blood in his hair. Lots of it. It seeped down his forehead and into his eyes. His lip was cut and his faded jeans were muddy.

"You're hurt!" I shot forward, terrified that the wound on his head was serious, but when he raised his eyes and looked at me, I stopped. His gaze was ice cold. His expression was lethal.

"Leave," he snapped, glaring at me across the distance.

"No," I said with more stubbornness than I felt.

Cash shook his head, furious. The muscles in his arm bulged around the soldier's neck. "Goddamn it, Cat! Leave!"

I stepped forward, fear forgotten, anger now taking over. "Over my dead body! Listen to me, Cash…"

"Cat, I swear to God—"

The soldier took advantage of our arguing, slamming his hand down on Cash's wrist with enough power to break it. But Cash was ready. His arm let go of the man's neck and the tip of his knife replaced it, pricking the skin below the soldier's jaw.

I shot forward, panic exploding in me when I saw the drop of blood ooze from under the blade. "No! Stop, Cash! Stop! I know him! I know him!"

Cash's eyes snapped up to mine, surprised.

"I know him," I repeated, glancing down at the soldier as I edged closer. For a man who was bleeding and had a knife near his jugular, he looked pretty calm, but something was telling me it was a lie.

"How?" Cash blinked against the blood dripping in his eye.

My heart beat faster. I couldn't tell him. God, I just couldn't.

"How do you know him, Cat?" he demanded when I didn't answer, his knife still against the man's neck.

The soldier stared at me with cool composure.

"I just do," I whispered, hoping I wouldn't regret it.

"Shit," Cash swore harshly. He removed the knife from the man's neck and shoved him away.

I stumbled back as the soldier fell forward. He caught himself on the palms of his hands, crunching the dead leaves in front of him.

Slowly, he raised his head. Twinkling blue eyes stared back at me.

"It's been a long time," he said in a deep voice, his gaze running over my body with interest. "A really long time."

Cash let out a low sound of warning, murder in his eyes. I could almost feel his anger growing, brewing, threatening to turn into a violent storm. Blood soaked his hair and ran down his face, giving him a wild, barbarian look. He needed medical attention but we had another problem.

Our new visitor.

I turned my gaze back to the soldier. What were the chances of running into him in the middle of the woods, years later after we met? I didn't believe in coincidence or fate or any of that other bullshit so it seemed suspicious.

"What are you doing here?" I asked, crossing my arms over my chest and sticking my chin up, trying to show some bravery. Inside I was shaking. My heart was pounding. My stomach was twisted into a painful knot. I knew Cash had a shotgun in one hand and a knife in the other, but I wasn't sure he could pull the trigger or throw the knife before the soldier could grab me and snap me in half.

He smirked as if he found my question funny then dusted off his hands and rose to his full height, towering well above me. With his eyes locked on mine, he rolled his shoulders and flexed his neck like an expert fighter ready to get back into the ring. Bones cracked and muscles bulged. Spreading his feet wide, he stretched out a hand, twisting his wrist one way then another as if he were testing it.

Glancing over his shoulder at Cash, his mouth quirked up. "Thanks for not killing me, man, but maybe you should have."

Cash didn't move a muscle. "Why?" he rumbled, his voice so low and cold that I felt a shiver run up my spine.

The soldier glanced back at me, his eyes roaming over my body slowly, his smirk growing. "Because I came for her."

Chapter Fourteen

-Cash-

I didn't have much honor left. Too much had happened since the war broke out and the land I loved became a graveyard of bodies and a battlefield of fighting. I learned quick that evil came in different forms. It could be terrorists shooting innocent people in the streets or men doing things that would turn a man's stomach. It was all done in the name of survival. I had seen it all, participated in some of it. I knew trouble and knew when it was in front of me.

The man was trouble.

I was fighting the urge to swing my shotgun up and fill him full of buckshot. He wanted Cat? He sure as hell would have to go through me first. That wasn't honor. That was the coldhearted part of me.

I tightened my fist around the handle of my knife. It felt like an extension of my hand. It was a hunting knife. Bone handle. Mirror finished blade. Deadly. Perfect. Something my dad never intended for me to use against a man when he gave it to me. But it had stopped the bastard. Who knows what he would have done to Cat if he had gotten free.

I kept my eyes off her, afraid if I looked at her I would lose it. I knew she was shaken and terrified. Ready to bolt. She was bleeding from a cut on her forehead and dirty from who in the hell knows. I needed to get her to David, have him check her out. I had a feeling the bullet wound was probably giving her fits, the way she favored her side. Hell, I probably needed some medical attention too but it could wait.

I had a stranger to deal with.

I raised the gun to my shoulder and peered down the barrel. The man didn't flinch as if he was used to being held at gunpoint. It didn't sit well with me. Neither did the fact that he was standing between Cat and me.

I started toward him, determined to kill him if he made one wrong move toward her.

"You came for her?" I asked, keeping him in my sights. "You mind telling me what for?"

The corner of his mouth quirked up. I was really starting to fume. I could say it was because he was here for her, but it was more than that. He and Cat knew each other. I wasn't a jealous man but I was starting to become one fast.

"How about you lower the gun and we'll talk?" he said, shrugging. "Just an idea."

Smartass.

"Stupid idea. Try again," I said, easing toward him. He didn't move but Cat scrambled back, tripping over a branch to get away.

He glanced at her and grinned. I wanted to kill him for that and the familiarity in his gaze when he looked at her. I might have told her it was over but no one touched her. No one but me.

"Call off your guard dog. I'm not a threat," he said to Cat with an edge to his voice that I didn't like when he talked to her.

Cat suddenly stopped where she was and raised an eyebrow.

"Not a threat?" she said with spirit and plenty of backbone. "Call me crazy but I don't believe you. You just said you came for me."

He opened his mouth to respond but she cut him off, narrowing her eyes at him.

"Why? It's been *years.*"

I wanted to ask if it had been years before her and I hooked up or after. It shouldn't be my business but it was. I was making it. He was trouble and I was going to take him out if he touched Cat. *Mine*, the savage part of me rumbled.

He turned to face her completely. "Doesn't matter why. When they finally catch up to me, all the guard dogs in the world won't be enough. He won't be enough." He jerked his thumb at me and started walking toward her. "They'll tie you up and…"

I had had enough. I saw what little blood was left in Cat's face rush out as he spoke. I could tell she was growing weaker, unsteady on her feet. I never should have told her to run. Not still recovering from a bullet wound. She had no more fight left in her.

But she had me.

I lunged. The stranger sprinted forward, going for Cat. He didn't get far.

I raised the gun over my head and slammed it down. The butt hit him in the back of the head. He crumbled to the ground, unconscious.

Cat seemed to fold in on herself. Her shoulders hunched forward. She started shaking. I wanted to grab her and run my hands all over her body, make sure she was alright and the cut on her head wasn't serious, but instead I kept my distance. Sheathing my knife, I crouched down near the man and started searching his pockets.

"You okay?" I asked her as I kept my attention on what I was doing. When she didn't answer, I glanced up. She was so pale that I thought she was going to pass out on me.

"Cat, answer me. Are you okay?" I snapped, worried.

"Yeah," she mumbled so low I almost didn't hear her. "I'm…I'm fine."

I went back to searching the man's pockets, keeping one eye on her. I could hear Tate and David in the distance, barreling through the woods like two hound dogs on a scent. They would be here shortly. I needed to get some answers from Cat before they arrived.

"Who is he?" I asked.

When she didn't answer, I jerked my head up, aggravation growing in me. "Cat? Answer me! Who is he?"

She licked her dry lips, hesitating. "A soldier."

I drew my brows together. *A soldier? What the hell?*

I hadn't seen a U.S. soldier in at least a year. What was one doing out here, wandering through the woods looking for Cat? It didn't add up. Neither did the guilty look on Cat's face.

I set my jaw in a firm line and turned my attention back to searching the stranger. There was nothing on him but a map and some bullets. *He must have hidden a stash of supplies somewhere.* I would search for them later. For now, I had to take care of Cat.

I climbed to my feet, planning to go to her but Tate burst through the trees.

"We heard three gunshots. Who the fuck is he?" he called out, jogging toward us as fast as the low hanging limbs and thick undergrowth would allow. David followed behind him at a slower pace, huffing and puffing, his face red with exertion. They both had rifles and I saw a pistol sticking out from under Tate's jacket.

"A soldier. He jumped me," I answered, wiping blood away from my eye as Tate stopped by the man. He looked down at him, his eyes going wide.

"Hell," he said glancing up at Cat. "You okay?"

Cat nodded and slid her gaze away, a telltale sign that she was feeling guilty as hell about something.

David kneeled down next to the man and checked his pulse.

"I know him," he said, sitting back on his haunches and squinting at the man.

"Seems like everyone does but me," I murmured. "Who is he?"

David pushed himself to his feet, frowning when he saw the blood dripping down my face. "He's one of Frankie's men."

Chapter Fifteen

-Cat-

"You really did a number on him. You sure he ain't dead?" Tate asked for the hundredth time, watching as Cash dumped the soldier on the cabin floor.

"I'm sure. He's just unconscious," Cash answered, standing up straight over the man.

It had made the trip back hard for Tate and Cash. They took turns carrying the soldier over their shoulders in a fireman's carry. He probably weighed a ton. I had stayed near David, helping him under low branches and over fallen trees when his knobby, arthritic knees wanted to give out. By the time we reached the cabin, the sun was setting and the chill in the air had increased.

Cash pushed the man to his side with the toe of his boot. "You still got that rope, Tate?"

Tate grabbed the nylon rope from his belt and handed it to Cash. "You gonna tie him up?"

"Yep," Cash answered, always patient with my brother.

He gathered the man's hands behind his back and looped the rope around his wrist. Giving it a firm tug, he tied it and made sure the knot was tight. Satisfied, he stood up and wiped a drop of blood off his forehead.

"You gonna let me look at that cut?" David asked, nodding at Cash's forehead.

"It's nothing."

I frowned. He had thrown his hat on the couch when we walked in. His hair was matted with blood and there seemed to be a lot of it. It was a little more than nothing.

He and David stood over the unconscious man, staring at him like they wanted to string him up from the nearest tree.

"So he's one of Frankie's men?" Cash asked, holding his shotgun in his hand, ready to use it if the soldier woke up fighting.

David scratched at his day's growth beard and nodded. "Yeah. One of Frankie's finest. I would know him anywhere. Frankie calls him his pride and joy. A real machine. He's an expert marksman and tracker. From what I gather, he's also a coldblooded, sly fellow. Folks say don't let his dry humor fool you. He's dangerous."

"You think he knows anything about Keely and Gavin?" Tate asked, looking from the soldier to Cash.

Cash shrugged and surveyed the man. "Guess we'll find out when he wakes up."

I looked down at the soldier, wondering what had happened to him. He wasn't so coldblooded or dangerous that night at the party or that day in Austin when supplies were being handed out. In fact, he seemed kind of young and green both times.

Now he seemed harder. Carved into a mercenary. He was better dressed than any of us and cleaner than all of us. His jeans didn't have holes and his jacket appeared to be neatly patched in places. Dirt didn't cake his hair or was smudged on his face. He looked prepared to spend days in the woods.

Tate had found his backpack. It was well equipped. I had no doubt where the supplies came from. The militia raided, killed, and stole for what they wanted. The soldier's clothes might have been taken off a dead man. A victim of their ruthless crimes.

"Was he in town the day we got out? Do you know?" Cash asked, peering at David.

David ran a hand over his mouth, thinking. "Don't reckon he was. I figure if he was in town, y'all wouldn't be standing here right now. Neither would I. The guy is just that good with a gun."

Cash looked over his shoulder at me, his eyes cold slates of gray. "And you know him, Cat?"

I nodded. "Yeah." I cleared my throat. "Kind of."

Cash stared at me, his gaze calculating. I felt stripped bare and left raw, all my past laid out for him to see, including the moments I had spent with the soldier.

"I remember him," Tate said suddenly. "He was that soldier in Austin, wasn't he, Cat?"

I nodded, afraid to meet Cash's hard gaze. I could feel it, burning holes in me. Judging me.

David squinted at Tate through the growing darkness in the cabin. "He's a soldier you say? U.S.?"

Tate scrunched up his face, thinking. "Yeah, I'm sure. Had the uniform and everything. He told us to get out of the city didn't he, Cat? Said bad things were about to happen." Tate shrugged. "So we ran."

The soldier let out a deep groan. I jumped back and Cash snapped his shotgun up, pointing it down at the man.

"Any sudden moves and I pull the trigger."

The soldier's eyelids fluttered. They rose halfway then lowered. Rose then lowered. Cash widened his stance, keeping his gun trained on the man as he tried to wake up.

"You sure he ain't got a concussion or something?" Tate asked, talking a mile a minute like he was so good at doing. "They say if you get hit in the head then fall asleep, you could have trouble waking up. You think you hurt him that bad, Cash? You got a mean swing. Could knock a man into yesterday and confuse the hell out of him. Concussions can do that. Am I right, preacher?"

The soldier's deep voice boomed out in the cabin. "I don't have a concussion but I do have a fucking headache." He squeezed his eyes tight. "Damn, kid, shut the fuck up."

Cash didn't move, pointing his gun steady at the man. "How about he shuts up and you start talking. Why are you here?"

The man peeled his eyes open and struggled to sit up, wincing. His face was battered and bruised, courtesy of Cash's fists. His right eye was swollen and turning black. His bottom lip was bleeding. He had a nasty bruise on his neck and a nick inches from his jugular from Cash's knife.

With his hands tied behind him, he looked around the cabin. The useless kerosene heaters were sitting against one wall, out of fuel. The last of our food was sitting on the table. His gaze skipped over Cash and touched on Tate then David. When he looked at me, I felt a chill run down my spine.

"Like I said, I came for her." His gaze slid from me to Cash. "I take it you're the boyfriend. I came for you too."

Cash smirked, a deadly grin. "Well, I'm here. How about you just leave her out of it and deal with me instead?"

The corner of the soldier's mouth quirked up in a smile. "Oh, I'll deal with you too but first things first. Her."

Cash peered down the gun. "You'll have to go through me first."

The soldier shrugged. "Okay."

David interrupted the standoff before things got out of hand.

"Frankie sent you, didn't he?" he asked with a loud, booming voice full of authority. "You're his killing machine and do the dirty work."

The man's gaze moved to David as if he just noticed the old man was there. "And you're the doc slash preacher. I heard you drove into town like an avenging angel to save the day. No one was expecting that. You got the whole town talking, old man. That makes you a target too. All of you are."

Tate glanced at me, his eyes wide with fear. I felt my skin crawl with a dark foreboding. A feeling that made me want to grab our meager supplies and run.

Cash held his gun steady. "What are your orders?"

The soldier ignored the question and looked at me. Before my eyes, he changed. He went from dangerous to someone harmless and nonthreatening. I wasn't sure if it was an act but the boy that had danced with me at a college party was back and the mercenary was gone.

"They said you had green eyes and black hair. I had no idea that you were the girl they were talking about." His eyes made a leisure path down my body and back up. "What are the chances?"

I shoved down my uneasiness, refusing to be afraid. "What else did they tell you about me?"

"They said you might be dead."

"Well, I'm not," I retorted. "I'm very much alive."

The soldier grinned, amused. "No, ma'am you're not. At least not yet."

A shiver ran over me as if a ghost walked through me.

Cash must have had enough because he eased his finger over the trigger. "Enough. I asked you a question. What are your orders?"

The soldier slid his gaze away from me to Cash. His eyes went hard. Lethal. It was then I saw the killer in him.

"My name is Adam and my orders don't matter. What matters is that they are coming for you. Run while you still can."

Chapter Sixteen

-Cat-

Cash didn't move, his gun still trained on the soldier's head. "How much time do we have until they show up?"

Adam peered up at him with his one good eye, ignoring the gun in his face.

"A week," he answered. "Give or take."

Cash frowned and jutted his chin out at Adam. "You know anything about a blonde and a black-haired guy that were with us?"

Adam shook his head. "Nope. Never heard of them."

Always the hothead, Tate snorted. "Why should we believe you? Hilltop is full of liars and thieves. You might be one of them."

Adam smiled wickedly. "I am. But you should believe me because I know these men and I know every move they make. I've fought beside them. I've trained them and taught them everything I know. They are a bloodthirsty group. They *will* find you and when they do, it won't be pretty."

"So why shouldn't we just kill you on the spot, then?" Tate asked, shrugging. "Leave them a little welcoming gift."

Adam didn't move a muscle, undercurrents of warning flowing from him. "Because, kid, once I saw her, everything changed. Orders can be damned and loyalty can be screwed. I don't kill people I know, at least the ones I care about." He looked at Cash. "Get her out of here."

Cash's muscles seemed to constrict and tighten more under his clothes as if he was debating whether to strangle the soldier or believe him. Finally, he lowered the weapon.

"I want someone outside at all times. I want to know if a leaf falls or a branch breaks. I don't want these fuckers to get the drop on us," he said, looking from Tate to David. "Be ready to leave."

Tate mumbled his understanding.

David cleared his throat, now that the tension had ebbed. "Cash, you and Cat are hurt. Let's get you patched up before we do anything else. Doctor's orders."

I reached up, touching the cut on my forehead as he headed to the kitchen for first aid supplies. I felt Cash staring at me, his own head bleeding. When his gaze touched on the gash on my forehead, he frowned.

"I'm okay," I assured him but his frown only deepened.

He handed his shotgun to Tate and started toward me. "He moves, pull the trigger," he said, pointing at Adam but keeping his gaze locked on me.

He reached for me but I scooted away. He was still the man who had said we were over. That wanted me to stop loving him. That had used sex to prove he was an asshole. I didn't want him touching me.

He let out a low rumble of annoyance and wrapped his hand around my upper arm. "You're bleeding, Cat. You're not okay."

I opened my mouth to argue but clamped it shut when he glowered at me with warning. I sulked, not happy, but didn't try to fight him when he started pulling me toward the kitchen where David was searching for the medical supplies.

"I'll take care of her," Cash muttered, grabbing the small box of first aid right out of David's hand as we walked by. David was left standing open-mouthed, staring after us.

"Let her take care of you too, son. You're a mess!" he called out as Cash pulled me toward the bedroom.

It was dark and cold. I could see little puffs of air as I exhaled. Cash led me over to the middle of the room and let me go. He sat the first aid kit on the bed and lit a candle then headed over to the corner of the room where a small gas heater sat. Kneeling down, he lit it. The little heater flared to life, a warm red glow illuminating the room.

Once the heater was working, Cash stood up and turned to face me.

"Sit down."

I bristled at his tone. I had one rule. Men couldn't boss me around. But somehow Cash always did.

"How about *you* sit down?" I retorted, growing angry. "You're still bleeding and I'm not."

Cash's gaze turned hard. His mouth tightened. "Fine," he muttered, stomping past me to the bed.

He sat down on the edge of the bed, looking pissed and impatient. The candlelight played over him, making him appear even more ominous and big. I took one tiny step toward him, suddenly nervous. We were alone. He looked so…sexy. It was a combination that always got me in trouble.

I hesitated, knowing my weakness.

He looked up at me, his knees spread. "Come here."

There he was again. The man he had become. The cowboy I couldn't resist. Strong. Demanding. A quiet strength that couldn't be denied.

I chewed on my bottom lip, glancing down at his hands. His long fingers were spread over his thigh. It was such an innocent pose but fuck, there was nothing innocent about what those fingers could do to me. Just seeing his hand lightly resting on his thigh made me wet and needy. Memories of him behind me, touching me with those fingers, making me cry out and come, had me burning on fire again.

Damn him! We were over. Finished. I wasn't going to be one of those girls anymore. No more sex for the sake of fucking. No more giving into my carnal needs. I was stronger. My heart was broken but my body didn't know that. I could ignore him.

Maybe.

I stiffened my resolve and went to him. He didn't speak or move. He just watched me walk toward him with those chaotic gray eyes of his, staying still as if he was afraid I might bolt.

The silence was heavy, sucking all the air out of the room. The murmur of voices outside the bedroom reminded me that no one was listening. We could do whatever we wanted.

On the bed.

The floor.

Against the wall.

In the chair.

God, I was crazy with need.

As I got closer to him, I grew hotter. My knees weaker. My fingertips tingled. My skin became sensitive. My palms grew moist.

Cash parted his legs, making room for me. I swallowed hard, seeing that space for me. So close to what could make me scream.

He looked up at me patiently, waiting. I pretended like he wasn't affecting me and stepped between his legs. I was just there to take care of his cuts. Nothing more. Nothing less.

He kept his hands on his legs in a safe place. One small inch and his fingers would be on me, sliding between my legs and going home.

This is not good. Not good. I ignored that little voice in my head and cleared my throat.

"Let me look," I whispered, reaching out to touch the bloody gash right above his hairline, trying to ignore how close my breasts were to his mouth.

He hissed and pulled away when my fingers touched the tear.

"Big baby," I whispered.

He grunted and peered up at me, the flickering light from the candle playing over his face.

I blushed and stepped away to grab the washcloth next to the large, ceramic bowl that Tate filled with hot water for me to bathe with. The apocalypse's idea of a bath.

I dipped it in the now cold water and turned back to Cash. This time when I returned between his legs, he touched the outside of my thigh. It was just a light touch, barely there, but I felt it down to my toes.

I went motionless, holding the washcloth halfway to his head. My heart beat faster. I drew shallow breaths. *He doesn't want to be with you*, I told myself. *Get over it!*

"How bad is it?" he asked, his voice a deep rumble of sex and desire and all the things I craved.

It's awful. Terrible. Delectable. Addicting. The words were on the tip of my tongue but I wasn't thinking of his injuries.

I cleared my mind and focused on what I was doing. I started dabbing the wound on his head, leaning closer to get a better view. The gash was gaping open, half of it disappearing in his hairline. I wanted to stalk out of the bedroom and punch Adam in the face a few times for it.

"You need stitches," I said, giving the wound a quick dab. "I'll go get David."

I turned to leave but Cash grabbed my wrist.

"No. Stay."

He pulled me back between his legs. Letting go of my wrist, he put his hand on the back of my thigh again, pulling me closer.

"Just patch me up. I need to go back out and make sure no one else was with that man."

"Adam," I said automatically, tilting Cash's head forward so I could get a good look at the gash on his head.

His gaze snapped up to mine. Heated fury swirled in his eyes. I let go of his head and cleared my throat.

"His name is Adam."

He didn't say anything for a few minutes. I went back to cleaning the wound and wiping blood away from his face. There were bruises on his cheekbone that were turning an ugly color of purple. A cut on his lip was already scabbed over. He was a mess but Adam looked a million times worse.

"How do you know him?" he asked as I leaned over to open the first aid kit beside him on the bed.

My stomach flopped. Oh shit.

I snapped open the box and rummaged inside, wondering what I would say. I almost had sex with him? I was drunk and trying to forget about you? Nothing seemed right, but I had to tell him the truth. At least part of it.

"I was with him when the EMP hit," I said before I could change my mind. "I met him that night."

Cash went rigid. What I said seemed to hang in the air between us.

I leaned over to grab a butterfly bandage from the first aid kit, my throat tight. Tears prickled the back of my eyes. I couldn't run from my past or forget what I once was. It would follow me, making me pay for every drunk, stupid decision I had ever made.

"Shit," I whispered, sniffing and trying to open the bandage package with shaky hands. I couldn't look at Cash. I was afraid to. If I saw the rejection in his eyes or hate, I might fall apart.

He took the package from me, his fingers grazing mine.

"Where were you, when the EMP hit?" he asked, opening the package and handing it back. His eyes were hard pieces of granite staring at me.

I didn't want to answer but I swore to always tell him the truth.

"I was at a party. I was drunk and—"

Cash interrupted me, his voice harsh in the silent bedroom. "Forget it. It doesn't matter. Just finish bandaging me up. I've got to go."

He hated me. He really did. I could see it in the rigid line of his body. In the way he held himself distant even though his hand stayed on my thigh.

I took a deep, cleansing breath and raised on my tiptoes to see the gash on his head better. "I didn't know him that well but I don't think he'll hurt me or lead them back here."

Cash scoffed. "You really believe that?" he asked, his forehead brushing against my chest.

"Yes."

He sighed with resignation. His warm exhale sent tingles over my skin. His fingers on the back of my thigh felt intimate. Familiar. I was reminded again of what Luke had said in my dream. *Cash was home.*

I put the butterfly bandage on his gash as carefully as I could. His hair was still matted with dried blood despite my best efforts to clean it. His skin was still tinged red from where I had wiped the blood away. The wound would probably scar but it would only add to his rugged appearance.

With the bandage in place, I lowered back to the heels of my feet and started to step away but Cash didn't let me go. His hand stayed on the back of my thigh. His eyes traveled up my body, taking their time, touching on every curve and slope.

Without a word, he eased me back a step so he could stand up. His body brushed against mine. His height made me feel small.

He reached back and grabbed gauze from the first aid kit.

"Your turn."

I stood still as he dabbed at the cut on my forehead until the blood was gone. Grabbing a Band-Aid out of the kit, he tore the package open and put it on my cut.

It hurt, watching him avoid looking at me. He was gentle and caring as he took care of me, but his body was tense as if he was about to explode.

Backing away, he shut the first aid kid. "Is it bleeding?" he asked, keeping his eyes off me.

I knew what he was talking about. The wound in my side.

I glanced down. "I'm not sure."

"Let me see."

He straightened up and returned to stand in front of me. Grabbing the lapels of his jacket that I still wore, he tugged it off me and tossed it behind him onto the bed.

I felt bare. Silly, I know. I still had on a shirt and jeans. But this was Cash and only a thin layer stood between him and me.

He lifted the edge of my shirt. The wide, square bandage over my left side was exposed but so was the curve of my breast.

He became motionless, his hand gripping my shirt. His knuckles brushed my nipple. The need that always existed between us flared. Like an obsession, I needed him. I wanted him in me, pounding me hard and deep until I screamed. I wanted to feel his hands on my breasts, squeezing and tormenting, holding them for his mouth. I wanted to feel him explode in me, soaking my insides until there was no doubt he had claimed me.

I parted my lips. A flush warmed my body. There was a man outside bruised by Cash's hands, warning us that men were coming. We were low on food. Cash said we were over. Sex with him should be the very last thing on my mind. War, death, violence, rage, heartache – none of it could stop me from wanting him. My need for him was that strong.

He gripped my shirt in his fist with self-possessed control. I stood frozen, unable to move, wishing he would just touch me.

He took a step closer. His thighs moved against me. His warm breath blew strands of my hair on the top of my head. I could almost see the war he fought with himself.

A second later, a curtain came down over him. Icy reserve took over.

"There's no blood. You're fine," he muttered, dropping my shirt back in place and moving away from me. Indifferent. Unfeeling. Remote.

I grabbed his jacket and thrust my arms through the holes with angry stabs. "So I'll survive?"

He pulled the pistol from his holster and opened up the chamber, checking for bullets. "You'll survive."

Aggravation made me want to yell and scream. I stuck my chin up in the air and hoped he couldn't see how hurt I was.

"And will you survive?" I burst out as he headed to the door.

He stopped, his back to me. I didn't think he would answer, but he turned around, taking his time. He had that gun in his hand and one hip cocked, looking like the cowboy he was.

"Will I survive what?" he asked in a chilly tone. "You? This? That man out there being here?"

I licked my dry lips and met his stare boldly. "Yes. Everything."

He took a step closer, his voice dropping to a spine-tingling tone. "As far as you and me, I'll survive. As far as him… He touched you, Cat. The real question is, will he survive?"

Chapter Seventeen

-Cash-

I walked out of the bedroom with furious strides. To say I was pissed was an understatement. Cat believed that asshole wasn't a threat. I didn't know which was worse – knowing she trusted him or knowing she had been with him not long after she was with me.

I hadn't been prone to anger or violence before the EMP hit. But afterward, I changed. Do or die. Kill or be killed. Take or be taken. They were sayings that had been burned in my brain since the electrical grids went down. This stranger…this man sent to hunt us down…had been with Cat. The more I thought of it, the angrier I got. The more I wanted to go apeshit on his ass.

I ignored David who glanced up at me and Tate standing nearby, picking at one of his fingernails with a pocketknife. I ignored the chill in the air and the way my mind nagged me to make sure Cat was warm enough. I ignored the flickering light from the candle someone had lit, chasing away the encroaching darkness. All I could think and pictured was the bastard touching Cat. Kissing her. Taking her clothes off.

He glanced up at me. His face was battered and bruised. His right eye was swollen shut and the left wasn't looking so good either. I didn't care. I was going to add some more black and blue to it.

Starting now.

I crossed the living room in three quick strides. If someone had tried to step in front of me, I would have thrown them out of the way. Tate was smarter than that though and so was the preacher. Can't say I was in that moment. When it came to Cat, I was reckless.

Adam wasn't surprised to see me barreling toward him. That just pissed me off more. I pulled back my fist and slammed it down on his face.

Bone crunched against bone. Adam's head whipped to the side, blood spraying across his jeans. David climbed to his feet and Tate shot forward.

He slowly turned his head back around. Blood oozed from his mouth. Staring at me, he worked his jaw back and forth, making sure it wasn't broken. Served him right if it was. Besides Cat, the man worked for Frankie. That was enough in my book to deserve a broken bone or two.

"Guess there's no reason to ask what that's for," he said with a thick Texas accent.

"Nope. Guess not," I muttered.

His gaze flicked to the bedroom behind me. I didn't have to turn around to know that Cat stood in the doorway, watching.

"Shit, honey," he chuckled, grinning at her. "Your boyfriend sure knows how to throw a punch."

"He's not my boyfriend," she countered.

I glanced over at her. She was leaning against the doorframe, looking cool as a cucumber in the candlelight. Her arms were folded over her chest and one of her ankles was crossed over the other. That little chin of hers was up in the air and her eyes were the color of grass on a summer day. She had never looked so good and her words had never hurt so much.

I turned and headed toward the door, feeling the sudden need to get the hell out of there. I was furious and was busting with pent-up rage. The best place for me to be was away.

"Sorry. I just figured you two were together. You got this vibe going," Adam quipped, sounding like a smartass.

"Doesn't matter. Stay away from her," I warned as I leaned over to grab my hat from the couch.

Adam grinned. "Oh, so it's like that, huh?"

I paused, my hat in my hand. He was trying to prod me and it was working. But I wouldn't let him know that.

I put my hat on my head and pulled the brim down low, conscious of Cat watching me. Glancing at the soldier, I gave him a cold glare. "Yeah, it's like that."

Adam shrugged. "Whatever. I'm not who you should worry about anyway."

"Who said I was worried?"

Before he could answer, I opened the door and stepped outside. Cold air greeted me. A full moon cast shadows on the trees.

I flexed my fists. My knuckles were red and scraped, just a little reminder of what this world had made me become. A violent man ready to bleed.

For survival.

For love.

For Cat.

Chapter Eighteen

-Cat-

I tossed and turned all night. The bedroom was too quiet. Too empty of Cash. I imagined Paul was outside, waiting. Smiling with anticipation. I dreamed Frankie caught Cash and killed him. I replayed Adam's words in my mind again and again, 'They're coming for her. Run.'

I blinked, the image of being chased by Frankie and Paul disappearing. It was midmorning and I was standing in the living room. Cash was gone and Tate was with him. David was untying the rope around Adam's wrists.

"You get ten minutes" he said to Adam.

"Thanks, old man." Adam smiled and rubbed his wrists, getting the blood flowing in them again.

"Don't make me regret it, son."

Adam gave a short nod and stood up. I watched from a safe distance as he stretched out the kinks in his back and rolled his neck after sleeping on the floor all night.

"You got any food around here?" he asked, glancing around as he rotated his shoulders.

David didn't answer and neither did I. The truth was we were down to almost nothing but we weren't going to tell him that.

"Guess that's a no," Adam muttered, bending down to rummage in his backpack.

He withdrew a bottle of water and took a long drink. Catching me staring at him, he lowered the bottle and wiped his mouth on the back of his sleeve. "You got a problem?"

"Yeah. I do." I looked at David. "Give us a minute."

"I can't do that, honey. Cash would skin me alive."

Adam chuckled which only made me angrier. I was tired, hungry, and broken up over Cash. To say I was cranky was an understatement. I was on bitch drive.

"Cash doesn't own me," I snapped, angry with David and Adam and all men in general.

Adam's lips twitched. "I'm not going to hurt her, Doc. Cross my heart and hope to die." He made a cross over his heart with his finger. Jackass.

David ignored Adam's attempt at humor and pointed his finger at him. "You better be on your best behavior if you've even got one. Me and my gun will be right outside, young man." He lowered his hand and looked at me. "You gonna be okay, sweetie?"

I nodded. I had a knife strapped to my waistband and I knew how to use it.

David gave Adam a dark look. "Ten minutes."

He walked to the door, looking putout at leaving. I waited until he was gone to face Adam again.

"Why did you do it?" I asked, crossing my arms over my chest.

"Why did I do what?" he said, leaning over to drop the water bottle back in his bag and grab a baggie of dried meat.

My mouth watered. God, I was hungry. My breakfast consisted of a single cup of stale oatmeal and some questionable looking canned peaches that had a little film on the top.

Seeing the piece of jerky in Adam's hand made my stomach rumble loudly. He must have heard it. He held it out to me with a raised eyebrow.

I shook my head. I wasn't that desperate for food. Yet.

He sighed and dropped the bag of meat back into his backpack. "I'm not going to hurt you, Cat. It's Cat, isn't it?"

"Yeah," I answered, feeling a tiny bit of shame. He didn't know my name and we almost had a one-night stand years ago. The people in my hometown were right. I was a slut. But I had been running from emotions. Running from pain. Running from a cowboy who made me hope and feel things.

"So where's…what's his name again? Cash?" Adam asked.

"He's out hunting."

I didn't want to talk about Cash with Adam. It felt wrong, like my past would taint my future.

I crossed my arms and changed the subject. "Why did you join Frankie's militia? You were military."

"Yeah, I was. But when Austin became a hellhole, the military lost control. We were fighting off insurgents every time we turned around and battling U.S. citizens who were attacking us for supplies. The government didn't have enough manpower to deal with it. We were getting slaughtered by the minute. My troop just fell apart."

"And that's when you hooked up with Frankie?"

"Yep. He was just sitting back and watching the shit go down. When he saw the military fall, he offered some of us a better, more secure life."

He grabbed his water bottle again and took a long drink. Screwing the top back on, he popped his neck and then continued.

"There were ten of us. We stood around a fire – tired, a few of us injured – and we listened to Frankie. He talked about the great, almighty United States of America and how it was the people's responsibility to take it back. We believed him. I mean, we were standing there starving and homeless, eating the meat that Frankie's men had killed and drinking whiskey we thought we would never taste again. It was more than we had had in months and he was charismatic – a natural born leader. We were itching to get back to the action and destroy some terrorist bastards." He shrugged. "So we joined up."

"And became Frankie's hired gun."

"Call it what you will. I did what it took to survive."

I scoffed. "You call tracking people for some maniac's sick revenge, surviving?"

Adam chuckled but he didn't sound amused. "Let me guess – you and your little posse here have been angels."

I didn't respond.

He smirked. "Yeah, that's what I thought."

I opened my mouth to tell him what I thought of his snarky attitude but he started walking toward me. Fear made me jittery but I held my ground. I refused to be intimidated.

He stopped a foot or two away and spread his legs in an aggressive stance. I pressed my arm against the knife under my shirt and stuck my chin up.

He looked down at my waist. "You got a weapon under there?"

I squared my shoulders, stubborn and brave. "Yes, and I can pull it out in seconds. I had to learn because of people like you."

He crossed his arms over his chest, amused. "You were a little she-devil that night at the party. Guess some things just never change."

I met his stare, unafraid. "Guess not because I'm not afraid of you."

He leaned closer. "But you should be."

I didn't flinch but I was shaking on the inside. Adam must have known what kind of effect he was having on me. His mouth twitched and amusement danced in his eyes.

"So tell me," he said, glancing up and down my body. "What's the deal with you and Cash? He's very protective of you. Is this some kind of unrequited love or something?"

"It's none of your business."

He tilted his head to the side at a jaunty angle. "The man has it bad for you and is willing to kick my ass to protect you, sweet thing."

"Don't call me that. And yes, he will kick your ass."

He laughed but sobered up when I winced and touched my left side.

"What's wrong?" He frowned.

His question caught me off guard. I rolled my eyes, covering up the surprise. "Not that it's any of your business but I was shot."

His eyes turned a dangerous sort of blue. "That's why they thought you might be dead. You took a bullet."

"Yeah. Happy?"

He ran a hand over the whiskers on his chin. "Not particularly. Why did they want you, if you were alive?"

"They didn't tell you?"

Adam shook his head. "I take orders. I don't question them, ma'am."

I pushed strands of hair out of my face, growing angry. I was tired of being afraid. Tired of being hungry and dirty. I wanted to go back home and find out it was all a bad dream, every damn day since the EMP hit and terrorists landed on U.S. soil.

I took a swift step toward Adam, undaunted by his big, bouncer body or the threat he posed. Who cared that he had tracked me? I had had enough.

"Maybe you should start questioning orders, soldier. You were hunting a girl one of them tried to rape. So maybe that's what they want with me. To finish what they started," I said bitterly. "That's who you signed on with. A bunch of damn rapist bastards."

Adam stared down at me, his mouth grim. I heard the cabin door open but I didn't bother looking up. It was probably David. Adam's ten minutes were up.

"I'm sorry," Adam said, sounding genuine. "I didn't know." He put his fingers under my chin and tilted my head back to look in my eyes. "I promise I'm not going to hurt you."

I didn't get a chance to respond. The sound of someone's boots scraping along the hardwood floor was like a chainsaw running in the tiny cabin.

I swung my head around and found Cash standing near the door. His cowboy hat was pulled down low on his head and his hard gaze was locked on Adam's hand on my chin.

I jerked away from Adam's grasp and took a quick step back. Adam turned to face Cash.

"Wondered when you were going to show up." He grinned like he didn't give a flying fuck if Cash caught him touching me or not.

If looks could kill, Adam would be lying at my feet, fast on his way to an early grave. Cash tore his gaze away from Adam and turned that heated stare on me. I felt caught and guilty but why should I? I hadn't done anything wrong. Adam had touched me not the other way around. Plus, Cash said we were over. He had no right to be jealous. None at all.

He started toward us, reaching under his jacket for the weapon I knew he kept holstered there. *Holy balls, what's he doing?* I gulped and darted a glance at Adam. He seemed relaxed. Too relaxed. I didn't trust him at all.

Cash pulled a scary-looking pistol out from under his jacket as he strolled closer. *What the hell is he going to do?*

Flipping open the pistol, he started removing bullets. One. Two. Three. Four. Five bullets. He looked up at Adam, murder in his eyes. Whatever he planned on doing, I wouldn't let him do it.

I stepped in front of Adam, protecting the soldier. How stupid was I?

Cash turned his leveled gaze on me, cold as ice.

"Whatever you think you saw, you're wrong," I claimed, falling back a step and running into Adam behind me.

Cash kept on coming.

"I'm not thinking anything," he said in a deceivingly calm voice. He looked at Adam. Dismissing me just like that.

I didn't know what to do but I wasn't going to move. I wouldn't allow Cash to kill or hurt Adam, even if he might deserve some more roughing up for working for Frankie.

He stopped in front of me, sandwiching me between him and Adam. It was a very bad place to be. They were two alpha males that wanted to tear each other's throat out and I wouldn't be able to stop them.

Cash's full lips were compressed in a hard line. His hat was tilted at an angle. My body reacted like it always did. Shortness of breath. Quickening of heart. Mouth dry. Lips suddenly tingly.

He snapped the pistol closed, leaving one bullet in the cylinder. Flipping the gun around he caught it by the barrel and reached around me, offering it to Adam.

"I believe this belongs to you."

I moved to the side. Adam eyed the gun like it might bite him but then he snatched it from Cash. As he opened the gun, Cash looked down at me. God, the coldness there almost made me drop to my knees.

I opened my mouth to tell him what he saw was nothing but Adam looked up.

"One bullet?" he asked, raising a dusty blonde eyebrow.

The corner of Cash's mouth lifted in a deadly smile. "Hope you're a good shot."

Adam let out a snort and snapped the gun closed. Reaching back, he shoved it into his waistband. "What now?"

"Now you leave and tell them we're dead."

Adam scratched the side of his nose and chuckled. "Yeah, that's not going to happen."

"I wasn't asking," Cash said in a low voice.

Adam crossed his arms over his chest and widened his stance, getting good and comfortable. "And what if I lead Frankie and his men straight back here? Right to your doorstep? You trust me enough not to do that?"

Cash pushed his hat brim. "I don't trust you at all."

Adam nodded at me. "She does."

I swung my gaze over to him, my mouth gaping open. *What? I never said that!*

Cash was still staring holes through Adam, ignoring me.

"Well, if she wants you here, I won't stand in your way. Just stay out of mine," he said.

"Cash, it's not like that!" I insisted, almost stomping my feet.

His eyes slid to me then away with indifference. That small sign of dismissal stung like nothing else.

Stupid, dumbass tears stung my eyes. If he noticed them, he didn't let on. He turned and walked away. Pain twisted inside me. I had always refused to feel anything. Now I was feeling everything and it hurt.

~~~~

I stared at the door, watching as it slammed behind Cash. I felt carved out and left to die. I ached. I hurt. A single tear ran down my face. I felt rage so strong that I went crazy.

Whirling around, I faced Adam.

"I *never* said I trusted you! In fact, I don't know you so how the hell *can* I trust you? You've been sent here to *hunt* me! To lead those men to me!"

Adam didn't move. He just stared down at me.

"You have a knife in your waistband. I could've grabbed it and slit your throat before you had time to blink. If I wanted to hurt you, Cat, I already would have. You can trust me."

I fisted my hands at my sides.

"I can't trust anyone but my brother and Cash!"

Adam snorted. "I think your boyfriend wants off that list."

This time I did stomp my foot. "Ugh!"

I spun around and marched across the room. Forget about my jacket. Forget about how cold it probably was outside or how crazy I was acting. I was sick of the random guy from my past that showed up. Sick of having the threat of Paul hanging over my head all the time. Sick of surviving. Of missing Nathan and my dad until I thought my heart burst. But more than anything, I was sick to death of Cash giving me the cold shoulder.

I shoved the door open and stomped outside. David and Tate looked up from the middle of the clearing in front of the cabin. Pieces of gathered wood lay around them, Tate dropping more at his feet. I ignored their curious stares and glanced around.
~~~~

There he was. The most aggravating man I had ever met.

Cash.

I narrowed my eyes at him. He was moving with his lazy, relaxed, irritating, and outrageously sexy stride toward the corner of the cabin. The old barn was back there along with David's truck. It was covered by a dark green canvas, blending with the trees and vegetation. That's where Cash was heading, forgetting about me just like that.

His back was outlined perfectly under his fitted jacket. His well-worn jeans hugged his ass to mouth-watering perfection and his stupid, dumb cowboy hat shielded his eyes from the sun. I wanted to run over there and snatch it from his head, fling it off into the woods. I hated the thing. No, scratch that – him in that hat made me achy for him and *that's* what I hated.

I raced across the porch and flew down the steps. *No time like the present.* I heard Tate call my name but I didn't stop. The air was still as if something was about to happen. The sun was shining. White, fluffy clouds flowed by. But I didn't see any of it. All I saw was that cowboy hat and the frustrating man who wore it.

I caught up to Cash as he rounded the frontend of the truck.

"Ask me," I said, following him to the driver's side.

He didn't seem surprised to see me.

"Ask you what?"

"Ask me if I slept with him. That's what you want to know, right? *That's* your problem."

He paused, reaching for the edge of the tarp.

"I don't have a problem and I don't care."

I crossed my arms over my chest and started tapping my foot, watching as he flipped the canvas back and reached into the bed of the truck.

"I didn't. Sleep with him, that is."

He didn't acknowledge that I had said anything but a tick appeared in his jaw. He rummaged in the truck bed, ignoring me. It made my rage triple. It always had. It drove me crazy and made me insane with a weird kind of desire. God, I was a mess. I wanted to punish him and push him until he lost control.

And I knew exactly how to do it.

"You want to know the truth?" I retorted, following him as he further moved down the truck. "I almost did. I was drunk out of my mind and he was there, dancing with me. I didn't know his name. All I knew was that he wasn't *you*."

When he didn't say anything, I kept talking. I wanted a reaction out of him. I wanted to make him mad. The words tumbled out of my mouth faster.

"He asked if I wanted to go somewhere private and I agreed, even though all I could think about was you. So we went to a bathroom and he started kissing me then—"

"Shut up."

I paused. Cash was gripping the edge of the truck bed with both hands, his arms straight out in front of him, his knuckles white. His jaw was clenched and one of his legs was bent, tension in every line of his body. He stared straight ahead, looking ready to explode.

I felt a little tingle of warning but ignored it. It's what I wanted, wasn't it? My lips turned up in a smug smile and I continued.

"He lifted me on the counter. Sound familiar, cowboy? And he started trying to get his hand down my pants. That's when—"

Cash let out an animalistic growl and lunged at me. *Holy shit!* I jumped away but he was faster. He grabbed my arms and hauled me back against the truck.

"Shut up, Cat. Just shut the fuck up," he growled, blazing down at me from beneath his hat. His hands rested on either side of me, locking me in. Pinning me against the rusted, old truck.

I met his stare and jutted my chin out. "Why should I? You said you didn't care."

His eyes turned a dark shade of gray. The one that indicated that he was mad.

"Yeah, I did say that, didn't I?" he said, his voice deceptively aloof.

It hurt but I covered it up in the only way I knew how – lashing out, acting up, and being the girl I used to be.

I stood up straighter then took a step closer.

"If you don't care, I'll just go back in there and pick up where I left off with him. Maybe I'll even sleep with him this time so I *can* forget about you." I shoved his arm out of the way and started past him, proud of myself for being so damn brave.

"Goodbye, cowboy," I said, walking away.

My heart breaking.

My soul shattered.

My world crushed.

But I should have known I was playing with fire.

He grabbed my arm and swung me back around. My breath hitched as he shoved me up against the truck again.

"You just made a big mistake, Cat."

I shivered from the predatory, lethal look in his eyes. I was vulnerable. Susceptible. Fragile standing before him. It scared me tenfold. But I stuck my chin up and met his stern gaze anyway.

"If you get out of my way, I'll go make another one."

He let out a low growl. "No one touches you but me."

I snorted. "Ha. Try again, cowboy. You have no power over me."

"We'll see about that."

One minute I'm standing on my feet and the next, his arm was around my waist like a strong vise. I cried out with alarm as he picked me up.

Oh, hell. I had just made an epic mistake.

Chapter Nineteen

-Cash-

I was so fucking mad, I couldn't see straight. First, I walked into the cabin and saw that stranger touching Cat. Shit, I would rather be dead and sitting by Lucifer himself than have to sit back and watch her with another man.

Second, I had to stand there and listen to Cat talk about the soldier. Fury and possessiveness rippled through me. My teeth were gritted so hard, I wanted to roar. She was mine and no one was going to have her. I would make sure of it.

Third, she said I had no power over her. It was true – I didn't. The girl was a spoiled brat. It was her that had the power over me and that made me mad. Time to change things.

Her ass hit my crotch and the back of her head hit my chest as I lifted her up.

"Let me go!" she shouted, kicking my shin with the heel of her boot. "You have no right to do this!"

"Oh, I have every right," I said in a cold voice. "Let me just show you how much."

I headed toward the old barn.

"Ugh! Put. Me. Down!" Cat shrieked, beating on my arm.

I paid no attention to her screams but, shit, she was beating the crap out of my shins with her boot heels and close to tearing my shirtsleeve to shreds with her fingers.

"Stop it," I growled in a low grumble, tightening my arm around her waist to prove I meant business.

"I'll behave when you put me down!" she screeched, hitting my forearm with her fists.

I snorted. "You don't know what the word *behave* means."

She let out a frustrated cry and hit me again. I struggled to maintain some self-control as her little round ass bounced against my dick again and again as I carried her to the barn.

Before I had got very far, David and Tate appeared around the corner of the cabin, both of them carrying guns and looking worried.

"What's going on?" Tate asked. His eyes grew round when he saw Cat struggling in my arms.

David lowered his gun, his beard twitching. "Lover's spat, son. Leave 'em be."

I gave David an evil look but didn't say anything.

"You need help, sis?" Tate asked, looking uncertain, his hair hanging in his eyes.

"Yes!" Cat piped up with relief. "This jackass here thinks—"

"She doesn't need help," I said between clenched teeth. "What she needs is a good—"

"Don't you say it, Cash!" she screeched, digging her nails further into my jacket sleeve. "Put. Me.—"

"Just give us some privacy," I told David and Tate like it was every day I carried a screaming girl around. "Someone needs a timeout."

"Timeout! Let me go, butthole!" she screamed, smacking me hard on the arm.

Okay, that was a new one for name-calling. This was getting amusing.

Tate stared at us, his eyes growing wider and wider. David grinned. I could care less. The preacher could think whatever he wanted. He might need to go say a prayer for my soul because I was going to hell for what I was about to do to Cat.

The barn was an old timber structure. Its roof was covered with leaves and dead branches. Weeds reached up the sides, camouflaging the building and taking it over. The corral side had collapsed but the rest of the barn was still standing. I had checked it out when we got here. It was small but big enough for what I planned.

"Put me down, Cash! Now!" Cat shrieked for the hundredth time, giving me a good, swift kick in the shin.

I sucked in a sharp breath at the sharp pain but kept a tight hold on her.

"Do that again, princess, and you'll regret it," I warned, flipping the latch on the barn door with my free hand.

"Are you really threatening me? Because if you are, you can kiss my…" She drew her leg as if she was going to kick me again.

I tightened my arm around her waist and shifted so she couldn't. Big mistake. My cock hit the middle of her ass, right in the cleft of her bottom like it was seeking entrance. Damn. It sent electricity through me.

She stiffened and I held back a moan.

"Told you," I whispered, sliding the barn door open. "You'll regret it."

She blew out a frustrated breath and quieted down as I carried her into the dark interior.

It was warmer inside. The smell of hay and old leather filled every corner of the barn. Loose straw covered the wooden floor. Beams of sunlight peeked between the slats of the walls, throwing light across the interior. The place hadn't been used for a while. The musty smell and the layers of dust and cobwebs proved it.

I slid the door closed, plunging us in shadowy darkness.

"You've made your point! You're a caveman. Now put me down!" Cat demanded, elbowing me in the side.

I grunted but didn't let her go. Her tone didn't have as much gumption as it did before and I noticed that she had kind of gone still. If she were afraid, she would never admit it. The girl was a powerhouse of bravery despite everything she had been through. Jesus, I loved her just for that alone.

The thought made me angry. I wasn't supposed to love her. It almost got her killed. No, I was only supposed to make her hate me.

Carrying her against my body, I strode to the tack room in the corner of the barn. It held old saddles and reins and also had a door and four walls. Just what I needed to teach the little hellcat what happens when she plays with me.

I kicked the door open. It swung open on rusted hinges. Particles of dust drifted on the air lazily as my boots churned up dirt and hay. A dusty stool sat in one corner, the oak stain long gone. Reins and ropes hung from numerous pegs on the walls and two old saddles had been thrown on the floor. A farm and ranch calendar from three years ago had been stapled on the wall to my right, the corners curled up and brittle.

Someone had spent a lot of time out there, taking care of horses and the gear that went along with them. But now it was mine to take care of something else.

I lowered Cat down. She tried to take off as soon as her feet hit the ground, but I wasn't letting her go that easily.

"I don't think so, sweetheart."

I spun her around and shoved her back against the wall.

She looked up at me, trapped against the wooden slats. Her nostrils flared. She curved one lip up in a snarl meant to look aggressive but only ended up looking sexy.

"What are you going to do, cowboy? Remind me again why I should never have fallen in love with you?" she spit with sarcasm.

I leaned closer, going nose to nose with her. The brim of my hat almost touched her head.

"No," I said, my warm breath mixing with hers. "I'm going to remind you why you're mine and just how much power I *do* have over you."

I grabbed her waist and flipped her around to face the wall. Her hands hit the warped boards on either side of her. A gasp escaped past her lips.

"Wha…what are you doing, Cash?" she asked in a whispery voice, wiggling against my palm on her hip and not sounding so high and mighty anymore.

I took off my hat and tossed it on the ground.

"I'm teaching you a lesson," I fumed. *She thought she could play with me, talking about Adam, threatening to finish what they started? Well, I'll show her who could play with whom.*

I spread my legs on either side of hers, caging her in. Grabbing both of her wrists, I forced them above her head and reached for some reins hanging nearby.

"Don't you dare!" she exclaimed, struggling to get away when she saw what I was going to do.

I tightened my grip on her wrists and leaned closer, my mouth going near her ear. "Oh, I'll do this and a whole lot more, Beauty Queen. Watch and learn."

I started wrapping the reins around her wrists, circling the delicate bones with the old leather.

She bucked against me, slamming her hip into my crotch. Trying to get away. I hissed with pain but recovered quickly and forced her back against the stall, pinning her body with mine.

She inhaled sharply when my cock nudged her ass again. Good. Maybe that would teach her to behave.

I pushed into her more. God, she felt good.

She stilled, afraid to move with me so close. I continued wrapping the reins around her wrists, taking my time. Going achingly slow. I wanted her to sweat. To grow nervous, wondering what I was going to do.

"You said we were over," she whispered, her voice shaky. "You told me to stop loving you."

I hardened my heart and finished tying her wrists. "We might be over, sweetheart, but we're far from done."

Her pulse beat strong and rapid under my thumb. The scent of her – something sweet and clean – filled my nostrils, almost making me groan.

She shuddered when I nudged her again with my cock, tying the reins off on a loose board near her head.

"This is not you, Cash," she murmured. "What happened to you?"

I ran my hand down her arm to her hip. "You happened to me."

She whimpered when I ran my hand under her shirt. My fingers traveled along her ribcage, feeling every contour and curve. I memorized every inch of her the first night we were together but I would never grow tired of touching the perfection that she was.

"Am I hurting you?" I asked, always mindful of her wound.

"No," she breathed.

"Good."

My fingers trailed over her skin, moving slowly to her waistband. She squirmed against my crotch, her cheeks flushing.

I ran my other hand up to cup the back of her head, tangling my fingers in the silky strands. I liked her like that – tied up and vulnerable. Just waiting for me to do what I wanted with her. People always thought I was a quiet, laidback kind of guy but I had a dark side that came out in the bedroom. Cat just seemed to bring it out even more.

"Cash," she said in a breathless whisper, wiggling against me.

But I wanted her writhing.

I swept my hand down and popped open the buttons on the front of her jeans. She pushed back, straining her bound wrists and pulling at the leather. I let go of the back of her head to run my hand up her arm.

"Don't move," I commanded in a low voice, easing her against the wall again.

She gave a small nod and licked her bottom lip.

Satisfied, I unbuttoned the last button on her jeans. The feel of it slipping through the hole under my finger made my mouth water. She was so damn enticing that I wanted to lick every single inch of her, making her wiggle and squirm with intense need. That asshole, Adam, had tried to get a hand down her pants. Well, I'd show her who was the only one allowed to do that.

Her breathing increased. I felt her battling to stay still. With her jeans finally unfastened, I eased my fingers down, my motions slow and torturous.

"Oh god," she murmured.

"Shhh," I instructed, moving my fingers lower.

She was wet and ready. I was desperate and barely hanging on. I made a slow circle around her clit then slipped my finger into her, sliding it in deep, her body welcoming me.

She threw her head back and whimpered. I loved that sound. I could listen to it every day for the rest of my life. It showed me how, with just a touch of my fingers, she would come apart for me.

With my cock right in line with her ass, I ran my other hand under her shirt as I worked my finger in and out of her tightness. She moaned and arched when my thumb grazed the underside of her breast, urging me to take it in my palm.

I did, unable to resist. But cupping it wasn't enough. I was too greedy when it came to her. I gave her breast a firm squeeze then rolled her nipple between my thumb and forefinger. It puckered to a more profound point, needing my lips around it.

Cat inhaled sharply but I wanted more. Much, much more.

I increased the rhythm of my finger plunging in and out of her. The wetter she became, the deeper I went.

She leaned her forehead against the wall and bit her lip to stifle the small whimpers escaping her. But I could hear them. Desperate. Needy. The sound of them made it very hard to keep my cock from busting.

She was close to coming – I could tell by the way her body clamped around my fingers and her breathing increased. But this was about power and I wanted all the control.

"Who do you belong to?" I asked, my mouth near her ear, my middle finger going deep inside her.

"You," she answered breathlessly. "Only you."

"And who gets to touch you like this?"

"You. No one else."

I ran my hand to her other breast, brushing my fingers over her nipple, causing her to jerk and hiss.

"Mmm. No one touches you. No one has you. But who gets to love you, Beauty Queen? Tell me," I demanded.

I heard her pant and saw her lick her lips.

"You. You're the one. The only one."

Her words caused a kind of warmth to flow through me.

"I'm the one?" I asked, my middle finger easing out of her then sliding back in.

She nodded, her breaths coming faster, her crotch grinding against my hand. Her arms pulled on the reins, going taut. I glanced at her wrists, making sure the leather wasn't cutting into her. Time to see just how much power I had.

I wrapped my arm around her, keeping her still while my hand worked between her legs.

"And you'd do anything for me?" I whispered, slipping my fingers out of her and running them over her clit.

"Yes," she said in a sultry voice, moving against my hand. "Shit, don't stop."

It was just the reaction I wanted. I drove my fingers into her hard, going as deep as I could as I held her up with my arm around her ribcage.

She bucked and rode my hand, so close to orgasm that I felt her insides quiver.

Just as she started to come – as her body started to clench at my fingers and her back arched – I slid my fingers out of her, leaving her wet and aching. Taking her to the edge and not letting her finish. The worse kind of torture and the best kind of control.

When she realized I had stopped, her eyes flew open and she looked over her shoulder at me. I took a step back. I wanted to swing her around and rip her shirt open. Take her nipple into my mouth and suck deep while I thrust up into her.

Instead, I pulled the slipknot I had tied, letting the reins fall away from her wrists. She lowered her arms as the leather fell away. Turning, she looked at me with confusion.

I blocked any feelings I had and gazed down at her coldly.

"Get on your knees, Beauty Queen."

Chapter Twenty

-Cat-

I wasn't one to follow directions well but when Cash said to get on my knees, I dropped like a starving woman.

A basic primal need took over, savage and uncivilized. I was desperate. Crazy. I needed him. I wanted him like never before.

With frantic movements, I unsnapped his belt buckle and unzipped his jeans. His gaze was scorching as he stared down at me. Not an inch of him moved. He was like a panther – sleek and dangerous – just waiting to eat its captured meal.

Except I was the one that was going to be fed.

Lowering my eyes, I reached for his erection. He was enormous. Long and thick, his manhood was stunning. My core quivered and clenched as I thought of him deep inside me, thrusting until I screamed from the pleasurable pain.

He tensed as I wrapped my hand around him. He was so wide, my fingers didn't meet. God, to have that in me again…

My mouth watered. I suddenly wanted to find out what he tasted like and run my tongue over the large veins that ran underneath his hardness.

I lifted my eyes, heat creeping down my body and pooling between my legs.

"Do it," he whispered in a hoarse voice, staring down at me. "Take me in your mouth."

He didn't have to tell me twice. I closed my lips around his tip, keeping my hand around the middle of his shaft.

"Shit," he moaned.

He rested both of his hands against the wall behind me, leaning his hard body over mine while I kneeled on the ground in front of him. His legs were spread. His jeans were hanging down on his hips, gaping open. I might have been on my knees, doing what he wanted, but I had the power. I had the control.

He was mine.

I peered up at him and ran my tongue over the head of his cock, licking up a drop of precum. He squeezed his eyes shut and hissed. The muscles in his arms flexed as he gripped the wood slats of the wall behind me harder.

"More" he groaned. "Take more of me."

I lowered my mouth, taking him deep in the warm recesses of my mouth. He was so big and long that I wasn't sure how much I could handle but I had never backed down from a challenge yet.

I relaxed my jaw and went deeper until he hit the back of my throat. A soft expletive left him and he leaned over more. I started moving my hand up and down on him while I sucked and licked, licked and sucked, taking him deep each time.

His breathing became erratic. His body clenched. A thrill of excitement moved through me. I wanted to give him every bit of pleasure possible. He was my euphoria and I was consumed by it.

"Jesus, Cat. Your mouth is amazing," he rasped.

I moaned around his hardness, his words sending a quiver through me.

"God, do that again," he demanded hoarsely, his voice sounding broken and nothing like the hard, cold person that he had become. "Moan for me."

I started to but a deep, guttural voice boomed from outside. "Son? You and your girl okay?" David called out on the other side of the barn door.

I froze. Cash stilled.

I removed my mouth from Cash's cock. The tack room was separated from the rest of the barn by walls and a door but I still felt exposed, down on my knees in front of Cash like that, his hard member in my hand and my mouth red and swollen from being around him.

Cash kept his hands planted on the wall behind me. He waited a heartbeat but then reached down and touched the back of my head, urging my mouth back on him.

I hesitated – there was a preacher right outside the barn! But when I looked up and saw Cash's intense gray eyes, staring down at me with heated warning, I obeyed. How could I not when he looked so amazing standing above me, his amazing manhood standing so proudly before me, his body primed and ready for anything I wanted to do to it?

Slowly, I lowered my mouth back down on him. He hissed and closed his eyes, his hand going back to the wall behind me, the muscles in his neck straining.

Wickedness slithered through me. There was something exhilarating about doing such a naughty act while others were nearby. It was one of the reasons I hadn't pushed him away when he cornered me in the public bathroom on our first date. It was just what Cash did to me.

"Son?" David called out again. "You two okay?"

"Shit," Cash whispered so low I was sure David couldn't hear him.

Clearing his throat, his erection pulsating in my mouth, he answered.

"We're okay. Just give us a minute."

His voice sounded scratchy, croaky even. It turned me on, knowing what kind of effect I had on him. I sucked harder and took him deeper until he hit the back of my throat. He reached down and grabbed the back of my head, silently urging me never to stop.

"Well, I know you love her. Remember that when you're…doing whatever it is you're doing," David called out. "Getting angry at her and such. If you two need to talk, I'm here." There was a chuckle. "I'm not going anywhere."

Hearing David say that Cash loved me – even if it wasn't true anymore – did something to me. I increased the stroking of his shaft with my hand and drew him deeper, coating him with my saliva and almost making me gag. I wanted him to be putty in my hands.

Cash clenched his jaw. "I'll keep that in mind, David," he ground out, his hand pushing my head down on him as I swirled my tongue over the thick, bulging veins under his hard silkiness.

"Okay," David said.

A second later, I heard him shuffling through the dead leaves, walking away. As soon as he was gone, Cash fisted a handful of my hair and pushed his cock deeper into my mouth.

"I'm almost there. Don't stop," he groaned, moving his hips in slow, hard thrusts. Taking over. Fucking my mouth.

I moaned and glanced up at him. His hand was tangled in my hair, the other flat against the wall. His muscles were tense, his body ready to explode. It was the most erotic thing I had ever seen, him so vulnerable. So into what I was doing to him. He had never looked so sexy before, every emotion played out on his face. It did things to me I had never experienced. But this was about more than me wanting to give him the orgasm of a lifetime. This was about us.

And control.

He quickened his thrusts into my mouth. I ran one hand up the back of his thigh as my other hand moved on him. He groaned, his manhood sliding past my lips and going deep. When his breath hitched and his fingers tightened in my hair, I knew he was close.

Time to give him a taste of his own medicine.

With a reluctant sigh, I removed my mouth from him and gave him one more squeeze before letting go, leaving him teetering at the edge. Close to exploding.

He looked down at me and growled low with displeasure. His cock stood at attention in front of me, red from my lips and looking painfully hard.

"You little tease," he whispered. "Get back here."

He tried to tug me back to him with the hold he had in my hair but I held firm and smiled up at him sweetly. I had him right where I wanted him. Achy and crazy with need.

"Haven't you heard, cowboy? Payback is a bitch and so am I," I whispered, using my best bedroom voice, dripping with honey and seduction and all those things guys loved.

But I forgot who I was dealing with. A cowboy that wasn't as calm as he appeared.

He grabbed my arms and yanked me to my feet. With a muttered curse, he pushed me against the wall, pinning me with his solid body. Gray irises of fire stared down at me, looking ready to throttle my backside.

"You're not a bitch," he rumbled in a dark, dangerous voice. "But you're right. Payback can be."

I didn't have time to think or freak out that he was going to repay me for teasing him. His mouth took fierce possession of mine, his body pressed against me from thigh to chest. I didn't fight him. I didn't wiggle or push against him. Instead, I gave in.

My muscles went weak as his tongue swooped past my lips, attacking me. I became lost, going further and further under the spell that seemed to control us whenever we were around each other. It didn't matter if we were in a dusty barn or in the ritziest restaurant in all of Texas. I couldn't resist him.

I grabbed the front of his jacket and pulled him against me. He became my anchor, my captor, holding me up against the slatted wall. His body pressed into me. I whimpered and wiggled against him. I wanted him now. I couldn't breathe until I had him.

I reached down and ran my hand under his shirt, brushing the tip of his cock pulsating between us. His mouth turned rougher on mine as I slid my hand along his abdomen and right above his open jeans.

He was all muscle, the ridges and valleys like silk under my fingers. A trail of hair ran from his belly button down, a trail I had to explore.

I ran the tip of my index finger along it. When my hand encountered the pulsating hardness between us, I didn't hesitate. I wrapped my fingers around him and squeezed.

He tore his mouth from mine and grabbed the waistband of my unbuttoned jeans in a tight fist.

"Take them off," he ordered, giving my jeans a hard yank. "Now."

I started to do as he said, but he was impatient.

"Fuck it," he bit out between clenched teeth.

He shoved my jeans down my thighs then dropped to one knee in front of me. I shivered as he grabbed my right boot and jerked it off then tossed it in the corner. He did the same to the left one then turned his attention to my jeans.

His fingers circled around my right calf and pulled my leg out of the worn pants. Leaving them attached to my left ankle, he stood up. Heated control flared from his eyes, all-consuming and undeniable. He looked hungry, ready to ravage me.

I held back a gasp as he wrapped his arm around my waist and lifted me up like I weighed nothing. My legs went around him automatically, my jeans dangling from one ankle. Taking a step forward, Cash pressed me up against the wall and did what I wanted most.

He thrust into me hard. I cried out and went stiff in his arms.

"Payback," he rasped, lodged deep in me.

Grabbing my bottom with both hands, he withdrew then thrust back into me.

I cried out again. Ripples of warm electricity zipped through me. My nipples felt like pinpoints of friction as they rubbed against my shirt. My slickness clenched around him, never wanting to give him up.

He buried his face in my neck, his mouth going to my throat.

"You've got me all tangled up inside, Cat," he whispered, his breath hot on my skin, his thick cock buried to the hilt in me. "All I can think about is you. All I want is this."

He withdrew and thrust again, pinning me against the wall. I wrapped my arms around his neck and hung on for dear life. My body burned, every pore suddenly sensitive. Every inch of me on fire.

"You're mine, Cat," he rasped. "All mine."

I ran my fingers through his hair and tugged his head to the side roughly. "Then make me come, cowboy" I whispered in his ear.

He sucked in a breath and slammed into me hard, making the wall behind me shake and tremor. The whole damn world could come down and I wouldn't care. When he thrust again, I came like never before, a violent orgasm ripping through me.

Stars burst. My vision blurred. He let out a low moan and thrust faster, my climax triggering his. I clamped down on his shoulder with my teeth, covering my cries as he exploded deep inside me.

My body jerked, rippling deep. I held onto him tightly as he continued to pump inside me, his essence soaking the tender walls of my body, emptying against my cervix.

Warning dinged in the back of my mind. We were playing with fire, using no protection. This was the third? Fourth? Fifth time he had come in me?

His nose and mouth was buried in my hair, sending little shivers over me. His hardness pulsating deep inside my body, still thick and semi-hard.

He was breathing fast. The muscles in his arms, holding me up, were bulging.

I don't know how long we stayed that way, with me held up against the wall and him still inside me. I wanted to stay that way forever but awareness slowly returned.

We were in a dusty barn. My pants were hanging off one ankle and my legs were around Cash's waist. His jeans were unbuttoned and hanging down around his hips. We were connected body to body. Cock to pussy. Tate or David could walk through the wide doors any minute and see us.

It was a wakeup call. A glaring reminder of reality. Cash must have realized the same thing. He eased out of me and lowered me to my feet.

My legs were shaky and my heart was beating too fast. I reached for the wall behind me and raised my eyes to Cash.

He was staring down at me with heat and a cool kind of wariness. I swallowed hard. From the broad set of his shoulders to the rugged five o'clock shadow that dusted his jaw, he was all male. The top of his head almost reached the low ceiling of the tack room. His tall, lean body was pure muscle, sleek and wound tight. His intense gaze pierced me down to my soul.

"Cash?" I whispered, wanting him to say something. Let me know that we were back to normal.

But he didn't. He slid his gaze away from me and stayed quiet. With his eyes downcast, he started tucking himself back into his jeans.

With my heart in my throat, I reached down and pulled my pants on. The barn was suddenly colder. My fingers were suddenly shakier.

He was so damn aggravating. One minute he was hot, the next minute he was cold. I didn't know whether to cry or punch something or better yet, someone.

Anger was better than weepy sadness any day. I leaned over and grabbed my boots, careful not to look at him. The leather reins caught my eye, laying in a tangled mess not far away.

How the hell had I allowed this to happen again? When would I ever learn my lesson? He said we were over. He didn't want me to love him. He pretty much said it was all about sex now. I was back to being a slut. Was that all I was worth? A good roll in the hay? Was I that pathetic that I didn't care as long as Cash fucked me?

The wound on my side pulled and ached but I didn't pay attention. It was just a harsh reminder of why he didn't want to love me.

Bending over at the waist, I shoved my feet into my boots, angry at myself and him. Mind-numbing sex was all I had wanted after Luke died. It was a way to escape everything. A chicken's way of dealing with pain and heartache. But that's not who I wanted to be now.

I jerked upright and flung my hair back, glaring at Cash as he leaned over to grab his cowboy hat. Standing upright, his eyes flicked to me as he sat the hat on his head.

"We're leaving tomorrow. Pack what you can find. We leave at first light," he said, turning to leave.

I watched him walk away, knowing how easy it was for him. I just wished it were as easy for me.

He made it to the door when the words burst from me.

"So that's it? Just fuck and run?" I asked, sticking my chin up. Hurt.

He stopped, his back to me.

"Yeah, that's about it," he answered in an icy cool voice.

Pain twisted my insides together. I tried my hardest to find some strength.

"Then it's over, cowboy. Stay away from me," I snapped, glaring at his stupidly, insane sexy back.

Slowly, he turned. His gaze was hard. His jaw was clenched to the breaking point. I had never seen him so pissed. So dangerous. Nothing like the man who had just used my mouth then came in me.

With predator-like slowness, he started back toward me, his hips rolling with each step. His body strung so tight, I thought he would burst.

The tack room was suddenly smaller. The air was thinner. I couldn't breathe. Couldn't run. Couldn't think of anything but him in me again.

Stopping right in front of me, he stared down at me, his gaze cool and detached.

"What did you say?" he asked in a quiet voice laced with warning.

I licked my dry lips, second guessing my intelligence. *No. Don't give in. Be strong.*

I cleared my throat and stuck my chin up more. "I said it's over. Isn't that what you want?"

Anger turned his eyes hard but he didn't say anything so I continued. Silence always made me uneasy.

"You don't love me but I'm completely in love with you, jerkface. And that's just not going to work. I refuse to be your fuck buddy. This body is closed."

I yanked the edge of my jacket down with precise, angry tugs, feeling much more in control now that I had his full attention and got those words off my chest.

"Jerkface?" he asked, raising one eyebrow. If I didn't know better, I might have seen one corner of his mouth twitch, fighting a smile. But that was impossible. He hadn't smiled in forever.

"Yes. Jerkface," I said with conviction, on a roll now. "Plus, another reason we're over is because we're not using any kind of birth control or protection. I don't even know if condoms *exist* anymore and pulling out isn't going to work forever. Not that you've been doing that," I added with a glare at him, the wetness between my legs a stark reminder. "I don't want to tie someone down who doesn't love me with a baby."

He slid his eyes over me, his eyebrows scrunched in a deep frown that only made him look more rugged and handsome. *As if he needs any help. Jerk.*

I blushed at his perusal and continued, feeling slightly sick at what I was about to say.

"Getting pregnant would be the dumbest, stupidest thing we could do and since you want us to be over anyway, I'll do what you said. I'll stay away from you. But you've got to stay away from me too. That's the only way this will work."

He stared at me like he wanted to punch a hole in the warped wall behind me. Not that I blamed him but it was his idea.

Can I really stay away from him? When he didn't say anything, I knew my answer. *Yes.*

I pushed away from the wall with a renewed purpose. I was strong. I had survived a car wreck, losing my best friend, my boyfriend, and watching Nathan die. I had lost my father to this damn war and my mother long before to greed and selfishness. I had fought off Paul and had to choose whether to pull the trigger and kill him or let him live.

I had lost everything. My home. My belongings. The things I thought made me, me. I had been hungry, dirty, and scared for months. If I could survive all of that, I could survive not being with Cash.

Maybe.

I pushed past him and across the tack room. I had to get away before I changed my mind. Before I made another stupid mistake and took back my words. He was too addicting and I was too far-gone. The best thing to do was go cold turkey.

I was almost to the doorway when he grabbed my arm and spun me around. I didn't have time to fight or yank away from him. He had me against the wall in seconds. My spine hit the warped boards. My hair fell into my face and stuck to my lips. Cash didn't care. He glared down at me, his eyes gray pinpoints of ice.

"Fuck the condoms and fuck what I said," he rasped, inches from me. "You're in my blood, Cat. When you bleed, I bleed. When you hurt, I hurt. I'm not staying away from you. Not until I'm ready."

With a tightening of his jaw, he pushed away from the wall and walked away. I watched, my heart beating fast.

The words '*not until I'm ready*' echoing in my heart.

Chapter Twenty-One

-Cash-

I walked out of the barn with angry strides. Why the hell had I admitted she was in my blood? Was I fuckin' crazy? I wanted her to hate me. To never again put her life on the line for me. I had to get away from her and that look in her eyes. I had taken her in the barn to teach her a lesson. But Cat had taught me one instead. I couldn't keep my hands off her no matter how hard I tried.

She had asked if it was a fuck and run. Damn straight it was. I was terrified of what I felt around her. No woman had ever driven me so irrational before. But what I said was the truth. I wasn't staying away from her. That was a problem.

I rounded the truck and stalked toward the front of the cabin, trying to keep my mind off the way Cat had looked down on her knees in front of me.

David and Tate paused in their wood stacking.

"Is he still here?" I growled, ignoring how David gave me a knowing look. So what if Cat was giving me the best blowjob I've ever had while he stood right outside the door? I was going to hell anyway for all the shit I had done since this war had started. There was no saving me now.

"That soldier?" Tate called out as I stomped toward the cabin. "Yeah. He's right behind you."

I swung around, my hand going to the knife attached to my belt. I must be off my game. I never heard the man. He was standing at the top of the porch, looking like he owned the place. Arrogant bastard.

"There's no need for that," he said with a grin, looking down at my knife.

I shrugged. "I don't know. There're some nasty snakes slithering around here. Best to be prepared."

He chuckled and started down the porch steps toward me.

I didn't move. Just watched him. Out of the corner of my eye, I saw Cat walk around the corner of the cabin and stop, looking pale and more fragile than usual. I afforded her a quick once over. Her hair was a mess, tangled curls lying softly on her shoulders. Her green eyes were wide and damn if there wasn't hurt written all over her.

I pushed down my concern. She was okay. I had made sure of it before I turned all cold and assholeish on her. It was better to be that way than to allow her to love me.

But it was hard to see her hurt. Really tore me up inside if I allowed myself to admit it. And fuck! Getting her pregnant? That left me weak and damn near shaky.

There was only one thing to do. The idea came as clear as day. I had to get her and Tate home safely then walk away.

It was the only way. I wouldn't be tempted by her. She would be forced to forget about me. There would be no more concern over getting pregnant. No more worry about her sacrificing herself for me.

Tate had been coming into his own and was capable of taking care of himself and Cat. He had learned how to handle his weapons and find what was needed to survive. She would be safe with her brother. Better off than almost dying for me.

It wasn't the best laid plan I ever had but it would work and she would be okay. I would make sure of it before I left. Then I wouldn't look back.

With my mind made up, I focused back on Adam, noticing the pistol stuffed in the front of his waistband.

"I told you to leave," I said in a low voice.

Adam widened his stance and glanced around, squinting against the sunlight.

"Now why would I do that? I kind of like it here," he said, his eyes moving to Cat.

Rage rolled through me but I remained still. I couldn't get her and Tate home if I was six feet in the ground. I had to keep my head straight and stay calm.

I let go of my knife and took lazy, relaxed strides toward the soldier. I was aware of Tate edging closer, pushing his coat back to expose his gun. Shit. The kid was going to get himself shot. I needed him to stay alive to take care of his sister when I left.

I shoved down the unease and focused on the threat in front of me. David said he was a killer. An assassin. I wasn't afraid of him. He could kill me for all I cared. Maddie always said I had no fear. She was right. I didn't. But I had someone else to think of. Cat. And this man needed to understand that I was willing to die for her but I would take him to hell with me.

He didn't move when I stopped in front of him but I saw his fingers twitch, wanting to grab his gun and use that one bullet on me.

"She's off limits," I said in a deadly voice that only he could hear. "I don't share. I don't back down. And I don't fuck around. You try something with her, the buzzards will be picking at your bones in minutes."

The smile on his face died. His eyes went hard.

"If I remember correctly, I didn't see a ring on her finger," he muttered past tight lips.

I ground my back teeth, wanting to strangle him. "Doesn't matter. She's with me."

"With you?" he scoffed. "Does Cat know you're marking your territory?"

The rage in me multiplied. He smiled with satisfaction. I wanted to punch the grin off his face. Instead, I kept my cool. It was time to settle this.

I readjusted the cowboy hat on my head and took a slow step toward him. Stopping right by his side, I stared at him under the brim.

"Mark my territory? Hell, I did that long ago," I drawled, my tone warning him not to go there.

But he did, the sonofabitch.

"Was that before or after me?" he asked, smirking.

Fury burst in me. I felt it travel to my fingertips and boil and brew. In the back of my mind, I could hear my father whispering that violence solved nothing. But things were different. I was different. The world had changed. The only person who was going down was Adam.

I pulled back my fist to punch him but Cat caught my eye. She stood in the same place. A cold breeze lifted the ends of her hair. Anxiety lined her face. Minutes ago, I had come in her. I had branded her as mine, giving her a part of me that I had never given any girl. She was mine until I walked away. After that…hell, I didn't want to think about it but after that she was free.

But not one second before.

The soldier needed to be reminded of that. I tore my gaze away from Cat and lowered my arm. Adam quipped one eyebrow up, looking surprised that I backed down.

But I hadn't. Sometimes words had more of a punch than a fist.

I pushed my hat back and glared at him. "The only reason you're still alive is because she stopped me from killing you. But I can change that. Just try me."

Before Adam could smart-off again, I turned and walked away. I wasn't going to wait around for another one of his snide comments. I had said my peace. He could take it or leave it but whatever he chose to do, I would make sure he never touched Cat.

"You want me to tie him up again?" Tate asked as I stalked toward him with furious strides.

"No. Just watch your sister and keep an eye out for trouble," I said over my shoulder as I continued walking. "I have something I have to do."

~~~~

Finding the chickens was easy. Catching one of them was the hard part.

When I was out earlier, I had heard the telltale clucking from a distance but hadn't investigated. I had been gone too long and didn't want to wander from the cabin. But now I needed the space and we needed the food.

I was being a real ass toward Cat. I knew it. I needed to be in order for her to see that loving me was a mistake. I wanted her to take care of herself first, not some bastard that broke her heart and used her. Despite my best intentions to be a card-carrying butthole, as she so eloquently put it, I was mindful of her wound at all times and tuned into her every need. When her stomach growled a few times in the barn, I knew she was starving. We had no food left except for what we could catch, kill, or find. I had done one. Now it was time to do the other two.

I crouched low and tried again to sneak up on the ugly orange chicken. There were four of them but I had my eye on the plumpest. I followed it around in a circle then
~~~~

dove for it. Its beady little eyes rolled back in its head and it let out a loud, startled squawk. I tried to snatch it again but, with a flap of its scrawny wings, it ran to safety in the midst of its friends.

"Damn," I muttered.

I took off my jacket and tossed it to the ground. It was cold but I was working up a sweat. I was going to get a chicken. Cat deserved a good meal after all the shit I had put her through.

I eased forward. The chickens scurried away but didn't go far. I saw my opportunity when the fat one stopped to poke at something on the ground.

I lunged and she squawked, the others darting in all directions. I was able to grab her by the neck before she could scamper away.

"That's my chicken you got there."

I froze. Someone was behind me and he sounded angry.

The chicken was going haywire in my grasp, feathers flying everywhere. I turned around slowly, holding the squawking bird away from my body.

A man stood between two trees. His legs were the size of tree trunks and his face was lined with wrinkles. He looked old enough to be someone's grandfather and young enough to move fast if I decided to run.

His beard was gray and hit him in the middle of his barrel chest. Layers of furs covered his meaty shoulders and potbelly middle. His clothes were patched and his shoes had duct tape wrapped around them to hold them together. Smudges of dirt and grime filled the creases around his eyes and made his John Deere cap a dark brown.

My knife was on my belt and David's pistol was in my waistband. I could drop the chicken and grab one of my weapons but I didn't want to. Cat needed food.

I held up my free hand, showing I was no threat.

"I didn't know they belonged to you. Would you be willing to part with one of them?" I asked, holding the struggling chicken as feathers floated around me.

The old man scratched his beard. "Welllll, I ain't sure if I can part. Times are tough and that's one of my finest."

I looked at the chicken in my hand. My mouth salivated.

"I can see that. She's a beaut. But my friends are hungry and we're out of food," I said, hoping he heard the desperation in my voice. "You mind if I have her? Please, sir?"

The word 'please' sounded funny coming from my mouth but I wasn't above groveling. We couldn't make a run for home if we were starving. Finding water would be hard enough. Finding food might be impossible.

The old man rolled back on his duct taped shoes. His beady little eyes looked me up and down. His unkempt beard twitched.

"Welllll, I'm open to trading. I sure am."

Shit. I had nothing on me but my clothes, my hat, and my weapons. When the EMP hit, I had a credit card and forty dollars in my wallet. At first, I exchanged some of the cash for supplies but money quickly became useless. I would have paid the man for the chicken but that was then and this was now. The only thing people wanted after the country went dark was water, food, weapons, and medicine, in that order. I had one of those things and I wasn't ready to part with it just yet.

"I don't have much. What do you have in mind?" I asked, hoping he was interested in my boots or my jacket.

The man looked me over carefully.

"What about that knife on your belt?" He jutted his beard-covered chin at the sleek, bone handle visible on my waist.

A sinking feeling filled my gut. My dad had given me the knife when I was twelve. It was all I had left of him. Just a memory.

"How about a pistol instead?" I asked, reaching for my gun. It was much more valuable than the knife and meant nothing to me.

The old man pushed his John Deere cap to the side and scratched a spot over his ear.

"Gun makes too much noise out here. I'll just take that knife," he said, indicating it with a nod of his bushy head.

Images of my dad teaching me how to use it filled my mind. I could almost feel his hand on my shoulder, showing me how to aim my throw.

"Steady," he had said. "Make it count, son."

I withdrew the knife from the sheath and walked over to the man, still dangling the chicken from my hand.

"Deal," I said, offering it to him, handle first.

He took the knife. "It's a beauty," he said, turning it over in his hand. "A real looker."

"Yeah," I said, feeling a tightening in my chest. "It is."

Before I could change my mind, I turned and headed back the way I had come. The chickens scattered and the one in my hand flapped its wings. The old man grumbled at them to be quiet as he shuffled away through the leaves.

My dad's words from that hot summer day rang in my head. *Make it count, son.* And I had.

I traded the only link to my past for a girl that had become my future.

Chapter Twenty-Two

-Cat-

I watched Cash stalk off toward the woods, his last words ringing in my ears, *'Not until I'm ready.'* They hurt. His coldness cut. Once again, he took what he wanted. Once again, I gave in.

But I was determined that it wouldn't happen again. I meant what I said. We had to stay away from each other and there was no better time to start than now.

I stayed near the corner of the cabin, watching him and Adam. I didn't know what they were talking about but it was heated. They had faced off like a couple of gunslingers, ready for a shootout in the middle of a dusty, western town.

Cash had that quiet stillness to him. The one that made me hold my breath and grow anxious and needy. Adam was a loose cannon. Someone not to be trusted. When Cash walked off, Adam was left standing. He must have felt me staring at him because his blue eyes met mine. I could see him for what he was.

Dangerous.

He slid his gaze away from me and turned back to the cabin. Something didn't feel right. Warning bells went off in my head. *Why isn't he leaving?*

I glanced at Cash as he walked toward the line of trees. His strong back was ramrod straight and his focus was set ahead. My body was still tender from what he did to me in the tack room and my heart was still hurting from what he said afterward. I shoved it all into that little box where I kept everything I didn't want to face. I would deal with what I could. If Cash wasn't going to stick around and see what Adam was up to, I would.

Keeping an eye on Cash, I hurried toward the porch. Adam was inside and I didn't trust him. The stash of guns was well-hidden and we had nothing else of value but I wouldn't put it past him to do something to make us more vulnerable.

I was almost to the porch steps when I saw Tate heading toward me.

"Save it," I snapped when he caught up to me.

I was angry and hurt about Cash. I was mad that Adam was here, drudging up old memories of who I used to be. I was scared because Frankie was hunting us. And I was worried we would never be free of the violence and need to always look over our shoulders. The last thing I wanted was to listen to Tate whine and complain.

His eyebrows shot up at my sharp tone. "You don't even know what I'm going to say."

"Yes, I do but that's besides the point. I'm not in the mood."

He opened his mouth to argue but I held up a hand, not finished.

"I have something to do and I know Cash told you to watch over me but that's just too bad. I don't need a babysitter so don't try to be one."

Tate snorted. "I ain't gonna try. You can kick ass better than anyone. Cash would argue with me but he's not here now so what he doesn't know won't hurt him." He jogged to keep up with my quick strides. "But that's not what I wanted to talk to you about."

"Okay. Spill," I muttered, stomping up the porch steps, super-aware of David watching from his position at the woodpile. Just because I couldn't look him in the eye didn't mean I felt guilty for going down on Cash when the preacher was right outside. I was glory-bound for purgatory anyway. A few minutes down on my knees or with my legs around Cash wasn't going to make a huge difference. I already had a fast pass to the fiery gates of hell.

"So…um…did Cash tell you we're leaving tomorrow?" Tate asked, following me up the porch steps.

"Yeah. Why?" My heart was twisting.

"Because…well…what if…at home…"

I stopped at the top and turned to face him. He was taller than me now. Not quite as big as Cash but he would be someday. I was sure of it.

"What about home?" I asked, growing impatient. "Are you worried we won't make it?"

I had never known Tate to worry but I could tell he was agitated. I could see it in the way he started chewing on his thumbnail and gazed up at me through strands of his hair.

"No. It's not that." He shifted nervously onto his other foot. "It's….do you think Dad made it home? He could be waiting for us right now, wondering where we are."

My throat clogged up. Heaviness settled on my chest like a pile of bricks. Our dad wasn't waiting for us. He was dead. I was sure of it. A nameless body in a mass grave. No one was wondering where we were. No one would greet us when we arrived home. No one was missing us. This was it. Just me and Tate. There would be no dad or mother. No family to hug us and welcome us. There would only be him and me.

Sadness made me feel a hundred times older. I had never had a close relationship with my father. He was always too busy traveling. Too caught up in his meetings and contracts. But I wished he had been with us when the

EMP hit. Maybe Nathan would still be alive. Maybe my dad would have saved Keely and me from Paul and Hightower.

Maybe. Maybe. Maybe.

Life was full of maybes. Maybe Luke and Jenna would still be alive if I hadn't been crazy and stupid. Maybe I never would have met Cash if my car hadn't broken down at Cooper's Bar. Maybe we would be safely tucked away at home if I hadn't run from my feelings. Maybe I would've stopped loving Cash when he pushed me away.

I glanced up at Tate. There was no maybe about this one. My dad was never coming back. I just had to convince my little brother of it.

"Dad was in Dubai when the EMP hit, Tate. Even if he's still alive, there's no way he could get home."

Tate got that look in his eyes. The one that told me he was about to do his favorite thing…argue.

"Adam said some countries have planes back in the air now. He could have hitched a ride. Would be easy enough with his overseas contacts," he snapped, his eyebrows drawn together. "If anyone could do it, Dad could."

I felt an inkling of anger. Just what was the soldier feeding my brother? Lies? Hope? Belief that the end of the war was in sight?

Before Tate, Keely, and I met up with Cash and Gavin, we tracked a group of men from a tiny town outside Austin. They had just exchanged some of their bullets for a case of homemade moonshine. It was the drink of the apocalypse, people said. We didn't care about the alcohol; we wanted the bullets. We were out and guns were our only source of protection.

The decision was simple – we would take what we wanted. Stealing wasn't above us. Tate, Keely, and I followed the men. Keely had become an expert pick-pocket. I was clever and cunning when it came to taking what wasn't mine. It's how we managed to survive.

By the time the men stopped, they had sampled the moonshine and were feeling relaxed. The three of us hid behind some trees to watch and wait. Maybe they would drink a little more and pass out. Maybe they wouldn't hear us sneaking into their camp.

But instead they started talking. A new president was in office. A different government was being formed. I didn't care about any of it. Politicians were the people who got us into the mess in the first place. But I did care about what they talked about next.

The electrical grid was being fixed.

It was a futuristic idea. As foreign to me as the idea of a man walking on the moon was to people at the turn of the century. But the men talked about it with anticipation. It was the hope of our new, fresh-faced country. A goal of the new president. Lines were being checked and restrung across the nation. Electrical stations were being repaired. Some cities had limited electricity with constant black out periods but it was working. Parts of the United States were finally seeing the light at the end of a very long, dark tunnel.

I had refused to get my hopes up. The country was large and places like Washington, D.C. and New York City were much more important than a little hicktown in nowhere, Texas. We would be the last to get electricity, I was almost sure of it.

The thought left me despondent. I was tired, hungry, and scared. I missed my home. Nathan. Diet Coke and showers. I missed clean clothes, coffee, and music. I miss everything I had taken for granted including my dad. But

I didn't think I would see him or anything else from my prior life again.

I glanced around at the woods surrounding the cabin, seeing nothing and everything that was my life now. Emptiness. Isolation. A stillness that couldn't be described. It was a pretty day despite the brisk chill in the air. The trees looked like they were on fire with their red and gold leaves. The sky was cloudless and the sun was bright. But here on earth, war and human evilness had left nothing but ugliness.

And I wanted to escape it all.

I took a deep breath and gazed back at my brother. "He was in *Dubai*, Tate. He's not coming back."

Tate's expression turned hostile. I knew underneath it, he was just as scared and upset as me.

"You ain't never believed in him, Cat. Not once. I remember you saying that Dad only cared about his money and we should only care about spending it. Well, you were wrong. He cares about us and he'll find a way to get home. So you can give up on him but I won't. I never will."

He stomped away from me with angry strides but stopped halfway across the porch and marched back.

"Do you even think Keely and Gavin made it home or did you lose all hope for them too?" he bit out, infuriated.

I narrowed my eyes at him.

"I haven't lost hope, Tate, but I also haven't lost touch with reality. Dad's gone and he's never coming back. Even if he were alive, the chances of him getting home are slim to none. I'm not going to pretend otherwise. This world is ugly and harsh and not all daisies and rainbows. But Keely and Gavin are safe, Tate. I'm almost sure of it."

"Almost? Geez, Cat, you should hear yourself. You trying to be positive is a joke. You're the most cynical person I know and you will never change," Tate said, rolling his eyes. "Just stop trying."

He was right. Positive didn't give me anything but letdowns, but I was worried about Keely and Gavin. What if Frankie and his men found them? What if Hightower caught up to them? There was only one way to find out. Adam. I had a feeling he knew more.

"Why don't we go talk to our visitor? He knows something he's not saying." I pushed past Tate, my fear and worry turning into anger. And it centered on one person.

I marched across the porch and flung back the rickety door. The cabin was dim, making it hard to tell what was man and object.

Unafraid, I stepped inside. A cold stillness seemed to permeate the cabin. Unlike the chill outside, this one was absolute, filling every corner of the small living room and kitchen. It sank deep into my bones, sapping me of warm. I shivered and burrowed deeper into my coat before going further inside.

"Where is he?" I muttered to no one in particular, glancing around the dark interior.

Tate appeared beside me. "What's that noise?" he asked in a hushed whisper.

I heard it too. It was coming from David's bedroom. It sounded like someone was rummaging through a box.

I was right. Adam was up to no good.

I reached over and grabbed the pistol from Tate's waistband.

"What the hell?" he whispered loudly, looking at me with outrage.

I ignored him and weighed the weapon in my hand as I eased forward. It was heavy, cold, and felt deadly in my hand. The feeling of holding something that could take a person's life made my stomach turn, but it was a necessary evil if I wanted to survive.

I held the gun out in front of me and started across the cabin. I heard Tate pull out his other gun, the sound of metal sliding against leather loud.

Taking careful steps toward the bedroom, I tried not to make any noise or step on a loose floorboard. If I could sneak up on…

"I can hear you," Adam's deep voice rang out from the room.

My steps faltered. Dammit.

I drew myself up to my full height. Taking a deep breath of courage, I stepped into the doorway and raised my gun.

"What the hell do you think you're doing?" I looked down the barrel of my weapon at the man who had been sent to hunt me.

He was kneeling near an old army cot, his big body resting on his knees. In front of him was a box that he had obviously pulled out from under the bed. Its contents were spilled all over the floor. Clothes. A couple of books. A bottle of whiskey.

David's things.

Adam looked up at me and smirked. "Just being curious, sweet pea."

"Don't call me that. Get up. I have a few questions for you." I motioned with the end of the gun for him to rise to his feet. I just wished that I didn't look like a girl who was still weak from a bullet wound and lack of food.

My stomach chose that moment to growl loudly. *Great.*

Adam chuckled and raised one eyebrow. "Hungry, *darling*?"

I gave him a sardonic, dry smile. "That's none of your business. I told you to get up."

Tate stepped around me. Lifting his gun, he pointed it at Adam's forehead. "I think my sister said to get up. You hard of hearing?"

Adam glanced at him, a deadly glint appearing in his eyes.

"Oh, I can hear just fine." He nodded at the gun in Tate's hand. "You might want to be careful with that thing, kid. Wouldn't want it to go off accidently and hurt you."

Tate didn't move a muscle. "If it goes off, it won't be accidental and it won't hurt me."

The glint flared brighter in Adam's eyes. He didn't appreciate the threat. But just as soon as it was there, it was gone. The easygoing man was back, covering up the killer he was with a smile.

He chuckled and climbed to his feet. "Are we really going to do this all over again? I told you that I wouldn't hurt anyone. You can trust me."

"Trust you?" I snorted. "You shouldn't have been snooping around." I stepped out of the doorway and motioned with my gun. "Move it."

He sighed. "Fine."

Taking his time, he strolled toward the door. When he got close to me, he stopped. Tate brought his gun up higher in warning. Adam ignored him and gazed down at me.

He was broad with bulky muscles and an in-your-face amount of lethal power. Cash was opposite – sleek and lithe, his underlying danger that stayed quiet until it brewed and simmered when provoked. The differences were there but they were both dangerous.

"Your boyfriend know you're doing this?" Adam asked.

"It doesn't matter," I said, hoping my voice didn't sound as shaky as it felt coming out of my mouth. "Move."

Adam narrowed his eyes but started toward the door. Giving my brother an arrogant glare, he walked out of the room.

Tate and I followed. To my surprise, David was standing in the living room, a shotgun cradled in his arms in an unstated warning.

Adam walked over to the couch and sat down as if it was everyday two guns were pointed at his back. Stretching out his legs, he leaned back and folded his hands behind his head, looking relaxed and right at home.

He looked from Tate to me then to David. "I take it he's not here?"

No one answered him. We didn't need to be told he was talking about Cash. But to admit out loud that he wasn't here was admitting how vulnerable we were. Cash was obviously the strongest one of the group. The one who would pull the trigger first and ask questions later. Without him, we were weaker. More of a target for Adam.

He looked at each of us again. "So no one is going to answer me?" When we kept quiet, he scoffed. "So he leaves a girl, a kid, and an old preacher alone with a killer? Good idea."

"So you admit that you can't be trusted," I said, peering down the barrel at him.

He turned his light blue eyes on me. "I didn't say that, sweet pea."

I arched my brow, not believing him and irritated with the names. He grinned knowingly and raised his own eyebrow, taunting me to argue.

I stepped forward to do just that but David intercepted me, limping closer and wincing at his bad knees.

"What was he doing in there?" he asked, nodding toward his bedroom.

I lowered my gun and started to answer but saw Adam reach under his jacket for something.

Tate shot forward and I lifted my weapon again as Adam pulled out a pistol.

"Calm down," he said, looking from me to Tate and holding his hands out to show he was no threat.

I eased my weapon down an inch and Tate relaxed but didn't back away. Satisfied, Adam set the gun beside him on the couch and looked at David.

"I was looking for bullets," he said. "I don't like being handicapped with just one."

I rushed over and grabbed the pistol then moved away quickly.

He watched me, not moving a muscle. "Is that really necessary?" he asked in a voice that held a note of warning. "I don't like being unarmed."

I gave him my best, smartass smile. "Too bad. It's necessary."

I handed the gun to David then faced Adam again. "Tell us about our friends."

"What friends?" he asked, sounding believable.

I resisted the urge to roll my eyes. "The blonde and a guy with her. Cash asked you already. You said you didn't know what happened to them but I have a feeling you do."

Adam leaned back against the couch and stretched his legs out in front of him and his arms along the back. He looked relaxed despite Tate's gun trained on him. I waited impatiently for him to get comfortable.

"What do I get for telling you?" he asked, raising one eyebrow and smirking.

"How about you get to stay alive," Tate said from beside me. "That work for you?"

Adam laughed at Tate's ferocity. "Okay. No need to get testy. I'll spill." He rolled his neck, popping the kinks out. Sighing, he answered. "A big brute, Hightower, went after them. That's all I know. Honest to God. Last I heard, he hadn't found them yet."

Oh, Jesus. The thought of Hightower chasing Keely left a bad taste in my mouth.

"You believe him, sis?" Tate asked, keeping his eyes on Adam.

I studied the man from my past for a minute. "Yeah, I do."

Adam's smile widened. "Thank you, sweet pea."

I frowned. "But tie him back up anyway," I told Tate, turning away.

Adam's low grumble of frustration sent a thrill of smugness through me. I heard Tate tell him to get to his feet and Adam mutter about bossy women. I was feeling pretty satisfied but it was short-lived. I was halfway across the room when his deep voice rang out.

"Your boyfriend said he marked his territory with you a long time ago. Threatened to put me in the ground if I treaded on what was his. Sorry, honey. Guess it's not going to work out between us after all."

Anger bubbled up inside me. I could feel David and Tate glancing at me. My cheeks burned. I wanted to scream with outrage and embarrassment, but my grandmother's cranky, old voice came back to haunt me.

"You can catch more flies with honey than vinegar, Catarina. Remember that when you feel like having one of your little fits."

I shoved her nasty memory to the back of my mind and plastered a perfected, sweet smile on my face. Turning, I faced Adam.

He stood big and tall across the room, a formidable opponent ready to battle. Not one ounce of him moved as Tate tied his hands behind his back. His mouth quirked up in a grin, seeing that he was getting to me, but in his eyes there was a dare. A challenge. It fed my courage and drowned any fear of him.

"There was never an *us*, soldier. But I do know how hard I am to forget. Good luck with that and I hope you and your right hand live happily ever after," I said.

Adam chuckled but his gaze blazed, warning me that I went too far. David cleared his throat, reminding me that he was still there and the reference to Adam jerking off wasn't appreciated. I ignored him and met Adam's stare, unwilling to back down.

He glanced up and down my body slowly. "You're a handful. I hope Cash has lots of energy to keep up with you."

"I do," a deep voice interjected from behind me. "And she's my handful."

The sound was like warm silk drifting across my naked skin. I felt safe instantly. Cocooned. Wrapped in seduction. Heated with need and angry because I wanted him.

Cash.

He stood in the doorway, sunlight behind him. His cowboy hat was pulled low, leaving only his jaw visible. His chin was cut from stone and his jawline was covered with stubble. I could still feel the roughness on my neck, leaving burn marks behind.

I suddenly didn't feel like the girl who had held a gun on a soldier. I felt like the woman who Cash had held up against the wall and whispered in my ear that I was his. And that made me mad and hurt all over again.

From one of his hands dangled a feathered, dead animal, limp and ugly. I wasn't sure what it was but my stomach growled in response.

He held it up. "Dinner," he explained as if reading my mind. "There's enough meat for everyone but Cat gets seconds."

"You found a chicken?" Tate asked with awe, forgetting about Adam at the mention of food.

"I traded," Cash said as if that answered everything.

Adam and Tate spoke at the same time.

"Traded? With who?"

"What did you trade?"

Cash didn't answer either of them at first but when he did, his voice held a quietness that sent shivers over my spine.

"Doesn't matter what I traded or who it was with. What matters is that we're eating tonight. We'll need the energy for tomorrow when we leave for home."

Chapter Twenty-Three

-Cat-

Dinner was chicken over an open flame. Cash had wrung the little thing's neck before bringing it to the cabin and David got the privilege of plucking it bare. I was glad not to do either.

I stared into the flames, watching the pieces of chicken cook on the makeshift skewer that Cash had made. As drops of fat sizzled and popped in the fire, my mind went back to the first time I had been forced to eat wild game.

It was right after Nathan died. Keely, Tate, and I roamed aimlessly for days, unsure where to go. The sun blistered our exposed skin. Heat exhaustion zapped our energy. Thirst and hunger slowed us down. Exhaustion made us weak and slow. We finally made camp along a two-lane highway, hidden in a thick cluster of trees.

"I'm starving," I had complained, hugging my knees to my chest as I sat on the ground. My lips were dry and cracked. My skin was red and burnt. I was covered with a fine layer of dust and dirt but my empty stomach was worse than feeling grimy and filthy. I had never felt so hungry before.

Tate poked a stick into the dirt, making a small hole, gaunt and tired. "Me too. It's been two days since we ate. My stomach is gnawing on itself."

Keely stared off into the distance. Her blonde hair was matted and her face was still marked with bruises from Hightower's fist. She hadn't spoken since that day. She just stared off into space and followed us. My heart twisted every time I looked at her. I felt guilty for not being able to protect her. She would wake me at night, screaming. I knew what he had done to her. There was no forgetting it. There was just going on.

One step further.

One hour more.

One day then another.

I glanced away from Keely and around the little grouping of trees we hid under.

"We need to find food," I said, squinting against the sunlight.

"How we gonna do that?" Tate grumbled past broken, dry lips. "We ain't seen a person in a day and there's nothing around but trees and more trees."

He was right. We were in the middle of nowhere. There was nothing. The truth was, we were lost. Yesterday, we got turned around and nothing looked familiar. We had tried backtracking but it had only got us more confused. I tried not to panic for Tate and Keely's sake. We would find our way back to a town.

But first we needed to find food.

"We can walk and see if we find a house," Tate said. It was risky, knocking on a stranger's door when the world had gone to hell. Two days ago, we had spotted a rundown shack sitting off the main road. Paper had been plastered over the windows and numerous cats roamed the rickety porch. I had knocked on the front door as one of them hissed at me from a broken chair. A second later, the end of a shotgun was pointed at my face and a man was roaring at us to get off his property.

"No, I don't think that's a good idea anymore," I muttered, resting my chin on my knees with defeat.

A breeze rattled the leaves above us. It felt good on my overheated skin. *This would be a good place to die of starvation. It's quiet. Peaceful. Away from the madness.* I sighed. I couldn't give up. Not yet.

Exhausted beyond measure, I didn't jump when Keely snagged the stick from Tate. But I did sit up straight and pay attention when she started writing something in the dirt.

I tilted my head to read it. So did Tate.

"Gun. Hunt," Tate muttered, reading the words.

I glanced up at Keely. She had anger in her eyes and held the stick like she wanted to whack someone with it.

She stabbed the stick under the word 'hunt' when Tate and I stared at her, dumbfounded and confused because of hunger.

"Hunt," I repeated weakly.

"What's there to hunt around here?" Tate grumbled. "I ain't seen nothing but a few little sparrows and a worm or two. I ain't gonna eat 'em."

I looked around. Waves of heat rose above the gray asphalt of the road. On the other side stood a barbed wire fence, half of it lying on the ground. Behind the fence was another clump of trees. As I watched, something scurried up one of the massive trunks.

"Squirrel," I said, the idea coming to me.

Tate turned and glanced across the road too, following the direction of my gaze.

"I'll do it," he said as if hunting squirrels was something he had done all his life.

Standing up, he dusted off his jeans (a useless act since we were filthy anyway) and dug in the backpack at his feet for a gun.

"Do you know what you're doing?" I asked, as he checked it for bullets. I was so tired and hungry that just saying that simple sentence took all my effort.

Tate rolled his eyes as he held the gun pointed at the ground. "Aim and pull the trigger. How hard can it be?"

Hard enough, I guessed later. It took half the day for Tate to kill the squirrel. He had to venture deeper into the field across the road and wait for long periods of time under the trees. One time, I lost sight of him. I kept my eyes glued to the place I had last seen him, praying for him to reappear again. My knee bounced with nerves as I waited. *Come back now, come back now.* Finally, he emerged between two straggly mesquite trees, a brown fuzzy animal hanging from his hand. A big smile lit up his blistered face as he headed back across the road toward Keely and me.

"Hit the sucker right in the head," he announced with pride, holding the squirrel out for us to see.

I squinted up at the furry thing. At a close range, I realized that squirrels were nasty looking little things.

I jumped to my feet and dusted off the seat of my jeans. "I'm starving. Let's eat." I was ready to tear into the squirrel.

Tate wrinkled up his nose and looked down at it. "You going to skin and gut it?"

I raised one eyebrow. "Uh, no."

Tate sighed and shifted onto his other foot. "Shit, me either."

In the end, Tate gutted the animal and I skinned it. We roasted it over a tiny fire we managed to start with a lighter Tate had found in an abandoned car. The squirrel tasted a little burnt and I found little hairs in my pieces, but it was the best tasting meal I ever had.

Starvation could do that to a person. Whittle you down to the basics. Make every little bite extraordinary. I no longer took food for granted. Instead, every meal was special, every mouthful incredible, because I never knew when I would eat again.

I was as hungry now as I was then. I bundled deeper into my jacket and glanced around, trying to focus on something else. Outside the ring of fire, it was pitch dark. The kind of night where you couldn't see your hand in front of your face. Thick clouds hid the stars and moon. The temperature had dropped, chilling the air to a bone-numbing temperature.

I glanced across the fire at Cash. He was sitting on a log on the other side of the fire pit. His elbows were on his knees and his hands were hanging between his legs. His hat was gone and his gaze was focused on the red and blue flames. I was wondering if I could really do it? If I could really stay away from him.

I studied him in the firelight, wondering what he was thinking. Was he going over the plans in his head that him and David had discussed earlier? Was he thinking about the road we needed to take that would lead us home? Was he contemplating the plan to stay clear of any towns or people? Was he wondering if David's old truck could get us home? The preacher was going with us. There was nothing left for him here but death and starvation. If Frankie and the militia found him, I cringed to think what they would do. No, the preacher had saved our lives.

We were going to save his.

I glanced over at David. He was sitting next to Tate, both of them talking in low tones as they waited for the chicken to cook. Like Cash, David had taken Tate under his wing. Many times I had heard him teaching Tate patience and the importance of being honest and respectful. I didn't know if it was sticking, but Tate seemed captivated by the older man and absorbed every word he said. He had no male to look up to anymore. Our father was gone and Nathan was dead. Cash and

David were it. But family is more than just blood. It is a kinship that even the worst can't tear apart. It is caring for each other through thick and thin.

I looked over at Adam, wondering if he had any family left. He was sitting off to the side by himself, his hands tied in front of him. He hadn't spoken much since earlier and no one had tried to talk to him either.

He was staring off into the darkness. His mouth was turned down in a frown and his body was wound tight. He seemed ready to spring into action at any minute, as if he was waiting for someone to leap out of the shadows.

I felt my pulse race. *Did he know something we didn't?* I wondered if Cash noticed Adam's weird behavior. If he did, he didn't show it or seem worried. He was staring at me instead.

Despite my best efforts to play indifferent, the air left my lungs in a soft whoosh. The world stopped. His gray eyes were fixed on me from across the fire. I couldn't look away. I was mesmerized, bound to him with just a look. We were suddenly a million miles away from the campfire and rustic cabin. We were back in the swanky bathroom on our first date. Back when he lifted me onto the counter. Back when I was lost, drifting aimlessly in a sea of self-destruction and self-absorption. But he found me.

And I would never be the same again.

"I think this little fellow is ready to eat," David said, leaning over to pick up the makeshift skewers the pieces of chicken dangled from.

"Hallelujah!" Tate said with a big shout, jumping to his feet and grabbing the stack of chipped bowls I had brought from the cabin. "Let's eat, preacher man!"

I tore my gaze away from Cash and smiled at Tate's enthusiasm. For the first time in a long time, he looked like a young boy again. Free. Happy. Lighthearted. Innocent.

My chest swelled. For that one moment in time, I felt whole. I had nothing. Not a home. Not another set of clothes. Not a dime to my name or fancy things to make me feel good. My future was a mystery and my present was a harsh reality, but watching my little brother smile filled me with something.

Peace.

I laughed out loud when Tate started doing a little dance, waiting for David to fill the bowls. Adam snorted with amusement and David started humming some fast song as he pulled off pieces of chicken and dropped them into the bowls. I felt the excitement. We had something to eat. We were leaving tomorrow for home.

We would be okay.

David joined Tate, dancing in place. They kicked up dirt and came dangerously close to the fire but they didn't care. David started singing, making up his own words, and Tate joined in, sounding off key.

I laughed, throwing my head back and letting the sound escape. God, it had been so long since I did that.

As I watched Tate and David, I felt Cash watching me from across the fire. His mouth was turned up in a gentle, lopsided smile.

My laughter died. My grin stayed. It had been so long since I saw him smile that I was blown away all over again. The cold against my cheeks was forgotten. The fear of leaving was ignored. It was just him and me and this thing between us that wouldn't let us go no matter how hard we fought it.

His eyes turned dark with heat. My body burned under my layer of clothes. I felt his gaze down to my marrow. The pull of him was undeniable. The effect indescribable.

He glanced away from me as David called his name. Rising to his feet, he walked over to where David was filling the bowls.

I lowered my eyes and smoothed a shaky hand over the leg of my jeans. *Holy shit.* The man could leave me breathless and shaky and all things that felt so right. He could do it all with just a word. Just a look. Just a smile. It was unfair and outrageous and I had to resist him.

"Cat."

I looked up. Cash was standing beside me, holding out a tin bowl. His voice was warm, smooth, and satisfying. My name on his lips sounded sinful.

I took the bowl from him, feeling nervous and jittery all at once.

He sat down beside me on the log, cradling his own bowl in his palm. The makeshift seat wasn't big enough for both of us. His leg rested against mine and his arm bumped my forearm and shoulder.

He leaned forward and rested his elbows on his knees. I stared at his profile as he started to eat, lost in the shape of his jaw and the fullness of his lips. He parted them and lifted a piece of chicken to his mouth.

David paused in handing Adam a bowl of steaming chicken and coughed, raising one eyebrow at Cash.

"I know you aren't a praying bunch but we should say a prayer before we eat," he said in a solemn tone, the man that had danced and sang forgotten and the seriousness of what we faced remembered. "We need all the help we can get for tomorrow, kids."

Reprimanded, Cash lowered his fork. David grunted with approval and lowered his head, He started praying in a solemn, deep voice, asking God to watch over us.

Tate started eating, glancing at the preacher every few seconds with amused interest. I gave him a warning glare and raised my eyebrow. He sighed and closed his eyes but still tried to stuff chicken into his mouth blindly.

I lowered my eyes but not before I saw Adam with his head down and eyes closed. I didn't peg him for a religious man but the war and EMP had changed people – some for the better and some for the worse. Some for a little of both.

Closing my eyes, I bowed my head. David prayed for our safety and our swift return home. He prayed for God to keep away evil and thanked Him for my recovery. I felt Cash shift beside me when David mentioned my name. Opening my eyes, I glanced at him.

His eyes were open and he was staring at the fire, listening to David's words. He shifted the bowl into his other hand and ran a palm over his thigh closest to me, his fingers touching my leg lightly. My heart beat faster. The friction between us grew.

Too soon, David finished and everyone started eating. Despite my hunger, I nibbled at the chicken. Nothing had ever tasted as good but my mind was on something else. The man beside me and his words from earlier. *'I'm not staying away from you, Cat. Not until I'm ready.'*

I felt his eyes on me in the firelight, watching me pick at the pieces of chicken.

"Eat," he demanded in a low voice, nodding at the bowl in my hand.

I decided maybe it was better to argue than to fight the magnetic pull of him. "Cash, I don't want to—"

He leaned closer, his voice dropping lower, sliding over me. "I wore you out today and I damn sure want to wear you out some more. Eat, Beauty Queen."

I stuck up my chin – something I was good at – and ignored the way my skin felt too hot. "I told you to stay away from me. Have you already forgotten that?"

His eyes narrowed. "No. Have you forgotten that you said you'd do anything for me or do you need to be reminded?"

I huffed and averted my gaze, hating how he was affecting me. "Trying to assert your dominance again, *cowboy*? It won't work this time."

Cash tilted his head. "Oh, really? Is that a dare?"

I rolled my eyes and shifted my knees away from him. "No, it's a fact. I'm immune. Your moves won't work on me anymore. These legs are permanently closed."

He grabbed my knee and pulled me back to him. Leaning over, he put his mouth near my ear. "As much as I want to talk about your legs, sweetheart, we need to talk about you doing anything for me. I want you to eat. If you can get down on your knees when I asked, you can eat when I insist."

I burned at the reminder. His voice caused me to shiver. Glancing around, I made sure no one was listening. They weren't, too busy eating to notice or hear.

I met Cash's gaze again and raised one eyebrow. "Insist all you want. It was a one-time thing. We're over just like you wanted." I started to take my bowl and get up but he put a hand on my leg, stopping me. A tick appeared in his jaw. I might have a love/hate thing with that.

"What I want and what I need are two separate things, Cat. Right now, I want you to eat."

"And later?" I whispered, unable to resist.

He glanced down at my lips then back up. "Later, I need you to hate me because I'm going to touch you again, Cat. I'm going to make love to you and listen to those little whimpers you make when you come. Afterward, I'll wish I never had touched you. I'll regret every second because it won't keep you safe or save your life and it damn sure will fuck with my brain. So that's what I need – for you to hate me because anything else is more than I can take."

Chapter Twenty-Four

-Cat-

By the end of the night, I managed to eat two bowls of chicken. How, I'm not sure because my stomach was in knots and my mind was replaying Cash's words.

I need you to hate me.

I'm going to touch you again.

I'm going to make love to you.

I'll regret every second.

Each was like a heavy weight dropped on me but the last ones were like shards of glass cutting into me.

He didn't say anything else the rest of the night but he kept an eye on me as he talked with David about the route we would take tomorrow, making sure I ate. He stayed near me when he questioned Adam on Frankie and his men. And he didn't venture too far when he told Tate to try to get some sleep. By the time I headed back to the cabin, the air between us was thick with awareness. One more look, one more accidental touch, one more word spoken in private, and we wouldn't be able to control ourselves.

We would shatter.

That wasn't an option. We were over. I avoided love, hope, and happiness before. I could do it again. They caused nothing but pain and heartache. Love tore your insides apart when the person you loved was yanked away from you. Hope made you feel dead inside when it was taken. Happiness left a bad taste in your mouth when it was abused. I understood what Cash was feeling too well.

But that didn't mean I had to like it.

I wrapped my arms around my middle and tucked my chin into my collar as I walked up the porch steps. Tate was already inside, tying Adam up for the night. David and Cash were still by the fire, talking in low tones.

I paused on the third step and glanced back at them. Cash was staring into the flames, listening silently as David spoke and nodding his head every few seconds as if he agreed or understood.

I studied him. He was quiet power and calm strength all wrapped up in one. He could kill with a look or calm me with a touch. He knew me like no one else and had touched a part of me that no one had since Luke. How I was supposed to stop loving him, I wasn't sure.

He looked up at me, his eyes piercing even from a distance. Tension lined his body. Coolness oozed from him.

David looked over his shoulder at me, following Cash's gaze. He said something and Cash gave a curt nod and looked away.

Confused, I watched as David headed straight for me. Cash was left alone, staring into the fire, his body all shadows and ridges in the light from the flames.

I tore my gaze away from him as David walked up the porch steps toward me.

"He's going to take first watch. Why don't you go on to bed, honey?" he said, more a command than a request.

I glanced at Cash again. "Is that your demand or his?" I asked David.

He chuckled. "What do you think?"

"His."

"Bingo," David said, walking the rest of the way up the stairs.

"Bingo," I whispered.

~~~~

A single candle burned on the bedside table. A chill was in the air. Adam was tied up in the living room and Tate was bedded down on the couch. David was in the other bedroom and Cash was on watch.

I couldn't sleep. I laid in bed and stared at the ceiling, thinking of everything Cash had said. The longer I laid there, the angrier I got. I let out a sigh of frustration and threw the covers off. Maybe a bath would help. I felt grimy and dirty. Getting clean might relax me and take my mind off Cash.

I climbed out of bed and glanced at the bowl on the bedside table. The water would be ice-cold but maybe it would cool my skin as I remembered him touching me.

With my back to the door, I began unbuttoning my shirt. One button. Two buttons. My fingers slipped them through the holes on autopilot.

We were done. Over. I could do this. I'll survive.

I pulled off my shirt and flung it on the bed. My chest rose and fell rapidly as my anger rose. *He wanted me to hate him? Then I would! Gladly!*

Goosebumps broke out along my arms but I ignored them. Standing naked from the waist up, I angrily grabbed the washcloth from the bowl of water that Tate had brought in for me.

"Damn you, Cash Marshall."

With furious motions, I rubbed the sliver of soap on the washcloth and started washing my neck. Drops of water ran down my chest and over my breasts. I sucked in a breath at the cold water but made angry swipes across my skin, trying not to imagine Cash touching my breasts. Cupping them. Lifting them for his mouth.

"Ugh!"
~~~~

I ran the washcloth lower with brisk, fast movements. "He wishes he never touched me? Well, I'll make him regret the day!"

I rubbed the cloth across my chest, irate and frustrated. Water drops ran down to my waistband and disappeared under the material. I dropped the washcloth back in the bowl, splashing water over the edge onto the nightstand. Grabbing it again, I ran it up my neck dripping wet. Rivets of water ran between my breasts and down my stomach.

"I will never, ever, *ever* give into him again," I said between clenched teeth, rubbing my skin vigorously. "Ever!"

The sound of a footstep came from behind me.

I gasped and swung around, holding the washcloth over my breasts, my skin pink with irritation at my quick, rough treatment.

Cash was standing inside the bedroom, looking larger than life and as dangerous as sin. He had on his hat and his eyes were dark pools of desire under it, wicked and focused on me.

I took a swift step back as he strolled toward me.

"You'll never, ever give into me?" he drawled, taking off his hat and flinging it toward the bed.

My bottom hit the bedside table, shaking the bowl of water on it. "Um, yes. Never," I mumbled, holding the washcloth over my breasts. Drops of water ran down my stomach, chilling my overheated skin.

Cash unbuckled his gun holster and dropped it to the floor as he advanced slowly toward me. His eyes moved down to the washcloth and my nipples puckered against the rough material. I swallowed hard as he stopped in front of me.

"Ever?"

"Ever," I whispered, my lips barely parted.

"Good."

He grasped the back of my neck and dragged me to him. My body hit his. A soft mewl left me. He caught the sound with his lips, sealing his mouth over mine.

The kiss was consuming, overriding all my better judgments and promises to myself. I kept my arm over the washcloth, trapping it between us and keeping my breasts hidden as his mouth conquered mine. It wasn't what he wanted and one thing I had learned – Cash always got what he wanted.

He reached up and jerked the washcloth away with impatience. I moaned softly as cold air hit my nipples. His tongue dipped inside my mouth as he reached around me to drop the washcloth in the bowl of water.

I shivered, standing naked from the waist up in front of him. His lips turned gentle on mine, tasting, barely touching. When he cupped my breast, I drew in a sharp breath.

"Resist me, Cat," he rumbled in a deep voice sliding his mouth from mine down to my jawline. "Tell me to go to hell. I can't stop wanting you and I don't know how."

I leaned my head back, exposing my neck.

"I said to stay away from me," I whispered, my eyes closed, the words holding no power as his lips moved to my throat.

He let out a low sound of irritation. "I can't."

"Not until you're ready," I added on a breath of air as his thumb drifted across my nipple again.

"Not until I'm ready," he said softly against my skin, catching a drop of water from my breast on the tip of his finger.

A soft sound escaped me as he rubbed it into my areola, grazing the point, at the same time he bit and licked at my neck. My breathing increased. My mouth went dry. I thought it was more than I could handle but I was wrong.

Very wrong.

He leaned over and caught a drop from my nipple with the warm, flat part of his tongue.

"Catarina," he whispered against the sensitive peak. "I'll regret this later but I've got to have it now."

I gasped as his mouth closed on my nipple. He sucked it hard than lapped at it, sending quakes through me. I was dying. I knew I was. His tongue swirled around the sensitive peak, licking up all the water and adding more wet heat. As if that wasn't enough, he cupped my breast and squeezed, holding me for his full, undivided attention.

My insides quivered. Need shot between my legs. I tangled my fingers into his hair, urging him never to stop.

He reached behind me and grabbed the washcloth out of the bowl. Drops of water fell to the floor as he brought it back to me and squeezed it over my left breast.

I hissed as the cold water ran down me in rivers. But his mouth was suddenly there, taking my nipple whole. He dropped the washcloth on the floor and suckled my nipple deep inside his mouth then licked up all the water and drank it down.

Pleasure traveled through me. I bit my lip, trying not to cry out but a tiny sound escaped me. It seemed to drive him crazy.

He reached down and jerked my jeans open with rough and impatient tugs.

"Those sounds fuck with me, Cat. Makes it damn hard to be civil about this."

"Then don't."

He groaned and slid his hand down the front of my jeans and took my nipple between his teeth. I hissed and tightened my fingers in his hair as his finger slipped over me with a slow, deliberate stroke.

"Are you always this wet for me?" he asked hoarsely against my breast.

"Yes. It's your fault you know."

He licked my nipple. "Hate me then."

"I do," I whispered on a sigh, closing my eyes again.

Cash growled deep in his throat, the sound escaping against my nipple as he swirled his tongue around the rosy tip.

Without even knowing what I was doing, I twisted strands of his hair around my fingers and held on tight as he ran a finger along my slick opening. If I was hurting him, he didn't care. He sucked my nipple deep into his mouth and skimmed his finger over my clit.

I bit my lips almost to the point of bleeding. *Oh god. Oh god. I'm going to come...*

He did it again, sliding his finger over the tender spot. When he followed it by slipping a finger into me, I shattered. My teeth pierced my bottom lip. Stars burst behind my eyelids. He held me as the orgasm rocked my body with force and made me jerk and shake.

"That's it," he said against my breast, sliding his finger deeper. "Come hard for me." He ran his tongue around my nipple then fastened onto it.

I let out a small cry and gripped his hair tighter. "No more," I mumbled incoherently as my body jerked. "Please."

"I'm just getting started, sweetheart."

He removed his fingers from me abruptly and swung me up into his arms. My eyes flew up and my breath caught. We were in the bedroom, only a sheet separating us from everyone else. Making me come was one thing. Fucking me while everyone else slept feet away was another.

"What…what are you doing?" I asked in hushed whisper as he carried me to the other side of the bed.

He didn't answer. Instead, he lowered me to my feet and leaned past me to grab the sheet and quilt on the bed. I watched with wide eyes as he spread it out on the floor between the bed and the wall.

"Cash! What are you doing?" I asked in a loud whisper.

His hand snapped out and grabbed the back of my neck. With a frustrated scowl, he pulled me toward him and put his mouth near my ear. "The bed makes too much noise. The only thing I want to hear is you."

His mouth covered mine. It wasn't gentle or kind or sweet. He took what he wanted. He owned it. What was rightfully his. I didn't care if I was supposed to hate him or if he would regret every second of it tomorrow. I wanted him to do his worst and best to me.

I grabbed the lapels of his jacket and tried to shove them down his arms. They didn't go very far. I wanted to stamp my foot and throw a tantrum. I was naked from the waist up and he was fully clothed. That was unfair and unkind and I wanted him to do something about it.

Without breaking the kiss, Cash let go of the back of my neck and shrugged out of the jacket like the thing was on fire. I smiled against his lips as he untangled his arms from it and flung it to the floor.

He growled a warning deep in his throat and grabbed the back of my head again, hauling me to him.

"Brat," he rasped against my grinning lips.

But then I forgot everything.

He plowed his fingers into my hair and yanked my head back. I whimpered and it was just what he wanted to hear. His tongue plunged into my mouth. His hand in my hair held me still. I could feel his erection between us, hard under his jeans and eager to please.

"On your knees."

His voice left no room for thinking or arguing. I slid my mouth from his and lowered to my knees. He watched me in the candlelight, my lips right in line with the hardness behind his zipper.

I licked my lips and looked up at him. The small area where I kneeled was secluded. Hidden from prying eyes. Perfect for me to take him to the back of my throat.

I glanced down at his zipper. My mouth watered. This time I would let him finish in my mouth.

Unable to wait, I reached for his belt buckle but he stopped me, his hand tangled in my hair.

"Lay down."

With my body flushing, I eased down to the faded sheet. I had never been the submissive type – I was more of a power-hungry kind of gal – but there was just something about Cash telling me what to do that made all my rules fly out the window.

He let go of my hair and watched me. His eyes were hooded, gray pinpoints of ice. He didn't just look at me with need. He looked at me with restraint. With the look of a man that always got what he wanted at any costs and without any sense of self-control.

When I was lying down, my legs outstretched, he kneeled at my feet and grabbed the legs of my jeans. With two tugs, he had them off and was tossing them to the side.

I grew nervous. "If someone walks in…" I whispered, afraid of him. Afraid of being discovered.

He looked up my body, taking his sweet, ever-loving time, damn him. "No one will."

God, his voice was so sexy.

I worried my bottom lip between my teeth and tried to ignore the way he gazed at my nakedness. The way heat radiated from him.

"How do you know?" I asked, trying to stay on topic, a shiver of arousal moving through me as he moved up my body.

His fingers spread over my stomach, forcing me to be still when I wiggled. "Because David and Tate are taking turns keeping watch the rest of the night." He paused. "And I told them not to come in here no matter what they heard."

What? He told them…

A little whine escaped me when he seized the back of my knee and shoved my leg high, spreading me open. I thought I was his before but now there was no question. He could do with me as he pleased and he wanted me wide open.

Lowering himself above me, his lips went to my collarbone, one of his hands held his weight off me.

I squirmed and thrust my breasts higher but he paid no attention to them. His mouth moved down between them, almost touching the curve of one.

I tried to keep my wits about me as his breath fanned over me in hot waves. As his mouth moved to my hip. As his tongue darted out to sample my skin.

When he kissed my inner thigh, inches from my wet center, I shifted on the blankets. He fastened his arm over my middle, keeping me still. Frustration, annoyance, and damn near everything else made me want to scream.

I licked my dry lips and tried to maintain some sense of control as the stubble on his jaw brushed against the sensitive skin of my inner leg. "But what if someone walks in?"

"You're safe."

He lifted my leg more, opening me. I burned with embarrassment as he gazed down at me with hunger and possession. "You're just not safe from me."

I hissed and arched my back as he buried his face between my legs. His mouth went straight to the slick cleft, devouring me.

My hips bucked and my fingers reached down to grab clumps of his hair. He licked and sucked then dived back in. I'd never felt so completely taken, consumed, enjoyed before.

He pinned me down with his arm across my stomach and pushed his tongue into me. I gasped and tried to thrust my hips up, unable to stop. Wanting more.

"Please. Please," I begged, squirming against him. The pleasure was killing me. I hated him for the torture. I loved him for the feeling.

He flicked his tongue over my clit. "I've wanted to do this forever. Now I never want to stop."

He drew my swollen clit into his mouth and applied the right amount of suction. At the same time, he slid a finger into me.

I convulsed. My legs opened wider. I let go of his hair and planted my hands against the wall above my head as he wreaked havoc on me. *Oh god.* I was his entirely.

My body arched when he hit a sensitive spot. A frenzy built in me. He kept a strong arm across my abdomen and glanced up my body, his eyes heated, watching me come apart as his tongue, fingers, and lips ravaged me.

Oh shit. Oh shit. I can't handle this.

I burst into a trillion stars, climaxing like never before. Silent screams tore from my throat. Powerful vibrations rocked my body.

My legs locked around Cash's head. He shoved them apart and went crazy on me.

I let go of the wall to grasp handfuls of the blanket under me. Cash never left the area between my legs. He held them open and feasted on me until I was a quivering mess and tears escaped from the corners of my eyes. My limbs shook and my body jerked violently.

When I finally went limp, his mouth left me and he started crawling up my body.

I was weightless, my mind nothing but a haze. I couldn't move. Couldn't think. I was afraid I would never breathe normally again. I had never had a man – any man – go down on me like that.

I managed to lift my eyes and watch as he crawled up my body. He had a predatory gleam in his eyes and moved with lion-like precision over me. I was trapped beneath him like a prized possession he was protecting so he could enjoy later. When he got to my breasts, he ducked his head and swiped at the tip with his tongue, reminding me of a dangerous carnivore who was sampling its dinner.

Anticipation made me squirm. Eagerness made me slide my fingers into his hair and turn his head so I could whisper in his ear, "You said a need and a want are two separate things. What am I? A need or a want?"

"Sweetheart, you're everything."

I arched when his mouth closed on my neck. I wiggled and squirmed, desperate.

"Make love to me, cowboy," I whispered.

A noise that sounded suspiciously like an animal growling erupted from his chest. He reached between us and unfastened his belt buckle. I felt him lower the zipper, reach in and pull himself out. His knuckles grazed against my abdomen as he fisted his length and rubbed it against me.

I rolled my hip, urging him in. He let go of himself to grasp the back of my knee. Lifting my leg higher, he shoved my other leg to the side. With his jeans pushed open just enough to allow his erection to jut out, he slid into me.

I gasped and arched my body. The size of him always surprised me. He was long and thick and stretched me to impossible limits. I was tender and sore from all the attention he had given me but it only added to the pleasure.

"Fuck, Cat," he rasped against my throat as he pulled out then eased back in, going deep and slow.

"You're so big," I whispered as he slid out and glided back in, letting me feel every inch of him taking me.

"You make me hard every second of the day," he rasped against my skin.

Reaching down, he cupped my bottom, tilting my hips up to meet his hard length. He held himself deep in me then eased out until only his tip remained.

He did it again and again, his wide head stretching me achingly slow. It made me berserk. I clenched strands of his hair and wrapped my legs around his jean-covered waist. "Harder," I breathed in his ear. "Please."

Burying his face in my neck, he tightened his hold on my bottom and started nailing me with wild, hard drives into my body. I got lost from the feel of him inside me.

Reaching down, I skimmed my hands underneath the back of his loose jeans, needing to touch him. His ass was tight and strong under my fingers, clenching as he dominated my body.

"Christ," he swore, pumping faster and faster in and out of me when I touched him. "I'm so deep in you."

His husky voice sent currents through me. "Mmm. I know," I moaned. "God, it feels good. Don't stop. I'm going to come."

A groan escaped him. "Fuck. Me too. Harder than ever before."

His hips jerked in powerful thrusts. His thickness glided in and out of me faster.

"I should pull out," he said breathlessly against my neck, fucking me with unleashed power that threatened to kill me.

I nodded, too lost to care. But I managed to say something. "You should definitely pull out."

He pulled his entire length out then plunged back into me. Hard. Fast. Pounding me. I bit off a scream and arched, almost coming up off the floor. My world exploded and tremors shook my body. Small cries bubbled up inside me as the orgasm ripped through me. I clamped my teeth on my lip to keep quiet. He claimed my mouth and took my lip himself, sucking it into his mouth and cutting off my cries. I could taste my blood on his tongue. Mine.

I whimpered against his mouth, the sound that drove him crazy. He lost control.

"Fuck, fuck," he whispered over and over again as he lunged in and out of me. His hips pounded against mine, driving me into the floor. My fingernails dug into his ass cheek and my body clutched at his cock.

He raised himself up on his elbows for leverage and pumped into me faster and faster. It changed the game entirely. It was now all about him.

He drove into me deep and hard, hammering me. There was an untamed, feral need in his thrusts like he was claiming and taking what was his.

His hips moved with ferocious strokes. I didn't think it was possible for his manhood to grow even more rigid but it did. I could feel the veins along its length bulge and pulse as my sex clinched him. I could feel the power and I wanted him to unleash it in me.

With his weight on his elbows, he lowered his head and claimed my mouth.

"*Cat*," he rasped against my lips, thrusting deep.

I gasped at the ripples traveling through me. His body stiffened and he started coming, pumping deep into me.

My body milked him, welcoming it. Needing it. Loving it.

He realized what he had done and so did I. I sucked in a shocked breath and he quickly broke off the kiss and reached down, pulling himself out of me. More hot fluid hit my opening as he finished coming against me, swearing softly.

"I'm sorry," he whispered in a broken voice as his body shuddered and the last drop left him.

I licked my lips and shook my head. "Don't be. I didn't want you to stop."

He let out a groan and relaxed down on me. His heart beat fast and he was breathing hard.

He stayed that way, spent. I ran my fingers up his back, over his nape, into his hair. He shivered. It was the first time I had ever seen him so completely…raw.

I wanted to stay that way forever, hidden in our little alcove, seeing him with his defenses down, but too soon his breathing slowed down and I felt his muscles tense.

He eased off me and sat up. Keeping his eyes off me, he tucked himself back into his jeans and zipped them up.

Without a word or a glance at me, he rose to his feet and disappeared around the bed.

I pulled a blanket over me and stared at the ceiling. Candlelight danced over it, casting soft, yellow glows along the rough boards. The area between my legs felt achy and wet. My breasts felt tender from the stubble on his chin.

I could hear Cash moving around. I squeezed my eyes shut tight. *He still has his boots on.* That bothered me. It meant he never planned on staying.

I turned on my side and pushed my hair out of my face. Nothing had changed. I couldn't resist him and he refused to be anything with me but a fuck and run.

He said he would regret every second afterward and I guess he wasn't lying.

I tucked my hands under my cheek and wondered if I could go on being just a convenience for him. Other men had been that for me but Cash was different. Was this my punishment for my past? I was getting what I deserved, as my grandmother would say?

I took a deep breath. I was right. Payback was a bitch.

I was wondering how I could deal with it when the candle was suddenly extinguished. The room went dark except for the moonlight streaming in through the small window.

I didn't move, wondering if Cash just left without saying anything. But then I heard his footsteps. He was heading back to me. His boots appeared in my line of vision, standing at the end of the puddle of blankets.

My gaze followed his jeans up. He was staring at me. His eyes were full of shadows. In his right hand was my shirt. In his left was his gun holster.

I held the blanket against my chest and sat up. "Are you leaving?"

"I should."

"It was a mistake. You regret it," I said, reading his mind.

"I said I would."

That hurt. My throat closed up. Tears clogged it.

Cash avoided my eyes and sat down at my feet. He put the holster on the floor and my shirt beside him. With his back to me, he tugged off his boots and left them at the foot of our makeshift bed. I was fighting off the tears when he turned, grabbing my shirt and my jeans. With a dark gaze on me, he started up my body.

I watched him, keeping the blanket over me. His eyes were cool, assessing, burning me through the thin, worn blanket. It was a tight fit between the wall and bed but it was away from the ugly world outside.

When he was close enough, he held my shirt open for me to put on. I hesitated but then said screw it.

I dropped the blanket and put one arm through the sleeve. If he already regretted what we did, he wouldn't care if I was naked. He wouldn't dare touch me again.

But I was wrong.

His eyes burned down at my breasts and the red blotches left from his stubble. I drew in a quick breath when he reached out and ran a finger across the top slope of my right breast, smoothing the red mark.

My body reacted but I shut it down real fast. I had always been someone's regret and I didn't want to be anymore.

I put my other arm through the sleeve and brushed his hand out of the way.

"Don't touch me," I snapped in a hushed voice.

His jaw clenched tight. His eyes went cold. He jerked the edges of my shirt together and started buttoning it, staring at me.

I stared back, ignoring the flush crawling up my body and the way he smelled so close to me. He finished buttoning my shirt and shoved my jeans at me. I grumbled about assholes and pulled my pants on, giving him my best dirty looks.

He looked ready to pull his hair out or turn me over his knee. I gave him a sickly sweet smile and started to lie down but he had other ideas.

He grabbed the back of my neck and hauled me to him. His mouth went close to mine.

"You want to know what I regret, Cat? I regret that I can't keep my hands off you. I regret that I want to come in you again and again and put you in danger of getting pregnant in this hellhole of a country. I regret everything, Cat, but I don't regret being here with you."

He kissed me so quick I didn't have time to blink. It was hard and fast and without apology. Letting go of me, he rearranged the blankets like nothing had happened and pushed me to lie back down.

As soon as I did, he laid down beside me. We stared at the ceiling, side by side. My shoulder was pressed against his arm. My leg rested against his. My mind was a confused jumble.

"Tonight I'm staying with you. Tomorrow we're going home," he said in a cool voice, his side resting against mine.

I nodded in the dark, trying to figure him out. He wanted me. He didn't. I was supposed to hate him. I couldn't. And of course we were going home. We had been preparing for it all day. Was he not going to stay with me after tonight? Was that what he meant by that?

I didn't think of it anymore. Cash turned onto his side and wrapped his arm around my waist. With a gentle tug, he pulled me to him and tucked me against his chest.

Warmth enveloped me. No matter what, I felt protected and sheltered.

But no one was really safe. Not anymore.

Chapter Twenty-Five

-Cash-

I put my arm around Cat's hip and pulled her closer. She fit into my body like a glove. I stared at the ceiling as her breathing slowed down. I had taken her like a madman, mercilessly.

And that scared the hell out of me.

She sighed in her sleep and wiggled against me. Jesus. I could take her again. But she was exhausted. I saw the circles under her eyes and the paleness of her skin earlier. She needed rest. I just needed her.

I shoved the thought away and closed my eyes. I needed to sleep. Tomorrow we would leave. I had to get her and Tate home safe. That was my only goal. I would make sure they could survive on their own then I would leave. Walk away from Cat for good. I would go to Ryder's and say goodbye to Maddie, Brody, and Gavin then set out on my own. I had always been a loner and that's what I would be again. It was for the best.

~~~~

For the first time in a long time, I slept deeply. At least for a little while.

My eyes opened slowly. Something woke me. A noise. A thud. Something wasn't right.

I didn't move. I hardly breathed. It was still dark. Cat was curled next to me. Soft snoring came from the living room. The patter of soft rain hit the window.

I listened again. *There. The sound.* A thump outside. Manmade, not natural.
~~~~

I eased away from Cat, careful not to wake her. She stirred and turned on her back but didn't open her eyes. I moved the covers off and climbed to my feet.

Grabbing my boots, I quickly slipped them on. The room was cold. I could see my own damn breath in front of my face. I thought about Cat but getting her warmed up would have to wait.

We had trouble and we weren't alone.

I grabbed my gun holster and was buckling it around my hips when I heard Cat move.

"What's going on?"

I looked over at her. She was yawning and sitting up. Her hair was tousled and red splotches still dotted her throat and jaw from my whiskered stubble rubbing against her. She had that drowsy look in her eyes that erased all her defenses and left her vulnerable. I wanted to grab her and kiss her until she couldn't breathe but first I had to protect her.

"Stay here," I ordered in a stern voice, leaving no room for argument.

She pushed her chopped-off curls out of her face. "Like hell," she muttered, throwing the blankets off.

I ground my molars and fought the urge to grab her and shake the living shit out of her for not doing what I said. But this was Cat and she was the most stubborn, bullheaded woman I had ever met. I gave her a dark look.

"I have a belt and there's a bed. I will tie you to it if I have to. Don't try me, Cat." Maybe that would scare her enough to do what I said. Her life might depend on it.

Typical Cat, she wasn't fazed. "Listen to me, cowboy. Just because we slept together doesn't mean…"

There it was again. The sound. A heavy footstep, maybe on the porch.

Cat froze, kneeling in the middle of the makeshift bed. I put my finger to my lips and eased my pistol out of my holster. With a finger near the trigger, I eased across the room. I could hear them. Men talking low tones outside the cabin.

"Oh god," Cat whispered behind me.

I swung around to tell her to get back on the floor but it was too late.

The bullet hit the window. It exploded into a million pieces, peppering me with glass. I threw myself on Cat and took her to the floor just as bullets whizzed past our heads.

She let out a muffled scream from under me, her body going rigid with terror. I was crushing her with my weight but there was no helping it. We were under fire and I damn sure wasn't going to let a bullet hit her.

I would die first.

I covered her head when more shots sprayed above us. Cat screamed and grasped my shirt, burying her face in my chest. The bullets struck the walls and shattered a picture, destroying the room.

When they died down, I heard a crash and shouts from the other room. *Tate and David! Shit!*

I climbed off Cat and grabbed her wrist. "They're reloading! Come on!"

She scrambled to her feet. We kept low to the ground, running for the doorway over broken glass and splinters of wood. She was barefoot but it couldn't be helped. There were worse things than getting shards of glass in your feet.

Like getting shot instead.

More shots pinged the bedroom walls. I put an arm around Cat and shoved the blanket in the doorway out of the way. We ran out. I held onto Cat's wrist with everything I had. No way in hell would I let her go.

The rest of the cabin was a scene from hell. Glass was everywhere and bullet holes the size of dimes dotted the walls. The smell of rain mixed with the scent of gunpowder. A slug hit the sofa, sending puffs of white stuffing flying.

David was plastered beside a broken window, grasping a shotgun. He eased forward to glance outside and a shot rang out in response. He darted back just in time, the bullet barely missing his head. He glanced over at Cat and me as we darted across the room. I had come to know the old man well. I could read his expression like he was my own father.

We were fucked.

Adam was still tied up where we had left him. His hands were secured behind his back and tied off around the base of an old, heavy chair. He had a calm expression on his face that bothered the hell out of me, but when he glanced at Cat, I saw it.

Concern.

I didn't have time to feel jealous or tell him that she belonged to me. I pulled Cat over to the corner of the room where a broken-down recliner sat at an angle. Letting go of her, I shoved the chair out of the way then grabbed her arm again.

"Stay down," I ordered, pushing her into the corner.

"What? No!" She grabbed my shirtsleeve when I started to push the recliner back in place but I unhooked her fingers from me.

"Do what I say! Stay down!" I snapped, pushing her back into the corner.

She gave me a panicky look but I didn't have the time to reassure her. I moved the recliner in front of her, trapping her in the corner. It wasn't much protection against a bullet but it would have to do. I just needed her to trust me.

With her as safe as I could get her, I started across the room. *Time to take care of these assholes.*

I pulled back the hammer on my gun.

"Untie me. I can help you," Adam said as I passed him.

I ignored him and kept going. I already had men shooting at us from the front. I didn't need one shooting me in the back.

"How many are there?" I asked David as I flattened myself on the other side of the window opposite him.

He looked over at me. "Ten if I had to guess."

Shit.

I peeked out the broken window, careful not to expose too much of myself for someone to use as target practice. The curtain whipped in the wind. The moon was bright. I could see the woodpile and the path to the outhouse and barn. Suddenly, the shape of a man darted across the yard.

I jerked my gun up and fired off a shot. There was a yelp and I saw the man stumble. I didn't wait to see if he went down. I swung back around and flattened myself against the wall again as a hail of bullets hit the cabin walls.

Adam ducked and Cat disappeared behind the recliner, covering her ears and squealing. I swung back around and returned fire, smoke rising from the barrel. David did the same, his shotgun sounding like a cannon going off in the tiny cabin.

We plastered ourselves back to the wall again when they returned fire. I looked over at David. He was struggling to get a shell out of his jacket pocket, his hand shaking bad.

"You okay?" I asked, glancing over him for a wound.

"Yeah." He dug deeper into his pocket. "Just shaky. Can you blame me?"

I ignored his question and glanced around. "Where's Tate?"

He waited until he had grasped the shell between two knotty fingers before answering. "He was on watch."

Fear crawled up me like little ants. The kid was like a brother. If he wasn't in the cabin that only left one place. Outside.

I flipped the cylinder open on my pistol and spun it. One more shot left. I needed more firepower.

I was about to go on a rescue mission.

Chapter Twenty-Six

-Cash-

"Cash, where's Tate? Oh god, where's Tate?"

I glanced at Cat over the spray of bullets. She was looking over the edge of the recliner, right where I had left her to keep her safe. Her eyes were wide with fear and panic. She was fine but she wouldn't be when she found out Tate might be outside.

"Stay down!" I shouted, ignoring her question. Crouching low, I rushed toward the middle of the room. I slid to a stop at the edge of the rug near Adam's feet. He looked at me with wild eyes.

"Hey, man. Untie me. I can help you, I swear."

"Sure, you will," I muttered, tossing the rug back and exposing the hidden compartment in the floor.

Adam let out a string of curses as more bullets peppered the cabin. The man was one of them. He could stay tied up for all I cared.

I opened the trap door and reached inside. The duffle bag of guns and ammunition was still inside. I hoisted it out and dumped it on the floor. An idea hit me.

I looked up at Cat. "Come here."

Her eyes went round but she let go of the ratty chair and squeezed past it. Staying low, she dashed across the room.

I grabbed her hand when she got to me and pulled her to the edge of the hole in the floor.

"Get in."

She shook her head and pulled back, resisting. "No. No. I can't…I can't."

I grabbed her under the elbow and hauled her closer again. "Yes, you can."

She was scared but there was no time. I could hear the men shouting outside. Something about surrounding the cabin and getting in.

I helped Cat down into the dank, cold hole. She was shaking. Goddamn, I had to stay cold. There was no room for concern. There was only room for deadly action. It was the only way to keep her safe.

I started to lower the door but a volley of shots rang out from behind the cabin. The small window in the kitchen exploded and bullets shattered the dishes sitting on the counter and a full plastic water jug. The container burst, spraying water everywhere. At the same time, a thud came from the bedroom. *Shit, someone's in the cabin!*

I jumped to my feet, grabbing a shotgun from the duffle bag. "David, take care of Cat!"

"Goddamn it! Untie me!" Adam yelled, struggling to get free.

I ignored him and checked to make sure the gun was loaded before I started to move away.

"No, Cash! No!" Cat protested, crawling out of the hole to grab me.

I avoided her hands and headed for the bedroom. More bullets sprayed the inside of the cabin. They were hitting us with everything they had so whoever was inside could get the jump on us.

Too bad. He had to go through me first.

I pumped the shotgun as I ran, hoping to God that Cat got back down in that hole and pulled the door closed behind her.

I was almost to the doorway when a man jumped out from behind the curtain. He was big and ugly with a revolver in his hand. He opened his mouth and roared when he saw me, charging like a bull.

I lifted my gun and fired. The shot hit him in the chest. He went down like a tree, his big body hitting the floor hard.

Peering down the gun barrel, I stepped over him and went into the bedroom. Glass crunched under my boots and moonlight spilled across the stripped bed but the room was empty. No one else was lurking around.

I turned to head back out and that's when I heard it. A shout from outside.

"CAT!"

Tate. Fuck.

"Send the girl out and he won't die," a deep voice shouted. Frankie.

That fuckin' sonofabitch!

I ran across the bedroom and rushed past the curtain. But I was too late. Too damn late.

"Tate!" Cat screamed, her bare feet smacking the hardwood floor as she crawled out of the hole and sprinted for the door.

I raced to intercept her, but the big man on the floor apparently wasn't dead. He came to, blood soaking his shirt. Seeing me, he scrambled forward on his belly and grabbed my ankle, stopping me.

I hit the ground hard, the shotgun went sliding across the floor. I flipped onto my back and kicked him in the head when he wrapped a hand around my calf and yanked me toward him. Bone crunched, blood squirted, and his eyes rolled to the back of his head. His face hit the floor with a smack.

With him out, I twisted around.

"Cat, stop!" I shouted, scrambling to get my gun.

But she didn't listen. She flung open the door and disappeared outside.

Goddammit!

I jumped to my feet and charged forward to follow. Gunfire erupted, blasting past my head. I threw myself to the floor again, narrowly missing a bullet to the brain.

"Untie me! Untie me! I can fuckin' save her!" Adam shouted, pulling at the rope around his wrists. "They trust me!"

Screw it.

Crouching, I jumped to my feet and ran to him.

"You better be telling me the truth or so help me God, I'll put a bullet in you myself," I swore, dropping down to my knees beside him. We ducked when a bullet zinged over our heads.

"I am. Trust me," he said in an impatient voice as I untied the rope around his wrists.

As soon as he was free, he dived for the duffle bag full of weapons. I wasn't going to wait. David was covering the window. I was going after Cat and Tate.

"Watch my back," I yelled at David, making a beeline for the door.

He gave a jerky nod and fired a few shots out the window.

I ran, staying low to the ground. In the doorway, I raised to my full height and brought the gun up to my shoulder. I had no fear. I only had Cat and her brother on my mind.

The porch was wet. The air still smelled of rain. I expected to feel the sting of a bullet as I stood in the doorway but suddenly they stopped. I was deadly calm as I headed down the porch steps but on the inside I was a mess. They had the one thing that I would kill for. That I would lay down my life for. That I would die to protect.

Cat.

I hit the wet ground with angry strides. If one person touched her, he would die by my hand.

My boots sunk into the soft earth. My eyes adjusted to the dark. The shadows took the shapes of men. There were fifteen of them fanned out in front of me.

And they had Cat and Tate.

Tate's hands were secured behind his back and two men stood on either side of him. One of them had a gun jammed under the kid's ribs.

He looked ruffed up and pissed but I couldn't see any bruises or blood on him.

Cat's hands were being held behind her back by a tall, skinny man. When I saw who it was, white-hot rage filled me. Paul. When he grinned at me and ran a hand up her arm, I saw red.

I swung my gun over, putting him in my sights, and headed straight across the clearing with quick, fearless strides. My cheek was against the gun, my eyes squinting down the barrel. I was outnumbered and outgunned but ice flowed through my veins. They would kill me if I pulled the trigger – *hell, they may kill me anyway* – but at least I would take him to hell with me.

I only had eyes for the man named Paul, but in my peripheral vision I saw an old man step forward, a large gun in his hand.

Frankie. The leader of this little shitfest.

I ignored him and focused on the man holding Cat. The motherfucker smiled and ran his hand around her neck, caressing her like a lover. Like he could break her with just a snap.

I scowled and tightened my finger on the trigger. His smile grew.

Staring smugly at me, he grabbed her chin and yanked her head up then leaned down and licked her ear.

Fuck!

"Let her go," I growled, stopping, my feet spread.

He smirked. His gaze moved behind me. I felt the skin on the back of my neck prickle. I knew without having to turn that someone was behind me.

Cat's eyes went wide. "Cash!" she screamed.

Before I could spin around, a blow hit me on the back of the head.

Pain exploded in my skull.

Then everything went dark.

Chapter Twenty-Seven

-Cash-

I woke up slowly. Consciousness returned. I became aware of the pain first. It radiated to every inch of my body and tunneled into my brain. Thinking was impossible and moving was out of the question. Just breathing caused sheer agony.

My hands were numb and tied behind my back. My arms hurt like hell. I moved my fingers, testing them. They were swollen, the circulation cut off. I tried moving my legs but my ankles were tied to the chair I sat on.

I slowly opened my eyes. Pain stabbed through my head like nails. I squeezed my eyes shut again and waited for it to ease. When it did, I peeled my eyes open. The first thing I saw was dark splotches of blood dripping from my nose onto my jeans.

I took a few deep breaths, testing my ribs. They hurt like someone had kicked me in the side. Wheezing sounds came from my chest and each breath hurt. If I had to guess, I had a few cracked ribs but if I could breathe, I could fight.

I glanced up. My vision was blurry. I was in an unfinished room of some kind. The floor was smooth, gray concrete. A pile of rope had been thrown in one corner. A single light bulb hung from a dirty wire above me and exposed rafters and pipes made up the ceiling. Wherever I was, it was an unfinished building but it had working electricity.

Shit. I was in Hilltop.

I fought the bad feeling in my gut and craned my neck to see behind me. There was nothing. Not even a window or another door. Just a wall that still had pipes left exposed.

I tested the rope on my wrists. It cut into me, rubbing my skin raw. I worked at it until it became slick with my blood. Until I felt the blood drop from my fingertips to the floor.

"Shit," I hissed. The rope was tied too tight.

Someone inserted a key into the metal door and jiggled it. I froze. *Fuck!* The door swung open and three men walked in.

The first was short with a mullet and mutton chops. He carried a deadly-looking weapon and reeked of cigarettes and body odor.

The second guy was huge. He had to stand at least six-foot-six and had arms thicker than a tree trunk. He wore a black hoodie and jeans that looked like he could fit two of the shorter man in them. His head was shaved to a smooth surface and his eyebrows were gone. Pale blue eyes that almost looked white fixated on me as he walked in and stood off to the side.

I narrowed my eyes. In his hand was my damn cowboy hat. *What the hell?*

It could wait. When I saw the third man who walked in the room, the anger I already felt turned into a dark, murderous rage.

Adam strolled in at a leisure pace. He carried a canteen and looked clean and well fed. He leaned back against the wall and crossed one ankle over the other.

"You son of a bitch," I spit, my lip curling.

He grinned. I wanted to kill him. He had said we could trust him. He lied. I didn't care much about me but what had he done with Cat?

"Where is she, asshole?" I snarled, wanting to get free so I could strangle him.

Adam opened his mouth to answer but Frankie walked in.

He entered the room like he was the goddamn king and everyone should bow down to him. His hair was combed back and his clothes were pristine but he looked like shit. His cheeks were hollow and the lower portion of his face was covered with a short, scraggly beard.

He strolled toward me, his bushy, gray eyebrows drawn together with irritation. "Good. You're awake."

I glared up at him, ignoring the blood dripping down my face. "Where's my friends and the girl?"

He didn't answer. Instead, he made a slow circle around me, taking his time. I stayed still, keeping my gaze locked ahead and letting him size me up. When I got untied, I would show him just what I was capable of. Until then, I could feel the rage churning in me, waiting to be unleashed.

He drew to a stop in front of me and started rolling up his sleeves. His henchmen stood on either side, almost licking their lips with anticipation to get to me.

Adam was still leaning up against the wall like the cool kid in a cheesy teen movie. He would be next on my list. I couldn't wait.

I centered my hate on Frankie for now. He finished rolling up one sleeve and started on the other. A cold warning slithered down my spine.

"Where is she?" I repeated, wanting to rip him apart.

He smiled. "That girl ain't any of your business anymore."

"She will always be my business. If you touched her–"

He chuckled and shook his head with amusement. "*If* I touched her? You mean when."

"I'll kill you," I roared, taking the chair with me as I ran toward him.

Smack! His fist shot out. Knuckles connected with my cheekbone. The chair slammed back to its feet. My head snapped to the side and the pain already in my head tripled.

I took a second, welcoming the pain. Letting it feed the vicious need coursing through me. It meant I was still alive. Still feeling something.

I had crossed a line long ago, doing things that would have made my dad cringe. But I was going to add to that list when I got my hands on the man in front of me.

Forcing the pain away, I turned my head back around. Blood streamed from my nose. My face throbbed.

I raised my gaze to Frankie. "That all you got?"

He swung again. This time, the punch hit me in the solar plexus.

I grunted and doubled over as much as I could with my hands tied behind my back. Black spots appeared in my vision. Oxygen was forced out of my lungs. If I thought my ribs were cracked before, I was now sure of it.

I tried drawing in shallow breaths of air. It hurt a helluva lot. Peeling my eyes open, I blinked a few times until the room stopped spinning.

Frankie was studying me, his mouth in a hard line. "You done being a smartass, boy?"

I grinned. "Nope."

His fist shot out again, striking me in my right eye. I felt my skin bust and the vision in the eye go completely blurry. Before I could recover, his knuckles connected with my jaw. The force sent the chair toppling sideways with me in it.

I hit the cement floor with a crack. Blood poured from my face and nose. I was wheezing badly. My eyes were swelling quickly. I forced them open and looked up.

Adam pushed off the wall and stared down at me, frowning. He had a certain look in his eyes that I should recognize but my brain was too muddled to figure it out.

I looked at Frankie instead. He was standing in the same place and breathing heavily. Thick strands of his hair had fallen over his forehead and the deep lines in his face were more pronounced. He pushed his hair back and held out his hand. The mullet man shot forward and laid a handkerchief in his palm.

Frankie wiped the blood from his knuckles. "String him up," he said calmly.

The big giant of a man shoved my hat on his head and went over to the rope on the floor. He grabbed it and walked back to me.

"Nice hat," I murmured, my eyes drifting open and closed.

The man didn't crack a smile. "Got it from a dead man," he said in a deep voice, throwing the rope toward the ceiling.

I let out a chuckle but it turned into a bloody cough.

The rope caught on an exposed pipe. The big man tied a knot than tugged on it, testing its strength.

I watched him, forcing myself to stay conscious. He withdrew a knife from his belt and cut the rope around my wrists and ankles then kicked the chair away.

The blood returned to my fingers and feet, sending a shooting pain into them. Here was my chance to fight and make a run for it, find Cat and Tate and get the hell out of here. But I couldn't get my body to cooperate and move. Frankie had beat me too badly.

The big man grabbed the rope hanging from the ceiling and started tying my wrists back together with it. The rough material burned and dug painfully into the cuts on my wrists. I struggled not to scream as agony shot up my arms. But it was about to get worse.

He tied the rope tight on my wrists. I winced but that hurt too. He started pulling on the rope, dragging me up until I was hanging by my hands from the ceiling.

Fuck! Fuck! Unspeakable pain moved through me. My arms felt like they were being pulled out of their sockets. Agony tore through my lungs. My wrists felt like they were being sawed in half. Blackness hovered. I felt consciousness slipping away.

They were going to beat the living shit out of me, maybe kill me.

"Wake him up," Frankie said.

Through the haze of pain, I heard someone walk toward me. I forced my eyes open and saw a pair of dusty, brown boots. They stopped in front of me. Ice cold water splashed down over my head.

I jerked my head up, spewing blood and water out of my mouth.

Adam stood in front of me. "Wake up. You need to hear this."

I glared at him between my swollen eyelids, swearing to god I would make him pay.

"Frankie," he said in a louder tone. "Can I get a piece of him for tying me up like a dog?"

"Go ahead," Frankie answered.

Adam scowled at the big guy beside me. "Move."

The man took a reluctant step back but didn't look happy about it. I had a feeling there was some animosity there. Good. Maybe they would off each other. One less job for me.

As soon as the big man was out of the way, Adam buried his fist into my stomach with a hard punch.

I hissed and my arms jerked as I swayed by my wrists. Blackness played at the corners of my mind.

Adam grabbed a fist of my shirt and yanked me back.

"She's safe but you're screwed," he whispered a second before he punched me in the stomach again.

I coughed with pain and saw stars. He let go of me and stepped back, letting me swing by the rope.

I was hanging there, my head on my chest, Adam's words rattling inside my head. I was screwed? Really? What gave him that idea? I wanted to laugh at the absurdity but shit, I hurt too damn much.

"You still with us, boy?"

I forced my head up. Frankie's face wavered in front of me. Water dripped off my head.

"Fuck you," I muttered.

Frankie chuckled and turned to glance at mullet man and Adam. "Can you believe this guy?"

Mullet rolled his shoulders and Adam wiped a hand over his mouth, looking like he wanted to say something.

Whatever it was, he missed his chance. Frankie strolled to me and yanked my head back. I heard the telltale sound of a knife being unsheathed a second before the sharp edge of a blade was thrust under my chin.

I didn't flinch. I was in too much pain. I just stared at him, daring him to do it. I wasn't afraid of dying. I was only afraid of never seeing Cat again.

He pressed the blade harder, pricking my skin. "You made an epic mistake crossing me, boy."

"Oh, yeah? How is that?" I wheezed, my eyes drifting closed as pain traveled through me.

Frankie jerked my head up, forcing my eyes open.

"My son was twenty-four years old and a helluva good soldier then you set foot in this town. The day you decided to open fire on my men, he was shot. For two days, he lay writhing in pain, screaming for his dead mama and bleeding out. He died. My only child." He jerked my head back more until I thought my neck would break. "*My* blood."

Spittle hit me from his pulled back lips. I winced as his fingers tightened in my hair.

"Sorry," I murmured with as much sarcasm as I could muster. "My bad."

With an angry roar, Frankie pressed the knife harder. I felt a drop of blood roll down my neck. I thought that was the end of me but he suddenly let me go with a disgusted shove and removed the knife from my chin.

He started pacing back and forth in front of me, trying to get himself under control. When he stopped, the grieving father was gone. The leader of Hilltop and its militia was back.

"I don't know if it was your bullet or that boy's—" he began.

"It was mine," I interrupted through gritted teeth, wanting Tate left out of it. I didn't know whose bullet had taken the man's son but I would take the blame if it would save Tate's life.

"That's what I thought." Frankie sheathed the knife then looked at me with superiority. "Here in Hilltop, we have rules. One of them is an eye for an eye. A life for a life."

I stared at him through my one good eye, waiting for the words I knew were coming.

"In two days, you will die for taking my son's life. You will hang. Until then, you will suffer like he did." Frankie glanced at the big man beside me. "Reed."

The giant stepped in front of me.

The last thing I remembered was a fist flying at me.

Chapter Twenty-Eight

-Cat-

I paced back and forth in the middle of the room.

"Breathe, Cat. Breathe. It'll be okay. It has to be."

I had been telling myself the same thing for hours, trying not to panic.

They had Cash.

I hadn't seen Tate or David in hours.

Paul was nearby.

And I was alone.

Adam had dumped me in Hilltop's hotel. To say I was scared was an understatement. I was terrified.

I wrapped my arms around my middle and hugged myself tight. I had no idea what was going on. I was back in the same bedroom Cash and I had shared when we were in town. In the same room where I had told him I loved him for the first time.

Morning light streaked across the floor, touching my bare toes as I walked back and forth. My eyelids felt like sandpaper. I hadn't slept since being woken up by Cash crawling out of our makeshift bed on the floor in the cabin. That had been hours ago.

Tears clogged my throat. I could still smell him on my clothes. *Oh God, where was he?*

I stared at the closed bedroom door. Adam had locked it behind him as he left. I had screamed and pounded on the thick wood until my voice grew hoarse and my hand went numb. Giving up, I had started pacing, my fear growing.

Tate and Cash were all I cared about and all I had left in this fucked up world. If something happened to them, I wouldn't know how to go on.

"Please God, let them be okay," I whispered, studying my toes. They were caked with dried mud. So were my jeans and strands of my hair. For the millionth time, I replayed in my mind the moment it happened.

When Cash fell to the ground and my world came crashing down.

~~~~

"Let me go! Let me go!" I screamed as Cash crumbled to the ground.

I struggled to get away from Paul but he chuckled and ran his fingers down the front of my jacket and across my collarbone.

"That's it, little bird. Struggle. You know I like it."

I tried jerking away from him but he had a tight hold on me. I wanted to fight and scream but hysteria bubbled up in me.

Cash was lying in the wet grass, unconscious. I didn't know if he was alive or dead.

Oh, God, I'm going to be sick.

I bent over at the waist and vomited. Paul yelped and let go of me. I fell down to my knees in the grass, heaving.

Tate shouted at me to run and started fighting to get free from the men holding him but I couldn't move. I was too sick and scared. Too frozen with fear.

David had his eyes tightly shut and was praying as his hands were being tied behind his back. Men were everywhere. Pulling weapons out of the cabin. Hauling
~~~~

out our meager supplies. Flinging the tarp off David's old truck.

I couldn't take my eyes off Cash. A big, militia soldier strolled out of the cabin wearing his cowboy hat. He walked over to Cash and nudged his limp body with the toe of his boot. When Cash didn't move, the man pulled back his foot and kicked him in the ribs.

"Nooo!" I screamed, scrambling to my feet. Paul grabbed me and yanked me back. I twisted and kicked to get away as the soldier kicked Cash again and again.

Paul ran his hand down my face, smearing the tears that rolled down my cheeks.

"Don't be sad. I'll take care of you," he said, nudging his nose into my hair.

I screeched and twisted in his arms. With as much power as I could, I drove my hand into his windpipe just like Cash showed me.

He gasped and grabbed at his neck, letting go. I spun around and took off sprinting. I had to get to Cash!

Glass from the broken windows slashed the bottoms of my feet. I slipped in the wet grass but managed to stay upright and run.

My hair flew behind me. I heard a shout but I only had feet to go.

The man kicking Cash looked up at me. Seeing I was no threat, he pulled back his heavy boot and kicked Cash again.

"Stop!" I screamed, running.

He looked up at me and grinned a second before someone tackled me to the ground.

The side of my face hit the wet earth. Pain exploded from the bullet wound in my side. I squeezed my eyes shut and gasped. Mud soaked my clothes and oozed between my fingers. I reached out to grasp a handful of grass and pull myself up but someone grabbed me by the back of my shirt and pulled up.

"Guess I need to clip your wings," Paul said, gathering my hands in front of me.

Weakness and pain made the blood rush from my head. *This was it*, I thought, my body going limp. *The end.*

But a sound woke me up. A grunt.

I forced my eyes open. Cash was looking at me.

Then the man kicked him again.

"No!" I cried out, trying to get away from Paul. *I need him! I need him!* I was Cash's and he was mine. I twisted and turned, fighting and struggling.

Frankie stepped in front of me, blocking my view of Cash. "Settle down, girl," he grumbled in an aggravated voice.

I drew back my head and spit in Frankie's face. He froze, saliva rolling down his leathery cheek.

His eyes went dark. His expression hardened. I wasn't just looking at a man anymore. I was looking at the devil.

His hand snapped out and grabbed my throat. I gasped but a second later I was struggling to breathe. He tightened his fingers on my neck, choking me. My toes scrambled at the ground as he lifted me up by his grasp. Blackness swam at the edges of my vision as my airway was cut off.

I heard Tate shout to let me go. David pleaded in his deep voice for heavenly intervention. But it was Adam who saved me.

"Let her go, Frankie. You can deal with her later. For now, we need to leave."

Frankie frowned. I didn't think he was going to listen to Adam but then his fingers relaxed on my throat. He set me back on my feet and let me go. I took big gulps of air, sucking in as much oxygen as I could get.

He peered over my shoulder at Paul. "Tie her up so she doesn't get loose again."

Paul stepped in front of me as Frankie walked away. He pulled a piece of leather from his back pocket and started wrapping it around my wrists.

"I hate to see my little bird hurt by someone else. I'm going to be the only one that touches you like that from now on."

I stared at Cash, tears blurring my vision, my hope disappearing. He was still unconscious. Frankie and the big man stood over him, talking. Around me, men were busy loading stuff in David's truck and pouring something on the porch of the cabin.

They're going to set fire to the cabin, I thought in a daze.

"Sis? Sis, you okay?" Tate asked as a man shoved him past me.

"Tate?" I felt dizzy and ill.

He stumbled and looked back at me as the man pushed him on. "He's not dead, Cat. He's not. You got to keep believing that."

I glanced at Cash but Paul spun me around. "Let's go, little bird."

He pushed me to follow the men heading into the woods. I tried looking back, to see where they were taking Tate and David and what they were doing with Cash, but Paul blocked my view.

At the edge of the clearing, I heard a whoosh and felt heat at my back. I glanced over my shoulder and saw the flames. They licked at the sides of the cabin and engulfed the roof. In minutes, it would be gone.

Paul pushed me into the woods. All I could see was right in front of me. All I could hear was Paul's hot breath behind me.

I was about to die.

The woods would be my graveyard. I wouldn't have a headstone or a final resting place. I would just have leaves as my coffin and wild, hungry animals as my companions. I would never see Tate or Cash again. I wouldn't feel worried or scared or hungry. I would feel nothing. At one time, that's what I wanted. But not anymore.

Paul hummed a song as he led me through the woods. Cold seeped through my clothes. I shivered uncontrollably. My teeth chattered loudly.

"I'll take her," a deep voice said somewhere beside me.

I jerked my head to the side as Paul drew me to a stop. I heard a match strike and flare to life. Adam was a few feet from me, looking ominous and deadly in the dark.

"Keep your hands to yourself. She's mine," Paul grumbled, tugging me a safe distance away even though Adam made no attempt to grab me.

He stared at Paul. "Finders keepers."

Paul snorted. "What are you? Twelve?"

The match went out and I heard the click of a gun being cocked a second before it appeared aimed between Paul's eyebrows.

"No, but I'm old enough to know my manners. Let her go. I'm not finished with her yet."

Paul's Adam's Apple danced up and down in his throat but he didn't move out of the way of the gun.

"Her and me got unfinished business. Stay out of it, killjoy. You had your chance."

Adam cocked his head to the side. "She's my finders fee. You don't like it, take it up with Frankie."

Paul opened his mouth to argue but Adam raised one of his eyebrows in question.

Paul let go of me and held both of his hands up.

"Fine. But you just made yourself an enemy. She's mine and I'm gonna have her, one way or another. I can guarantee it." He glanced at me then backed away, disappearing a minute later.

As soon as he was gone, Adam hooked a finger in the leather band around my wrists. "Come on."

I jogged to keep up with him as he pulled me around trees.

"Where…where are they taking Tate and David?" I asked, stumbling to keep up.

He didn't answer so I tried again. "Is Cash okay?"

Again, nothing. I grew angry and yanked back on my bound wrists he held, stopping him.

"You either tell me or you have to drag me."

Adam sighed and grabbed a fistful of my shirt, jerking me closer.

"Paul was taking you *away* from where everyone else is at, you realize that, don't you?" he asked, almost yanking me off my feet.

When I stuck up my chin and didn't say anything, he scowled. "You are such a little—"

"Paul says there's a problem. Is there?"

Frankie was in front of us, his arms crossed over his chest and a deadly knife hanging from his belt loop. Terror made me start to shake, remembering how he had almost strangled me.

Adam let go of me and faced Frankie. "There's no problem. Paul just doesn't understand the logistics of my job."

"And what would they be?"

I could feel the tension in Adam. He might work for Frankie but he didn't like being questioned.

He grabbed the leather around my wrists again. A warning to stay quiet.

"I do your bidding – no matter what it is – and I get paid nicely for it. Whatever I want." He shrugged. "I want her. She's my trophy. Paul seems to not understand that."

"Did you ask my permission?" Frankie ground out.

"No. But I got you what you wanted so I get her."

Frankie frowned, considering it. "Fine. Do what you want with her. But then hand her over to Paul. I don't want any discourse in my unit. Understood?"

Adam nodded. "Yes, sir."

Frankie turned to leave but then paused. "I have to ask. Why her? The girl's more trouble than she's worth. There are plenty of women in town—"

Adam interrupted in a cold voice. "I want to teach her a lesson. America won't become great again unless people know their place and pay for their crimes. You taught me that. She needs to pay."

Frankie smiled with pride. "That's why we're here. The lawless shall suffer and the righteous shall thrive. But be warned – Paul's obsessed with her. That's the only dang thing I've heard for days."

"Obsession can get you killed," Adam muttered, dragging me past Frankie.

"So can a possession," Frankie said as we walked away.

~~~~

The militia had left four running vehicles hidden in the woods. Seeing so many working trucks in one place made me stumble and almost fall as Adam and I approached the small clearing. It brought back memories of better times. Better days when I wasn't fighting for my life or struggling to survive.
~~~~

"Where's Cash?" I asked Adam for the hundredth time. "Is he alive?"

"Don't know." Adam pulled me over to the nearest truck, yanking on my wrists.

"I hate you right now," I muttered as he heaved me up onto the tailgate.

"I don't particularly like you very much either," he said, following me up into the bed of the truck.

I glowered at him. He sighed and put his hand on my shoulder, shoving me down.

I fell to my bottom on the cold, slick metal of the pickup. I had no coat, jacket, or shoes. I was going to freeze to death or get myself killed before the night was over. I was sure of it.

"Where's my brother and David?" I asked, glancing around at the men throwing weapons in the trucks and climbing in.

"They took them in David's truck and will meet us back in town," Adam said, stretching out his legs and nodding at a man climbing up in the truck bed.

I eyed the stranger carefully as he sat down across from us. Deep scars crisscrossed his face and his hands looked like weapons.

I eased further back against the truck.

"What's going to happen?" I asked Adam, tearing my gaze away from the man.

Adam kept his eyes on the soldier. "No talking."

I bristled, the man forgotten. "No talking? Tell me what they are going to do with Cash and tell me if he's still alive. Now or I'll scream my bloody head off and tell them everything!"

The man raised an eyebrow.

"Hell," Adam sighed, smiling at him. "Women."

I shrieked and flew at him, my claws unleashed despite my wrists being bound together. The next thing I knew, I was flat on my back, Adam was holding me down, and the truck was bouncing over rough terrain.

Leaning down, he put his mouth near my ear, causing our heads to bump together when the truck hit a deep hole in the ground.

"I'm this close to turning you back over to Paul," he whispered. "So shut up and be a good little captive, okay?"

"A good little captive?" I shrieked and kicked at him. He climbed off me and sat back, smirking and putting his arm on the edge of the truck.

I couldn't stand it any longer. I got to my knees and slugged him as hard as I could with my hands tied together as the truck bounced and flew around trees.

His head jerked to the side. I felt smug until he looked at me and I heard a click.

I turned my head slowly. The man sitting across from us had his gun cocked and pointed at me.

"You gonna shut her up or am I?"

Adam looked at me, his gaze blazing. I lowered myself back down and scooted into the corner.

We rode the rest of the way in silence. The wind whipped my hair into my face. The woods gave way to abandoned homes. I tried to look for Cash or Tate in the other vehicles around us but their headlights were too bright and we were going too fast.

I shivered and sank deeper into my little corner, wishing I could get out of the wind. It cut through my shirt, chilling me from the inside out.

I had resigned myself to freezing to death when the truck slammed to a stop.

We were at Hilltop.

I stared at the wall in front of me. It surrounded the community like a barricade. Hilltop wasn't a town. It was a prison.

A loud screeching sound came from the big, metal gate that kept the crazies in and the sane people out.

"Home sweet home," Adam muttered beside me as the gate slid open.

I swallowed hard and felt fear choke me as we drove into town. Nothing had changed. The grass was still cut neatly. The streets were still clean. The war hadn't touched Hilltop. They had power and food and anything else they could steal. Hunger didn't exist there and neither did diseases. It was a fortress where we thought we could find supplies. Instead, we had found trouble.

Our truck followed the others into the town square. Even though it was the middle of the night, people were gathered outside, waiting for us. They glared at me as we drove by. I was never one to cower but I felt like doing it then.

The truck rolled to a stop in front of the hotel. I looked up. The old water tower still sat on top, the words *Hilltop Hotel* proudly written in green paint.

"Let's go," Adam said, jumping out of the truck and reaching for me.

I ignored him and slid off the tailgate myself. The other man jumped out and headed elsewhere. Adam watched him leave with a raised eyebrow.

"You really know how to make friends around here," he said, grabbing the leather rope around my wrists.

I glared at his back as he started leading me into the hotel by the leather. "And you fit in perfectly with all these crazies."

He grumbled something under his breath and stepped up on the curb. I jerked back on my wrists, wanting to buy time before he dragged me inside. I needed to find Cash and my brother. Plus, where was David? The townspeople wouldn't be happy that one of their own had switched sides. If Adam got me inside, I may never see any of them again. I had to stall.

"I'm not going in there!" I said, taking a step back.

Adam sighed and turned, still holding onto the leather around my wrists. He started to say something but his gaze snapped to someone behind me.

"Bitch!"

I swung around. A woman was racing across the street toward me, fury on her face. It was one of those moments where you were so shocked, you didn't know how to react. I had never seen the woman before and had no idea why she would call me a bitch.

She raised her arm as she ran toward me. My mind screamed at me to run but my legs didn't get the message. A rock hit me in the hip.

"Ow!" I shouted, glaring at her.

But she snatched another rock from the ground.

Adam stepped in front of me and scowled at the crowd that had gathered. "Back off!" he roared.

I recoiled. In front of my eyes, he turned into something else. The killer David said he was.

He was big and wide and a wall of muscle. I backed away into the hotel entrance as he stood in front of me. He glared at the crowd one more time then looked over his shoulder at me and frowned.

"You're a pain in my ass."

I stuck my chin up. "And you're just an ass."

He rolled his eyes and turned. Grabbing my elbow, he hauled me into the hotel with angry strides.

"Why do they hate me?" I asked, glancing over my shoulder at the crowd.

Adam flung open the hotel door and glanced over his shoulder. "I think you should be asking yourself how you're going to live through this instead?"

Chapter Twenty-Nine

-Cat-

"You gotta eat."

"No, I don't," I mumbled, staring out the window, not seeing anything. It was morning and the inhabitants of Hilltop were out and about. As for me, I was still locked away in the hotel room. Still away from Cash, Tate, and David. It had been hours since Adam had pulled me inside. Hours since the woman threw the rock at me.

"You can't just waste away," Mary whined. "I won't allow it."

I didn't need to turn around to know that she was wringing her hands with worry and her double chins were shaking. Since being allowed in my room this morning by the muscle-head stationed outside my door, she had been teary-eyed and apologetic. Blaming herself for the mess we were in and the bullet that had hit me.

"You can at least take a shower. Ladies should be clean," she said in a motherly tone, buzzing around, straightening up the bed I hadn't slept in last night. Wiping her still wet eyes.

"I'm not a lady," I muttered, staring down at the sidewalk below and wishing she would just leave me alone. A little girl skipped beside her mother, both of them looking like it was just another day. Another world that hadn't collapsed. It was as if they didn't know that people were struggling to survive on the other side of the wall.

That was the eerie thing about Hilltop. The people were brainwashed. Oblivious to what was really happening outside their town. And I knew exactly who was responsible. Frankie.

I pulled my knees to my chest and curved further into the window-seat. I could still feel his fingers on my neck. Tightening. Constricting. Cutting off my air supply.

Reaching up, I touched my throat. My windpipe was tender. Even swallowing was painful. My voice was raspy, thanks to my screaming and Frankie's choking. It wasn't the lack of oxygen that had scared me. It was the bloodthirsty look in his eyes.

Mary stopped beside me and clicked her tongue. "You're a mess, sweetie. Those clothes need to be burned. I've laid out some new ones for you."

I glanced at the bed. A white shift dress lay on the faded quilt along with clean underthings. Soft ballet flats sat on the floor. They were almost duplicates of the ones I had been given to wear when I was there earlier. Before I was shot. Before Keely and Gavin had to flee without us.

I looked away from the dress. "I'm not changing."

Mary huffed, making her ample bosom move up and down. "You're a smart girl. Pretty." She leaned closer, dropping her voice. "You can use that to your advantage."

I jerked my head around to look at her. If she was suggesting…

"I'm with Cash."

Sadness crossed her face. "Oh, child."

There was something about the way she said it that made the bottom drop out of my stomach. I eased my legs off the windowsill.

"Where is he? What do you know?"

Mary wiped the sadness off her face and spun around. "Oh, Lord. I've been rattling on. I've got to go. I have beans soaking and there's wash to be done." She waddled toward the door, her voice shaky and nervous.

I jumped off the windowsill and rushed to follow her. "Mary, please. Is he okay? Is he here somewhere? Where's my brother and David? What do you know?"

She hurried to the door and opened it quickly before I could get to her. The guard stood right outside, staring at us with a frown. I ignored him and raised my voice.

"Mary! Tell me! Is Cash still alive?"

Her shoulders fell. When she turned to look at me, the pity on her face hit me square in the chest.

"Oh god," I whispered, staggering to a stop in the middle of the room.

She looked at me with sympathy. "I'm sorry."

Tears welled up in my eyes. I didn't hear the door click behind her as she left or the low murmur of voices as she talked to the guard.

All I heard was my heart shattering.

~~~~

I buried my face in my knees and squeezed my eyes shut. Tears soaked my jeans. My throat was so tight, I could barely breathe. I was sitting on the floor, my back against the door. The silence was killing me. The not-knowing was eating away at my soul. I wasn't sure how much more I could take. Luke. Jenna. Nathan. My dad. I had lost them all. But I couldn't take losing Cash or Tate. That might just be the end of me for good.

I pushed back my grimy hair and swiped at a tear. My eyes were swollen from crying and my hands were shaky from worry but I had to be strong. *Cash is still alive and Tate is okay.* I told myself that again and again until I thought I might go crazy.
~~~~

"They are okay," I whispered to the empty room for the hundredth time. "They have to be."

I hadn't seen Mary or anyone else since morning. It was early evening and the room was dark. My stomach growled. I was tired but I refused to close my eyes, not even for a minute.

I was staring at my bloody toes, cut by the shards of glass on the cabin floor, when the sound of footsteps and voices came from the hallway. Was it Frankie, coming to deal with me? Or was it Paul, wanting to finish what he started?

Turning, I laid my ear against the door. It was hard to hear over my pounding heart but I could make out the sound of two men talking. I listened but couldn't understand what they were saying. The words were too mumbled, the door too thick. I could hear the authority in one of the voices and the subordinate tone in the other.

Only one man walked around here with authority. Frankie.

Kneeling on my hands and feet, I scrambled away and stared at the door. He would kill me but I wouldn't go down without a fight. I would scream and kick and scratch his eyes out.

The footsteps drew to a stop in front of the door. I looked down and saw two shadows. The lock jiggled. I crawled back like a wounded animal. My hair hung in my eyes and dried mud covered me.

The door swung open and a large man walked in.

Adam.

"God, you look like a wild animal," he said with disgust, stopping right inside the room and looking down at me.

"Ugggh!" I jumped up and flew at him. "Where are they? Where the hell are they?" I cried, hitting him on the chest with my fists. "Tell me nooooow! Where. Are. They?"

He grabbed my wrists and yanked me off him. "Calm down," he hissed through tight lips. "You want to get yourself and Tate killed?"

I froze at the mention of my brother. Adam raised an eyebrow and let go of my wrists. Before I could ask where he was, there was the sound of a struggle. Tate appeared in the doorway, led by a man in camos and combat boots.

"Let me go, bitchass!" he swore, jerking his arm away from the man and glaring up at him.

"Tate?" I whispered, so scared and weak that I thought I was seeing things.

Tate froze, the man forgotten. "Sis?" he asked, his voice breaking.

In seconds, I had my arms around his skinny body and was hugging him so tight, I thought I would crack his ribs.

He still smelled like dirt and smoke from the cabin's fire. He needed a haircut badly and a change of clothes desperately. His flannel shirt had more holes than buttons and his jeans were brown with dirt instead of denim blue. Despite it all, I had never been so relieved to see him and didn't want to let him go.

After a minute, he wiggled away. There was a small cut across his right cheekbone and his bottom lip was swollen and purple. A dark blue bruise had formed under one eye.

"What did they do to you? You're hurt!" I grabbed his arms and looked him up and down. "Did they hit you anywhere else? Are you okay? What happened?"

Tate brushed off my hands. "They tried to hurt me, sis, but I fought them. Asshole sons of bitches," he scowled, looking back over his shoulder at Adam.

Adam smirked and crossed his arms over his chest. I ignored him and glanced over my brother again, looking for injuries. With his long hair hanging in his eyes and smudges of dirt on his face, he looked wild. Untamed.

He glanced over me too – always the protector – and frowned.

"What?" I asked. He looked pissed. I knew I looked bad with my dirty clothes and matted hair but…

He reached out and pushed my shirt collar out of the way. "That man left bruises when he tried to strangle you. I tried…" He gulped. "I tried to get to you."

I brushed his hand away. "I'm okay. It's just a couple of marks. Where's David?"

"They locked him up down the hallway. He's fine. A little pissed for a reverend, but fine. Do you know where Cash is? They beat him pretty bad, sis."

I swallowed past the bile raising in my throat. "I don't know. I haven't seen him." I gave Adam a nasty look. "And Adam won't tell me."

Adam smirked but shouts came from outside.

He uncrossed his arms from over his chest and started across the room.

"What's going on?" Tate asked.

Adam went to the window and pulled the curtain to the side.

"I don't know," he said glancing down on the street in front of the hotel.

I saw the gun sticking out of the back of his jeans and wondered if I could grab it. Get out of the hotel and find Cash.

I was thinking of different scenarios and my chances of fighting with only one gun when Adam dropped the curtain back in place and walked over to where Tate and I stood.

"You want to see Cash?" he asked, staring down at me.

"Yes! So he's okay? He's alive? Let's go now!" I turned around to leave, desperate to see him, but Adam grabbed my arm.

"It's not going to be that easy. You'll have to do what I say and play along."

I nodded. "Okay, I will."

Adam studied me a second then pushed past me to go to the door. He stopped when the handle rattled.

"Shit," he swore under his breath. He looked back at Tate. "Kid, keep quiet and keep your cool. No sudden moves."

The door opened and Frankie walked in. Behind him was Paul and the big, skin-head that had kicked Cash again and again in front of the cabin.

Frankie's eyes – so hard and cold – landed on us from beneath his tightly-drawn brows.

I shrunk back, happy Adam was taller than Tate and me both. Paul gave me the chills but there was something about Frankie that was just plain evil. He had the look of a man who had no qualms about taking a life or destroying a future. A man that seemed to be looking to prove he had power.

"Adam," he said in way of a greeting, not surprised at all to see his number one soldier in the room with us.

"Frankie." Adam gave a short nod but didn't move.

Frankie glanced past him to me. "Cat, is it?"

"Meow," Paul said with a grin, giving me a wink.

Frankie's hand snapped up, quieting Paul. The shadows under his sunken cheekbones deepened as he frowned at me.

He had lost weight since the last time I had seen him and looked like he had lost sleep too. Dark circles surrounded his eyes and the lines in his forehead were more pronounced.

He rubbed a hand over his whiskered jaw and strolled over to the bed, leaving Paul and Skin-Head to guard the door.

"I'm feeding you," he said, glancing down at the untouched food left on the tray. "Clothing you. Providing a bed and shelter for you." He rubbed the dress between his thumb and finger. "I'm giving you hospitality that most people would kill for."

He let go of the dress and looked up at me. "I've been thinking about how you could repay me."

Chills broke out across my skin. His gaze moved up and down my body, not like a man who wanted me. Like a man assessing my potential.

Tate took a step forward but I put a hand on his arm, stopping him. No way would I let my little brother fight my battle. This was between me and Frankie.

"Let my friends go and I'll do anything you want," I said, meeting his eyes, suddenly calm and sure of what I was saying. "Just let them walk past those walls and I'm yours."

Adam stared at me like I was insane. I ignored him, never breaking eye contact with Frankie. Something told me he respected courage and I had tons of it if it meant Cash and my brother would go free.

The expression on Frankie's face didn't give anything away but he looked over me carefully. "Hmm," he said, glancing down my body, assessing what I offered.

I stood tall, letting him look his fill. I had used men for my own selfish reasons before. He could use me for Tate, David, and Cash's lives now.

"Men. This lady is the epitome of brave," he said in a boisterous tone, pointing at me as he walked back across the room. "Take note, gentlemen. You could learn something from her." He looked at me and smiled. "You got a deal, lady."

Paul grinned and made licking motions at me with his tongue. Adam eased his hand near his gun and Tate stepped in front of me.

At the door, Frankie stopped and looked over his shoulder at Adam.

"Clean her up and take her to him. I'm going to enjoy this goodbye."

Chapter Thirty

-Cat-

I smoothed down the dress. It hit me at the knees and hung on my body like a gown. The neckline was scooped and dipped below my collarbone. Tiny lace lined the edges, delicate against my body.

"You can do this, Cat," I whispered to my reflection in the rusted mirror above the sink.

For a long time, I believed what people said about me – I was spoiled and selfish. I didn't care about anyone and had a heart of ice. It helped me hide from reality but the blackout and war forced me to face the truth. I cared and was willing to die to protect those I loved.

At any costs.

That cost was about to come in the form of me turning myself over to Frankie. But first, Adam was taking me to see Cash. To say goodbye.

Taking a deep breath, I turned away from the mirror and slipped my feet into the ballet flats. "I can do this. I can do this. I can do this."

I opened the door. Adam was standing right outside.

He turned and looked me up and down. "Ready?"

I wasn't sure if I could trust him but he had saved me from Paul and Frankie. I nodded and stepped out of the bathroom. A single bulb lit up the hallway. Muted sounds came from outside. I followed Adam past the guard stationed at my room and down the hallway. My heart pounded harder and harder with each step. I could feel the guard staring holes into my back.

Adam stopped at a door halfway down the hallway marked number 3. He knocked once and waited, tense beside me.

The door flew open. Tate was standing there, his brown hair matted and dirty. He was lean and tall, on the verge of becoming a man but still a kid to me. I forgot about being nervous or scared. I would wear a ridiculous crown of daises and twirl around in circles for Frankie's entertainment if he and Cash walked free.

"You two ready?" Adam asked Tate, his voice sharp.

"Wait. What?" I stammered, looking from him to Tate with confusion. *Two?*

"Hello, kiddo."

I drew in a sharp breath. *David!*

I rushed past Adam and Tate into the room. The preacher was sitting on the bed. He climbed to his feet as I rushed toward him. His gray hair was sticking up all over and bruises marked his face.

"I'm so glad you're okay," I muttered, throwing my arms around him and pressing my cheek against his warm, flannel shirt.

He wrapped his arm around me. "I'm glad you're okay too."

I squeezed my eyes shut, feeling safe. When we first arrived at Hilltop, I thought David was the enemy. He had smiled and welcomed us with opened arms but it hadn't felt real. Just like with me, what others saw and believed wasn't the truth. He had saved us. I would've died if he hadn't dug the bullet out of me. I owed him my life and I was about to pay up.

"Sis, this is a bad idea," Tate said, standing a few feet away. "I'm not just going to let you turn yourself over to Frankie. No way in fuckin' hell. He'll kill you."

I let go of David and went over to my brother. Staring up into his eyes, I lied and told him what we both needed to hear.

"I'll be okay, Tate. Don't worry. Frankie will just keep me prisoner and maybe scare me a little bit. I'll get out after a few days and find you."

He shook his head, blinking against the sudden wetness in his eyes. "No, he'll kill you, Cat. I know he will."

I took a step closer and grabbed the front of his shirt. "Listen to me, Tate. Get Cash and get out of town. Find Keely and Gavin. *I'll* find you, I promise. Trust me."

He shook his head and backed away, swiping angrily at his eyes. "Fuck, Cat. You can't ask me to do this and you know Cash will never leave you."

"Cash won't have a say," Adam interjected from the shadows of the room.

I looked over at him. His face was set in stone. The gun in his belt gleamed in the moonlight.

"We need to go. All of us," he said, uncrossing his arms and striding toward me. "It's time." He grabbed my upper arm and dragged me toward the door.

"Stay close," I said to Tate over my shoulder. "And remember to go when it's time. Don't look back and don't fight. Just go. Promise me, Tate!"

He nodded and looked away, mumbling, "Yeah. Whatever."

I felt panic. He wasn't going to do it. I could hear the stubbornness in his voice.

Adam didn't give me time to argue.

"Do what I say and everyone will get through this in one piece," he muttered, grasping my upper arm tight and tugging me through the doorway like I was a prisoner.

I didn't resist. I had agreed to this and there was no going back.

Adam led us down the stairs. In the dining room, there were two guards. Each was cradling a gun in their arms and looked out of place against the faded rose wallpaper of the hotel. They stepped toward us when we appeared.

"Back off. I got this," Adam snapped, tugging me toward the door.

This was it. There was no going back. I would see Cash one more time, hug my brother goodbye, and let Frankie do his worst.

A cold wind wrapped around my legs as Adam pulled the door and pulled me outside. Townspeople lingered around. No trash littered the streets. No dead cars were parked at odd angles where they had died like in other towns. Hilltop was a utopia. Solar panels lay here and there, gathering power for the inhabitants. Near the corner of each building was a water barrel to collect rainwater from rooftops. Structures lay untouched, surviving the worst time in American history. But underneath the perfection was an unsettling feeling that something wasn't right.

Across the street, a group of men stood in the town square talking. The old street lamp above them was broken but there was still enough light to see. One of the men looked at me then nudged the guy next to him. One by one, they all turned to look at us as Adam led me across the street.

My hair whipped into my face and my dress flattened against my legs as the cold wind hit me. Adam tightened his hold on my arm and led me in the direction of the men. My heart rate increased. These people hated me. What was stopping one of them from putting a knife in my stomach? Killing me to avenge the men who had been shot that day on the street?

One of them spit on the ground and glared at me as we approached. Another man pushed his jacket back, exposing the gun attached to his side. They all looked at me with hate.

I looked away, almost tripping in my nervousness. All I had to do was stay alive long enough to turn myself over to Frankie then they could have a go at me. It didn't matter what they did as long as Cash, Tate, and David could get away.

I glanced over my shoulder at Tate, making sure he was staying close. He was and so was David but the two guards from the hotel were also following us. Tate looked edgy, glaring at the people on the street. I started to tell him to calm down but suddenly one of the men broke from the group and hurried toward us.

Adam leaned down and whispered in my ear, "Do what I say." I drew a sharp breath when the end of his gun poked into my rib.

"Hey," the man said, swaggering toward us with a cocky grin.

"Back off, Brewer," Adam said, pulling me around a small grassy area sectioned off from the rest of the town square by chicken wire. Dead stalks of corn and other brown, leafy plants sat wilted in the enclosure.

The man started walking beside us. "You taking them to the hanging tree too?"

I gaped at him. *Hanging tree? What was he talking about?*

The man grinned at me like I was about to be put on a skewer and served as dinner. Half his teeth were gone and deep pockets of pimples crisscrossed his face.

Adam ignored the man and pulled me across the town square. I stumbled and almost fell when I saw where he was taking me.

The courthouse.

"Cash is in here?"

It was a turn of the century building, made up of red bricks and green trim. A tattered American flag hung on a flagpole in front. It was a symbol of what our country was now – faded, worn, damaged and torn – but like its people, it was still hanging on and flying.

"Yeah," Adam answered. "Ironic isn't it?"

I had no idea what he was talking about but I didn't bother asking. I kept my eyes on the double doors as he led me up the stone steps. Above us, the flag whipped in the wind. Below us, our shoes made shuffling sounds on the steps. Tate was breathing heavily behind me. David coughed. The men in the town square talked in loud voices. I heard it all but my attention was focused on what lay in front of me.

The way that led to Cash.

Adam nudged me inside with the gun in my back. I faltered when I saw the men inside. There had to be twenty of them. They were lounging in recliners and playing cards on broken-down tables. Some were smoking handmade cigarettes and others were passing around bottles of liquor. They stopped what they were doing to look up as we walked in.

I realized it was the militia's headquarters. The heart of the organization. The smell of men and sweat was overwhelming. The scent of alcohol and piss worse. I swallowed against the need to vomit and moved carefully between men as Adam pushed me on. They stared at me with hostility, refusing to move.

A big man stepped in my path halfway across the room. His leather jacket was tight and his goatee was greasy. I stepped back into Adam as he stared down at me with cruelty.

"Royce," Adam said in greeting, pulling me to the side to go around the guy.

The old man stepped in front of us and crossed his massive arms over his chest. With a dark look, he stared down his nose at Adam.

"Pussy isn't allowed in here, killjoy."

A shiver went up my spine from the man's voice alone.

Adam cocked his head to the side in that annoying little way he had. "You're here, aren't you, Royce?"

The man growled. I swear he was part animal.

"I don't like you much, killjoy. Take your pussy and that traitor – David – and leave."

Adam's fingers tightened on my arm until I thought it would break.

"Get out of my way," he said between clenched teeth.

Royce considered it but still didn't budge.

Adam sighed and shook his head. Just when I thought he would give up, he swung the gun away from my spine and pointed at the man's forehead.

"Move."

I held my breath. Every man climbed to their feet and pulled out their guns. Royce didn't flinch, even with the gun in his face.

"Frankie know you brought them here?"

Adam scoffed. "Who do you think told me to? I'm sure not doing this for fun and I know this is a no pussy zone. This woman is a pain in my ass and so are these two." Adam jerked a thumb back at Tate and David. "But orders are orders and I follow them. Now move or Frankie can have your head instead of my balls."

Royce hesitated but then moved out of the way. Adam stuck the gun back in my spine and nudged me to go.

I moved past Royce, silently thanking Adam for not getting us killed. Tate and David stayed close behind us, watching the men for any sudden moves. They were white as a sheet. I couldn't blame them. I was shaking in my little flats.

Adam steered me toward a dark staircase near the back of the room. As we drew closer to it, I noticed the stairs only went down. *To the basement, maybe? Is that where Cash is being held?*

The thought of spiders and darkness made goosebumps break out on my arms. But I was about to find out that there were worse things than eight-legged bugs and shadowy, damp corners.

Chapter Thirty-One

-Cat-

My fingers slid over the cold handrail as we walked down the marble staircase.

"He's down here?" I whispered, trying to see into the darkness up ahead.

"Yes," was Adam's only answer but it was enough to send chills over me.

Cash was down in the ancient basement. Probably cold. Probably hungry. Probably fighting to get away. I could practically feel him nearby.

My heart beat faster as we went further down the stairs. Adam had let me go and removed the gun from my back. Free, I hurried as fast as I could, careful not to slip in the flats. They weren't made for running or getting away from bad men with guns. I wanted my old boots back but they were long gone, probably burnt to a crisp in the cabin.

I pushed the depressing thought away and hunched my shoulders forward, wishing Mary had provided me with a jacket. The air was colder the closer we got to the bottom and had a kind of dampness to it that made the chill go right through my dress.

My nose twitched at the smell of the ancient building. I hated that smell. It reminded me of my grandmother's home and of her plastic flowers and old photos of the prestigious Phillips family. She called me a disgrace to the family but where was the family now? Dead? Homeless? Hungry? None of that money or the big houses mattered now.

Our footsteps were loud in the stairway. I concentrated on that instead of the past and my uncertain future.

The bottom of the stairwell appeared. I started to hurry, flying over the marble steps. Just as I stepped off the last step and saw the rows of metal shelves in the basement, Adam grabbed my arm and spun me around.

"Listen to me. There's something you need to know first."

I tried jerking my arm away. "Let me go! I want to see him!"

Adam let go of my arm and pushed me back against the wall with his arm across my chest.

"I don't think so, sweet pea."

I winced at the pain in my spine from the stair rail behind me, but pulled my lips back. "Don't call me that!"

Adam glared down at me, his usual playfulness gone. "I have a gun and I put my neck on the line for you. I'll call you anything I damn well please. Now, calm down and listen to me."

"Let go of my sister."

Tate appeared by Adam's side, David behind him.

Adam froze. "Where did you get that?"

With my back pressed up to the rail and Adam's arm across my chest, I couldn't move but I glanced at Tate. He held a kitchen knife at Adam's side.

"Ms. Mary thought I might be dealing with some tough meat soon and thought I would need it," he said, looking at Adam through the hair hanging in his eyes.

The corner of Adam's mouth lifted in a grin. "That was nice of her. I hope you said thank you."

"I did," Tate said, still keeping the knife against Adam. "Told her I couldn't wait to use it either. Knew just the right person I would share it with."

Adam grunted with amusement and eased his arm off me. He turned slowly to face my brother.

"You could hurt someone with that, kid. Put it away."

Tate didn't move. "I'm not a kid. I'll put it away when I'm good and….argh!"

Adam's arm swung out and struck Tate's wrist. He grabbed the knife and had it up against Tate's throat in seconds, fisting the handle and pushing my brother against the wall.

"Always go for the jugular. If you stab in the side, you might hit a rib. Your opponent will have a chance to kill you if you only wound him."

He whipped the knife away from Tate's throat and flipped it around, handing it back to my brother handle first.

"Other than that, you're fast, *kid*."

"Mmm…thanks," Tate said, taking the knife like it might bite.

Adam turned his attention back to me. "You need to listen to me very carefully, Cat. Things have happened. I need to know just how strong you can be."

I stuck my nose up and squared my shoulders. "I'm very strong. I survived a bullet, Paul, the EMP, this town, *you*. Why?"

"This might be worse than all those combined. I need to know that you can keep it together."

I swallowed hard. "Why? What's happened? Is Cash okay? Is he hurt?"

Pain twisted Adam's face.

"They're going to execute him tomorrow."

Chapter Thirty-Two

-Cat-

My vision faded. My heart stopped. "Oh god," I whispered, sucking in a breath of air. "I think I'm going to pass out."

"Oh no you don't," Adam muttered, grabbing my elbow and keeping me on my feet.

The stairway was spinning. All I could hear was the roaring in my ears. I didn't struggle when Adam hauled me away from the wall and started dragging me into the dark basement. My legs worked and my eyes were open but my mind was in a fog. I couldn't hear anything but the same words again and again. *They are going to execute him. They are going to execute him.*

Cash was going to die because he had been trying to protect me.

The world spun. I stumbled. Adam yanked me up and kept walking. Tate and David were behind us, talking in low, angry voices. Adam led me down an aisle then another. A small, still coherent part of me realized that the basement was a maze of metal shelves. I started to notice details, my mind's way of dealing with the pain.

A chill radiated from the concrete and swept under my dress.

Legal file boxes lined the shelves on either side of me. They were marked with dates. 1945. 1976. 1982. Evidence boxes? Closed cases? It didn't matter.

They were going to kill Cash.

Adam pulled me around a corner past the metal shelves and dusty cardboard boxes. I almost missed a step when I saw the newly constructed room in front of me.

It stuck out like a sore thumb in the ancient government building. Unfinished dry wall separated it from the rest of the dank, dark basement. A heavy metal door faced us and in front of it stood the big, bald man who had kicked Cash again and again in front of the cabin.

"Reed," Adam said in greeting, leading me straight to the man.

The man crossed his trunk-like arms over his massive chest and widened his stance. "What are you doing here, killjoy?"

Adam rolled his eyes and muttered, "I really hate that nickname."

Reed looked down his wide nose at us as we approached. "It fits. You didn't answer my question. What are you doing down here?"

Adam yanked me to a stop in front of the man, his fingers biting into my skin. "Frankie said you could take the night off and get ready for tomorrow. I'm here to relieve you."

Reed glanced at me with disgust then at Tate and David behind me. "And why are they here? They need some roughing up too?"

Adam's gaze turned hostile. "No. Frankie wanted a show. He should be here soon to enjoy it."

The man grunted and studied me. I stood still, letting him. If it got me into the room and to Cash, he could stare all he wanted.

Finally, he stepped away from the door. "He won't be a problem for you," he said, nodding at the room behind him.

"That's good to know," Adam muttered, hauling me past the man roughly.

I didn't have time to prepare myself for what was on the other side of the door. I thought I was strong but I was about to find out that I was very wrong.

~~~~

He was hanging by his hands. A rope was tied around a pipe exposed in the ceiling. His wrists were bloody and raw. His head was hanging down, his chin resting on his chest.

"Cash!" I screamed, pulling my arm from Adam and running into the room.

He grunted and opened his eyes as I wrapped my arms around his middle.

"Cat?" he whispered, staring down at me as if I wasn't real. His right eye was full of blood, the vessels broken in it. The left eye was swollen shut and surrounded by ugly black and blue bruises.

"It's me. It's me," I cried, trying to hold him up and take the weight off his tied wrists. Blood ran from them, soaking the sleeves of his shirt and coating the rope.

Tears fell down my cheeks unchecked. I heard Tate, Adam, and David rush into the room behind me.

"Cut him down! Cut him down!" I screamed, struggling to hold his solid weight up.

Adam whipped out his knife and slashed the rope above Cash's wrists. Cash grunted again and started to crumble on me but Tate and Adam caught him and lowered him to the floor.

I knelt down beside him, afraid to touch him, afraid to see how badly he was hurt.

"Cash. Cash." I took his face in my hands. He had been beaten. His face was black and blue. One cheekbone
~~~~

was puffy. His lips were cut. Dried blood was encrusted under his nose.

"Kid, right outside is a box labeled 1996," Adam said to Tate, kneeling on the other side of Cash. "Find it and bring it in here."

Tate jumped up and left at a run.

"What've you done, boy?" David asked Adam, lowering himself down to one knee by Cash's head.

Adam shrugged. "A few of my men are still on my side. They hid a backpack of supplies in the box for us."

I didn't care. I was too worried about Cash. He had lost consciousness when the rope was cut away. Who knew how long he had been tied up by his wrists, the blood cut off from his fingers.

"Let me look at him, honey," David said, giving me a reassuring glance.

I let Cash go and backed away enough to give David room. He started poking and prodding Cash, checking for injuries, feeling for broken bones. When David touched his ribs, Cash hissed and opened his eyes.

"How you doing, boy?" David asked, leaving his ribs to examine the deep cuts left by the rope in his wrists.

"I've been better," Cash muttered, barely moving his lips. They were cut and coated with dried blood.

David gave a weak smile and prodded Cash's side again. "They broken?" he asked, referring to his ribs.

Cash groaned. "At least a few of them."

Tate reappeared carrying a cardboard box. He set it on the floor inside the room and flung the lid off. Grabbing the backpack inside, he took it over to Adam. Adam ripped open the zipper and grabbed a water bottle from inside. Unscrewing the top, he put an arm under Cash's shoulders and lifted him up high enough to drink.

Cash drank greedily as soon as the bottle touched his lips. Water ran down his chin and onto the floor under him. God, had they not let him have any water? He was dying of thirst.

When he coughed and water sprayed from his mouth, Adam took the bottle away and David went back to examining him.

"Best thing is to leave your ribs alone. What about the rest of you?" David asked, carefully poking Cash's cheekbone. "Anything else broken?"

Cash winced and closed his eyes. "No."

"Good. How about your insides? Any pain? Tenderness?" David poked around on Cash's abdomen. Cash hissed when he hit a sore spot and stiffened.

I let out a little cry, thinking of terrible internal injuries he might have. Cash's eyes flew open at the sound. Stone gray irises looked at me.

"What are you doing here?" he muttered between cracked, bloody lips.

I grabbed his hand and scooted closer. "Where else would I be?"

His other hand was lying by my leg. I drew in a soft breath when his thumb lifted and stroked my knee. "Always so stubborn," he whispered, his eyes drifting closed.

A sob escaped me. To see him so…broken…broke me.

He forced his eyes open and licked his cut lip. "Take Tate and go, Cat. Now."

I shook my head, unable to see past my tears. "No. I'm not leaving you."

His thumb made another slow pass over my knee. "You have no choice, sweetheart. Go."

New tears bubbled up in my eyes and ran over my lashes. My chin quivered while my heart broke.

I leaned closer and squeezed his hand harder. "We always have a choice, cowboy, and I'm choosing you."

Slow clapping came from behind me. My blood went cold. Cash didn't move but his eyes went hard.

"What a touching scene. Exactly what I wanted to see," someone said behind me.

The hair raised on my arms at the sound of Frankie's voice. I let go of Cash's hand and glanced over my shoulder. Through strands of hair hanging in my eyes, I saw the leader standing inside the room. On either side of him was Paul and Reed, fanned out in front of the doorway. Behind them were four other men. We were outnumbered and surrounded. I felt rooted to the spot.

"Exactly what you wanted to see?" I spit at Frankie, avoiding looking at Paul. "You're sick, you know that? You're not a leader. You're a dictator. A murderer. A Hitler all over again and you deserve to die."

Frankie smiled and strolled into the room. "I'm sure you believe that, honey, but I'm not a Hitler. I'm just ridding the United States of men like him."

"And who's going to rid the world of people like you?" I hissed.

Frankie shrugged. "Not you or your friends."

I curved my shoulders inward, becoming as small as possible as he circled around Cash and me. I had seen what he was capable of. I still had the bruises on my neck to show it. I was terrified of him. My body was shaking. My hands were clammy.

He studied us a minute then stopped to check out what was in the backpack. "Adam has y'all set up pretty good. Liquor. A blanket. You can pay him back for that later, girl."

Cash tensed. Tate cursed under his breath. Any minute one of them was going to lose it and attack. I couldn't let that happen.

I averted my gaze from Cash and looked up at Frankie.

"We had a deal. I turn myself over and they go free. So let them go free." I raised my hands in surrender. "Take me now."

Cash struggled to push to his elbow. "What are you doing, Cat?"

I ignored him and kept my gaze on Frankie.

He chuckled. "Oh, I plan to take you, girl, but first we're going to have a little fun." He glanced at the big man at the door. "Reed."

I heard heavy footsteps a second before someone grabbed me under the arms and started dragging me back. I shrieked and kicked.

Tate pulled his knife and started forward, but Adam grabbed the knife and wrapped an arm around Tate's neck. "Calm down, kid."

"No! No!" He had the knife against Tate's jugular!

I dug my heels into the floor and tried to get free as Reed dragged me toward the door. The other men rushed into the room, two of them grabbing David and slamming him back against the wall when he would've helped me.

Paul grinned, watching me struggle. "Little bird is a fighter, isn't she, Reed?"

The big man grunted. I kicked and twisted. "Let me go!" I screamed.

Reed slapped a hand over my mouth and pulled me a few more feet on my bottom.

Cash struggled to sit up. "Let her go," he rasped, holding an arm across his ribs and breathing hard.

Frankie smiled and crouched down beside him. "She's pretty, isn't she?"

"Mmmm!" I screamed behind Reed's palm, trying to yank away. When that didn't work, I clawed at his hand over my mouth.

He grunted and let go of my arm.

I had my chance! I was free. I jerked my mouth away from his hand and scrambled away on all fours.

But he caught me.

"NOOOO!" I screamed.

He grabbed a handful of my hair and yanked me back. My eyes watered. His grip in my hair pulled painfully. I howled and reached up, trying to peel his fingers away, tears rolling down my cheeks.

"You're a dead man." Cash held his side and stared at Reed behind me.

Frankie chuckled. "Paul, have a little fun with her." He leaned close to Cash. "Watch this."

Paul strolled toward me, a lusty grin on his face. He ran his tongue over his bottom lip. "Mmm, mmm, mmm, I'm going to enjoy this."

I thrashed about like a wild animal. "No! No! Don't touch me!"

He giggled like a school kid and reached out to touch me. I bared my teeth at him and kicked out. He danced away, laughing. "Don't touch me. Don't touch me." Mocking me in a high-pitched voice.

I let out a shriek and kicked again. He pranced away then lunged at me, hooting with laughter.

He was doing it on purpose, tormenting me. Each time he got closer. I grew desperate, kicking out without aiming. My frustrated shrieks turning into hysterical tears.

"Okay," Cash ground out. "Enough! Leave her alone!"

But Paul wasn't giving up. He dodged my hands and feet with cat-like ability and went for my thighs. I fought harder, frantic, but Reed grabbed my wrists and restrained me.

I screeched and cried as Paul's hand slid along the edge of my dress.

"Get your hands off her."

Cash crawled to his knees and tried to get to his feet. The beating he took made moving almost impossible. His breathing was ragged, forced. He winced and held his side as he swayed on one knee. I became frantic. He was weakened. They would kill him. I had to do something.

Paul was distracted, watching his hand as he ran it up my thigh. He licked his lips again as he moved his fingers higher. I waited a heartbeat and mustered all the nerve I had. *Now!* I kicked him as hard as I could in the shin.

He howled and stumbled back. I twisted my wrists to wrench them away from Reed. He grasped my hair tighter, pulling the strands. Making me cry out.

"Fucker." Cash started to push to his feet.

Frankie grabbed a handful of his hair and yanked his head back.

"Look at her," he said near Cash's ear. "All that dark hair and pretty skin. Do you love her?"

I went crazy, hanging from Reed's hand like a puppet. *I have to get away! I need to get Tate and run! They're going to kill Cash!*

I kicked and hit. Cash said my name, low and smooth from across the room. "Catarina."

I stilled, my heart racing a mile a minute. His voice was laced with iron and steel, a quiet command for me to follow. It could make me do anything he wanted and demanded. Right now, he wanted me to stop fighting.

When I did, Reed relaxed his hold in my hair but didn't let go.

"Do you love her?" Frankie asked, jerking Cash's head back by his hair.

Cash didn't wince or show one hint of being in pain. He just stared at me and answered, "Yeah. Yeah, I do."

Frankie frowned. "My son loved someone too."

He shoved Cash away with disgust and rose to his full height. My face went white when he pulled a gun from his waistband and started pacing in front of us, wound tight as a rubber band.

His men stayed quiet, waiting for instructions. Adam kept Tate out of the fight and David watched from where he was being held against the wall.

Cash was staring at me. *He loves me.* Oh god. I wanted to hear it again but not like this. Not forced or coerced.

Frankie dropped back down beside him and grabbed a fistful of his hair again. He yanked Cash's head back and sneered.

"I think what we've been doing has been child's play. I want you to suffer, boy, just like my son did. So here's what we're going to do. My son had just married a girl. Pretty little thing. He loved her. I swear he would die for her, the fool. But he won't ever get to see his wife's face again. He won't ever get to hold her or crawl between her legs. You're going to feel that loss, boy. You're going to marry the woman you love then tomorrow I'm going to put a noose around your neck. You will have to stare at your wife's face, knowing you will never see her again. Just like my son did while he lay dying."

I went slack, all the fight gone. Cash's blood-filled eyes became dark with fury. Violence hummed in him, just waiting for an outlet. His eyes flicked over to someone beside me, the muscles in his discolored jaw clenching.

"Stay away from her," he warned with a predatory look in his eyes.

Paul edged closer and reached out, touching my hair. "She'll make a pretty bride but an even prettier widow."

My skin crawled. I jerked away from him. A deep, furious sound came from Cash across the room.

"One day, I'll catch you alone. And when I do, I'm going to kill you."

Paul fingered a strand of my hair between his fingers and smirked at Cash. "You gonna kill me from the grave? You'll be dead."

Cash's lips lifted in a deadly grin. "Maybe, but not before you."

Paul frowned. His face went white. His fingers paused on my hair.

Frankie stood up and waved Paul away with his gun. "Hands off. You'll get your turn."

Paul's smirk returned. He let go of my hair and backed away, winking at Cash. "*My* turn."

Frankie sighed and turned to where David was being held. "Bring him here."

One of the men shoved David toward the center of the room. His knee gave out but he caught himself and stumbled to a stop in front of Frankie.

"Preacher David, marry these two young people," Frankie said, waving his gun at Cash and me.

I trembled, seeing the gun carelessly swung around. Cash didn't move or flinch. His gaze stayed on me. His body was stone cold still.

"Well, I…I don't normally marry folks against their will. That isn't how marriage works," David stammered, looking at Frankie and wringing his hands.

Frankie popped his neck, taking his time and growing angry. I swallowed hard, worried about David. Worried what the leader would do.

He let out a gruff chuckle and scratched his chin with the gun. When he looked at David, his patience was gone.

"I don't really give a damn how marriage works, Preacher," he said, aiming the gun at David. "In the eyes of God, they will be married tonight and tomorrow, this boy will meet his maker while I welcome his wife to my fold. Family got to take care of family, you understand. So do it or else."

When David didn't say anything, Frankie grinned and spread his arms wide, taking in Adam, Tate, and his men. "Come on, Preacher! We are all here to be witnesses to this joyous occasion. Do it." He pointed the gun at David again, his smile disappearing.

David gulped and looked from me to Cash. Frankie sighed and cocked his gun.

"I don't have all day, Preacher."

"Okay, okay." David wiped the sweat from his head. He cleared his throat and looked around. "I…I don't have my Bible." He patted his jacket pockets and frowned.

Frankie rolled his eyes. "You've done this a million times, Preacher. You married my son and Gloria without a Bible just a few weeks ago. Get on with it." He waved his gun at us. "Now."

David coughed and folded his hands in front of his chest. "Dearly Beloved, we are gathered here today to join this man and woman in holy matrimony. Um, what's your legal name, Cat?" He looked at me, his forehead wrinkled with fear.

No. I shook my head. *No. This isn't real.*

Reed pulled my hair. Frankie sighed and pointed his gun at me. "Legal name?"

"Catarina Phillips," Cash answered in a voice deathly calm.

"Thank you." Frankie lowered his gun. "Continue preacher."

David wiped his brow again. "Okay. So we're here to celebrate the love of Catarina Phillips and Cash Marshall?" He looked at Cash in question. Cash gave a small nod and David continued.

"Do you, Cash Marshall, take Catarina Phillips to be your wife? Do you promise to love her, honor her, cherish her, in sickness and in health, for better or for worse, till death do you part?"

Oh god.

A muscle ticked in Cash's jaw. Frankie sighed and raised his gun, pointing it at Cash's head.

"Answer the question, boy."

Cash's eyes flicked to Reed, still holding me hostage. "Not until the bastard lets her go."

Frankie nodded at Reed. The big man let go of my hair but put his massive hand on my shoulder, stopping me from scrambling away.

"Your answer," Frankie demanded, peering down his gun barrel at Cash.

Cash's gaze returned to mine, full of fury and heat. "I do."

"Your turn, honey." Frankie swung the gun to point at me again.

"Wait! You can't force people to get married!" Tate shouted from the corner, struggling to get away from Adam. "This is crazy! I object! Isn't that part of the ceremony? Who objects to this wedding? I do!"

"Not in this ceremony," Adam grumbled, jerking Tate back. "Cool it, kid."

Frankie narrowed his eyes at Tate with impatience. "Kill the kid if she doesn't agree." He looked at me and raised an eyebrow. "Should we continue?"

Trembling all over, I nodded, feeling sick. "I do."

"Let the preacher ask you first. Gotta do this right."

David shifted to his other foot. "Hmm. Do you, Catarina Phillips, take Cash Marshall to be your husband. Do you promise to love him, honor him, comfort him, in sickness and in health, for better or for worse, till death do you part?"

I nodded. "I do." I sneered at Frankie. "There. You happy?"

He smiled. "Not. Yet."

David coughed and looked at Cash then me. "By the power vested in me, I now pronounce you man and wife."

"And?" Frankie asked, a smile on his face.

David flushed. "You may kiss the bride."

Frankie motioned to Cash with his gun. "Go get your bride."

Cash glared up at him. Frankie gestured with his gun to get up. Cash's steely eyes never left Frankie as he climbed slowly to his feet. A sob left me as he wobbled, bloody and beaten, his arm wrapped around his side.

"He gonna do it, boys?" Frankie chortled, watching Cash take slow, painful steps toward me. "He gonna get his girl?"

"Fuck you," Cash said. "I'll always get her."

He limped toward me, holding his ribs. Reed yanked me up, wrapping an arm around my middle. The room was silent. I had eyes only for Cash. He was wounded and hurt, but he was coming for me.

Stopping a foot away, he looked Reed dead in the eyes. "Let go of my wife."

The big man removed his hand from my hair. I took an unsteady step toward Cash. He didn't touch me. Didn't move. He just stood there and watched me, one eye swollen and the other bloody.

"You okay," he asked when I stopped in front of him.

I nodded. "You?"

He gave a small nod.

"Get on with it. Seal the deal," Frankie boomed out in his gruff voice. "Kiss the bride."

Cash scowled but leaned down, keeping an arm around his ribs. "I'm sorry, Cat," he muttered before kissing me, light and quick on the lips.

Frankie let out a groan. "That's not a proper kiss, boy. Give her a good one like you mean it. Might be your last chance."

Cash got that look on his face. Dark, angry, dangerous. My heart pounded against my ribs as he took a step closer. We had an audience. My brother. A preacher. A whole lot of bad men. But suddenly it was just us. Him and me.

He let go of his side and cupped my face in his hands. "This is for us, Cat, not them."

His lips touched mine, gentle at first. It was soft and sweet, making my throat swell. Then he deepened the kiss. I became lost in the feel of his rough hands holding my face and his mouth on mine. There was something intimate about our not-so-intimate kiss. I could drown in it forever but we didn't have forever. We just had today.

When slow clapping interrupted, Cash's lips slid from mine and his hands left my face.

"Very good. Very good. Congratulations," Frankie said, clapping slowly as he walked toward us. "Now you will suffer like my son did."

Cash pushed me behind his back, putting himself between me and Frankie. "You got what you wanted. Now, let them go." He jerked his chin at the door, standing at his full height and towering over the leader.

Frankie cocked his head. "Nah, I don't think so." He strolled past us to the door. "Let's go, boys."

The men that had held David sprung forward and grabbed his arm. They pushed him toward the door, unmindful of his older age. Adam nudged Tate to follow, glancing at me with pity.

Tate turned to look over his shoulder at me, struggling against Adam. "Sis? Sis? What's going on? What's happening?"

I rushed around Cash to go to my brother, but Frankie held up a hand, stopping me. "No, darling. You stay."

Adam gave me a look as he led Tate out the door. One that told me to calm down, he'd watch over Tate.

The men piled out of the room, one by one. Soon there was only Frankie, Cash, and me.

Frankie stood in front of the door, arms crossed over his chest and feet spread with authority. He smiled at Cash. "You got one night with her. Enjoy it. Revel in it. Soak it all in because tomorrow you hang."

Chapter Thirty-Three

-Cat-

"Oh Jesus," I whispered staring at the closed door. They were really going to kill him. It wasn't just a bad dream.

I squeezed my eyes closed. When Luke died, I felt empty. Incapable of feeling anything. With the threat of losing Cash, I felt everything. Pain, anguish, heartbreak, and anger. I wanted to wail and scream. He was bruised and I was breaking. I couldn't take it any longer.

"Cat."

I squeezed my eyes tighter at the sound of his voice. I couldn't take it, the thought of losing him.

My grief turned into anger. *They couldn't do this! They couldn't!*

I ran to the door and slammed my fists against it. "Frankie! Open the door! Open the fucking door!" I shouted, banging on it with my balled-up fists. There was no answer. Only dead silence.

I pounded harder, tears streaming down my face. I wanted to see my brother. I wanted to beg and plead with Frankie not to hang Cash. "Open the door!" I screamed, smacking the door as hard as I could. "Open it NOW!"

"Cat," Cash said calmly behind me again.

"No. They have to let us out!" I banged on the door harder then grabbed the handle and shook it. "They can't do this! It's wrong!" I shouted, smacking the door with my palm.

"Stop."

The word was like a whip, striking me. I could feel Cash's eyes boring into my back, his ire rising. But I hit the door again and again. My eyes were red and puffy and my nose running.

Cash let out a low sound of irritation. "You're going to hurt yourself. Stop or I'll stop you myself, Beauty Queen."

I flattened my hand against the door and dropped my chin to my chest, breathing hard. I tried to block out his voice. It irritated me like never before. He might be mad but he was still calm. I wanted him to lose control. Fly off the handle. Yell *fuck you!* at the world. Instead, he stood there composed. It made me mad. *Didn't he care that we had been forced to marry and they're going to kill him?* I turned around and faced him, a complete mess of anger and ugly cry.

He was standing in the middle of the room, a prime example of control. His arm was around his ribcage, his face was a patchwork of bruises. His shirt and jeans had seen better days, torn here and there and splotched with dark blood or smeared with mud. His eyes were on me.

I kicked off my shoes – I hated the things – and stomped over to him, stopping only when the tips of my toes touched the edges of his boots.

"How can you stand there, cold as ice, knowing they might kill you tomorrow? Don't you care? Don't you feel anything?" I shrieked.

He glowered down at me. "I feel things, sweetheart."

"Then show it! Yell, scream, do something!"

He clenched his bruised jaw, making the muscle under his day's growth of beard tick. "What do you want me to do, Cat? Throw a fit? Hit a wall?"

"Yes!" I yelled, throwing my hands up. "It's better than being so unemotional!" I pushed past him and stormed across the room on bare feet.

Cash turned and watched me through his swollen, blood-filled eyes. I paced with furious strides. Back and forth, back and forth, from the wall to the center of the room. I felt like a caged animal, eager to get out and run. The chill of the room didn't register with me and the cold under my feet didn't matter. I crossed my arms over my chest and stormed one way then another.

Cash sighed. I turned just in time to see him grab the backpack and limp to the wall. With his back to me, he was a study in male perfection. The broad shoulders. The muscular back. His bruised body was coiled taut. He did everything with grace and strength, from walking across the room to making love to me in a barn.

He leaned against the wall and slid down, grimacing and holding his side. Sitting, he bent his knees and pulled the backpack to him. I chewed my bottom lip, pain hitting my chest at the sight of his battered face.

He unzipped the backpack and pulled out a small blanket. Tossing it aside, he reached in and withdrew a package of crackers and a bottle of liquor. Whiskey. The good kind, if my dad had taught me anything.

He unscrewed the bottle, his gaze flicking up to mine. "Tell your boyfriend thank you for me."

I rolled my eyes and tried not to stare as he tipped the bottle to his mouth and took a long drink. Brown liquid splashed past his lips. His strong throat worked to swallow.

Glancing away, I started pacing again. I had to think. We needed to figure a way out. There were four walls. No windows. A bucket for bathroom needs. *Fuck. Great.*

"Come here, Cat."

His voice sent tingles up my spine. I could feel his eyes on me. "No."

I paced to the wall then back around. *Ignore him. Ignore him.* When I turned, his eyes pinned me in place.

"Don't make me get up, Beauty Queen. Come here and sit down."

"No," I said again, marching to the middle of the room and back. "We've got to figure out what we're going to do."

"There's nothing we can do."

His tone was so final, so absolute. I felt a punch to my gut that almost doubled me over. I turned around. He was lowering the liquor bottle, the sound of whiskey sloshing against the glass loud.

Angry and hurting, I crossed the room in quick strides. "Are you just going to give up? Just like that?"

Cash peered up at me as I approached, his bloodshot eyes swollen. "No. I'm facing reality, Cat. There's nothing we can do."

I flung my arms out in frustration. "Of course there's something we can do! We can fight. We can try to get out. We can't just give up and allow them to hang you!"

"Yes, we can," Cash mumbled, raising the bottle to his mouth again.

I clenched my fists and started pacing again. "Ugh!" I was angrier.

Cash watched me, sipping the whiskey and holding his side. I ignored him and thought through different scenarios. Could we hold someone hostage when they came to get Cash? Maybe we could grab a gun and escape?

"What did you mean when you told Frankie you had a deal?" Cash's voice rang out in a deep rumble.

I paused. My heart pounded. He sounded furious. Irate.

"I..um..." I started pacing again and sneaking peeks at him. "I agreed to do anything he wanted in exchange for your freedom along with Tate and David's."

Cash set the bottle down slowly. His gaze was hard, his voice deadly quiet. "Over my dead body, Cat."

I snorted and rolled my tear-filled eyes. "Jeez, did you hear what you just said?" Swiping a tear away from my cheek, I started pacing again. "It doesn't matter. Frankie's not going to let you go."

"Oh, it matters, sweetheart. This is exactly why I wanted you to stop loving me."

Hurt tore through me. I spun around, livid. "Well, too bad. I'll never stop loving you."

Anger radiated off him. He clenched his fists and clamped his jaw with barely controlled fury. A heartbeat passed then two. He deflated and shoved a hand through his hair. "Fuck," he hissed. "Damn, Cat, I don't know what to do."

Seeing him so broken destroyed me. All the anger left me in a whoosh. I went to his side and dropped down. He lifted his eyes and looked at me. I took his face in my hands and scooted closer. The bruises. The dried blood. New tears formed behind my eyes. They had hurt him – this man that was so strong. If they could do that to him, what else were they capable of?

"Don't give up, Cash," I whispered, finding strength for both of us. "I'll do whatever you say. I'll tell you I don't love you. I'll say I hate you. I'll do whatever it takes. I just need you to fight."

"Then leave me. At the first chance you get, grab Tate and run."

I shook my head, dropping my hands and lowering my gaze. "I can't."

He lifted my chin, forcing me to look at him. "Yes, you can. I was going to leave you. Does that make the decision any easier?"

My mind went blank. Pain squeezed my chest. "No." I forced the word out.

He let out a soft curse and let me go. Grabbing the whiskey bottle, he took a long drink.

I waited. Afraid. Terrified. Hurt.

He lowered the bottle and sat it back down beside him. Regret and pain crossed his face. "I thought it would be for the best, leaving you. I was going to get you and Tate home then take off." He scoffed and shook his head. "I was a fucking fool. There's no way I could walk away from you – I know that now – but you gotta leave me, sweetheart. I can't have you stay and watch what's going to happen tomorrow."

Tears blurred my vision. My chin quivered. My throat closed up until I thought I would suffocate.

Cash cupped my face in his palm. Swallowing hard, he wiped a tear away from my cheek with his thumb. "Go with Adam. He'll get you out before it happens and make sure you and Tate get somewhere safe. And – *shit* – I want you to stay with him. He'll love you and keep you safe. I can die knowing you'll be okay."

"No." I shook my head, the tears so thick that I couldn't see now. "I…I can't do that, Cash. Don't ask me to."

He put his hand on the back of my head and pulled me closer. His voice dropped to a rugged rasp and his gaze became heated.

"Do you think I want to suggest or even *think* of him touching you? *You're mine.* You have been ever since I stood between your legs and took you on that bathroom counter. But I don't want you to be there when I die. I want to close my eyes as they put the noose around my neck and know you're somewhere safe, away from this hellhole. I want the last thing I think about to be the way you looked the night we met, standing in front of Cooper's in the rain. I want to die knowing you'll be okay. Give me that *please.*"

I shook my head, tears falling down my cheeks. "I won't be okay, cowboy. Not without you."

He swore and pulled me closer, putting his forehead against mine.

"I know, sweetheart, God do I know. But I need you to do this. Leave me. Go with Adam. Run."

I cried and grasped the front of his shirt. He tightened his fingers in my hair and pressed his lips against my forehead.

"Forget about me, Cat. Forget about me and move on."

Chapter Thirty-Four

-Cat-

I threw my leg over Cash and climbed into his lap. I needed to be as close to him as possible.

My dress slid up my thighs. Goosebumps rose on my arms from his heat in front of me and the coldness behind me. Grasping his face, I cupped his cheeks with my hands. I couldn't talk. Couldn't agree to what he said. All I wanted to do was be as close to him as possible.

"Cat—" he groaned, his hand going to my waist.

"Don't talk," I whispered. "Do this instead."

I lowered my head and kissed him, my mouth sliding over his. He tasted like malt whiskey. Intoxicating. Heady. Drunkenly good. I glided my tongue over his lower lip, sampling the taste. He let out a low sound deep in his throat and grasped the back of my head. His mouth angled over mine, taking over. He urged my lips apart with pressure. When I gave in, his tongue was immediately there, dipping inside.

I moaned against his mouth, melting and falling apart, as he licked and consumed. When the cut on his lip brushed against me, I started to pull away. A deep growl of displeasure erupted from him. He fisted a hand in my hair and held me tight. There was no escaping but I wasn't going anywhere.

His tongue plunged back inside while his fingers kept me captive. I let go of his face and ran my hands up his chest. When my fingers grazed his ribs, he drew in a sharp breath.

I froze and pulled my mouth away. "I'm sorry. We shouldn't do this. You're hurt and…"

He seized my mouth again, cutting off the rest of the sentence. This time there was no mercy. No romantic overtures. I didn't know where I ended and he began. We were desperate. We had to touch. Nothing would have stopped us, not even the end of the world.

He reached down and ran his hand under the edge of my dress. His fingers were warm. Rough. Strength against softness.

I reached between us and lowered his zipper. He let out a low groan against my mouth when I wrapped my fingers around him and freed his hard-as-steel erection. Holding him in my hand, I rose to my knees. He pulled my panties to the side.

We couldn't wait. Like two high school kids doing something forbidden, we were feverish to have each other.

At least one more time.

I aimed the tip of his cock at my opening and slowly lowered down. He sucked in a breath against my lips and wrapped his arm around my waist. A little mewl sound of pleasure escaped me as I was filled inch by inch by his hardness.

It was heaven; it was hell. I pulled my mouth from his and bit my bottom lip as I started moving on him. His arm was banded around me. He gave me all the control.

I started breathing harder, moving on him. I was close to tears, letting out little sounds of frustration, but beneath the sensations lay harsh reality. This was it. Our last time.

A broken sob tore from me. Cash grasped both sides of my face and looked into my eyes.

"It's okay," he whispered, sliding in and out of me. "It'll be okay."

Tears rolled down my cheeks.

"Hell," he whispered seeing me cry. He slipped his hand around to the back of my neck and pulled my mouth to his. He kissed me gently. Tenderly. Heartbreakingly sweet. We made love leisurely, soaking in every moment, every thrust of him in me. We touched. We reveled in every sensation. He took his time. Filling me. Going deep. I wanted it to last forever but forever wasn't possible.

Little shockwaves started building in my body. I whimpered incoherently against his mouth. My tears were captured by the rough stubble on his chin and cheeks.

He grasped my hips tighter, his fingers digging into my hips. Against my lips he whispered, "You make me want to never give up, Cat. You make me want to live."

Just like that, I exploded. A cry escaped me. He moaned and grasped me tight to him as spasms rocked my body.

Rapid, little breaths left me as I convulsed around him. Cash tangled his fingers into my hair and moved faster in and out of me. I buried my face in the curve of his neck as the orgasm shook me. The muscles in his arms tensed. I kept moving on him. He was close to coming; I could hear his breathing increase.

I lifted my head. My hair was plastered to my skin, my cheeks wet from tears. His eyes were closed as I rode him, savage pleasure twisting his beautiful, battered face.

I kissed his jaw. "I'm yours always," I whispered against the rough stubble.

He groaned and his fingers tightened in my hair. His body went stiff under me. White hot cum erupted deep inside me.

"Fuck. Fuck." He continued to come in me, his thick cock ejaculating. My walls clamped around him, forming a snug seal, as he continued to gush into me.

He let go of my hair and slid his hand down to my hip, leaving imprints on my skin as he held me tight and pumped into me until every drop was released. Only then did he stop, buried to the hilt and nudging my cervix with his wide head.

My pulse was racing so hard I couldn't hear it. He let out a deep rumble of masculine satisfaction and let go of my hip to curve his hand around my neck. Pulling me toward him, his mouth covered mine with fierce possession. I had no choice. No reason to resist. I melted against him and let him claim me, my body weightless, throbbing around his pulsating hardness.

Every emotion was behind his kiss. Desperation. Insatiable need. A demand to remember him and this. I answered them all. I would give him anything. Everything. I already had and I would do it again.

After a minute, his kiss gentled. His cut, bruised lips brushed over mine. Sorrow at remembering why they were hurt made me want to cry.

He let go of my neck and eased out of me, moving my panties back in place with all the tenderness in the world. As soon as he was tucked into his jeans, he pulled me to his chest. I went willingly, exhaustion winning out. My body went limp and my eyelids were suddenly heavy as his arm cradled me close.

The world slowed down. The roaring in my ears dissipated. I could hear Cash's heartbeat under my ear, strong and powerful. It was as familiar to me as my own. His masculine scent invaded my senses and his warmth surrounded me.

I felt small. Protected.

Terrified suddenly.

New tears prickled the backs of my eyes. I realized it might be the last time he would hold me. Make love to me. Whisper my name.

I buried my face in his neck and breathed him in, a tear falling down my cheek and landing on his skin.

He ran his hand up my back to the area between my shoulder blades. "Don't cry," he whispered against my hair. "It kills me when you do."

I sniffed and tried to stop for him but the tears kept on coming. He didn't say anything else. He just held me as I cried.

We stayed that way for a while, me straddling his lap, him holding me close. I wept until tiredness pulled at me. When my eyes started to close, I forced them back open. I wasn't ready to fall asleep yet. I didn't want to wake up and it be tomorrow.

But I had been through too much in the past twenty-four hours. My body was worn out. My emotions drained. When I lost the battle and sleep started to win, Cash seemed to know. He lowered me to the ground and stretched out beside me. Putting his arm under my head for a pillow, he grabbed the small blanket and pulled it over us.

I watched him through half-closed eyes. His full lips were firm. His sharp jaw was covered with a day's growth of beard. Bruises marred his face and I could see more peeking out of the collar of his shirt.

He tucked the blanket around me and rolled onto his back, bringing me with him. I snuggled against his chest.

"I'm scared to close my eyes," I murmured, sleep pulling at me.

Cash pressed his lips to my forehead. "It's okay. No one's going to hurt you. I'm right here."

"But what about tomorrow?"

He stilled. I felt him swallow. His breathing stopped.

"It doesn't matter. We have tonight," he whispered against my forehead, his voice hoarse. Broken.

My throat was thick with tears. They fell down my chin and soaked into his shirt. He kissed my forehead again and mumbled something. I wanted to ask what he said but exhaustion finally won out. I fell asleep, my cheeks wet.

And dreamed that he had said 'I love you.'

~~~~

I imagined ice crystals on my skin. Shivering in my sleep, I burrowed closer to the immense heat next to me. Warm fingers pushed my dress higher up my thighs. Lips kissed the area below my ear.

"Open for me," a deep voice whispered, his hand easing up my leg.

I moaned and bent one knee, somewhere in that place between wakefulness and sleep. Rough stubble brushed my throat. A male sound of appreciation rumbled in my ear.

"God, you're perfect."

I smiled sleepily and snuggled closer to him.

The rough pads of fingers traveled higher. His mouth brushed along my neck.

"I need you again, sweetheart. One more time then you can sleep."

His fingers found me. My body bowed, desire shooting through me like lightning.

But it wasn't just one more time. He made love to me again and again during the night. Sometimes he took his time, driving me crazy, memorizing every inch of me. Other times he took me with raw need, fast and hard like
~~~~

he couldn't get enough. Time didn't exist. What was coming tomorrow didn't matter. He let me sleep then wake me, whispering in my ear.

I was used completely and given everything wholeheartedly. Every part of me was touched or kissed, revered by Cash's mouth and body. I had never felt so loved before but nothing lasts forever. It was the story of my life.

I was sleeping soundly, deeply. In some part of my brain, I realized that Cash was no longer lying beside me. He was sitting up, his body tense, staying close to protect me.

"Wake up, Cat."

His voice wasn't gentle like it was during the night. It was hard, the words ground out. Angry and dark.

My eyes flew open. My stomach twisted. The bliss of last night disappeared in a snap. Darkness still shrouded the room but in the doorway there was light.

And Frankie.

He looked at Cash, his gray eyebrows drawn together in a scowl.

"Get up, boy. It's time to die."

Chapter Thirty-Five

-Cash-

I crouched like a feral dog, guarding Cat as Frankie strolled into the room. He wore an army jacket that was patched and tattered. His salt-and-pepper hair was slicked back. I smelled coffee on him that made my stomach rumble and told me that it was probably early morning. *Fuck*. My time was up. He had plans for today and it had to do with me swinging by a rope. I was screwed.

That might have seemed a pretty lame statement to be making, but there it was. I was screwed. I hadn't slept a wink last night. I had racked my brain to figure a way out and came up empty. I had no allies in Hilltop except Tate, David, and maybe Adam. The preacher and kid couldn't fight a militia. Hell, I'm not sure who could.

I glanced over at Cat. No, the reason I hadn't slept last night was because of her. If I wasn't touching her, I was watching her sleep and thinking of touching her. If I wasn't making love to her, I was thinking of making love to her. Knowing I was going to die made me greedy. I couldn't get enough of her and kept her up all night. I felt guilty as hell when I saw the circles under her eyes but I couldn't get enough of her. I still couldn't.

But it was time to die.

Frankie strolled into the room like the cocky bastard he was. Four men followed him in, fanning out in front of the door.

"Have a nice little honeymoon, boy?" Frankie asked with a smirk.

I didn't answer. Just stayed in front of Cat, feeling savage and bloodthirsty.

He frowned and glanced behind me at her. "She looks tired. Guess you worked her over pretty good. Enjoyed yourself did you, honey?"

"Don't look at her," I warned through gritted teeth.

A vein pulsated in the middle of Frankie's forehead. "You ain't in no position to be given orders. Not if you want her to live." He jerked his chin in Cat's direction. "Answer me, honey."

I let out another low growl in my throat and eased in front of her some more.

Frankie chuckled, a deep, hoarse sound. "Aww look, fellows, he's protecting her. Ain't that sweet?"

As if on cue, the other men chuckled. I checked them out, one by one.

Adam was standing just inside the doorway, looking bored out of his mind. He had his arms crossed over his chest and an *it's-too-early-for-this-shit* expression on his face. I wanted to wring his neck for not getting Cat and Tate out of town sooner but I had to trust him. He was Cat's future. *Fuck!* To think of the two of them together made something inside me pull and tighten.

I forced the emotion – whatever it was – away and focused on the next man. It was that big asshole, Reed, who had fucked me up and enjoyed every fuckin' minute of it. He was standing to the left of Frankie, looking like he wanted to add a few more bruises to my collection. *Get in line, douchebag.* I was still sore and tender, my body still feeling every punch. I felt like I had gotten ran over by a truck. My face was a mess and my arms hurt like hell from being hung by the ceiling. Having sex all night hadn't helped my broken ribs or battered body but I couldn't keep my hands off Cat.

Two other guys that looked like they would bend over and take it up the ass for Frankie if he asked, stood to the right. A few more appeared outside the door.

I scowled and glared at each of them from behind my swollen, busted eyes. They could do whatever they wanted with me but if they attempted to touch Cat, I would snap some necks and bust some balls. *Just watch me.* No one touched what was mine, not as long as there was breath left in my lungs.

I kept one eye on them but turned all my attention back to Frankie. He walked closer, not giving a shit if I looked ready to go postal on his ass or not.

"Come here, sweetie," he said, looking past me to Cat and motioning with his hand.

She started to scramble back but I stopped her with a hand to her leg. I wanted her as close as possible to protect her. The men would have to go through me first.

Frankie looked down at us and frowned. "Get her up, boys."

I let out a low sound of warning as two men broke from the group and started toward us. They were big and mean-looking but I was deadly when it came to safeguarding Cat. My muscles bunched, ready to attack. My fists curled against the ground. I felt my adrenaline rise and the murderous urge to hurt someone rushed through me. I was going to protect what was mine or die trying.

The two men paused, seeing the lethal look in my eyes.

Frankie glowered at them. "Pieces of shit. What are you waiting for? Get her! Do it!"

The men watched me with uncertainty but crept forward, the fear of their leader propelling them on.

I curled my lips at them but turned my attention to the one who got a lusty look in his eyes when he glanced at Cat behind me.

He was my first target.

Cat grabbed a fistful of the back of my shirt. "Caaash."

I changed my mind. I wanted her at a safe distance. I was about to unleash hell on these guys and I wanted her out of harm's way.

"Get back, Cat," I muttered, keeping my gaze on the men.

She let me go and scrambled away. I didn't need to turn around to know there were tears streaming down her face. I was so attuned to her that I knew every move she made and every breath she took. All attempts to stay away from her after she was shot hadn't taken that ability from me.

I hardened my heart to thoughts of her scared and vulnerable. Ice filled my veins. The man who had held her last night and made love to her was gone. The man that slowly stood up to protect her with his life was cold and deadly.

The guy drooling over Cat wiped a hand across his mouth and stared at her. He was big. More fat than muscle. Double chin. Beady eyes. His attention was on her, not me. Big mistake. When he licked his lips and whispered, "Come to papa," he signed his own death warrant.

The other man edging toward us was short and stocky but packed with muscle. His arms looked like logs and his neck was as wide as a jock's on steroids. He only had eyes for me and according to the knuckles he kept on cracking, those were for me too. They would both be easy pickings. But first asshole number one.

I waited for him to get closer. Didn't move a muscle. Didn't even blink. This was what hunting was all about. Waiting. Watching. Knowing when to take the shot. It was all about timing and precision and studying your prey.

I kept everyone else in my peripheral vision. Reed, Frankie, Adam.

Frankie stood a safe distance away. He wasn't stupid; he knew I could take him down without much effort. I gave him brownie points for knowing that. Smart man but he was still dead.

Adam stood to the right of the door, his feet spread, his arms crossed over his chest. He watched me with a cool expression. The kind that said he could care less what these men did to me as long as he didn't have to get his hands dirty or clean up the mess. He was just cold-hearted enough for me to know he would protect Cat and not think twice about what he had to do. I told her last night to stay with him. That he would care for her. It was the fucking hardest thing that I had ever said in my life but I had seen the look in his eyes when he looked at her. He cared for her. He would keep her safe. To think of him stepping in and taking my place tore me apart but he was Cat and Tate's best hope if Frankie got a rope around my neck.

Fuck. Just thinking of it left me in a cold sweat.

I had to be callous if I was going to get Cat through this. Forget about me. It was her I had to save.

My gaze slid over to the man on my left then to the guy on my right. They were getting closer. Four feet. Three feet. They were almost even with me. Just one more step…

I heard Cat climb to her feet behind me. I knew her shoes were clear across the room and the little dress she wore left nothing to the imagination. It had screwed with my mind earlier but the thought of what these men saw and were thinking when they looked at her just fed the fury in me more.

The man ogling Cat whistled low at her and went to step past me. I saw my opening.

That's when I became a madman.

My fist snapped out, slamming into the man's throat. The jab was fast and swift, hitting its target like a bullet. My knuckles connected with his windpipe. The blow was point on. He let out a gurgled gasp and grasped his neck, choking as he stumbled backwards.

I whirled to face the other man. With a fast move, I punched him in the side of the head then threw a quick one-two stab to his ribs.

He was solid but the hits were hard. He doubled over and I turned back to the first guy. Two rapid punches to his nose landed him on the ground in seconds. I was hurting from the beating I took yesterday but I was running on pure adrenaline. Cat was scrambling back and other men were flying into the room. This was my chance. I had to give her time to get out of there.

The man rolled around on his back, crying like a baby with blood bursting from his nose. I was in bloodbath mode. There was no stopping me. I swung to attack the second man when I heard the scream.

"Let me go!"

Cat! Shit!

I started to spin around but the cold press of a gun barrel nudged the back of my skull.

Well, fuck me...

"You done, boy?" Frankie boomed from behind me.

Coldness filled my veins. He had her. I could hear her crying, little sounds that gutted me. I could sense him holding onto her as she tried to get away. My fingers flexed with the need to wrap them around Frankie's neck or better yet, grab the gun and flip it around.

I stood still, breathing hard, letting the fury pump in my system. Adam strolled over, pulling out his gun at the same time. Stopping an arm's length from me, he aimed the Glock between my eyes and gave me a look that said to calm the hell down.

"I got him, Frankie," he said in a cocky voice.

I looked down the barrel at him as Frankie pulled the gun away from the back of my head. I wanted to rip Adam's head off and feed it to the brainless Hilltop zombies outside but I remained motionless and silent. Whatever he had up his sleeve, I was game if it got Cat out of there.

Frankie's gruff voice barked out behind me. "Keep a bead on him. If he so much as twitches, empty your chamber in him."

My back went stiff. My fists clenched at my sides. If someone had told the skinny, gangly boy I was back in high school that the future me would be itching to kill in order to protect the woman I loved, I wouldn't have believed it. But there I was. Deadly and willing.

My chest rose and fell faster, adrenaline pumping into my veins like a drug-induced high. A soft cry and the sound of small fists hitting a solid body came from behind me. I tried not to go apeshit crazy, thinking of Frankie manhandling Cat.

Adam must have noticed the thin hold I had on my rage. He gave me a small shake of his head that I would have missed if I had blinked. His message was loud and clear. Cat was in trouble and if I didn't want anything to happen to her, I had to stand down. But when she let out a pained yelp, I was ready to take him out.

Adam tilted his head and raised an eyebrow at me. *Don't be a fuckard*, he was pretty much saying. I glowered at him but stood ramrod still as Frankie dragged Cat around me. I was scared to death to look at her because I knew it would tear me up inside.

Tears tracked down her face and fear made her green eyes bright. She looked too skinny in the dress she wore and shit, she looked cold. Her teeth were chattering and her nipples were sticking out for all the world to see. I wanted to cover her up but one wrong move, that dress she was wearing would be covered with my blood or worse.

The two guys I had put on the ground were slowly climbing to their feet. They looked at me with murderous expressions but they could go to hell. I only had eyes for Cat and the man that held her.

She dug in her heels but Frankie was stronger. He yanked her past me roughly, his hand wrapped tight around her upper arm. I could see the red indentions on her flawless skin. She would have bruises from his fingers. Just one more reason to rid the world of Hilltop's leader.

"Me and your man got an appointment to keep," he said to her between clenched teeth. "I'll deal with you and our little arrangement after he's hanging from a tree."

"No!" Cat screamed, struggling to get away. She tried yanking her arm out of his grasp and kicked at Frankie's shins with her bare feet. But he was a strong old man and held onto her tightly. She turned and scraped her nails down the side of his face.

"Uuuuughhh!"

Frankie let go of her and grabbed his right cheek. Red streaks ran from his cheekbone down to his jaw.

"*Fuck*," Adam muttered, his gaze flicking to Cat but keeping the gun pointed in my face. He knew as well as I did that she was in trouble.

I started to lunge and grab her before Frankie could retaliate for the scratches with a backhand across her face, but she was already flying toward me.

"Grab her!" Frankie roared, holding his cheek in his palm.

Cat threw herself against me. "Don't let them do this, Cash! You can't die!"

I wrapped an arm around her in protection. Men were rushing toward us. I only had seconds. Not enough to say what I wanted to say but it would have to do.

I cupped Cat's face between my hands and forced her to look up at me. "Remember what I told you. Stay with Adam. Go."

She shook her head, tears running down her face. "No," she whispered. "I'm not leaving you. They'll have to kill me too."

I swore as someone grabbed my arms from behind and yanked them back, away from Cat. *I'm not done!* I wanted to scream. *I have other things to say to her! Things I never said!*

The man behind me started to wrap a piece of rope around my wrists, making my muscles scream and my torn, raw skin burn. It was Reed. Shit. The guy had a thing for dispensing pain.

I didn't fight him because, hell, the guy was a machine. I wouldn't put it past him to turn on Cat. He would have no qualms about hitting her but one punch from his meaty fist might kill her. No, I would stand down for her. Anything for her.

As he tied my hands behind my back, I leaned down and kissed her with everything in me.

Saying goodbye for the last time.

She held on to my shirt tightly. I could taste her tears. They were salty on my lips. A part of her I would take with me when I died.

She was torn from me too soon by Adam. He wrapped his arm around her waist and pulled her away.

"Noooo!" she screeched, fighting him, clawing at his arm as it clamped around her waist and reaching for me. *God, reaching for me.* I got choked-up.

I almost went full-on savage, seeing Adam take her away from me. But I knew it was for the best. I was a dead man walking.

Frankie scowled at all the racket Cat was making.

"Get her out of here," he snapped, wiping the blood away from the nail marks she had left behind on his cheek. "I'll deal with her later."

I set my jaw tight. My tendons pulled in my arms, testing my bindings. Wanting to break loose.

Adam fought to hold Cat. She had always been a fighter and wasn't going to stop now despite being upset and afraid. She screamed and bucked against him, ramming her elbows into his abdomen and even head-butting him once. He hissed with pain but didn't loosen his grip on her. When he lifted her up and started carrying her to the door, she let out a shriek and started kicking him fiercely.

I fought the urge to go berserk. Ally or no ally, Adam was taking her from me. Fuck. I couldn't deal with it. I growled low, deep in my chest, and made a move to step forward but the cold end of a barrel poked against the base of my neck again. Reed. Shit.

"Boss wants a rope around your neck but I'll put a bullet in it instead," he rumbled, his voice so deep it was almost inaudible over the sound of Cat's screams.

I went completely still. My gaze stayed on Cat, praying Adam got her out before something bad happened like Reed pulling the trigger.

She wasn't going easily. She grabbed the doorframe with both hands as Adam carried her under it.

"Let me go! You can't kill him. Please! Let me go!" she cried. "I'll do anything!"

The man who had been salivating over her and received a broken nose from me for it, wiped away a drop of blood from his nostrils and started toward her. "I'll help him, boss."

The hackles raised on my neck. I ducked my head like a bull ready to charge.

Standing near me, Frankie raised his gun and pointed it at her. "You move, she dies."

I was breathing hard, taut with fury. The pull to go to her was strong. The need to protect her was consuming. But I knew her life depended on my actions. If I moved, Frankie wouldn't hesitate to pull the trigger. And if he did…

I would want to be dead too.

Adam lifted his gun and pointed at the guy's head as he approached, his arm still wrapped around Cat.

"I got this, Pearson."

The man lifted his hands and moved back a step.

I looked at Adam, my expression hardening, my voice cold. "Get her out of here," I snarled.

"No. No." Cat shook her head frantically. "Don't do this, Cash. Please. I need you."

My jaw tightened. My eyes flicked to Adam's. "Leave. Now."

He unwrapped Cat's fingers from the doorframe, his expression grim. She let out a shriek and kicked back at him. My muscles tensed like a tight band, ready to snap any second as Adam wrestled to hold her. I fought to stay still. My fists clenched painfully behind my back. I wanted to rain hell down on everyone, but I held myself in check.

With a lump in my throat the size of Texas, I watched as Adam heaved Cat up and carried her away. It hit me like a freight train, making me want to puke my guts out. I wouldn't see her again until a noose was around my neck.

I wanted to squeeze my eyes closed and block out her cries as Adam carted her through the basement. Her curses mixed with tears, hitting me in the solar plexus and stealing the air from my lungs. I had never felt so helpless before. I didn't know whether to drop to my knees and scream or throw back my head and roar.

As the sound of her struggles and cries faded, Frankie stepped into my line of vision. My blood went cold, all my emotions shutting down.

He crossed his arms over his chest and looked down his nose at me. His thick brows drew together.

There was no help for me now. I was going to die.

~~~~

Frankie rubbed a hand over his chin and stared at me. "Everyone out."

The men scrambled to do his bidding. The last man shut the door behind him but Reed stayed, keeping the end of the gun pressed against the bottom of my neck.

I stared at Frankie through my busted eyes, wondering what hell he was going to put me through now.

"Let him go, Reed," he ordered gruffly.

The gun disappeared from my neck. I could breathe easily again. I still didn't move. I didn't trust the fucker in front of me.
~~~~

Frankie studied me with a disgruntled frown. I stared at him, my muscles bunched to attack.

He snorted at the murderous expression in my eyes and strolled behind me to the blanket lying on the floor.

Blind rage built in me as he leaned over and grabbed it. Bringing it to his nose, he turned back to me and took a big whiff. "Hmmm. Smells like her. Something sweet and heavenly. I'm going to like breaking her in and beating the fight out of her."

A low sound erupted from my throat. Something animalistic. Not human. More demon than man.

Frankie lowered the blanket and raised one bushy eyebrow. "You say something, boy?"

I curled my lips. "Yeah. Stay the fuck away from her."

He grinned and sauntered back to me. "Nah. Don't think I will."

Stopping in front of me, he took another big whiff of the blanket and closed his eyes, enjoying the smell.

My biceps tightened. The tendons in my neck bulged. I scowled. "You fuc—"

He dropped the blanket and swung. I never saw it coming. His fist connected with my stomach. I doubled over.

For an old man, Frankie had the punch of a powerhouse. I had been fucked up by the asshole behind me – Reed – and was still tender. I felt Frankie's fist all the way to my spine.

As I breathed through my nose and let the pain roll through me, Frankie smoothed back his hair and looked down at me. "Hold him, Reed."

The monster behind me grabbed my arms again and forced me to stand up straight. I gritted my teeth against the pain and glared at Frankie from between my swollen eyelids. "That all you got?"

Frankie rolled his neck and studied me. "I'll break you if it's the last thing I do. Get him on his knees."

Reed forced me down. I didn't go easily but the pain in my stomach got the best of me. My knees hit the cold concrete hard. Sheer agony radiated up my body.

Frankie grabbed a handful of my hair – that must be his thing – and jerked my head back to look up at him.

"I want you to grovel." He hit me in the face. *Whack!* "I want you to cry." He hit me again, this time causing blood to spurt from my nose. "I want you to shit your pants with fear and beg for your life and hers." He hit me again, this time in the cheekbone that was already screaming with pain. "I want you to bleed like my son and scream like he did when they tried to dig that bullet out of him."

His knuckle connected with my temple. My brain rattled in my skull. I wavered on my knees. Blackness wavered at the corners of my vision but I shook it away. If I passed out, Frankie would kill me. Hell, he was going to kill me anyway. But I wouldn't go by his hand. I wouldn't give him that pleasure. A rope was much better.

He punched me a fifth time then a sixth. Blood filled my mouth.

"You got nothing to say, boy?" he grumbled, pulling my hair by the roots and forcing me to look at him. "Hmmm?"

When I kept my mouth shut, he backhanded me. I would have fallen over if Reed didn't grab me and hold me up.

Frankie let out a frustrated snarl, disgusted with my stony silence. I knew it made people sweat. Half the time its why I did it. But mostly it was just me being me. Nothing was going to change that.

Reed let me go and stood stoically behind me. I swayed on my knees but stayed upright. I was dizzy as shit but still had my wits about me. At the first sign of weakness from Frankie or the beast behind me, I would take it.

Gladly.

Frankie started pacing in front of me. I kept my eyes on him and spit a mouthful of blood on the floor. So far, he hadn't got to me but that was about to change.

"Get him up," he muttered to Reed, rubbing at the whiskers on his chin, deep in thought.

Reed jerked me to my feet. I winced. Shit, I couldn't help it. The room spun and those black spots in my vision turned into splotches. I blinked and cleared them away. If it was my last day on earth, I was going to stay conscious as long as possible.

Frankie glanced over at Cat's shoes, left where she had taken them off last night. My back stiffened, wariness putting me on edge.

He stopped in front of me and looked me up and down. "So tell me – did you fill her belly with a baby last night? Will she grow round with your son in nine months?" He smiled and took a step closer. "Don't worry. If you did, I'll raise it as my own once you're dead. I'll teach him to lead this army and I'll call him my son. He will be in good hands and so will she. I promise."

The fiery pits of hell couldn't be as bad as his words. I bared my teeth and shot toward him but Reed grabbed my shoulder and jerked me back.

Frankie chuckled. "Ah, there's your sore spot."

I became a feral animal, struggling to get free from Reed's hold. I wanted to kill Frankie. No one threatened my unborn child, whether Cat was pregnant or not.

Frankie watched me with amusement. "That bother you, boy, the thought of me raising your son? You don't like the idea of me running my hands over your woman's tummy, feeling your baby growing right there? Vulnerable. So small and tiny."

I growled and yanked at my bindings, wanting to tear him apart limb by limb.

Frankie spread his legs and looked down his nose at me. "Beg."

I went still, my heart racing a mile a minute. My face went white. I could feel all the blood drain from my body. It's what he wanted – to see me plead. Fuck, I didn't know if I could do it. But for Cat and a baby that may not even exist, I would do anything.

Swallowing hard, I said the words. "Don't. Please."

Frankie cupped a hand around his ear. "I can't hear you. Say it again."

I wanted to kill him over and over again just to see him suffer. Instead, I ate my pride. For Cat. God, for our baby that she might be carrying now. "Kill me. Just don't touch her or my child if she's pregnant. Let them go free."

Frankie smiled. "And?"

I swallowed, knowing what else he wanted. "I killed your son."

Frankie walked up to me and slapped me on the back. "Now that wasn't so hard was it?"

I felt vomit rising in my throat. He gave me another solid pat on the back. I stood motionless, feeling every last hope leave me.

The heavy door opened. I flicked my eyes up, disinterested. Adam walked in.

His face blanched when he saw me. I must've looked like crap. I looked at him bleakly, hoping he could read my mind because I sure as hell needed him to get Cat out of town as quickly as possible. The thought of her being pregnant and Frankie claiming my child made me sick to my stomach. I wanted to vomit on his shoes but I had nothing in my stomach but fear and whiskey. It was a foreign feeling for me – this vulnerability – but only concern for Cat could make me experience it so heavily.

Adam recovered from his shock and a mask of indifference fell over his face. He sauntered into the room with a relaxed gait as if he was going for a morning stroll. "All set, boss," he said to Frankie with a laidback tone.

Frankie turned to face him, the wrinkles on his leathery face deepening as he frowned. "Where's the girl?"

Adam shrugged and kept on walking. "I handed her off to Montague. Her and the kid are down in the yard just like you ordered. Front and center for this little dog and pony show."

Who the hell is Montague?

"Everything is ready?" Frankie asked in a gruff voice.

Adam stopped in front of him. "Yeah. Crowd is gathering out front. Everyone is here just like you wanted."

Frankie nodded. "Good. They want retribution and they will have it." He headed to the door, saying over his shoulder. "Reed, come with me. Adam, bring the prisoner out in ten minutes. I need to prepare."

Adam crossed his arms over his chest and stared at me as Reed went around me. The big man hit my shoulder with his as he walked by, muttering, "fuckhead," under his breath. I glared at his back as he followed Frankie out of the room.

As soon as the door closed, I looked at Adam and hissed, "Where is she?"

He looked at the bruises on my face and the blood under my nose. "You look like shit again. Can you *not* stay out of trouble?"

I shot toward him, tired of beating around the bush. "Where is Cat?"

Adam didn't move. For all his smartass remarks, he could be as cold as a dead fish sometimes.

"Her and Tate are with one of my guys. She's safe," he said.

I swore softly. Was he a moron? Did he live in la-la land? "Safe? What does that mean? Her and the kid aren't safe here at all."

Adam didn't blink. "She's okay. Trust me."

Shit, I had no choice.

I took a deep breath. "Fine. Get her out of town and…hell…I need you to—"

Adam interrupted, not moving one muscle. "I know and I will."

But I still had to say it for my own peace of mind.

"Stay with her and make her happy. She deserves it after all she's been through. Keep her safe and if…if she's pregnant…" Christ, I couldn't even finish the rest of the sentence.

Adam didn't bat an eye. "You don't have to tell me twice."

I swallowed past the solid lump in my throat and squared my shoulders. "Then let's do this."

I walked past him and headed toward the door, my hands tied behind my back and my face feeling like someone had taken a meat hammer to it.

"You that eager to die?" Adam called out, turning around to watch me.

I stopped and looked over my shoulder at him. "Do I have much choice?"

He didn't move or answer my question. Instead, he said the one thing that got my attention. "We need to talk."

Chapter Thirty-Six

-Cat-

I tried not to wail and sob. What I did do was fight.

Adam carried me out of the basement but not without receiving some scratches and a bitten finger.

"You little witch!" he roared when I clamped down on his digit. It was there as I struggled against him to get free so I latched on.

In anger, he wrapped his other arm around my chest and covered my mouth with his huge palm, carrying me facing away from him in front of his body. I attempted to bite his hand too but he smashed my lips so hard against my teeth, I couldn't move them without hurting myself.

I raised quite a ruckus as he carried me through the courthouse and out into the bright sunlight. My teeth started chattering and shivers shook my body as the cold air of early morning washed over me. But nothing would stop me from trying to get free.

I kicked and screamed behind Adam's hand as he carried me down the courthouse steps. Panic at Cash dying made me wild, impossible to control.

Adam grunted when I got a good kick to his shin but when I saw all the people gathered in the town square, I became immobile.

There had to be a hundred of them. All I could do was stare. The sun blinded me. A cold wind went straight through my dress and lifted the hem above my knees. I could care less. *They're all here to see Cash hang.*

My face paled. I didn't need a mirror to know it. My breaths came out in quick puffs of foggy air. Adam pushed his way through the crowd, holding me on his hip like a rag doll. And that's how I felt. Boneless, my arms and legs flopping uselessly against his body.

He didn't say anything which was bad in itself. It meant he could feel it too – the underlining current that something awful was about to happen and we had no way to stop it. It seemed to permeate the air and cause the little hairs on my arm to stand up.

"Where's my brother?" I managed to ask, my voice meek and afraid, just a whispered breath.

"Here," was his answer, spoken with a curt nod at the crowd.

Men in hunting jackets and women in old-fashioned flowery dresses and heavy coats turned to look at us. They frowned. They scowled. One or two spit at Adam's feet. He ignored them and moved on, toward the front of the gathering. My gaze swept over everyone, terrified, looking for a friendly face.

There were none.

The crowd's animosity was too thick, the looks too hostile. I clung to Adam's neck like a monkey, practically climbing up his body. He grunted and pulled me back down.

"Stop it," he ground out.

I calmed down except for my racing heart. It pounded like a jackhammer out of control. Every breeze or murmured voice seemed like it was coming from far away. *They're going to kill Cash. They're going to kill Cash.*

The words replayed in my head as Adam pushed his way through the throng of people, carrying me. Near the front of the crowd he drew to a stop in front of a big man with pitch black hair and caramel colored skin. "We set?"

The big Latino man nodded. "Yes, Sergeant."

"Good." Adam set me on my feet and gave me a push toward the man. "Watch her."

The man caught me as I fell against his huge, plump stomach. He must have been one of the soldiers that served with Adam in the military. Adam said some of them still took orders from him.

I scrambled off the man and spun around to plead with Adam to help Cash but the Latino caught my arm with thick, stubby fingers. "Un momento, chica."

Panicking, I tried to tug away. "No. I need to talk to Adam." He was Cash's only chance. But the man wouldn't let me go.

"You stay," he said in heavily-accented English.

My breath burst in and out of me. I felt like I was going to hyperventilate. I needed to find help. I couldn't just sit here and wait.

Grass poked up between my cold toes. My shoes were back in the basement but that was the least of my problems. I wrapped my arms around my middle and shivered violently. *Help. I need help.* I glanced back, looking for Adam but he was gone, disappearing into the crowd. All I could see was handmade stocking hats and dirty ball caps, most of the owners glaring at me. I searched for a friendly face. Mary? David?

"Sis!"

I whirled at the sound of the voice, going light-headed with happiness. "Tate!"

He was rushing around the Latino, pushing him out of the way. His long hair was damp and combed back off his high forehead, worry in his eyes.

"Oh God, I'm so happy to see you," I said, wrapping my arms around him as soon as he was close.

He leaned over and buried his face in my hair, his tall, lanky body almost toppling me over. "Are you okay? I worried about you all night. What happened? Where were you?"

New tears filled my eyes, soaking into his jacket. "I'm fine. I was with Cash last night. Are you okay?"

He shook his head, sniffing. "No. They're going to hang him, Cat. They took my knife and I…I don't know what to do to help him."

I clutched him tight. "I know," I whispered against his shirt. It was spotless and smelled like flowers. Mary. She would've made sure he ate and given him clean clothes. I sent a silent thank you to her wherever she was.

"Here, chica."

I let go of Tate as the Latino nudged my arm. He was holding a hoodie out to me. It was faded blue and didn't look warm enough to protect against the chill. The man nudged my arm again with it, urging me to take it. I looked down at it with disgust. I would rather feel the bite of cold on my skin than take anything that belonged to Frankie or his men.

The Latino nodded at the hoodie in his hand. "You're gonna need it. It's cold."

A powerful shiver shook me but I stuck my chin up anyway and glared at the man. "I don't want anything that comes from Frankie."

Tate let out a frustrated sigh. Grabbing the jacket, he yanked it from the Latino and thrust it at me. "Take the damn jacket, Cat. Don't you think Cash or Nathan would want you to if they were here right now?"

Pain squeezed my heart. If our older brother, Nathan, were alive, he would grumble at me for being stubborn and stare at me until I gave in. And Cash? Cash would tell me in that smooth voice he had to put the jacket on before he made me.

I sighed and took the jacket from Tate. My legs were like blocks of ice and my fingers were red. I stuffed my arms in the sleeves and zipped the jacket up under my chin.

As soon as I had it on, the Latino grabbed my arm and muttered in a thick accent, "My name's Montague. Come with me, por favor."

He didn't give me a chance to argue or even agree. Holding onto my arm, he dragged me through the crowd. Tate followed behind us, almost stepping on my heels to stay close. People scowled as we passed. One woman reached out and yanked my hair painfully as we walked by.

"Bitch!" she swore.

I yelped and turned to fight her off but Montague gave her a look of warning and she let me go, taking some strands of my hair with her.

He didn't seem disturbed by the animosity brewing in the crowd. He led Tate and I on, nudging his way through the people. I glanced back over my shoulder a time or two, peering at the woman. I was afraid she would attack again but she hadn't moved. Her dirty, brown hair fell in her face in limp strands. Her oversized dress hung on her gaunt body like a sack. She was staring at me with malice. It was obvious she wanted to do more than just pull a few strands of hair. She wanted me to suffer. It was there in her eyes.

I stayed close to Montague. He was big enough to clear a path in the angry, eager mob and protect us against people like the woman. But something told me he would hurt Tate or me on command if Adam – his sergeant – ordered it.

I shivered beneath the jacket. The crowd created a warm pocket but the cold still swept around my legs. Montague led us toward what appeared to be the front of the crowd. We were almost there when I saw it.

The tree.

It was a huge oak, maybe a hundred years old. Its massive branches spread out over the people. Dead leaves clung to the limbs – a few fell as we approached. But it wasn't the tree that held my attention.

It was the rope swinging from it.

My vision blurred. I felt boneless, my knees going weak. I tripped and bumped into a man. He was tall and muscular, towering over me by a foot or more. He wore a dark jacket. The hood was pulled low over his head, leaving only his chiseled jaw exposed. He exuded danger and a don't-fuck-with-me attitude. Looking down at me, he frowned. His face was shadowed under the hood but I could see bright blue eyes staring down at me with icy reserve. *Another person who hated me, I presume?*

I recoiled away from him, afraid he would pull a knife or yank his hand out of his jacket pocket and hit me, but Montague tugged me forward.

"Boss wanted you here."

He set me in a particular spot in the grass like we were rehearsing a damn dance number. When he was satisfied, he snapped his fingers at Tate and pointed to the ground next to me. My little brother gave the big Latino a *suck-this* glare but stepped next to me, standing in the place the man indicated.

I could care less about where I stood or if Tate was giving the man attitude. My gaze was fixed ahead. My fingers went cold. A great weight settled on my chest.

Tate deflated and seemed to forget about being defiant when he saw what was in front of us. "Shit."

The cold wind whipped my dress, plastering it against my body. A shiver passed over my skin. I didn't feel any of it. There was a disconnect between my brain and my body. All I could do was stare at the rope hanging in front of me.

The wind made it swing gently. Little creaking sounds came from it. Bile rose up in my throat. I was going to be sick. They were going to hang Cash from the rope.

And they were going to make me stand there and watch.

Oh god. The murmurs of people behind me faded. I felt dizzy and had trouble swallowing. Memories bombarded me, hitting me from all sides.

I was back in Luke's car. It was wrapped around a tree. My neck hurt. Blood dripped from my nose. I could still feel the pain if I closed my eyes tight enough. Every muscle had ached, every inch of me had been bruised.

I had managed to get the door open and fall out. Gravel bit into my palms. The wind had been whistling through the trees that night. I remember aching all over as I limped around the Mustang. One minute Luke had been telling me to put my seat belt on and the next…

I was screaming.

Then I was in an old house, fighting to get Paul off me. I heard the boom. I saw the gun. I watched a red blossom spread over Nathan's shirt. My older brother – the one that always watched over me – was dying.

And all I wanted to do was scream.

I wanted to do that now as I stood in front of the hanging tree. I wanted to scream at the top of my lungs. Shout at God to stop taking people I loved away from me. But I couldn't do anything but stand there and watch that swinging rope.

Waiting to take someone else away from me.

A choked sob caught me unaware. I slapped a hand over my mouth to cover it but another one escaped then another. Tears burst from my eyes. My chest hurt like someone was tearing into me. I cried. I struggled to breathe.

Tate put his arm around me when I would have fallen to my knees. Montague sidled closer and looked down at me with worry. I could feel the tall man in the hoodie behind me, looming close and staring at my back. I wished he did have a knife. Then he could end my life before I had to watch what was about to happen.

A shout of excitement went up around me. I glanced back like everyone else around me. Through a blur of tears, I saw Frankie leading a group of men through the crowd. There were six of them and they were being welcomed like saints. People slapped Frankie on the back and he stopped to shake hands with a few. As I watched, one mother held her swaddled infant daughter up proudly for Frankie to touch. He ran his finger over the rosy cheek and smiled, catching my eye from across the crowd. His gaze was full of merriment and a sort of dark satisfaction. Turning away from the mother and child, he strolled through the crowd toward me.

"Revenge, how sweet it is," he boomed out above the excited chatter of the crowd.

A shiver that had nothing to do with the cold traveled over me. Passing me without a word, Frankie nodded at me. I didn't even have the strength or courage to glare.

The hooded man behind me stared at Hilltop's leader with revulsion. His fists flexed and clenched. I could almost feel the hatred rolling off him in waves. I blinked, wondering if I was seeing things. One of the town's men wasn't brainwashed by the almighty militia leader? I tilted my head and studied him closely. His blue eyes flicked to me then slid away.

I turned my attention to the men following Frankie, dismissing the man in the hood. Behind Hilltop's leader was one of the men Cash had punched that morning. His nose was tinged red and he looked disgruntled, glaring at everyone as he walked by. When I saw the next man in line, I sucked in a breath. It was David.

He looked older than he had last night. His face was a stark white and dark circles were under his eyes. He looked haggard. Lost of all hope. Glancing at me, he tried to smile but it only came out as a grimace instead.

I looked down. In his hand, he held a Bible. My face turned ashen. My stomach rolled. He was going to pray over Cash's hanging.

My knees started to buckle. The world started to tilt. Tate gripped me harder and held me up. Without him, I would have fallen to the ground.

Frankie stopped in front of the rope and gave it a good tug. I thought I would lose the contents of my stomach – which wasn't much since I hadn't eaten in twenty-four hours. Tucking my chin into the jacket, I said a silent prayer that a miracle would happen and Cash would be spared.

Frankie turned to the crowd and held up a hand. "Friends, family. Quiet please."

The people quieted. A baby cried. The tree above us moved in the wind. Frankie waited until all attention was on him then cleared his throat and began.

"We have all suffered since the war began. We have all known heartache and hardship. But as a community we have pulled together and made a new beginning. A place of welcome. We have opened our arms to our fellow man and shared our bounties with them. But as we have learned, sometimes our generosity and love is abused and destroyed through crimes too painful to discuss. These people must be punished so they don't commit the same wrongdoings on other great Americans like us. Killing a man is never a glorious thing but the country must have laws. We must have consequences. That is why we are gathered here today. Consequences."

He turned at the sound of men approaching. Tate stiffened beside me. A murmur went through the crowd. I followed Frankie's gaze and felt like a bullet hit me all over again.

It was Cash.

His hands were tied behind his back. Adam was behind him, pushing him toward the tree. New bruises covered his jaw and cheekbones. Blood was crusted under his nose. His eyes darted over the crowd until he found me. I took a step toward him but Montague stopped me with a hand to my arm. Cash never took his eyes off me as Adam shoved him to the rope.

I choked back a sob, shaking. Cash heard it and gulped, his Adam's apple bobbing up and down in his throat. His gaze drifted over the crowd, all emotions hidden. But I saw it – there in his eyes – worry. It was there quickly then disappeared, replaced by acceptance. He was ready to die.

He faced the crowd proudly, his shoulders straight, his gaze ahead. *No. No. This is not happening. This is not happening.* I put a hand over my mouth, muffling my cries. My eyes brimmed with fresh tears. My body shook with more than just chills.

Frankie pointed at Cash, his voice gruff and booming over the wind. "This man took a life that would've led us to victory. He ended a soul that would have brightened our future. That's why he needs to be hanged today. Consequences, my friends. We have laws and he broke them. He must pay for his crimes."

The crowd cheered. The people on the other side of Tate shook their fists in the air. Tate eased closer to me and looked down at me with fear.

I grabbed his hand and squeezed it tight. My heart raced. Tears fell down my icy cheeks. I watched as Frankie turned and walked behind Cash.

Cash met my eyes as Frankie placed the rope over his head. I let out a sob and put the back of my hand over my mouth, cutting off the sound.

Cash didn't flinch when Frankie tightened the noose around his neck. He didn't blink when the crowd grew louder. He just kept his gaze on me, unwavering and unmoving.

I started shaking my head, my lips trembling. *This isn't real. It isn't real.* Frankie walked back beside Cash and faced the crowd.

"Ladies and gentlemen, this man killed my son. It is time for him to hang."

He motioned to two men standing on the other side of Cash. They stepped forward and grabbed the rope hanging from the tree branch. One wrapped the end around his waist for leverage and the other grasped the rope just ahead of him.

I dropped my hand from my mouth and looked into Cash's eyes. The world seemed to stop. It was just him and me.

"I love you," I whispered right before the men pulled the rope.

Chapter Thirty-Seven

-Cat-

It happened in seconds. The men pulled. The rope went taut. Cash jerked.

And the world exploded in a rain of gunfire.

The crowd went crazy. There were screams and shouts. People started ducking and running in all directions. I was pushed and shoved and almost fell to the ground. A shot rang out over my head.

Confusion and fear caused mass chaos. The thundering sound of galloping horses came from behind me. Amid the screams, I heard a yelp. One of Frankie's men fell to the ground, an arrow buried in his heart.

A rider on horseback came barreling through the terrified crowd. He had a crossbow raised and aimed at the men surrounding Cash.

Gavin.

I had never been so happy to see anyone in my life before. He peered down the bow and released another arrow, hitting a man in the chest. Before the man fell, Gavin was yanking a gun from his holster, looking like an outlaw on a rampage. He raised the gun and fired off a shot as his horse danced under him nervously.

Tate grabbed my arm and yanked me out of the way as a man roared and sprinted past us toward Gavin. I glanced back at Cash in enough time to see Adam withdraw a knife from under his jacket and slashed it through the ties binding Cash's wrists. As Cash untangled his hands, Adam turned in enough time to avoid being attacked by a militia soldier. Ducking, he swung hard, catching the man with a powerful uppercut. When the man went down, Adam tossed the knife to Cash.

Cash caught it in one hand and yanked the rope off his neck with the other. He palmed the knife and turned just as Frankie charged him.

"You piece of…!" Frankie dove at Cash, his face twisted in fury.

Cash moved so fast, I didn't see it. His arm whipped out. The knife went flying. Frankie stumbled to a stop. His eyes went wide. He stared down at his chest, open-mouthed. For the first time ever, I saw fear in his eyes. The blade was buried to the hilt in his torso, a red blossom spreading.

He dropped to his knees and sank back on his haunches. Cash reached him in two quick strides and grabbed a wad of his gray-streaked hair. He yanked the leader's head back and reached down for the knife handle sticking out of the man's chest. It made a sickening, sucking sound as Cash pulled it free and laid the blade against the the older man's jugular.

"This is for my unborn son."

I squeezed my eyes shut as he dragged the edge along Frankie's throat. A second later there was the sound of gurgling and the thud of a body hitting the ground.

As shouts and screams came around me, I peeled my eyes open. People were running and fighting everywhere. Tate was pushing a man away. Montague was standing guard over me, ready to attack.

I avoided looking at the figure laid out under the old oak tree and focused on Cash. He was trying to get to me but someone jumped in his path. A man in overalls and a John Deere hat. Cash threw a punch and caught the man in the temple but the stranger recovered quickly and pulled a pistol.

"Cash!" I screamed.

He swung and knocked the gun out of the man's hand with a swift sweep of his arm. The man made a dive for his weapon but Cash was on him in seconds. He threw the man onto his back and buried his knife into the man's shoulder.

The man screamed and thrashed under Cash. Cash slid the knife out of him just as David let out a hoarse cry. He was wrestling with a short, stocky man on the ground. The man had the upper hand. He was at least a decade younger and he had a gun in his hand.

Cash jumped to his feet. The preacher had saved our lives. Now Cash was going to save his.

David wasn't the only one in trouble. Adam was fighting off the giant, Reed. He had lost his weapon and Reed had him in a deadly chokehold. Adam's face was turning purple by the second and his feet were scrambling to get a foothold on the ground. He fought the big man vigorously but Reed was a bull instead of a wolf like Adam. Stronger but not so smart.

Montague let out a growl at seeing his sergeant in trouble. He pulled out his gun. "Stay here with your brother, little chica," he muttered before sprinting through the crowd to Adam.

People shouted with fury. In front of me, two men pulled out guns and raced forward. Tate grabbed the front of my jacket. "Get behind me, sis."

He shoved me behind him and widened his stance, protecting me from the violence and mayhem. We were on our own. Cash and Adam were fighting. Gavin was taking out men from atop his horse yards away.

I glanced around frantically, looking for Cash and a way out. That's when I saw him. A man with hate in his eyes charging toward Tate and me. I clasped the back of

Tate's jacket and tried to yank him out of the way but he was holding steady, waiting…

"Tate! Go! Go!" I shouted.

His fist shot out, a solid punch to the man's nose. The stranger's eyes rolled into the back of his head and he toppled backwards like a downed tree.

Tate shook his hand. "Damn, fuck. That was like hitting a fuckin' concrete wall."

I let go of his shirt and searched for Cash. *Where is he? Where is he?* Growing frantic, I raised up on my toes. *There.*

He had taken out David's attacker and was fighting other men. They seemed to be descending on him in droves. I shot forward to rush to him but someone grabbed me around the waist and yanked me back. I fought and scratched at his arm. He growled and spun me around.

It was the man in the dark hoodie.

Tate whipped around to save me but the man gripped his shirt and wrenched him close.

"Cool it, kid," he rumbled in a raspy voice.

I tried to smack him in the face but he let go of Tate and grabbed my wrist in a bone-crushing grip. With his other hand, he yanked the hood off. Blue eyes the color of a cloudless sky stared down at me. A whiskered jaw clenched and flexed. I was held spellbound for a second, staring back at him, until I realized he wasn't going to let me go.

His fingers tightened on my wrist and he glanced at Tate. "Both of you, come with me."

Another time, another place, I would have had to pick my jaw off the ground. The man was gorgeous. He had unruly, sun-kissed brown hair and was rugged and his eyes were so piercing blue, they were breathtaking. He was tall and muscular as well, but I didn't know him and he wasn't Cash so that made him my enemy.

Tate seemed be willing to go with him but I dug in my heels and clawed at his hand wrapped around my wrist. "Let. Me. Go!"

He let out an impatient sigh and peeled my fingers off his hand. "Settle down. I'm here to help you. My name's Ryder."

Like that means anything to me.

"Well, fuck me," Tate whispered, staring at the man in wonderment.

Seeing my blank expression, Ryder rolled his amazing eyes and scoffed. "Shit, the little fucker didn't tell you about me? Figures. Cash is a…friend. Let's just leave it at that. Now, are you going to come with me or do I have to carry you? Your choice."

I furrowed my brow. Ryder. There *was* something familiar about his name… My gaze flicked behind him at movement.

"Watch out!" I yelled.

He swung around just as a man came at him with a knife. Ryder raised his gun and fired. A stream of smoke rose from the end of the gun, blinding me for a moment. The boom muffled my hearing, making the shouts around me muted. When the smoke cleared, I saw the man. He was laid out on the ground but there was another one charging right behind him.

It was like they were multiplying around us in the dozens. Ryder and Tate fought them but we were surrounded. Outnumbered and outgunned.

"Stay behind me!" Ryder yelled, pushing Tate behind him and dodging a fist.

I turned to find Cash, to get help, and that's when it happened. An arm snaked around my waist. A cold nose buried in my hair, right over my ear.

"Told you I'd have you one way or the other."

My face went white. My stomach bottomed out. It was Paul.

He shoved the hard end of a gun into my side. "Let's go, little bird."

I looked at Ryder and Tate. They were too busy fighting off men to notice. I opened my mouth to shout at them but the gun jammed into my side painfully.

I winced and curved my body away – it was my side with the still-healing bullet wound – but Paul yanked me back to him. He leaned down and whispered in my ear again, his hot breath fanning over my hair.

"Scream and I'll put a bullet in your brother's spine. He'll never walk again."

I closed my mouth. Tears from the gun wedged in my ribs and the fear for Tate's life, filled my eyes.

"Good girl," Paul hissed in my ear. He grabbed my upper arm in a bruising grip and started dragging me through the crowd.

I stumbled. I almost fell. I blinked away the tears. He used the chaos to his advantage and hauled me through the mob of people. The gun poked into my side and his fingers pinched my arm. I tried to turn around and look for Cash, Tate, or Adam – *somebody* – but I couldn't see anybody in the fighting.

I had fought off Ryder like a madwoman but fear froze me with Paul. My mind shut down. I couldn't fight. Couldn't breathe.

At the edge of the crowd, Paul steered me toward the hotel. I woke up from my terrified stupor. If he got me inside, the worst would happen. I had to do something.

I ignored the gun in my side and tried to yank out of his grip. He frowned and held onto to me tighter but I wasn't giving up yet. I started to turn and scream for help but Paul lifted the gun and pressed it against my temple.

"You yell, you get a bullet. If anyone comes after you, they get one too."

I swallowed my scream and stilled.

Paul smiled. "Good, good. I knew you were a brave little one. I want to play with you some more."

He jammed the gun in my side again and tugged me toward the hotel entrance. I shook violently as he yanked open the door and pushed me in. The interior was dark and cold. Empty and eerie quiet. I shivered and tried to shrink away but Paul's broken and long fingernails bit into my arm painfully and held me still as he flipped the lock on the hotel's door.

My heart pounded. I struggled to breath. He was locking us in. I could taste the terror, rising on my tongue like bile. No one would find me. No one would know where to look. I wondered if I could fight him off again or if this was it. The end.

Paul shoved me into the dining room. I listened for any signs of Mary but all I could hear was the hum of a heater and the rushing of blood in my ears.

He prodded my side harder with the gun as we headed toward the stairs. "Your man foiled my plans, escaping the noose like some damn escape artist. But when I saw my opening, I took it. We got business to finish, little thing, and I'm looking forward to it."

I found my voice and some courage. "He's going to kill you," I hissed, trying to jerk out of his grasp. "But I hope you suffer first."

Paul laughed, a high-pitched squeaky sound. "Ain't lost none of that sass have you? Well, I'll beat it out of you and teach you a thing or two about respect. First, let's get somewhere more private."

He gave me a hard shove up the stairs. I almost tripped on the bottom step but caught myself, grabbing onto the railing. My hands shook. I could hear the faint sounds of gunfire and shouting outside.

I took my time going up the dark stairway, trying to buy time. Maybe if I went slow enough, someone would show up. I just needed to distract Paul and keep him from getting me into a room alone.

"They are going to figure out I'm missing. It's only a matter of time until they come looking for me," I said, moving slow up the stairs.

Paul snorted behind me. "Let 'em. By the time they show up, I'll be done with you and you'll be no good for anyone anymore."

He gave me a hard shove at the top of the stairs. I fell to my knees but he yanked me up and dragged me down the hallway. I fought and twisted but he buried his hand in the back of my hair and jerked me to him. Tears prickled the back of my eyes as he pulled strands of hair. He shoved the gun up under my jaw.

"That's enough, little bird. I would hate to splatter these walls with you."

I shivered with fright. I didn't know what to do. When I calmed down, Paul lowered the gun and pushed me the rest of the way down the hallway until we came to the last door. Pushing it open, he propelled me inside. It was colder. Darker. The room had been shut up, the warmth from the heater not able to reach it. The blinds had been drawn, only small beams of sunlight getting in.

Paul let me go and gave me a hard shove into the room. I staggered forward and stopped in the middle of the room. Turning, I faced him, shrinking back.

He kicked the door closed with the heel of his boot and locked it. Setting his gun down on a small side table by the door, he strolled into the room, licking his lips and looking me up and down.

"Take off that dress, honey," he said in a smooth voice, a lecherous look in his eyes. "I want to see all of you."

I backed away, my bare feet so cold I couldn't feel them anymore. "No. Go to hell."

He chuckled, sounding fascinated by my refusal. "Say that again – no. I like it."

I gulped and took a step back.

"Come on. Say it again. 'No' sounds so sweet coming from your mouth. I love it when you refuse. I *really* love it when you struggle. Makes me all horny and hot. Really gets my dick hard. You wanna see?" He reached for his zipper.

Bile rose in my throat and I shook my head, moving back slowly.

He giggled and popped open the top button of his jeans. "Oops. How did that happen? Your turn, little bird. Take off your dress."

My hip hit the bedside table, making the lamp on it shake. "Screw you."

Paul shrugged, his gaze lustful and hungry on my legs. "Guess I'll have to do it myself then."

I screeched as he leaped at me and tried to dart away but he was fast.

"NOOOO!" I screamed as he grabbed me and flung me to the floor.

My head hit the hard surface. Stars appeared behind my eyes. Before I could recover, he was on me. Pulling my dress up. Yanking my underwear down. Vicious. Painful. His nails scraping the back of my thighs.

"There it is," he murmured, his thick middle finger finding me.

I came alive. Thrashing. Crying out. I tried to buck him off me but he had me pinned to the floor, grating my hipbones into the cold, hard wood with his crotch.

I screamed and fought, becoming a madwoman. He restrained me with an arm across my back and leaned off enough to unzip his pants. I went berserk, digging my fingers into the floor and trying to crawl out from under him. Screaming until my throat was raw.

He held me down and pushed his jeans out of the way, muttering obscene things that he couldn't wait to do with me. A warm, fleshy object smacked my leg. Oh god. Oh god. I was going to be sick. *Run, Cat, now!* That voice in my head screamed.

I gagged and tried to crawl out from under him, but he was stronger and determined to get what he wanted. He grabbed a handful of my hair and tucked me back under him.

"You're so soft, little bird." He trailed a finger over my bottom, despite my struggling. "Time to make you sing."

When he leaned close to my ear, I saw my chance. It was either fight or be raped. Do or die.

I threw my elbow back as hard as I could. It caught him in the jaw, the pointy bone hitting its mark. *Smack*!

He let out a yelp of pain and let me go, his head snapping back and his jaw cracking to the side. Knowing I had only seconds, I pushed to my feet and started to run but he recovered quick.

And went crazy.

"Bitch!" He grabbed the hem of my dress and yanked.

I heard a tear but scrambled to get away, the collar of the dress choking me as he held on. He gave the dress another hard tug and dragged me back. I screamed and fought but he grabbed a chunk of my hair and slammed me down to the floor.

I cried out and flailed. He was breathing hard, angry. Insane. He pulled my head up and slammed it down. My cheek hit the floor. Pain exploded in my head. I struggled to stay conscious and tried to crawl away. He lifted my head up and slammed it down again. Harder. Pulling strands of my hair out, muttering under his breath that I was his.

He was killing me. I knew it in some part of my brain as he rammed my head onto the floor. Everything went fuzzy. The room faded in and out. My muscles shut down. Blackness started to take over. The metallic taste of blood filled my mouth.

Paul grunted with approval when I grew limp. He shoved my dress around my waist and crawled on top of me. "God, I'm going to love this."

My eyes drifted closed as he shoved my legs apart. Unconsciousness was pulling me under, sheltering me from what was about to happen.

Cash would find me like this.

Tate would see what the monster did to me.

I wouldn't survive.

I heard Paul's rapid breathing in my ear a second before the world went black and I passed out.

Chapter Thirty-Eight

-Cat-

The sound came from far away. *Whaaack! Whaaack!*

"Cat!" a voice roared followed by a swift kick to the door.

My eyelids lifted slowly. Pain exploded in my head and left cheekbone. I wasn't sure how long I had been out but it hadn't been long. Paul was still on top of me but he hadn't done anything.

Yet.

"Fuck!" he swore when another solid kick landed on the door.

He was doing something. Fumbling. He couldn't get it up and someone was trying to get in the room.

I wanted to shout for help but my jaw hurt and every time I swallowed, I tasted blood. I tried to focus. The room wavered in and out, making my stomach roll and my head spin.

"Goddamn it! Cat!" an angry voice bellowed on the other side of the door. "Answer me!"

The door shook on its hinges as another kick landed on it, angry and violent.

Cash! He was here!

I had to do something. Paul was distracted. Cash was right outside the door. I licked my dry lips and tried to yell but my head felt like it was going to burst and my lower jaw felt dislocated.

"This is bullshit," Paul swore as Cash pounded on the door. He rammed my head down on the floor and shoved my legs apart when I locked them together.

Fumbling to push his jeans down further, he grumbled. “He can’t get in but I swear I’m getting in you, little bird, one way or another.”

Flattening his hand down on my head, he shoved my face into the floor and kneeled between my legs.

I let out a broken cry and struggled to crawl away.

Paul leaned over and covered my mouth with his hand. “Shh. Shh. It’ll only take a minute. Next time we’ll take our time and *really* play, I promise.”

Vomit heaved in me. I screamed against his hand and thrashed.

“CAT!” Cash roared.

The desperation in his voice propelled me. I bit Paul’s finger, chomping down on the meaty part as hard as I could. He shouted a curse and yanked his hand away.

As soon as my mouth was uncovered, I screamed. “Cash!”

A hard kick hit the door. The hollow wood shook. A cheap picture of a meadow fell to the floor and shattered.

I screamed again. “Cash! Help me!”

Another swift kick to the door had it flying open. It slammed back on its hinges and hit the inside wall.

“You son of a bitch!” Cash roared, charging into the room.

Paul scrambled off me. “Hey man. Hey man. She wanted it, I swear.”

He held up one hand and fumbled to pull his jeans up with the other.

A bellow burst from Cash. He flew at Paul and swung.

His knuckles connected with Paul’s face. Paul’s head snapped to the side. He teetered on his knees near me but shook off the hit and snarled at Cash. “She’s—”

Cash hit him again, shredding the skin on Paul’s cheekbone and rattling the teeth in his head. I had never seen him so vicious before or glimpsed such a fatal look in his eyes.

"I told you I would kill you," he scowled, his knuckles bloody and raw as he swung again.

Paul grunted as the punch caught him on the jaw and snapped his head to the side again. He recovered quickly and spit out a tooth on the floor. "I'm not dead yet, motherfucker."

He roared and dived for Cash. Cash hit him in the ribs with a hard blow but Paul wrapped his arms around Cash's middle and took him down to the floor.

Before Cash could get up, Paul was on him. He hammered away at Cash's ribcage, his fists flying nonstop.

Cash tried to curl his body inward and protect his bruised and broken ribs but Paul laid into him like a professional, pummeling him.

My limbs shook and every part of me hurt but I pushed myself up. I had to help Cash. He was hurt and bloody. Paul had the upper hand.

I pushed myself to my feet unsteadily. The room spun and my head ached. Paul didn't notice me. He was too busy nailing Cash's face. "She's my little bird! Mine! Get your own!" he screamed.

A thick strand of his hair fell across his forehead as he hit Cash again and again. A wild look was in his eyes. He started talking incoherently but his fists were spot on. "Mine! Mine!"

Blood burst from Cash's nose. He fought, catching Paul in the ribs and spleen but Paul was a lunatic. A loose cannon on speed.

Cash grunted with each hit. I realized as I stood wavering on my feet, that he was taking the punches and not fighting back, letting Paul beat him to a pulp.

I took a wobbly step forward. *What is he doing?*

As I watched, he reached down and pulled a deadly looking blade out of his boot. He turned it over slowly in his hand as Paul pounded him.

Oh fuck. Oh fuck.

"She's mine! She's mine!" Paul shouted as he punched Cash.

Cash glared up at Paul, his bruised jaw hard and his face bloody. "You're wrong, asshole. She's mine."

He thrust. The blade went deep into Paul's kidney.

He howled and arched his body, reaching back for the knife. Blubbing like a baby, he sucked his lower lip in and out of his mouth and grasped the handle with a cry.

Cash crawled out from under him, bleeding, bruised, but far from weak. He got to his feet and stumbled to me.

"Go, Cat. Get out of here," he said, grasping my arm and breathing hard.

I shook my head. My gaze flicked past him as Paul let out a hiss.

Like a bad horror movie with a villain that wouldn't die, Paul squeezed his eyes closed and grimaced as he pulled the knife out of his back. Blood started running down his jacket and turning his jeans red.

He gulped and turned as white as a ghost but he wasn't done yet. Still on his knees, he grasped the bloody knife and slashed out at Cash's leg.

Cash darted back, inches from getting cut. Paul bellowed in frustration and lunged again. The knife made another wide arch through the air, almost grazing Cash's stomach.

Shit! Shit! I have to do something! I glanced around the room – frantic and terrified. About to lose the lunch I never had. Then I saw it. The gun that Paul had set down by the door.

I flew across the room, ignoring the way my legs shook or how things went in and out of focus. My hip hit the small table. A knickknack fell off and shattered. I grabbed the gun and slipped the safety off. My hands were trembling and damp from fear.

From behind me came the sound of a body hitting a wall. I swung around, the gun held out in front of me. Paul had Cash up against the wall, trying to bury the knife in his neck. The tip nicked Cash's neck. A drop of blood appeared.

Cash grasped Paul's wrist, keeping the knife from slicing his jugular. The tendons in his neck stood out in the struggle. His muscular body was pinned to the wall. His lip was bleeding and a cut on his cheekbone was dripping. One slip of the knife and he would die right in front of my eyes.

I didn't think. I didn't consider my options. I was going to save the man I loved.

I took three long strides across the room and stopped an arm's length away from Paul. With a suddenly steady hand, I lifted the gun and pointed it at his head.

"Drop it, asshole."

He froze. Sweat dripped down his face despite the cold. I ignored my own goosebumps and stared at him.

Glancing over at me, he smiled. "Hey, sweetie. Just give me a second and I'll get to you." He winked and turned his attention back to Cash.

Cash grabbed his arm and twisted. The sound of bone breaking was followed by the clink of the knife hitting the floor.

"OWWWW!" Paul screamed, cradling his broken arm and stumbling away.

Cash pushed off the wall and swung, striking him in the nose with a sharp, fast punch. Bone crunched. Blood spurted. Paul shrieked and grabbed his broken nose.

"Motherfucking bastard! I'll show you!" Dropping his hand, blood pouring from his nostrils, he turned toward me and charged.

Shaking, I pulled the trigger. The gun kicked back in my hand, throwing me back. The bullet exploded from the end, deafening me.

The slug hit Paul in the chest with a sickening thud. He froze and looked down at the blood spreading on his shirt. I fell back a step, swaying. With one arm wrapped around his ribs, Cash grabbed me and held me steady. I watched – feeling like I was having an out of body experience – as Paul reached up and touched the hole in his shirt. He looked up at me with confusion and dropped to his knees.

A broken sob escaped me. I lowered the gun. But I couldn't take my eyes off Paul. What he had done to me, what he had tried to do, kept replaying in my mind. He had touched me, said things to me. He had taken my brother from me and almost taken Cash.

I raised the gun.

Cash's voice sounded like it was coming from far away, telling me to give him the gun. Saying I didn't want it on my conscience. But I did.

For Nathan.

When Paul looked at Cash and lunged one more time, I did it.

I pulled the trigger.

Chapter Thirty-Nine

-Cat-

The gun exploded. Paul toppled over. I couldn't move. The gun was still in my hand, still pointed straight ahead.

Cash ran his hand over mine, cupping the weapon. "It's okay, Cat. Give me the gun, sweetheart" he said in a gentle voice. "He can't hurt you anymore."

I couldn't let go. My fingers were stiff around the cold metal. Cash looked at me and pried the gun from my cold hand, his touch careful and slow.

As soon as it was gone, my arm fell limp to my side. I stared straight ahead and took a deep, shuddering breath. "Oh god."

Still holding his ribs, Cash's other arm went around me, pulling me to him.

"Fuck, Cat. Fuck," he said hoarsely against the top of my head.

I stood stiffly beside him. My mind was blank except for four words.

I killed a man.

Cash moved his hand up to the back of my head, cradling me close. His lips touched my head.

"You're okay," he whispered, holding the gun pointed down. "Thank God you're okay."

His voice was hoarse, the words broken. I realized with a start that he was shaking, his hand trembling as he stroked me. Knowing this rugged, tough cowboy could be frightened by the thought of almost losing me, made the flood gates open. I buried my face in his chest and cried.

I don't know how long we stayed that way. Cash held me as I cried. It was as much for him as for me. We needed each other. Words weren't required; touching said it all.

He pressed me to him closer. I breathed in the scent of him. His whiskers grabbed at my hair. My fingers clenched his jacket.

When I started shaking with cold and my chilled nose pressed into his chest, he let go of me and crossed the room in two quick strides, stuffing the gun in the back of his waistband.

I stood in place, trembling, watching as he yanked the blanket from the bed and retrieved my underwear from the floor. Color burned my cheeks and my stomach tightened painfully. I was suddenly back on the floor, Paul forcing me down to touch me. I could remember his hands on me, making my skin slither.

I whimpered and fell back a step. Cash returned quickly and wrapped the blanket around my shoulders. then dropped to his knees and held out the underwear.

"You're okay, Cat, you hear me?" His voice was hard, determined like he was saying it as much to convince himself as he was to convince me.

I nodded numbly. He frowned and dropped to his knees in front of me, holding out my underwear for me to step into. I didn't. I couldn't.

"Cat, please."

His tone was so heart wrenching, so pain-filled. I put my hands on his shoulders for balance and stepped into my underwear. We were more than just two people who couldn't keep their hands off each other. We took care of each other even in the toughest of times.

He pulled my underwear up my legs, the backs of his knuckles warm against my chilled skin.

"You're the most stubborn woman I know. You don't take shit from no one and that's what I lo—"

I hiccupped, a tear falling down my cheek. "Cash, he tried to…"

"Fuck," Cash swore under his breath and shot to his feet. He cupped my cheeks and bent down to look in my eyes. His throat worked hard, pain crossed his battered face.

"Did I…" he gulped and closed his eyes. When he opened them again, there was anguish in his gaze. "Did I stop him in enough time?"

I nodded. "Yes."

"Thank god." The words were said on a rush of air. He wiped a tear away and glanced over my features. My forehead. My eyes. My mouth and lower. His face was a patchwork of black and blue. His nose bloody. One eye still swollen and the other blood-filled.

I hissed with pain and pulled my chin away when he touched the edge of my jaw.

"What happened? Your jaw is bruised."

I licked my lips. "He slammed my head against the floor."

Cash swore, his hands dropping to my arms. "If you hadn't killed him, I would've just for those bruises alone."

I started to peek around Cash's arm. I had to look, to make sure Paul was really dead and he wouldn't hurt me again. But Cash stepped in front of me, blocking my view.

"Don't."

I looked up at him through the tears in my eyes. He was so tall and imposing. So strong. I remembered how he looked, with the rope around his neck. I took a step closer. He drew in a sharp breath and his body went tense, aware of me like I was of him.

"You're alive," I whispered, holding the blanket around me.

He didn't move. "Yeah. Gavin snuck into town and found out that they were going to hang me. He cornered Mary and she got Adam. They made plans to get us out."

I drew my brows together. "When did that happen? Adam led me to believe they were going to hang you." I took a step closer, suddenly angry. "Do you know how terrible it was, watching them put that noose around your neck?"

Cash stared down at me, his gray eyes haunted and cold as he remembered. "I didn't find out until seconds before Adam dragged me out of the basement. If he told you, you wouldn't have been upset. Frankie would have known something was up. He was smart and tuned into you like a hawk. You were our key to make it play out right. I needed to be out in the open and the only way to make that happen was for them to almost hang me."

"Did Tate know?"

Cash shook his head. "No. We needed him to be a hothead like Frankie expected."

I was angry that no one told me and let me worry but something nagged at me. Something Cash said…

"Right before you killed Frankie, I heard you say it was for your unborn son."

Cash's gaze went dark. The muscle in his jaw ticked.

"He said if you were pregnant, he would raise the baby as his own after I was dead." His eyes moved down to my stomach and back up. "I don't know if you're pregnant or not, but the thought of that monster touching my son or daughter—"

Angry voices cut him off. He let me go and swung to the open doorway, the gun in his hand. I heard running footsteps. Many of them. Pounding up the stairs. Heading our way. We were still in a town full of bloodthirsty people. We were the hunted. The prey.

Standing close, Cash slipped a knife out from under his jacket and pressed it into the palm of my hand. He held a finger to his lips, telling me to be quiet, then started toward the door.

He closed it quietly, hardly making a sound. The sound of men got closer. Fear made me take a step back then another. I raised the knife in front of me and avoided looking at Paul's body. I kept my eyes on the door instead and prayed.

The footsteps got closer. Men. Big. Running with purpose. Terror made me shake along with the cold that found its way under my dress and the blanket.

I glanced from the door to Cash nervously. His profile was in shadows as he listened for the men, the gun was clasped tightly between his fingers.

I gulped with fear, my heart beating so hard I was afraid the men could hear it. The footsteps were louder. Closer.

"Sis!"

My gaze flew to Cash's. *Tate!*

I flew forward just as Cash opened the door. Tate appeared in the doorway and pushed past Cash.

"Where is she? Where the fuck is she?" he shouted, rushing inside.

"Here," I said, lowering the knife.

He let out a small cry and ran to me. I almost fell back as he wrapped his arms around me and hugged me tightly.

"Easy, kid. She's banged up," Cash said, watching from the door.

Tate didn't let up. He squeezed me tight, his lanky body almost bending me backwards.

Someone else appeared in the doorway. The man in the hoodie. Ryder.

"You found her," he said, walking into the room and slipping the safety back on the gun he held in front of him.

Cash shot to Ryder and had him up against the wall in seconds. "No thanks to you, Ryder. Where the fuck were you? You were supposed to grab her and run."

Ryder glared at Cash and shoved him away. "I was trying not to get killed so I could save her hide and yours."

Cash let him go but didn't back down. "You fucking owed me."

Ryder got in Cash's face. "Like you wouldn't have saved Maddie anyway."

I let go of Tate and stared at Cash with confusion. I knew who Maddie was. He had told me about her, but why was there jealousy in Ryder's voice. What was going on?

Ryder gave Cash a fuck-you glare and strolled in, his gaze pinning me in place.

He was big and tall and his attitude sucked but I refused to be scared. He had a backpack over one shoulder and a shotgun slung on the other. Where Cash was calm and deadly, this guy was a lit bomb ready to go off. He strolled into the room with a roll of his hips and stopped right in front of me as Tate stepped away to look at Paul's body.

"You okay?" he asked, looking down at me with his crystal clear blue eyes.

I nodded, aware that Cash was watching, looking anything but happy.

Ryder stared at me a second longer then went to the window, dismissing me without another glance.

As soon as he was gone, Tate was back in front of me, looking at the bruises on my jaw and cheek. "Holy shitballs, Cat. What did that man do to you?"

Before I could answer him, more people filed into the room. Gavin. David. A man with short brown hair who looked like he belonged on a high school football team instead of fighting in a town from hell. Adam appeared last, looking like a soldier with his mouth set in a rigid line and an assault rifle in his hand. They piled into the room one by one, tense and roughed up.

Alive.

David and Gavin headed straight to me, shooting questions at me nonstop.

"Are you okay?"

"Where are you hurt?"

"What did he do?"

I had been okay but it was too much. They were crowding me. Intimidating me with their size when I had never been afraid of them before. I hunched my shoulders and drew away, cowering. It was an automatic response, one I wasn't proud of. I was imagining Paul's hands on me. Touching. Trying. Invading. I whimpered and started shaking, feeling pathetic but unable to control the fear.

Tate frowned at me. "What the fuck, sis?"

Cash stiffened by the door. Adam was talking to him in low tones but when he heard me whimper, he pushed past Adam and over to me.

"Back off," he told Gavin and David, muttering and not happy.

David moved away but Gavin didn't go anywhere.

"Cool your engines, Romeo. I was an EMT and she needs to be looked at. Her face is a mess." He leaned down to peer into my eyes. "What did he do to you, pussycat? Talk to me."

I glared at him, feeling my fear dissipate. "Don't call me that. I hate it."

Gavin grinned and reached for my chin. "Works every time. Make a girl mad enough and she forgets to be afraid."

"You're an expert at doing that, Gavin. I wouldn't be proud," Ryder muttered from the window, peeking out between the blinds.

Gavin snorted and grasped my chin. I flinched but he grabbed it anyway and turned it right then left, studying me. His grin disappeared. He glanced up at Cash. "What happened?"

Cash frowned down at me, crossing his arms over his chest. "He slammed her head against the floor, among other things."

"Damn," the High School Football Star whispered, rubbing a hand over his face with uncomfortable irritation.

"Shit, sis," Tate mumbled, shifting from foot to foot beside me. "Did you kill him?"

Cash told him to shut up. Gavin got closer to study my pupils. It was too much. I felt like a subject under a microscope – bared and exposed for all to see. Plus, there was a body feet away. Someone I had killed. Combine that with the fact that I hadn't ate in over twenty-four hours, I almost watched Cash get hanged, and I probably had a concussion and…oh god, I was going to be sick.

I pushed past Cash and Gavin, dropping the blanket. I didn't make it very far before my stomach emptied, right in front of High School Football Star's dusty boots.

Cash was immediately behind me, holding me upright and tucking my hair behind my ear. The room grew quiet. A clock ticked somewhere in the hotel.

I looked up. Mr. Football Star was slightly green as he stared down at me.

"We haven't met yet. I'm Brody." He attempted a smile and failed.

Gavin kneeled down beside me and looked up at Cash. "You want me to look at her now?"

Before Cash could answer, Ryder's brusque voice cut in. "Make it fast, Gavin. We're about to have company."

I looked over at him. He was holding the blind open enough to peer out. Sounds of shouts came from outside the hotel, right below.

Cash nodded at Gavin. "Make sure she's okay."

Gavin reached for my chin again and turned my head one way then another. He studied my eyes and whispered an apology when he touched my jaw. I winced and whispered that it was okay, studying him myself.

He was very handsome despite his annoying attitude. His hair was pitch black and his eyes were the same bright blue as Ryder's. He had a small cut on one cheek and an old scar that ran through one eyebrow. His easygoing attitude seemed to be a rouse. I had seen the serious side of him which reminded me…

I licked my dry lips and asked the one question that hadn't left my mind in weeks. "Is Keely okay?"

Gavin's fingers paused on my cheek. "Yeah." His voice softened. "She says hi."

I smiled. A weight lifted off my shoulders.

Gavin let go of my chin and looked up at Cash. "She's banged up and will probably be hurting worse tomorrow but I think—"

Ryder interrupted from the window. "No time. We've to go *now*."

Cash pulled me up and grabbed the blanket. Wrapping it around me, he grasped the front and pulled me to him. "Stay close."

I nodded and we rushed out of the room. Ryder led the way followed by Gavin, David, and Tate. Cash and I hurried to keep up with Adam bringing up the rear and watching our backs.

We rushed down the cold, dark hallway and down the stairs. In the dining room, we could hear voices outside. A group of men. Angry. Close. Coming our way.

Ryder went over to the window and peered out. "They're here."

The front door knob jiggled. Cash pushed me behind him and raised his gun. Tate stood beside him, pulling a gun from the back of his jeans and providing extra protection for me too.

Gavin, Brody, and Ryder had their weapons up and cocked. David eased to the window and peered out.

"Six of them. Armed to the hilt." He looked over his shoulder at us. "They're mighty mad, boys. It'll be a fight to get out."

I back away, my heart thumping with fear. Cash looked back at me, his gaze moving over my body quickly.

"I'm not going to let anything happen to you, Cat. I promise."

I nodded. I believed him. But the door handle wiggled some more. My heart knocked against my chest harder. Suddenly, the kitchen door flew open. Everyone swung their guns around.

It was Mary. She rushed in, ignoring the weapons pointing at her and spotting me immediately.

"Oh, child. Oh, child. This is just awful," she cried, running to me, pushing Cash and Tate out of the way.

Her flabby arms went around me. Her soft body hit mine. The smell of the outdoors and freshly baked bread wafted up from her curly, gray hair.

"It's okay," I whispered against the wiry strands. "We're alive."

"For now," Ryder grumbled, peeking past the lace curtain on the window.

Mary patted my back very motherly then pulled away and sniffed, wiping her nose on the back of her flowery, quilted jacket. "You have to leave now. Here—" She grabbed hold of the blanket around me and started pulling me toward the kitchen door, glancing back at Cash. "Go out the back. It's the only way out. They've got the front surrounded."

She pushed open the swinging door and pulled me through the kitchen. Cash stayed right behind me, never letting me get far away. Everyone else followed, guns at the ready.

Near the back door, Mary let go of the blanket and turned to face me. "You stay safe, you hear me?"

I hugged her again. "Come with us, Mary," I whispered against her gray hair.

She shook her head and patted my back. "Oh no, child. This is my home. My people need me. You go on. You and your man. You'll be okay, you'll see."

She gave me another strong pat and pulled away to look me over.

I wasn't one to show another woman affection – I had had so little of it in my own life – but she had quickly become like a mother to me.

"Thank you for everything, Mary," I said as she looked me over.

Her eyes watered all over again. She gave a sharp nod and ushered me to the door.

"Go now. And young man..." She raised one eyebrow at Cash.

Cash looked at her. "Yes, ma'am?"

She narrowed her eyes at him like an overprotective mother hen. "You take care of her. You hear?"

Cash tipped his absent hat at her and drawled, "Yes, ma'am. I will."

David hugged her goodbye and Gavin gave her a playful slap on the rump. It was bittersweet, saying goodbye. But we had to go. Loud banging sounds were coming from the front as the men tried to break down the door.

"Go! Go!" Mary shooed us out the door.

Sun blinded me as Gavin pushed it open.

It was now or never. Time to run.

Chapter Forty

-Cash-

I wasn't a praying man. Growing up, I had heard my dad do it enough to know it sometimes didn't work. He would pray for rain and there would be a drought. He prayed for the crops to come in and they died out. He prayed for the price of feed to go down and they skyrocketed, emptying his pockets and leaving our bank account dry. But as I stepped outside of the hotel with Cat beside me, I prayed.

I just hoped this time God was listening.

He had when Adam told me Gavin, Brody, and Ryder were in town to rescue my sorry ass. He was when I found Cat before it was too late. I prayed He would hear me one more time and get us out of the hellhole that was Hilltop. We needed all the help we could get.

We headed down the alleyway behind the hotel at a quick pace. Shouts from the street made us move faster. It was déjà vu all over again except this time we had extra guns and help plus Keely wasn't with us.

It was the first thing I had asked Gavin when I met up with him back in the town square.

"Where's my sister?" I had bit out as he appeared beside me in the crowd.

He raised his gun and fired before answering, taking out a man that was charging toward us with his shotgun raised.

"She's with Maddie. Don't worry, she's safe," he had answered, swinging around as another man roared behind us.

That one I took care of myself. A right hook to the jaw.

Gavin had avoided my gaze and didn't say more about Keely but I had questions. Lots of them. It wasn't the time or place. I was fighting to stay alive and I realized quickly that Cat was missing. Ryder had lost her in the crowd. I went berserk, shouting and screaming her name. Throwing men out of my path and taking out a few with the knife Adam had tossed me. No one would stop me from finding her.

Shit. My hands trembled again, thinking of how close I had been to losing her. And when I found out Paul had her…fuck, I almost died right then.

I blocked the thought from my mind and the way she looked under him when I burst in, all pale and afraid. I focused on getting her out of town. That was all that mattered now.

I could see horses tied up ahead. We ran faster, gravel crunching under our boots. My ribs hurt like hell.

I could hear Cat breathing hard beside me, her cheeks flushed with the cold and exertion. Paul had banged her up pretty good. For that, I wanted to kill him all over again.

I grabbed her arm from under the blanket and pulled her along with me when she started to slow down. We shot past one building and was almost to the corner of another when men appeared behind us.

"Hey!" one of them yelled.

I dropped Cat's hand and turned, firing off a shot. Ryder and Brody did the same. Guns blasted. Bullets sprayed. The sound was deafening, the smoke from the guns filling my lungs with an acidity sting.

The men ducked and returned fire. More showed up behind them.

"Run!" I shouted, pushing Cat to go.

Panic filled her eyes. She grabbed Tate's hand and bolted forward. I followed right behind them, turning to get off a shot.

Ryder, Brody, and Adam sprinted down the alleyway and turned at the same time to open fire on the men. Gavin stopped up in the middle of the alley and started loading an arrow into his crossbow.

"Fuck the damn bow! Come on!" I yelled, passing him. Damn idiot was going to get himself shot.

He ignored me and settled the bow into his shoulder, taking his time. Sighting his target, he waited for the right moment. Bullets pinged around his feet. The men got closer. He pulled the trigger. An arrow went flying.

One of the men let out a sharp cry as the arrow embedded in his shoulder.

"Bullseye," Gavin muttered, lowering his weapon. Turning, he smirked at me. "Do that with your damn knife."

I rolled my eyes and took off running to catch up with Cat. She was a few feet in front of me, running in front of Adam, Tate right by her side. She had lost the blanket, back a few yards, but it would have to stay.

Adam was protecting her from the shots. I saw him grab her and yank her in front of him when she weaved to the right. I felt jealous but reminded myself that there was no need to worry about him taking my place. Only death would keep me from her.

He looked back at me and nodded when he saw I was catching up. Stopping, he took aim at the men to give me cover to get her out of there.

I caught up to Cat and grabbed her waist, pulling her to run in front of me. Her bare feet flew over the ground and her dress and dark hair flowed behind her. Looking back over her shoulder at me, fear made her green eyes go wide.

"Oh my god. Oh my god. Cash!" she cried, afraid.

I grabbed her hand. "I've got you. Don't stop."

We ran as fast as we could, our hands clasped tightly together. Fifteen yards. Ten yards. We were almost there.

I could see the horses, dancing around nervously as gunfire boomed and shouts ripped through the air. Brody made it to them first.

"Here." He handed me the reins of a big quarter horse. "We gotta ride double."

I would have insisted on it even if it wasn't necessary. I wrapped my hands around Cat's waist and helped her up into the saddle.

"Hold on, Beauty Queen. We're about to go on the ride of our lives."

I held onto the saddle horn in front of her and swung up into the saddle, wincing when my bruised and broken ribs protested. Holding the reins in one hand, I wrapped my other arm around Cat's waist and tugged her closer, fitting her against me. Her dress rose higher up her thighs. The horse danced under us, panicked and ready to run.

David heaved himself into the saddle of a big gray mare. He reached down for Tate's outstretched hand and swung him up behind him. Gavin fired off another shot as Ryder mounted up. Brody handed off a horse to Adam then got on his own.

The men had thinned out. Only one or two remained. As Adam's horse danced under him, he aimed and fired. As the last man dropped, Gavin mounted up. We took off at a gallop. All I could hear was my breathing and the beat of the horses' hooves on pavement. I noticed a backpack was tied behind each saddle. Ours bounced on the horse's rear flank, heavy with supplies.

The gate in the wall was up ahead. The same one that we had walked through, now we would ride out of for good.

Shouts came from the town square. I held onto Cat tightly and glanced over that direction as our horse ran at a flat run. Men were racing toward us, a few of them sighting us in their scopes.

"Shit." I dug my heels into the horse's side, urging him to go faster.

Cat held onto the saddle horn as we flew toward the gate.

A man was stationed there, looking scared to death but determined. He started to raise his gun but Brody slid his horse to a stop inches from the man and yanked his shotgun to his shoulder.

"I'll be mighty appreciative if you open that gate," Brody said, peering down the barrel at the man.

Our horses neighed and danced around, their eyes rolling around crazily as we waited. Cat stiffened in front of me. I pulled back on the reins, trying to control our horse and keep an eye on the men running toward us. My knuckles brushed her stomach. The thought of her being pregnant made me tense.

I raised my gun and pointed it at the man. "Open it up now."

The stranger looked like he was about to piss his pants. He jumped and hurried to open the gate, getting tangled in his own feet. As soon as it was opened, we were through it, riding at a flat out gallop.

The land was rough and the terrain uneven. I held Cat tightly as we flew across the land. The wind was cold as it hit our faces. The sun was high in the sky, blinding us.

Cat shivered against me and bundled closer. We were free.

And we were going home.

Chapter Forty-One

-Cat-

We rode for days. The militia tracked us for a while but we lost them by the third day, covering our tracks, backtracking, and traveling up a stream to lose them. Adam led the way, an expert at moving without being seen or leaving a trail.

Our nights were spent on the ground, huddled together under saddle blankets and the meager belongings we carried. We ate homemade jerky that Ryder's mother had made and shared three cans of baked beans between the eight of us.

The backpacks tied behind the saddles were ours. Mary had gathered them from the street the day I was shot. She had kept them safe, hoping she would see us again.

My bag was packed just as it had been the day I dropped it on the sidewalk. A change of clothes was inside and an extra pair of shoes I had found a few months ago. My prized toothbrush and toothpaste were also there along with my hairbrush, a ball cap, and my coveted, treasured box of tampons. It was all there, just as I had packed it.

The weather got worse as we rode and winter reared its ugly head. The sky turned a turbulent gray and gusts of bitter, cold wind whipped against us.

I bundled deeper under the blanket that Cash had thrown over me. My chin was frozen and I could no longer feel my fingers or toes. The horse walked at a rolling, relaxed gait, rocking me gently to drowsiness.

I leaned back against Cash's warm body. His chest was hard against my back. His arm stayed rigid around me as he held the reins in front of my abdomen with one hand. His left hand rested on his muscular thigh, inches from my leg.

For the past day, he had seemed restless. Edgy. Quieter than usual. He didn't say much to me. I shivered as his biceps brushed the outside of my arm.

"Cold?" his deep voice above my head.

I nodded, aware of every inch of him against me.

He reached under the blanket and wrapped his arm around my waist. I jumped, a kneejerk reaction to being touched. Since we left Hilltop, I recoiled when someone accidently brushed against me. I flinched when Adam reached out one time to grab a twig out of my hair. No matter how much I tried, I couldn't forget about Paul's hands on me.

Cash stiffened and slid his arm from around me. "Sorry," he whispered near my ear.

Tears clogged my throat. He hadn't touched me since Hilltop except to help me on and off the horse. At night, he slept close but kept a few feet between us. During the day, I rode in front of him, his hard body behind me but his hands staying off me unless necessary.

We hadn't discussed the wedding or what happened back at the courthouse. Since Cash hadn't said anything or addressed it, I assumed the marriage was a hoax – for Frankie's benefit only. For some reason it hurt, knowing it wasn't real, but I needed to be realistic. Cash had wanted me to stop loving him. He had insisted on it, even telling me to be with Adam if he died. No, Cash wouldn't want to be married to me. I was almost positive.

We also hadn't talked about what would happen when we arrived home. I knew we were going to Ryder's ranch first, where Cash had been staying.

After that I didn't know what would happen. Would Cash take me home? In the courthouse basement, he confessed that he had planned to leave me. He said it was for the best. That night, he admitted there was no way he could walk away from me. He even called himself a fool. But what if he had changed his mind? What if he believed it was the best thing to do again? The threat of dying could make a person say things. Things that may not be true. Now that he knew he wasn't going to die, the idea of staying with me might be daunting. Something he didn't want to do.

My throat went thick. I stared ahead, not really seeing Ryder's straight back or the faded ball cap he wore. I didn't see my brother or the smile on Gavin's face when he said we were getting closer to home. All I saw was my future looming ahead of me. A future that may not include Cash.

~~~~

The rest of the day was spent riding down empty roads overgrown with weeds. We were five days away from Hilltop and the men who wanted to see us dead.

The temperature dropped even more. My stomach rumbled nonstop. By midday I was so hungry, I dreamed of food when the gentle sway of the horse lulled me to sleep.

I wasn't sure how long I slept. The next thing I knew, I was being jolted awake. We had stopped at an old farmhouse.
~~~~

I lifted my head off Cash's chest, embarrassed I had snuggled into his warmth as I slept. He controlled our horse with his thighs and one hand holding the reins in front of me. His other hand curved around my waist and kept me in the saddle.

I sat up straighter when I saw Gavin and Brody climb off their horses.

"What are they doing?" I asked Cash as I looked from the rundown house to them.

"We need food," Cash answered. "They're going to see if we can trade for some."

Gavin and Brody approached the house with wariness. There were no signs of life except for some chickens pecking around the yard.

I held my breath, watching as they marched up the porch steps and knocked on the door. Cash let me go, moving his hand toward his gun.

Whoever lived here could open fire on us from one of the windows any second. We could be dead in minutes, lying on the ground. Since the EMP, people protected what was theirs at any cost. Most shot first and asked questions later.

We watched and waited, Ryder and Adam ready with their guns. A minute ticked by. Cash pulled his gun out of the holster.

The door creaked open slowly. A very pregnant woman appeared. She had a baby on her hip and a small child hid behind her skirt. I couldn't hear what she said but she talked to Gavin and Brody a minute then disappeared back inside the house, shutting the door firmly.

A few minutes later she returned and handed a bundle to Gavin. Brody gave her a cloth-wrapped package.

She shut the door firmly and Gavin and Brody headed back to us.

It seemed we were going to eat again. My stomach would be happy.

~~~~

After eating stale bread and handmade cheese, we rode in silence again. Cash's body kept me warm but he kept his hands off me. Pain wrapped around my heart and squeezed.

He demanded that I be with Adam if he died.

He said that he planned to leave me.

I shut my eyes tight and breathed. Tate would say it was one big cluster fuck. I didn't know what to do. But I had another problem. One that had been nudging at the back of my mind for days but I had tried to ignore. When I saw that pregnant woman, it hit me.

I had skipped my period.

I first realized it when I saw the tampons in my backpack. I couldn't remember the last time I used them. I tried counting the days in my head, thinking I was wrong. The time I was unconscious from the bullet wound was fuzzy but Cash had told me I had been out for a week. *That meant…* I counted back. *No. It couldn't be.*

The blood drained from my face. I counted again, trying to visualize a calendar and the days on it. *Oh god.* I most definitely was late.

Cash's knuckles brushed my abdomen as the horse stepped in a shallow hole. I jumped and almost fell out of the saddle.

His hand snapped and grabbed me around the waist. "You okay?"
~~~~

I nodded. "Yeah." But I wasn't. Not if what I thought were true.

I eased away from Cash's arm. He let me go, his body going rigid.

I told him at one time that I didn't want to tie someone down with a baby. And I wouldn't. I refused to.

I stared at the empty, dirt road in front of us, looking for anything familiar. Something to take my mind off a baby. I looked for a house. A sign. Anything to tell me that we were close to home.

Gavin said we were almost there. My heart hammered, thinking of walking into the town that hated me. I hadn't been there in three years. Would they still look at me with scorn, the girl who caused her boyfriend to die in a car crash? The woman who had partied and been with men to forget?

We turned a bend in the road and the horse's ears perked up. Its gait increased, no longer tired. I grabbed hold of the saddle horn as the horse trotted at a canter. Cash kept his hands off me but I felt the muscles in his legs, keeping me in the seat.

Brody and Ryder sat up straighter. Gavin turned at the waist and grinned at me.

I squashed the hope that we were close. My grandmother used to call me cynical. I guess she was right. I would believe we were home when I saw it. Until then it was only a hope and a dream.

We turned down a narrow path that once was a road. Two tire tracks were visible in the tall weeds and grass. Farmland stretched out on either side of us as far as the eye could see. A small herd of cows grazed in the distance. It looked peaceful, something I didn't trust.

Cash kept the horse at a trot when it wanted to gallop. But Gavin, Brody, and Ryder took off, their horses kicking up grass and dirt.

I glanced over at Adam riding beside us. His face was covered with a thick beard and his hair was sticking up all over. He had been quiet the last couple of days. Something was on his mind.

David was doing better on the trip than I thought he would, considering he had arthritis and was older than any of us. He was jolly at night and excited to share stories of his youth during the day. He rode like he was an extension of the horse, holding the reins loosely in his big, gnarly hands.

For me, each plod of the horses' hooves brought me closer to facing the truth. Cash and I might be over. This might be the end of us.

I looked over at my little brother, riding behind David. He was so antsy to get home, he didn't sleep much at night. Since we left Hilltop, he hung on every word Ryder said and watched him with fascination. Ryder kept his distance and didn't seem to notice. He wasn't what I would call very approachable.

The five of us rode in silence. Gavin, Brody, and Ryder were now out of sight. The wind picked up and a big crow coasted above us, riding the gust and cawing out at us as if we were trespassing on its land.

When an old farmhouse came into view, I stared at it. "Maddie's old home." Cash said before I could ask.

A twinge of jealousy uncoiled in me. Cash was close to her – Maddie – and now we were here. At her home.

I stared at the house until it disappeared from sight. The overgrown road grew narrower, the weeds and grass thicker. Within minutes, another farmhouse appeared, this one bigger.

In the yard stood strangers, greeting Gavin, Ryder, and Brody with hugs and cries of relief. I became very self-conscious as they turned and stared at us as we rode closer. I didn't look my best. My clothes were grimy and I smelled like horse and smoke from a campfire. My hair was matted and there were still bruises on my face from Paul.

Cash pulled the horse to a stop a short distance from the group. Swinging his leg over, he dismounted, wincing from the pain in his ribs.

I immediately missed him near me. I wondered how I would ever live without him. But I might have to if he still wanted to leave me.

I bit my lip to keep from crying. When he reached up to help me dismount, I slid off the horse without his help. He looked at me with irritation but covered it up quickly and replaced it with cool aloofness.

"I don't want you to hurt your ribs," I whispered in way of explanation.

His eyes darkened. Before he could argue, a childish squeal ripped through the air.

"Cass!" a little, dark-haired girl shrieked, wiggling out of Ryder's arms and down to the ground.

She held out her chubby arms and ran toward us. Dark brown curls danced on her tiny shoulders and tossed about in the wind. Her little blue dress bounced against the ground and tiny shoes peeked out as she ran.

Cash bent down and caught her as she flung herself at him. Sweeping her off the ground, he winced from the pain in his ribs but it was such a quick expression – there then gone - I doubted anyone would have noticed.

"Hello, Emma," he said, holding her in his arms. He cupped one hand around her waist and the other around the back of her head and those curls.

The girl – Emma – pulled away and looked at him. "What happened?" She poked at one of the bruises on his face.

He grimaced. "Nothing you should worry about, Emma."

Emma scrunched her delicate brows together and glanced up at his head. "Where your hat?"

Cash gave her a lopsided grin and tugged at one of her curls. "I lost it, Em. You got one I can borrow?"

Emma scrunched her face then shrugged and buried her little fingers in Cash's hair. "Nope. Ask Daddy."

Cash chuckled and lifted her higher to rub his nose in her round tummy. She giggled and grasped his hair tighter, her cheeks going rosy.

When Cash stopped tickling her, she saw me. "Who that?" she asked, sticking a finger in her mouth and staring at me with round blue eyes.

Cash looked at me. "That's Cat."

Emma's eyes got bigger and she pulled her finger from her mouth with a wet plop. "She's a *cat?*"

There were a few chuckles from the group. I grew red and looked at the onlookers just as a woman headed toward us.

She was gorgeous. Dark hair fell down her back. She was petite and had delicate, perfect features. Her eyes were dark brown. Her skin was porcelain white. She was breathtaking.

And she was very pregnant.

She walked to us gracefully – none of that duck walking that pregnant women tended to do. Stopping in front of Cash, she took Emma from him. "Okay, nosy. That's enough questions," she said. Even her voice was beautiful.

The little girl stuck her finger back in her mouth and eyed me with wonder as her mother took her from Cash and set her on her hip.

The woman stepped closer to Cash and wrapped her arm around his neck. "I missed you so much," she whispered, pulling him to her for a hug. She stood on tiptoes, her big, protruding belly resting against him.

I knew who she was instantly.

Maddie.

Cash wrapped his arms around her and hugged her close.

"I missed you too. You okay?" His voice was thick. Intimate. Caring.

Maddie closed her eyes and nodded, ignoring her wiggling daughter on her hip. "Yes. I'm fine. Just worried about you. Are you okay? You look terrible."

"Just a few bruises. I'll be fine," Cash said against her hair.

I felt like a voyeur, watching a private scene. I glanced over at Ryder. His face was set in stone as he watched Cash and Maddie. Reaching up, he pulled his ball cap further down on his head, half-listening to what the older man and woman next to him was saying. His gaze flicked to me – cold, hard, imposing. As jealous as me.

I studied him but Maddie let go of Cash and turned to face me.

"Hi, I'm Maddie," she said, a dazzling smile on her face. She held out a delicate hand for me to shake. I wanted to hate her but I couldn't. She seemed so nice and friendly.

I took her hand, shaking it. "I'm Cat."

"She's my wife, Maddie," a smooth voice interjected beside me.

A tingle went up my spine. Maddie looked from me to Cash. She let go of my hand and raised an eyebrow.

"Wife?"

I glanced at Cash. He was staring at Maddie, his jaw set hard. "We're married."

Maddie glanced from me to him. "When did this happen?"

Before he could answer, Ryder walked up and interrupted. "It's a long story. You can hear it later. I want you inside where it's warm." He took Emma from her arms, giving Cash a warning glare.

Maddie gave Ryder a smile but then glanced back at me. Her smile faltered. I saw uncertainty and distrust in her eyes but then she stepped toward me.

"I never expected Cash to come home married but welcome to the family, Cat." She hugged me tight, her extended belly pressing into my body. "We're happy you're here."

Despite my jealousy, I hugged her back. When she pulled away, I still saw apprehension in her eyes but she smiled warmly.

Ryder grasped her arm. "Inside now, before that baby decides to come right now."

Maddie rolled her eyes but let him pull her away. She was a few steps from me when she glanced over her shoulder. "Really, Cat. I'm glad you're here."

She turned back around when Ryder pulled her close. I watched as he slid his hand around her hip and leaned down, kissing her head as he held Emma on his hip.

I felt that familiar pang of anguish – Ryder seemed to love Maddie so much. Turning my head, I found Cash staring at me. His eyes were intense, his body set in stone.

"You love her," I said, wrapping my arms around my middle as a cold wind blew past me.

Cash nodded and looked over at Maddie as Ryder led her away. "Yeah, I do," he said, his voice sounding like he was remembering something from long ago.

My chest felt tight, seeing the softness in his eyes for her. With shaking hands and tears in my eyes, I turned away.

"Cat."

Cash reached for me. I moved out of the way, reaching for my backpack tied on behind the saddle. It was stupid really, feeling jealous or worried. I had survived a lot. I could survive watching him loving someone else.

He appeared in front of me, towering over me and blocking my view of everyone else.

"She's my friend, Cat," his voice rumbled, low and raspy beside me.

"I know," I said, untying the knot that held my backpack with a jerk. I kept my eyes off Cash. I couldn't look at him and see pity or guilt.

He grabbed my arm and spun me around to face him, glaring down at me. I let go of the backpack and stared up at him, suddenly angry and tired of what life always threw at me.

I yanked my arm out of his grasp and went back to untying my backpack. Disgusted. Mad. Furious. All at myself.

"You told her I was your wife," I snapped. "There's no need to pretend, Cash. They were just a few words said for Frankie's benefit. It meant nothing."

Cash stepped closer. "Nothing?"

I swung my backpack down and looked up at him. "Nothing."

I started to push past him when an ear-splitting shriek rang through the air. Tate shouted. Cash flew into action, grabbing me and throwing me against the horse's side. The wind was knocked out of me. He held me in place with a hand against my breastbone and yanked his shotgun out of the scabbard on the saddle and then let go of me to swing it up to his shoulder.

I glanced around, terrified. And that's when I saw Keely.

She was running toward us from around the corner of the house. Her blonde hair was bouncing on her shoulders and glasses sat on her nose. Gavin was behind her, a big grin on his face, and another blonde woman followed them with Brody by her side.

Keely ran across the uneven ground and threw herself at Cash. He caught her with a grunt, holding the gun in one hand.

"Cash," she said in a broken whisper, her arms around his neck. "I missed you. So much. What. Happened?"

Her voice was fragmented. Awkward like she was learning a new language. But hearing her talk left me speechless. My mouth gaped open. Cash squeezed his eyes shut tight.

"Just a little trouble," he answered, his voice thick. "I'm sure glad to see you, little sis."

She smiled, her eyes misty. "You. Look. Like. Sh…Shit."

Cash grinned and hugged her tighter.

"Keely, you're talking," I said in awe, taking a step closer.

She let go of Cash and looked at me, smiling. "Cat."

I shot toward her and wrapped my arms around her tightly. Her wispy blonde hair tickled my nose and her skinny arms squeezed my neck until I thought I would choke.

"Now I can tell you. How much. You drove me crazy," she said in a voice that could only be described as angelic. Soft, light – it fit her personality perfectly.

"I killed Paul, Keely," I whispered, squeezing my eyes shut. "He tried again and I killed him."

Keely hugged me tighter, smelling like sunshine and vanilla. "It's okay. You're alive."

Something about hearing her say that filled me with peace. They couldn't hurt us again. We were going to be okay.

She gave me another squeeze then stepped away. Gavin walked up behind her, grinning like a lovesick fool.

Cash glared at him, still holding the gun by his side. "Do we need to have another shotgun wedding, Gavin?"

Pain sliced through me.

Gavin looked at Keely, his gaze growing warm. "No. No, shotgun wedding. I've got this handled."

Keely smiled wider then moved away to hug Tate and introduce herself to Adam and David.

Cash crossed his arms over his chest and widened his stance, staring at his friend. "I'll kill you if you hurt my sister."

Gavin smirked. "You'll kill me? With what? You told me you traded your dad's knife for food for Cat?"

I turned my head and gaped at Cash. He narrowed his eyes at Gavin.

Gavin's grin disappeared. He ran a hand over his face and stepped forward. "Listen, man. You're not just my friend. You're my brother. I'm happy you're home and alive."

He held out his hand for Cash to shake.

Cash hesitated then shook it. "Yeah. Thanks for coming back for me."

Gavin grinned. "Anytime. Just try not to get hung again."

Cash smiled and let go of his hand. "I'll try."

Gavin snorted and turned to leave but I stopped him, stepping forward and touching his arm.

"What happened between you and Keely on the way home?" I asked.

He smirked, his bright blue eyes twinkling. "Maybe I'll tell you one day, Kitty Cat."

Chapter Forty-Two

-Cat-

I was introduced to everyone. There was Ryder and Gavin's parents – Janice and Roger Delaney – and the pretty blonde, Eva. Janice immediately took me under her wing when she noticed me shivering and swaying on my feet.

"Let's get you inside where it's warm," she said, leading me to the farmhouse.

I glanced back to see Cash. He was leading the horse to the barn and talking to Ryder with Tate following close behind. His eyes flicked to me. But a second later, he turned away, dismissing me.

"I'll put you in the room where Cash stays," Janice was saying as she led me up the porch steps.

I forced myself to pay attention but at the back of my mind it nagged at me that I may not be staying. Cash might be taking me home.

Inside, Janice ushered me into the room where Cash stayed. A single bed and a small chest of drawers took up most of the space.

I lowered my backpack to the floor as Janice went to the small closet. She started gathering clothes for me to change into, talking the whole time about Cash.

"We love him so much. He's like a son to us. How long have you known him?" she asked, smiling and walking over to me, holding out a pair of jeans and a shirt.

I took them from her slowly. Her question had sounded very curious as if she didn't trust me. "Um. I've known him a long time," I answered.

She tilted her head to the side and studied me. “Maddie said you were married. When did that happen? Cash never mentioned you before?”

My cheeks grew red. I looked down at the shirt in my hands and fidgeted with a loose thread. I couldn’t do it. I couldn’t talk about our fake marriage with this woman.

The walls started to close in on me. The welcoming strangers and warm house felt wrong, as if I had landed in an alternate universe where I didn’t belong.

I picked up my backpack and slung it on my shoulder, holding the clothes against my chest. “Do you have somewhere I can wash my face?”

She smiled, a little too forced. “Sure. Down the hall on your right. Cash rigged up a system for running water.”

I muttered a thank you before hurrying from the room. In the hallway, I walked fast, keeping my eyes downcast.

I was moving quickly past an open door when I heard a deep voice. I looked up and that’s when I saw them. In a room. Maddie and Cash.

They were standing close together. Cash had one hand on his hip and as I watched, he thrust the other through his hair with frustration.

I darted back against the wall as Maddie put her hand on his arm.

“What happened?” she asked in a worried voice.

I waited, eavesdropping. Listening closely.

“He forced me to marry her. Fuck, it was awful, Maddie,” Cash said in a rugged, hoarse voice.

Tears filled my eyes. A sob broke from me. I leaned my head back against the wall and slapped a hand over my mouth to stop it.

I didn’t hear what else they said until a second later.

“So what are you going to do?” I heard Maddie ask.

Cash sighed. “What can I do?”

Tears rolled down my cheeks. Anguish tore through me. I wanted to scream. Wail. It was just too much and I couldn’t handle it.

Maddie and Cash continued talking but I had heard enough. I pushed off the wall and ran down the hallway, swiping at the tears on my face.

Janice appeared, stepping out of Cash’s room. “Did I say something wrong?” she asked as I rushed by with my backpack and change of clothes.

I thrust the clothes at her. “No. Thank you for your hospitality.”

She took the clothes and gaped at me as I hurried away. I held onto the strap of my backpack and ran.

Tears blurred my vision but I knew the way out. I rounded the corner into the living room and slammed into the blonde, Eva.

“Whoa. What’s wrong?” she asked, turning as I sped past her.

I gave her a quick glance over my shoulder, ignoring the tears on my face. “Have you seen my brother?”

She frowned and took a step toward me. “You’re crying.”

“My brother? Have you seen him?” I asked, my tone biting. Impatient.

She nodded. “Yeah. I saw him go outside. Why?”

I didn’t answer her. Cash’s deep voice and Maddie’s gentle one came from down the hallway.

“Shit,” I whispered. “I’ve got to go.”

I rushed across the room, ignoring Eva’s attempt to stop me. I had to hurry. I didn’t want to face Cash, knowing how he felt.

‘Fuck, it was awful,’ he had said.

Remembering made the tears start up all over again. I felt like I was suffocating.

I needed to find Tate and run. We could make it on our own. We didn't belong in the fucked-up town that hated me. We didn't belong here, two charity cases with no home. We belonged out there. Alone. Making it on our own. If I was pregnant, I would raise the baby and we would survive without Cash. It would be hard but I could do it. I already had to do so much since the EMP and war.

I opened the door and ran outside. Cold air entered my lungs and cooled my overheated skin.

Breathing hard, puffs of chilled air leaving me, I held onto the backpack strap and jogged down the porch stairs. The sun was still high in the sky but the temperature was dropping, keeping everyone inside. Leaving a warm house and friendly people was hard but I would survive. I always did. Tate and I would find our way to a new home.

I spotted my brother quickly. He was walking toward the house. No one was with him, thank goodness. The last thing I wanted was to have to listen to someone try to stop me.

Tate's eyes widened when he saw me running toward him.

"What's going on?" he asked as I grabbed the sleeve of his jacket.

I held onto him tight and dragged him along. "We're leaving."

My mother once said that I ruined everyone's life. She was right. I had ruined Luke's and Nathan's.

But I wasn't going to ruin Cash's.

Chapter Forty-Three

-Cat-

I pulled Tate with me in the direction of the barn.

"Why are we leaving?" he asked, tripping over his feet to keep up with me.

"Because we don't belong here," I said, convincing myself to believe it.

Tate frowned down at me but I ignored him and took long strides, almost running. The faster we got out of there, the less likely someone would try to stop us from going.

At the barn, I unlatched the door and slid it open. The smell of cow manure and horses bombarded me. The livestock warmed the dusty barn to a toasty temperature. The hay on the floor insulated it against the cold. In one corner sat an old truck. Against the walls were horse stalls.

I rushed inside, dragging Tate with me. In the middle, I let him go and hurried over to the first stall.

A big, black horse nickered in greeting and stuck his soft nose out to smell me. He was a massive horse – the top of my head reached only his shoulder. But he seemed friendly and harmless. He would be perfect for a fast getaway.

Tate stood in place and watched me. "You're not making any sense, sis. Why do we not belong here?"

"Because," I said, dropping my backpack on the ground in front of the stall and unlatching the small door. "This is not our home."

"But it could be," Tate reasoned as I cautiously stepped inside by the stallion, hoping he wouldn't stomp me.

"It's not," I said, running my hand over the horse's nose.

Tate sighed. "Ryder says they have enough land for you and Cash to build a house. We could live in it. The three of us. If you want me to live with you two, that is."

Agony clamped down on my chest. I couldn't tell my brother that Cash and I weren't going to be together. There would be no house. No three of us sharing a table at night. It would kill Tate to leave but I couldn't stay, knowing how Cash felt.

I shoved the pain down deep and reached for some reins hanging nearby on the stall. "Do you think I'm the type to settle down, Tate? Wear an apron and make cookies?"

Tate shrugged. "Yeah. What's wrong with that?"

I shook my head and scoffed. Tears welled in my eyes. Through the wet blur, I slipped the bridle on the horse. When he didn't fight or rear up, I felt relief and left the stall to find a saddle.

Tate watched as I checked one enclosure then another. I kept my head ducked so he couldn't see the wetness on my face. I cursed the tears for making me feel weak.

Just as I started to grow frantic and worried that we would have to ride bareback, I found an old saddle tucked away in a corner. I heaved it up and carried it back to the horse.

Tate frowned and nodded at the stallion. "So what? Now we're horse thieves too?"

"Yes, if that's what it takes."

Tate let out a curse and kicked at the hay on the ground.

I ignored him and tried to lift the heavy saddle on the horse. It weighed a ton.

It took me three tries but I finally got it on. The stallion stomped its feet and shook his head, unhappy with the idea of a ride.

Tate blew his long hair out of his eyes and glared at me. "Fine. You win."

He marched to a stall where a light-brown quarter horse stood quietly. Flipping the latch on the door, he glanced over at me.

"But just so you know, I don't like the idea of leaving. They have food."

Typical of him, thinking with his stomach.

I tightened the straps on the stallion and led him from the stall. His big hooves thumped on the barn floor and he yanked his head up at the tight hold I had on the reins. He seemed bigger outside his stall. Powerful and strong. I wasn't sure if I could handle him but I was about to find out.

I tied him to the stall door and picked up my backpack. Lifting it up, I started tying it to the back of the saddle.

"Tell me again. Why should we leave?" Tate asked from the other stall. "I need it to soak in."

I rolled my eyes and started to answer him but a cold voice came from behind me.

"Yeah, Cat. Tell me. Why should you leave?"

I froze, my fingers stopping on the rope. My mouth went dry. I stopped breathing.

I could feel him behind me. His heat. His anger. I turned, holding onto the horse for support and swallowing hard.

He was wearing a cowboy hat. I wondered briefly where he got it. He glared down at me, his gaze frigid.

His lean body was coiled with tensile strength. A few week's worth of growth covered his jaw. Bruises still marked his cheekbones and around his eyes but now they were green instead of blue and black.

"I'm waiting," he said in a voice that made me wince.

I became angry. He was mad at me! I wasn't the one who said the marriage was awful. The one who didn't know what to do.

I stuck my chin up and faced him, getting right in his space.

"I should leave because it was *fucking awful* and *what can I do*," I spit sarcastically, repeating his exact words.

His face went white. He flinched like I had hit him.

Pain crushed my chest when he didn't deny it. New tears popped in my eyes. I blinked past the moisture and stared up at him.

"I'll tell you what you can do, *cowboy*. Let me leave."

His nostrils flared. His lips thinned. He let out a growl and grabbed my upper arm. I yelped as he dragged me past my brother who was leading the quarter horse out of a stall.

"Get out of here, Tate," Cash snarled, hauling me by the arm.

Tate looked at us with wide eyes. "Uh. Okay. Sure."

"And leave the horse," Cash whipped over his shoulder. "You're not going anywhere."

I looked up. He was pissed. A dangerous tick appeared in his jaw. His fingers were tight on my arm.

I jogged to keep up with him as he dragged me toward the old farm truck parked in the corner.

"Let. Me. Go," I ordered through clenched teeth, trying to yank my arm away.

"Not on your life, sweetheart," Cash growled, tugging me forward.

I gave my arm another good jerk just for the principal of it and glared up at him with anger. He paid no attention and hauled me to the passenger door of the truck.

Keeping a firm grasp on me, he wrenched the door open. “Get in,” he ordered in a cutting voice that slashed through me.

I jerked away from him. “No. I’m not going anywhere with you, jerkface.”

He growled and clasped my waist when I started to go around him.

Pinning me back against the truck, he put his hand behind me and leaned closer.

“Do I look like I’m kidding, Beauty Queen? Get in the fuckin’ truck or I’ll pick you up and put you there myself.”

Oh god.

With a glare, I pushed past him and plopped down on the seat. But I kept one foot on the ground just to be stubborn.

“Fine. I’m in. Do your worse,” I said, crossing my arms over my chest.

His gaze slid down my body. “Oh, I plan to. Get your leg in too, princess.”

I pouted and pulled my foot inside the truck, huffing.

“Thank you,” he clipped out, slamming the passenger door closed.

It completely caught me off guard, him being so nice. It made the lump in my throat triple.

But I wouldn’t let him get to me. I wouldn’t be that girl anymore that couldn’t resist him.

I hand-cranked the window down as Cash stomped to the back of the truck. Resting my arm on the door, I leaned out and looked at him.

"What are we doing? I'll get out of this truck right now if you think you can take me somewhere and change my mind. I'm leaving, cowboy, and you can't stop me." I grabbed the handle to open the door just to prove I meant it.

He glared at me over his shoulder. "Do it and I'll find some reins and a private little corner of this barn, Cat."

I clamped my mouth shut and stared at his jean-covered ass as he walked away. He stopped by the back of the barn and grabbed two handles near a seam in the wall. Giving them a yank, he slid the doors open wide enough for a tractor to drive through. Bright sunlight spilled in along with a brisk cold air.

Pushing the door all the way open, Cash then went over to the driver's side of the truck. It rocked on its axles as he got in and slammed the door.

The vehicle had seen better days. Springs poked out of the pickup's seat and the windshield had a crack that ran from one corner to another. Papers and an old blanket were stuffed on the floor. An old stereo had an ancient cassette tape sticking out.

Cash popped the visor down. A pair of keys fell into his lap. He grabbed them and put the key in the ignition. The truck roared to life.

He gave it the gas a few times then put it into reverse. Resting his arm on the back of the seat, he twisted his upper body around to look out the back window.

His thumb grazed my shoulder bone. Volts of electricity went through me. His gaze shot to mine, heated. Piercing.

Shit.

His eyes moved to his fingers, his other hand gripping the steering wheel tightly. I didn't move. Couldn't think.

All I knew was that he said it was fucking awful, marrying me.

But then there was this. The unexpected wave of desire that always consumed us when we were close. I could hear Cash breathing, almost sense the tension rolling off his body. There was something about sitting in a truck with him that brought back memories.

Our first date.

Me in his lap, whispering for him to touch me.

I drew in a ragged breath. His eyes moved down to my parted lips then slid away. A shadow passed over his features. His thumb moved off me. Looking out the rear window, he backed the truck out of the barn as if the moment hadn't happened. As if the desire between us didn't exist.

I folded my hands in my lap and took a deep, cleansing breath. "Are you going to tell me where we're going or do I have to guess?"

Cash didn't answer. Instead, he backed the truck out then put it in drive. He turned the wheel and floored the gas. The pickup shot forward, bouncing over rabbit holes and mounds of gopher dirt.

I grabbed the door handle, hanging on for dear life.

"Put on your seatbelt," Cash muttered, staring out the cracked windshield.

I looked at him and scoffed. "Really? We're out in the middle of nowhere. No one has a car but you."

His hand clenched around the steering wheel harder until his knuckles turned white. He looked at me and raised one eyebrow.

Message received.

I sighed and pulled the seatbelt across my lap but it wouldn't click into place. I tried again just as the truck hit a large hole. I bounced up. My side hit the door.

"Shit." Cash slammed on the brake and threw the truck into park. Reaching across the seat, he grabbed the seatbelt out of my hand and snapped it into place. His gaze ran over me quickly, making sure I was alright.

"Thank you," I whispered, hating that my heart was racing and his nearness could make me sweat.

He let out a humph and sat up. His fingers brushed my leg as he slid his hand away.

I narrowed my eyes at him and muttered under my breath, "But I'm still leaving."

He let out a sound of aggravation and faced forward again. Slamming the truck into drive, he stomped on the gas.

We flew past the house and out to the road – or what used to be a road. The truck's engine roared loudly and the body vibrated so roughly, I thought every screw and hinge would fall out of it.

We sailed at a neck-breaking speed. The land blurred on either side of us and the sun glinted off the windshield.

We drove for a while. The roads were more like abandoned trails. Large tree branches reached across them and it was slow going for a while. A few times Cash had to slow down to go around a downed limb or an abandoned car. The emptiness of the land made me feel like we were the only two people left on earth. But I started to get nervous. *Where's he taking me?*

I was about to ask him when he slowed the truck down and turned onto a narrow path leading back into some thick woods.

Branches grabbed at the pickup, screeching like nails on a chalkboard as they slid by. A sign lying on its side caught my attention as we drove past it. *Turner's Lake.*

The place Cash and I had gone on our first date.

My pulse started racing. My palms grew sweaty. I glanced over at Cash, wondering what he was planning.

His jaw was clamped hard and his gaze was set straight ahead. He didn't speak or look at me as he maneuvered the truck through the dense woods.

Foliage darkened the truck's interior as it blocked the sun from reaching us. Just when I thought we would drive forever, the trees opened up to a clearing.

The same spot where we had made love.

My mouth went dry. My hands trembled. Cash threw the truck into park and turned off the engine. Without a word, he opened up his door and got out.

I tried to get my seatbelt unhooked as he made his way around the truck. The damn thing was stuck again.

When I realized Cash was heading straight toward me, I tried faster, my fingers numb and useless. Oh, Jesus, I couldn't take him touching me.

Before I could get free, Cash swung open the door. I glanced up at him, still working on the seatbelt frantically.

He reached across me to unhook it. His arm brushed my stomach, his face inches from mine. He smelled masculine. Earthy. Delectable.

Perfect.

I let my eyes run over every line, every cut, every healing bruise on his face. I wanted to run my fingertips over the short stubble on his chin. Smooth out the grimness around his mouth.

He unclipped my seatbelt and let it slide across my lap and back into place. I held my breath, thinking he would move away, but he stayed close, leaning over me in the truck. I could see the pulse in his neck, steady and strong. His eyes were dark and turbulent like a dangerous storm approaching.

He slid his hand down my leg to my knee, grasping it with firm fingers.

"You're my wife, Cat. I fucking love you. Yeah, I told Maddie I was forced to marry you. And yes, I said it was awful. But I was talking about the thought of dying and leaving you. Christ, Cat, it was torture."

I couldn't form words. Blood pounded in my ears. I wanted to believe him – I really did – but there was a part of me that was scared.

I jerked my head up and narrowed my eyes at him. "You wanted me to stop loving you since I got shot. You told me to be with Adam. And now we're married?" I shook my head. "Let's just be honest. There was never a happily-ever-after in our future. That joke of a wedding ceremony were only words. Don't try to sugarcoat it and tell me they weren't. They meant nothing. Stop pretending they did. You are off the hook."

"There's that word again. *Nothing*," he ground out with a tightly clenched jaw, gripping my knee tightly. "You really believe that?"

I stuck up my chin. "Yes."

He growled and shoved my legs apart. His hand whipped out and grabbed the back of my neck. Heat swirled in his eyes. Possession consumed them. Fierceness made his muscles tense.

"It was real, sweetheart," he swore vehemently inches from my mouth. "Every single damn word. Love. Honor. Cherish. Protect. I said them all and I meant it. You're my wife and you're right where you're supposed to be. With me. I wouldn't change that. Fuck, do you want me to say them again? I, Cash Marshall, take you, Catarina Phillips, to be my wife. To have and to hold, from this day forward, for better, for worse. Until death do us—"

I pulled him down. His mouth captured mine. The kiss was brutal. Punishing. I should have been afraid – memories of Paul hovered close – but I wasn't. I was lost in Cash and him in me.

It was just like years earlier. I had sat in his truck and he had stood between my legs. We had been different then. I had been wild. He had been sweet. But the desire was the same. Heady and intense. It never changed.

I gripped his jacket and pulled him closer. He groaned and sank against my crotch. I kissed the corner of his mouth gently. "I, Catarina Phillips, take you, Cash Marshall, to be my husband. To have and to hold—"

His mouth covered mine, cutting off the rest of my words. He slid his hand from the back of my neck to my cheek. His body pressed into mine. I moaned and threaded my fingers into his hair, tasting his lips and tongue.

Too soon, he slid his mouth from mine and grabbed my hand. "Come here. I want to show you something."

He tugged me out of the truck and closed the door behind me. Holding my hand, he led me to the edge of the lake and the very same spot where he had laid me down on our first date.

The water sparkled under the sunlight. Little ripples danced across it when the wind picked up. If I closed my eyes, I could still hear the party across the water and the rustle of my clothes as Cash pushed them out of the way.

"I come out here sometimes," he said, staring across the crystal water. His profile was turned, his rough stubble dark on his face. "I pictured you here, lying on that blanket. So many times I wondered where you were. If you were okay. If I would ever see you again."

He turned to face me. His thumb caressed the soft pad between my thumb and forefinger. "I thought I was crazy, asking you out. You were so far out of my league. I had no money. No future except for farming. And I had no chance at giving someone like you the lifestyle you deserved. But when I laid you down on that blanket, everything that should have kept us apart didn't matter. I wanted to strip away all that pain I saw in your eyes and give you the world."

My throat got thick. "That was a long time ago," I whispered.

"But nothing has changed. I still want to give you the world. Forever."

He opened his mouth then hesitated and shut it. Rubbing a hand across his jaw, he gazed out across the water, looking unsure.

I stepped closer. "What is it?"

He swung his gaze back to me. "I've got something for you. A wedding present."

I drew my brows together, confused. His mouth turned up in a lopsided grin. God, that could leave me weak every time.

Letting go of my hand, he turned and went back to the truck, leaving me standing near the edge of the water.

I watched him, reminded of another time, when he left me on the blanket to go back to his truck for a condom. We thought the world would go on as it always had. That nothing would change. Now here we were, stripped of everything but each other.

I stared at him, wondering what he was doing. He went to the driver's side and opened the door. Reaching in, he disappeared for a second, only the very top of his head visible.

I waited, little breaths of cold air leaving my mouth. Suddenly, music blared from the truck. I gasped. I hadn't heard a song in years except for once when Tate, Keely, and I heard the national anthem played over a shortwave radio. This one was an old country western song. Something slow and romantic.

Cash stood upright and strolled back, his gaze pinning me in place. Stopping in front of me, he held out his hand.

"Dance with me, Cat."

I looked down at his hand and placed mine in his. He pulled me closer and wrapped his arm around me.

We started moving slowly. The grass was our dance floor and the lake our audience. My body fit against his like we were meant to do this from the beginning.

His hand moved to the small of my back, urging me closer. He tucked my head against his chest as we swayed to the music.

"I love you, Cat," he whispered. "I want to grow old with you and have babies with you. I want to wake up in the morning and see your face and go to sleep at night with you by my side."

He let me go and cupped my face, looking into my eyes.

"If you want to leave, we'll grab Tate and go. Make our home somewhere else. I'll follow you anywhere—"

I shook my head. "I love you, Cash. As long as we're together, it doesn't matter."

I was right where I wanted to be.

I was home.

Epilogue

-Cat-

Two Weeks Later

I walked through the house with slow steps. Cash had brought Tate and I home.

He told me the story of how he had come here looking for me after the EMP hit, bleeding and burning up with fever. How he had hallucinated and saw me.

The house was still standing but it was covered with vines and hidden by weeds. Cash and Gavin had boarded up the windows. Cash admitted that he had hoped I would show up one day and if I did, he wanted me to have my old home.

The pool was green, only rainwater in the bottom. The cabinets were bare. The furniture was still in the same place but covered with a thick layer of dust and grime.

I walked over to the kitchen and stood there, imagining Nathan leaning against the counter, smiling at me. Tears filled my eyes. A hand went to my hip.

"He's here with you," a deep voice drawled behind me.

"I know," I whispered as Cash stopped next to me, his face shadowed by his cowboy hat.

Pulling me close, he leaned over and kissed my temple then let go of me and returned to the living room.

I took a deep breath and turned to follow him. Tate was upstairs, going through his room. I wanted to do the same.

With Cash behind me, I went up the stairs. The hallway was dark, the silence eerie. I glanced at the expensive artwork still on the walls and remembered when my mother had bought them. They were layered with dust and hanging crooked now, useless material things.

That had seemed so long ago, in a time that seemed like an alternate reality. But I still got choked up, remembering my life then and how I missed Nathan and my dad.

In my room, I stopped and looked around. The past came back in a flood of images. Lying on my bed, listening to Tate and Nathan argue. Thinking of a cowboy with gray eyes and a crooked smile.

The clothes were gone – stolen Cash said – but the old me was still there. I could almost hear my laughter and remember my tears.

Cash leaned against the doorframe and watched as I walked into the room.

"I always pictured you in here, pulling on those boots you wore on our first date, strutting in front of the mirror." His eyes ran over me. "Looking gorgeous as always."

"I thought I was too good for a cowboy like you," I said, smiling at him over my shoulder.

He pushed off the doorframe, a predator look in his eyes. "You were," he rumbled, walking toward me. "Still are."

I blushed, something I only did with Cash.

He stopped in front of me and slid his hand over my stomach. "Have you told Tate?"

I shook my head. "Not yet. I'm waiting for the right moment."

"Told me what?" Tate asked from the doorway.

I looked up. He was standing in the hall. I swear he had grown a foot taller in the last week. Janice was filling him full of food and Ryder had taken him under his wing, teaching him all he knew about hunting and...women.

Emma followed him around like a puppy dog. He grumbled about it but I saw the look in his eyes. He had grown to love her.

I smiled at Tate, wondering what he would think when I told him he was going to be an uncle. "I'll tell you later," I said, easing away from Cash's hand and going to the door.

"Oh, hold up," Cash said, turning away from me. "I think there's something still here."

He went over to the grime-covered dresser and opened the top drawer. Reaching inside, he pulled out a small piece of paper. *A photo?*

Turning, he headed back to me. "I found this when I came here looking for you."

He stopped in front of me and held it out. With shaking hands, I took it.

It was a picture of Luke and me. He smiled back at me, frozen in time. His arm was around my shoulders. I was grinning at the camera. I remembered the day perfectly.

It was the day he was killed.

"It's him, isn't it?" Cash asked, standing close.

"Luke? Yes. Earlier in the day before the accident," I said, my voice hoarse and thick.

Cash looked down at the picture. Suddenly, he grew stiff. "Holy shit."

"What?" I asked, alarmed, looking from him to the photograph.

Cash's throat worked hard. He went a little pale. "I saw him."

"What? No, you didn't. He died," I said, feeling faint.

Cash shook his head and looked at me. "I saw *him.* It was the second night after you were shot. You cried out and I woke up. There was a man standing over you. *That* man." He pointed to the picture. "Before I could grab my gun, he was gone. I thought I was dreaming. It had been days since I ate or had a good night's sleep and I was worried you were going to die…I just figured I was imagining things but it was him. I know it."

'I'll always be with you, Cat.'

A shiver passed over me, remembering Luke's words. He had been there, urging me to live. I smiled down at the picture and ran my finger over his face. I still missed him after all these years.

"Y'all are freakin' me out. Can we go?" Tate grumbled from the doorway. "I'm starving."

I smiled and tucked the picture in my pocket. "Okay. Let's go home."

Cash touched my elbow in passing and led the way down the hall and stairs. We would be back. Cash had already talked about spending more time here, to get away and be by ourselves some more.

Ryder's ranch was getting crowded. David had been given a small patch of land on Maddie's old farm; Eva and Brody lived in the old house. Keely, Tate, Cash, and I were staying in Ryder's parents' home until we could build a house. Gavin was bunking with Ryder and Maddie even though Ryder wasn't happy about that.

And Adam?

He had said goodbye three days ago. I still felt sadness, remembering his goodbye. He was going to find someone he had wronged, he said.

He promised to come back. I told him he better. I already missed his smirk and teasing.

Tate was still grumbling about being hungry as we walked through the living room. I turned to tell him to stop cussing and watch his language when suddenly a man appeared.

He was stepping through the boarded-up door, the same way we had come in. His skin was leathery and his tall frame was gaunt. He wore a heavy flannel coat, big clunky boots, and tattered pants. His hair was a mass of gray and black that stood up everywhere. Most of his face was covered with a thick beard that reached the top of his chest.

His gaze snapped up at us. Surprised, he paused as he stepped over the threshold.

Cash pushed me behind him and snapped the shotgun he had been carrying to his shoulder. "Stop right there, mister."

I peered around Cash's arm. The man's eyes went from Tate to me. There was something about him…

I stepped around Cash but he grabbed me and pulled me back. "I swear, princess," he muttered under his breath with frustration.

But I wasn't listening. I was staring at the man. His eyes. I knew those eyes.

"Dad?" I whispered, pushing Cash's hand off my waist.

The old man blinked. "Catnip?"

"Oh god! Oh god!" I threw myself at him, sobbing.

The man's thin arms caught me. He smelled awful and I was sure there was something alive in his beard but he was here. My dad was alive.

He started crying as he hugged me, his thin body shaking against mine.

"Cat! I can't believe…I've looked…" His voice was thick and scratchy, thick with tears and rough from disuse but I would recognize it anywhere.

Cash eased closer but kept his gun trained on my dad. "Cat? You sure it's really him?"

I sniffed and pulled away, looking over my shoulder at Cash. "It's him. It's my father."

Cash lowered the gun and relaxed but still looked wary.

"Where have you been? Are you okay?" I asked my dad, looking over him. Making sure he wasn't injured.

He brushed my hands away and smiled. "I'm fine. I…I hitched a ride on a cargo ship leaving Dubai. I've…I've been traveling for years, trying to get home to you. I…I just hoped you were here."

I hugged him again, unable to believe it. He patted my back, his beard tickling my face, and looked over my head at Tate.

"Tater Tot?" he asked in a whispered, surprised voice, his arms dropping away from me.

I glanced back. Tate was shifting to his other foot, looking uneasy.

He stuck his nose up and sniffed. "No one calls me that anymore."

Our dad walked over to Tate and stopped in front of him. Tate glared at him then looked away with an angry frown.

"I missed you, son," our dad said in a tear-choked voice, his beard twitching as his chin started quivering.

Tate's eyes filled with tears. Our father reached out and grabbed him, hugging him tight. At first, Tate resisted but then he wrapped his arms around the man and squeezed his eyes shut.

After a minute, my dad let him go and looked around. "Where's Nathan?"

I glanced at Tate. He looked at the ground and kicked at the edge of a dusty rug.

My dad looked at me. "Cat? Where's your brother?"

Tears welled in my eyes. Cash stepped next to me and slid an arm around my waist, giving me strength with his quiet presence.

I took a deep breath and looked at my father. "He was killed, dad."

"Oh God." He drew in a sharp breath and looked up at the ceiling, blinking quickly as his eyes watered.

Tate wrapped an arm around my father's shaking shoulders. I went to them and hugged my dad, missing Nathan like never before.

After a moment, my father drew back and sniffed. Clearing his throat, he looked at Cash and glanced at the shotgun in his hand. "Who are you?"

I started to answer but Cash beat me to it.

"I'm Cash. Her husband."

~~~~

A little bit later, I stood in the doorway, staring out at the land. Tate and my dad stood at the fence, their arms resting on the top rung. They were gazing out at the pasture and talking. Tate wanted to be the one to tell my dad how Nathan died. I was thankful. I didn't want to relive the moment and feel the pain.

There would always be a hole inside me, missing my brother. But as I stood there, watching my dad and Tate, a warm feeling filled me. I was safe. Happy.

"Cat."
~~~~

Tingles went up my spine at the voice. I turned. In the shadows of the house, he stood there, silhouetted against the sun. His cowboy hat was pulled low. His sharp jaw was dusted with whiskers and his eyes were a light gray under the brim of the hat.

My cowboy.

I went to him, wrapping my arm around his middle. He kissed the top of my head and whispered, "I love you, Beauty Queen. Let's go home."

~

This was the story of my life. A story of love. Of finding strength when there was none. Of living when the odds are stacked against you. It all started on a rainy night when a quiet cowboy helped a spoiled brat fix a car…

ABOUT THE AUTHOR

Paige Weaver lives in Texas with her husband and two children. Her love for books became a love for writing at a young age. She wrote her first book as a teenager and continued writing throughout the years. Encouraged by her husband, she finally decided to self-publish. Her debut novel, *Promise Me Darkness*, was released in April 2013 and quickly became a *New York Times* and *USA Today* bestseller. When she is not writing, you can find her reading or chasing her kids around.

Find out about future books and connect with her on:

Website: authorpaigeweaver.com
Twitter: @AuthorPWeaver
Instagram: AuthorPaigeWeaver
Facebook: AuthorPaigeWeaver

~~~~

BOOKS BY PAIGE

Promise Me Darkness
New York Times and *USA Today* bestseller

Promise Me Light
USA Today bestseller

Promise Me Once
The beginning of Cat and Cash's story

Sweet Destruction
A stand-alone novel
~~~~

Made in the USA
Columbia, SC
26 July 2023

20947844R00255